Lovers in London

Lovers in London

By A. A. Milne

London
ALSTON RIVERS, Arundel Street, W.C.
1905

BRADBURY, AGNEW & CO., LD., PRINTERS,
LONDON AND TONBRIDGE.

Contents.

Contents.

Lovers in London.

CHAPTER I.

A FAMILY GROUP.

LADIES and gentlemen: Amelia. Amelia's father and mother. Amelia's dog. Absent through illness: Amelia's brother.

Amelia, you will observe, is in the centre of the group. She has in her hands a book, evidently a work of great lore. No doubt it is a history of the American War of Independence. Amelia, you are at liberty to suppose, contemplates the publishing of an American Encyclopædia. *W.* War. See *I.* Independence. It will be a valuable dictionary of reference, and you are invited to subscribe for it now, before it is too late....

One can notice the length and beauty of her eyelashes. She is looking at the book carelessly. May be it is only an album of the photographer's family.

She is wearing (for the benefit of the male novelist) "a simple dress of some soft, white, clinging material." There is "a red rose at her waist, and another at her hair." (These, too, are for the male novelist's benefit. This is as far as he will venture.)

She has, one gathers, the bloom of youth upon her cheek. Her mouth turns down delightfully at the corners. Her nose, if one may speak of it, is well shaped.

This gentleman on the right is Amelia's father. He has his hand to his brow. We conceive him thinking out next Sunday's sermon. His hair and beard are white; a kindly-looking young old man.

Amelia's mother on the left. She is glancing over Amelia's book. Is that the photographer's wife? My dear, what a fright she looks!

Amelia's dog. Query: Is it really a dog?

So far the photograph. Amelia's brother, says the letter, was down with a broken leg. He is at Cornell. One remembers how they play football in America, and is glad it is only a leg that is broken. We feel sure that he will work hard at the University, in order to please his parents.

And now to put the letter and photograph carefully away in our most private drawer....

It is Amelia who writes the letter—rather shyly, and in places at second hand. "Mother wants me to write and tell you that, after all, we shan't reach England until the beginning of the year.... Mother thought you would like to see the enclosed photograph of us all. It is a good one of father. Isn't Toddles just too sweet for words?... I look a sight."... (Toddles must be the dog.) She begins, "My dear Teddy," crosses out "Teddy," and puts "Edward," and finally "Teddy" again. I rather like it.

The letter is headed "*S.S. Antelope* at sea." Amelia has not been very well, so they are coming to England by way of San Francisco and the Pacific and other places. I must look them up on the map. I never was much at geography....

But who is Amelia?

When I am reading a book of adventure, I turn over quickly the pages which describe the beautiful scene spread before the hero's gaze as he lay hidden in the cocoanut tree. I turn over the pages until I come to the words, "But George had no time for these things now. Already the Malays ..." I am like George for the moment. On the other hand, when I am reading a humorous work, I go solemnly through the dullest looking page, lest it should hide one of the author's jokes. Now this is not a book of adventure, and if you omit a page which looks dull I cannot promise that the next one will be more exciting. Nor should I care to call this a humorous work. Wherefore you need not be afraid of missing inadvertently a hearty laugh. So that you may do as you please with the short explanation of Amelia's parentage that impends, having nothing to hope for, nor anything to fear.

Very well then. I first met Amelia's father at a christening, when he gave me the names of William Edward. (He also presented me with a solid silver napkin ring. I look at it sometimes now.) As he was then my godfather, so he is now, and for many years has been my guardian. By birth an Englishman, he married an American, settled with her in the States, and soon became naturalised. Nearly every year, however, he would come over to England to see after my education. (Generally he came alone, occasionally he brought his wife. Twice Amelia has come herself; at the ages of six and twelve.) I have a good many aunts and cousins and things who looked after my domestic affairs when I was a boy. (Arranged about my socks and so on.) Amelia's father did the other part. He selected my school and college, spent my money for me till I was of age (about £300 a year it is), and was the sole court of appeal in time of trouble.

Finally, he is a Presbyterian minister whom I call "Father William." I owe him a good deal one way and another.

Amelia's mother and I have never got on well together. She is "going" rather quickly. When I last saw her (four years ago) she gave me the idea that she was a little upset at having a grown-up daughter. A little soured, I think. A little jealous. "Aunt Anne" she is—and kisses me on the forehead.

As for Amelia and myself, if you are kind enough to take any interest in us, you will have learnt all that there is to know by the time you have finished the last chapter. (Amelia's favourite waltz is mentioned in the fifteenth chapter, her favourite live poet in the sixth.

In the fifteenth also is named her hero in real life, but perhaps the twenty-fourth will give you another impression.)

Amelia, then, is the heroine. If you had seen her you would say so. But for my own position in the lime-light, I can only plead that as actor-manager I have precedent for it. I have taken all the best lines for myself. . . . And, besides, I was in love already! In love with Amelia's photograph—with Amelia of the family group.

But Amelia herself was on the sea. I had a mind to buy an atlas.

CHAPTER II.

A DREAM OF ISLANDS.

IN a certain shop in the Strand there is a large map of the world on somebody's projection. Little models of ships are dotted over the sea part, and if you have a cousin who left last month for the gold-digging, you look at this map and realise at once where he is. Perhaps you find him stuck in a Suez Canal or so; perhaps you are not keen on the Suez Canal, nor yet on the cousin; certainly you have no expectations from him. So you leave him there, nor trouble yourself further about the matter. Only when people talk of the chances of the Baltic Fleet getting through the Canal, and of other things connected with the laws of neutrality, you say, "My dear fellow! My dear fellow," you say, "I have a cousin there, so I ought to know."

But suppose it is not a cousin, but—the daughter of somebody's godfather! Suppose she is going round the world for her health, which is weak. Daily you watch her glide over the Pacific; and your heart beats high, for there are so many islands in the Pacific where a girl of good family may be wrecked. At last you come down to the window to see that there is one particular little island directly in the way of her ship. It looks uninhabited on the map; but there is something about the shape of it which speaks eloquently of coral-reefs and cocoanuts. . . .

This is your moment. You go back to your rooms—well, it is useless to deceive you—I go back to my rooms, and put on a pair of white flannel trousers, a soft-fronted shirt with a double collar, and a pair of pumps. I have long ago decided that I will be shipwrecked nohow else.

My hair, I need hardly say, is parted to perfection.

Then I close my eyes. . . .

* * * * *

Half carrying, half dragging Amelia, I fought my way up out of the tumbling waves, until at last I could lay her down on the dry sand beyond the reach of harm. . . .

I stood up, but dimly conscious of the heaving waste of waters before me. Suddenly a terrible suspicion flashed across my mind. I looked down. Yes, it was only too true. One of my pumps was missing. . . .

I glanced seawards. All at once I spied it upon the crest of a wave. To plunge in after it was the work of a moment. . . .

I have a confused remembrance of breakers crashing over me . . . of being pulled down and down and still down. . . .

Of wondering if this were indeed the end. . . .

Of Amelia, and of sunny days when we played together in the paddock. . . .

And then—a blank.

* * * * *

It was a glorious morning when I opened my eyes again. (One of those wonderful tropic days which we get so often in the Pacific.) Amelia had already gathered some sticks, and was busy lighting a fire.

"You've been asleep hours and hours," she said, when she saw that I was awake. "I thought you were dead. This was going to be your funeral pyre."

"I wasn't asleep," I protested. "I fell into a swoon. You'd have done it if you had been through all I went through last night. I forget how many times it was I saved your life."

"Well, but for me you wouldn't be here at all. So come and find something for breakfast."

Breakfast, I must confess, was a failure. Five shell-fish and a young lizard sounds all right from a distance; but, actually, the lizard preserved his *status quo* through the intercession of Amelia, and of the shellfish only one was obliging enough to come undone. The loss of the lizard was a great blow to me. All the time we were struggling with the clams I could catch Amelia out of the corner of my eye throwing wistful glances at it.

"You'll spoil that lizard," I said at last, "if you make eyes at it. It will begin to give itself airs. A while ago it was content to be a breakfast dish; now it will aspire to nobler things. All the same," I added bitterly, "if it thinks it's come here to be a pet it's jolly well mistaken. The necessities of man"—and I took up the toasting fork.

"Just when I've christened him William Henry," sobbed Amelia. "Come to your mother, darling." And she took him up in her hands.

"It only makes it harder for him to leave us. You shall have the tail. Epicures say it's the best part."

"Spare my child," wailed Amelia. "Strike, but hear me. He's going to find truffles for us; aren't you, sweetest?"

So there, of course, we left it.

After breakfast we started to tour the island. You must imagine us: I led the way with the gun over my shoulder; Amelia came next, bare-headed and short-skirted, carrying the box of matches; behind waddled William Henry, officially looking for truffles.

"What do we do first?" asked Amelia.

"The first thing to do is to find out whether this really is an island, or just part of an ordinary continent."

"Fancy, if it's really Brighton, and we didn't know," giggled Amelia.

"Incidentally we must find the bread-fruit tree, and shoot something."

"Bags I the turtle's eggs, then."

"Amelia," I said sternly, "you are very frivolous

about it all. Little wot you that at any moment we may be surrounded by yelling savages."

"Wot what?"

"Savages!" I said, in a hoarse voice.

"Oh, I say, and I haven't got a hat on! What *will* they think of me?"

The caustic reply which I had prepared froze upon my lips, for at this moment we plunged into the depths of an impenetrable forest. In a little while there was a silence as of night. Through the tangled undergrowth we fought our way for what seemed hours. There appeared to be no living creature there save ourselves. The ghostly stillness worked upon our nerves until we hardly dared to speak to each other. What catastrophe was about to happen?

Suddenly I put my hand to my brow, and staggered back. Directly in front of us was a "blazed" tree! I moistened my lips, and spoke in a voice which I barely recognised as my own.

"Whose footprint is that?" I gasped.

"Please I cannot tell a lie. I done it with my little hatchet. I thought it was the proper thing to do."

"Amelia," I said, "you have saved our lives."

We lunched on the sands off bread-fruit and a peculiar kind of bark which I had discovered, William Henry having had no success. After the meal was over Amelia announced her intention of going to sleep for an hour. . . . .

"Very well," I said; "I'll leave you here, and you shall have William Henry to guard you."

"What are you going to do?"

I looked at her in surprise.

"Find the india-rubber tree, of course," I said, simply.

"What do we want india-rubber for?"

"My dear girl," I said, "what else are we here for? You don't seem to realise the strategical importance of finding the india-rubber tree."

"No, I don't; nor does William Henry, do you, dear?"

"Well, any how, it's got to be done. Good-bye, Amelia."

"Good-bye, dear."

I had a premonition of coming evil as I left her. But duty came first. I turned away, and struck inland.

It was lonely without her. Every tree, every little shrub brought back the incidents of the morning with a sudden stab of regret. Something seemed to have gone out of the day. I threw stones idly at a group of monkeys playing in the trees, and wondered that Amelia was not there to laugh at my bad aim. The whole place now seemed alive with the chattering of birds and the hum of insects. But they brought no sense of companionship. . . .

I don't know what can have happened. Perhaps I fell asleep, for suddenly I realised that it was late and cold. There was a wind in the air. I shivered, and ran down to where I had left Amelia. I must have wandered miles that afternoon. I began to wonder if I should ever get there. Ah! the sea at last . . . .

Somehow I knew she would be gone. Perhaps she had only moved away to find shade. Yet, as I told myself that, I knew that I did not believe it. What had happened?

Suddenly I saw her. There was a little hillock of palms half a mile away, may be; and she was standing there among the trees, with the dark blue sky behind her, looking out over the sea. I followed her eyes.

Canoes! Half a dozen of them. I knew what that meant. They were near the shore, but I could get to her before they were beached. There was no danger if I was with her.

Yet I couldn't! Simply I couldn't! I see her there now as I write, looking calmly on while her fate drew nearer. And I, powerless to move a limb! Tall and queenly, she stood lined out firmly against the wind. She pushed her hair back from her face, and half turned her head, as though she wondered why I was not with her. . . .

* * * * *

That was the last I saw of her. My pumps gave out, and I had to return to London and the realities again. Yet that evening, as I walked down the Strand, I looked half fearfully in at the window, and when I saw that the island was left well behind, I heaved a sigh of relief.

CHAPTER III.

GREETINGS AND ARRANGEMENTS.

THEY had been in London for three days before I saw Amelia. Her father had written asking me to meet them at Southampton; but I had pleaded urgent business. I much regretted, I wrote, that owing to extremely urgent business, I should be unable to return to London until the Saturday after their arrival. On Saturday afternoon I would give myself the pleasure of calling on them, and I hoped that they would recognise me.

Now, the truth must be told, there were two reasons for this urgent business. First of all, I refuse absolutely to be anywhere near Amelia's parents when they are catching a train, or landing from a boat, or going up the Great Wheel, or doing anything of that kind. Amelia's father is the sort of man who goes into church half-an-hour before the service begins, who gets to his train half-an-hour before it starts, who pops his head out of the window at every station to see how his luggage is getting on. . . . He worries. You know the kind of man. Of course, the young should make allowances for the weaknesses of age;

but—I know my own weaknesses too, and to save unpleasantness I stay away.

Also I had been growing a moustache, and I wanted to give it as long as I could. By Saturday it would be "taking notice," I hoped.

On Saturday afternoon I called. They had taken a house near the South Kensington Museum. I was shown in, and soon there appeared what was evidently Amelia. I rose from my chair.

"It's a dream," I murmured to myself, "a beautiful dream. I shall wake soon and have fish for breakfast. Ugh!" (They always give me fish for breakfast.)

"Hullo, Teddy," said the vision, "I've been just longing for you to come. How are you?"

"Pinch me," I said. "Ow! Not there."

"Aren't you glad to see me? You've grown a heap."

"Is it really you?"

"Yes. You are Teddy, aren't you?"

"Oh, I'm all right," I said. "The only question is whether you are—they must be awfully bad photographers in America."

"Oh, I see what you mean. Did it flatter me so?" Amelia laughed.

"Flatter?" I said, indignantly. "You've—you're—" she said she was longing for me! Oh lord!

I cannot attempt to describe Amelia. I don't know how it is with other people, but when I read that Lady Clara, daughter of a hundred earls, had an oval face, pearly teeth, a slightly *retroussé* nose, and a dimpled chin—it conveys nothing at all to me. But if the author says simply that she is just sweet, then I think of the prettiest face I know, or have ever known, and, be it country maid's or town madame's, there is my Lady Clara. So now, if you will think of the loveliest girl you ever saw, if you will remember that she spoke with the divinest American accent, and forget (if it makes it easier) that she had been "longing for me," then there will be Amelia for you to the last chapter.

"When I last saw you I was twelve," said Amelia.

"Ten years ago, so you're now nineteen."

"I'd rather be twenty-two, if you don't mind. Fancy! we're both grown up. Now, Teddy, you've just got to show me London. Everything."

"Things like the Zoo and the Tower, and—"

"Yes, everything. Oh, except the South Kensington Museum."

"You've seen that?"

"I went this morning."

"Then, let's shake hands again," I said. "But I should love to take you to the Zoo, or anywhere else."

Amelia's father and mother also remarked on my growth, looks, and age. It seemed to please them. At tea I made myself agreeable, I hope. I talked about the fiscal question to Father William, pointing out that there were two ways of regarding it, and that one must not come to a hasty conclusion. I also told him in what way Togo had lost his opportunity. War had just been declared then. I gave Aunt Anne information as to the best chapel for the family to attend, throwing in details about the private life of the minister. He kept a canary called Percy. I talked to Amelia herself—about everything. I had no idea what I was saying.

But afterwards I saw her alone for awhile.

"We start on Monday," she said.

"Where?"

"Round the world. Round London. You can spare the time?"

"Certainly, my dear Holmes. I have an obliging friend who can take my practice. Where do we go to first?"

"Where do you want to go?"

"The Zoo. I love the Zoo."

"Then we'll go. But I've been twice already—yesterday and Thursday. I'm just crazy on it."

"Amelia, how could you? Why weren't you unpacking? And who did you go with? Of course we won't go—if—"

"Of course we'll go, and I'll introduce you to someone. A darling. I love him already."

"I like reptiles," I said; "but I loathe insects. If it isn't an insect I shall be glad to meet it."

"Him, please," said Amelia. "Good-bye. Two o'clock on Monday. And we'll go in a hansom. I adore hansoms."

I got home somehow.

CHAPTER IV.

LONDON IN BED.

I LAY awake that night thinking of Amelia. I imagined us in wonderful situations. One of the most ferocious lions in the Zoo had escaped. There was a panic. Cries and shrieks rent the air. Amelia and I in another part of the grounds heard the noise, and wondered idly what was the matter. Suddenly we turned the corner, and there—there was the king of beasts. . . .

I took off my coat and rolled up my sleeves.

"Amelia," I called, "save yourself! I will rejoin you outside the opossums' cage."

"Teddy!" sobbed Amelia.

I seized her umbrella, and waving and shouting, dashed at the animal. Some of my past life rose before my eyes—the more satisfactory parts. I thought of Amelia. I thought of Livingstone. There used to be a picture of the intrepid missionary underneath a lion. Livingstone was pretending to be dead, and the lion was gnawing a piece of his arm, and pretending too. One gathered from the text that the sensation was pleasant rather than otherwise—from Livingstone's point of view, I mean (and probably from the lion's, if hungry). I thought much of that. It cheered me. I shouted and waved. . . .

Would the animal turn? . . .

And then, just as I was upon it, the lion remembered that it had left its cage open, and went back to close it. We were saved.

I turned to Amelia, putting on my coat. A grand moment! . . .

They clean the roads at night. I found myself listening to the sound. The horses' feet—clod—clod-clod—clod-clod—clod; the whish—sh of the brush as it goes round. Then "Woa-*back!* woa! woa-back! woa, carn't yer? Get ba-ack; woa!" Whish—sh—sh. Clod—clod. "Woa-*back!*"

I was seized with an unreasoning rage. I cursed the driver. Never did I loathe anybody so much. I wanted to get up and hit him hard with his own whip several times across the face. I concentrated my mind on that man. Man? Reptile. If there is anything in telepathy, he must have felt that I despised him and ground him under my feet.

"Woa-*back!*" he shouted again; and all through the night. Why couldn't he talk gently to his animal? A vulgar man.

They print the newspapers at night. Newspapers are all around. How have I ever managed to sleep here with that noise of engines outside. There goes the *Daily Mail.*

"No stomach-tax, no stomach-tax, no stomach-tax, no—." Then it changes. "Oh, it's *not* a stomach-tax; no, it's *not* a stomach-tax; oh, it's not a stomach-tax; no, it's not a stomach-tax."

There goes the *Daily News*. Mark how smoothly. No betting news, no drink advertisements there. Nothing but peace. Pe-e-e-ace. Hallo, what's that? A little harsh and violent, is it? Ah, that's because it's giving a much-needed lesson to the Yellow Press. It's rebuking the *Daily Mail* for bringing about war between Russia and Japan. What, you actually thought that Russia brought on war? And your friend says it was all the Japanese's fault, and that they've been preparing for war for seven years? Nonsense, my dear man. It was the *Daily Mail*. Russia and Japan weren't even consulted. Listen! Can't you hear it? "The *Daily Mail* again, the *Daily Mail* again, the *Daily Mail* again." . . .

Directly opposite works the *Sun*. Hark to its motto grinding away. "If you see it in the *Sun* it is so. If you see it in the *Sun* it is so. If you see it in the *Sun* it is *not* so." Hallo! something in the machinery caught there. Ah! that's right. Now it's working properly again. "If you see it in the *Sun* it is so."

"Toot, toot!" comes from the river. I suppose Amelia will want the exact spot in Westminster Bridge on which Wordsworth composed his sonnet. Well, she can't have it.

And I refuse to go up the Monument.

And she shan't see the Lord Mayor's Show. I haven't. My one achievement.

Let's see. There's the Zoo, and the Tower, and the Abbey, and the British Museum. Hang the British Museum! It always gives me a headache.

And Earl's Court and the National Gallery. Hang the National Gallery! I seem to be in for headaches.

Anyhow, there's Amelia. She may go and see the National Gallery if she likes, and I shall go to the National Gallery to see her. That's fair.

Toot, toot, whish-sh-sh, clod-clod, clod-clod. "Woa there, can't yer? Get ba-ack!" It suddenly became clear to me that I was not going to sleep that night. I went into the other room and turned on the light. Then I took out the family group.

It wasn't a bit like her, you know. Fancy thinking I was in love with that! Bah! Some men are fools.

CHAPTER V.

AN AFTERNOON WITH THE ANIMALS.

AMELIA'S friend turned out to be a racoon, and so on Monday afternoon we went to call on him. He is known as the Crab-eating Racoon—no doubt because he eats crabs. We, however, call him "Charles." (I was allowed to call him "Charles" on the very first day.) Those in the know may refer to him as "Procyon Cancriverous," but to us it seems an unwarranted familiarity.

Charles wanted to see us about four o'clock, so we strolled through the gardens first.

The polar bear is a love and a darling and a sweet thing. Likewise he is just a dear, and rather a pet. There you have our united criticism. The "rather a pet" was my own idea; I threw it in, as Amelia appeared to be getting heady over the animal. Unfortunately you can't stroke him without breaking a by-law. But we blew kisses to him, and hoped he would sit up and take his fish nicely at dinner.

At the back of the bears' cages are the hyænas'. The worst noise in the Gardens comes from the spotted hyæna at lunch-time; the most plaintive from the seal at all times; the most surprising from the one-wattled cassowary when we happened to pass him. Amelia said it was because he was disappointed at only having one wattle. But after all a wattle is a wattle, and many of us haven't even one. His christian name is Casuarius Uniappendiculatus. Perhaps that will explain why he barks so well.

As we went under the bridge to get to the elephant-house Amelia insisted on buying buns for the rhinoceros.

"But they don't eat buns," I objected.

"He will if I offer it to him," said Amelia confidently.

"My dear Amelia," I said, "it is a matter of common knowledge that the rhinoceros, belonging as it does to the odd-toed set of ungulates, has a gnarled skin, thickened so as to form massive plates, which are united by thinner portions forming flexible joints. Further, the animal in question, though fierce and savage when roused, is a vegetable feeder. In fact, he may be said to be herbivorous."

"I don't care," said Amelia defiantly; "all animals in the Zoo eat buns."

"I can tell you three that don't."

"I bet a shilling you can't—not straight off."

I instanced the electric eel, the ceciopian silk moth, and the cocoanut crab. So Amelia paid for our teas. But in the elephant-house the rhinoceros took his bun with *verve*—not to say *aplomb*.

Beyond this is the canal bank aviary—a wonderful

place. All sorts of birds mix up together here. We were witnesses of a scene between two herons and a little green bird—name unknown. Suppose we call him a green-cheeked amazon—because there is such a bird.

He sat on a branch, and the two herons strolled up to him.

Said the first: "What on earth is it?"

The second looked the amazon over carefully. "Upon my word, I shouldn't like to say. It's a mistake of some sort."

"Go away!" said the amazon nervously.

"Very inferior place the Gardens are getting," said the herons, "not like they were when we were boys."

"I wonder if that green comes off," said the first one reflectively.

He proceeded to try. . . .

Then Amelia clapped her hands, and they all flew away.

In the next house we found the Somali wild ass. "There used to be another," said Amelia. I explained that he had fled into Italian territory, and no one could say when he would return.

Just here is No. 58a, "The Meerkats' Cages." Next comes No. 59, "The Superintendent's House." You are requested not to feed the superintendent.

We made a similar mistake a moment later. My guide-book spoke about a téa-house. "I don't remember ever seeing the te-as," said Amelia? "what are they like?" I didn't want to confess ignorance.

"The téa," I said, "is a cross between an emu and a wild goat. Something like a rhea, and something like a thar, you know."

"Yes, I remember now," she said; "where is it?"

We went all over the place, looking for the common or herbaceous téa. We grew wonderfully keen on it. I pointed out to Amelia that it was probably a very rare animal, and that we might have to pay extra to see it. . . .

Then it suddenly struck me. As I have said, Amelia paid for both.

After tea we saw the reptiles. A donation to the man at the wheel, and for the first time in her life Amelia wore a real boa. Quite a young one, and like linoleum to feel. (I shall not advertise it any further. I leave this to the puff adder.)

We came back by way of the eagles. They like having their heads scratched. One of them is called the "vociferous eagle," but luckily he did not vociferate.

Space forbids me to tell of the hairy-nosed agouti and the two-toed sloth. I may not refer to the Indian darter that I left behind me. Nor can I say a word for the grunting ox, nor pronounce an opinion (or anything else) on Prjevalski's wild horse. I have only a moment for Charles.

The racoon may be stroked with the first finger—and with impunity.

"Tell me, dear," said Amelia to him, "you don't really like horrid crabs, do you?"

"Never touch 'em," said Charles, with a wink at me.

"And your name isn't really Proki—what was it, is it?"

"What's in a name?" said Charles, airily.

"Procyon Cancriverous," I suggested.

Charles looked uneasy.

"A family name," he said hastily; "my great-grand-father's. I haven't an idea what it means."

"Charles!" I said, sternly.

"It doesn't mean what you mean," he said.

"You're making Charles angry," said Amelia. "Did'ums, was they horrid to him, then?"

"They was!" said Charles, stiffly. "Send him away."

Amelia looked appealingly at me.

"The glutton is next door," said Charles, vindictively. "That's more in his line."

CHAPTER VI.

WESTMINSTER WAY.

WESTMINSTER Abbey is to the American what—a moment ago I had a simile, but I have forgotten it now. It is to the American as—well, it doesn't matter much, so long as you realise how greatly Amelia wished to see it. She had heard of it; she knew its direction from Marble Arch. (Amelia reckons from Marble Arch, not knowing London very well.) To get from the Bank to Liverpool Street she would make for Marble Arch, and then enquire the way. Policemen, shedding tears of anguish in their futile attempts to direct her, brighten up when they hear that she knows Marble Arch. Something of this sort happens, you may say.

Amelia : Say, how do I get to St. Paul's, please?

Policeman (thinking he has a soft thing on) : It's just at the top of Ludgate Hill, ma'am. You can't mistake it.

Amelia (innocently) : Ludgate Hill?

Policeman : Yes. That's at the bottom of Fleet Street. Go straight up the Strand.

Amelia : Fleet Street? Strand?

Policeman : Yes. You know the Strand?

Amelia (with a charming smile) : No! Where is it?

Westminster Way.

Policeman (*getting anxious, but feeling that now at last he has touched bottom*)*:* Well, you know Charing Cross, ma'am ?

Amelia (*brightly*)*:* But I don't. (*Thinking to please him.*) But I've *heard* of it!

Policeman (*desperate*) *:* Trafalgar Square, then ?

Amelia : No-o.

Policeman : Well, ma'am, what *do* you know ?

Amelia (*beaming all over*) *:* I know Mar-rble Ar-rch.

Looking up, I see that this dialogue started life as a parenthesis. Well, well, it is lost now. . . . But it was a mistake. All Amelia's sayings and doings should come into a main sentence. They do—for me.

We went over and through and round the Abbey. The Nave, the Choir, the Poets' Corner. Into the Triforium, the Waxworks, the Chapels. Perhaps one may be permitted a smile at the Waxworks; but, for the rest, Amelia was quiet—almost frightened. We spoke in the lowest whispers, for fear of rousing the dead kings and queens. . . .

There is a monument to Sir Isaac Newton. For a long time it was supposed that the Binomial Theorem was written on it. As many a poet has composed his own requiem, so it seemed possible that carved on Sir Isaac Newton's tomb was some mathematical truth. Now Deans and Chapters are not mathematicians as a rule, and to the Classic the Binomial Theorem is a mystic thing—connoting, according to his personality, a new star in the heavens, a definition of quaternion fluids, the sign for infinity; whatever, in fact, is outside his vision. So, when they wished to find out the truth of the legend, they knew not what they went out for to see.

At last, quite a few years ago, a mathematician of eminence was called in. Armed with a step-ladder, a microscope, and an Algebra, he made his examination—to find . . .

Nothing. There was not even an Arithmetical Progression.

In the Cloisters afterwards Amelia said: "Teddy, do you know Silas Kerranhappuch Bloggs?"

"What is it like?" I asked, for you can never be sure from the name what these American drinks are going to be.

"It! He's a man! Oh, a man!"

"Oh, a man? A friend of yours?"

"A friend of *mine?*" asked Amelia in amazement.

"No? Then tell me. Does he pack pork, or is he a Gum King?"

"He's a poet. The greatest American poet."

"Is he a good poet?"

"The only poet. *He* ought to be in that corner of yours."

"Is he still alive?" I asked anxiously.

"Oh, yes."

"Then I agree with you. He ought."

American poets have such funny names. An Englishman called Bloggs wouldn't dare to turn out verse.

But they do it in the States. You can never tell with an American what he is going to be.

In the Cloisters there is a piece of statuary; a figure turning over the pages of a book. I told Amelia the legend. If you come down the Cloisters facing this, as soon as you turn to the right and have your back to it, the figure turns over a page of his book.

Frankly, Amelia didn't believe it.

"All right," I said; "try it."

We walked past, and then looked suddenly back.

"There you are," I said, "he's just turned over. If we had been a moment sooner we should have seen him."

"How many pages are there in an ordinary book?" asked Amelia.

"About four hundred," I ventured.

"Then I shall walk past it four hundred times, and just show you how absurd it is. You say the book will be finished by then."

"May I sit down?" I asked.

After the tenth time I thought I ought to interfere.

"He will never get to the end," I said. "There are an infinite number of pages in that book. All you will prove is the existence of the number infinity, a thing which has bothered many mathematicians of the highest credentials. I will write to the British Association about it."

We walked into Little Dean's Yard.

Westminster School is not an easy place to find. Nor

when found is it always understood—by the ladies at least. I have a friend who was at school there, and this frequently, he tells me, is the sort of remark in which he is involved.

"Oh, so you were at Westminster," she says. "Were you in the choir?"

My friend then explains with great heat and fervour that no Westminster boy has anything to do with the choir.

If she does not ask him about the choir then she is thinking of something else, and the conversation takes this turn.

"Oh, were you really? Did you know George Jones?"

"I don't seem to remember the name."

"Oh, I know he was there. He left about three years ago."

"Oh yes, that's all right. But he wasn't in my house. Of course you can't expect to know everybody."

"Oh! He was very good at games. In the eleven, I fancy. He got his colours, didn't he, Arthur?"

"Who?" says Arthur.

"George."

"Oh yes, rather!"

"Well, that's very funny," said my friend. "I was in the eleven three years ago, and there was certainly nobody called Jones in it. There was a fellow called Smith, who was twelfth man."

"Oh, I'm certain his name was Jones."

My friend still looked mystified, so Arthur was called in again. It then transpired (as the papers say) that she was thinking of Winchester. My friend says that among the fairer sex this often happens.

Amelia says, "How can women be expected to know?" For her own part she can hardly distinguish between Marlborough and Nelson—or is it Wellington?

We came round by the Houses of Parliament. Amelia wondered, as so many have done, whether Richard wasn't feeling tired after holding his sword up so straight for so long. Perhaps he has writer's cramp by now, in which case the ancients had all the diseases, as well as all the virtues. "King Richard and I," I shall observe to my friends. . . .

"And is the House of Commons sitting now?" asked Amelia.

"Yes; they are making laws for us."

"For us? For you; they can't touch me."

"But, perhaps, some day it will apply to both of us," I hazarded.

"You mean, I might become naturalised."

"Well, yes."

"Why?"

"Legally," I began. . . . "It was just an idea," I said. "Come and have some tea."

CHAPTER VII.

A. B. C.

WHEN Amelia was twelve her uncle gave her T at an A. B. C. I am not certain how many scones it was that she ate. Legends grow up around one's early adventures, as you know. In the Amelian circle the reference to it is general rather than particular, and proverbial. "Amelia and the scones" is as historic, and teaches as important a lesson, as "Alfred and the cakes." (Dear old Alfred and the cakes !)

This, of course, was the Amelia of years ago. Since that almost fatal day she had never been to an A. B. C. So, after leaving the Abbey that afternoon, she persuaded me to give her tea there. "It must be the identical dépôt," she said, and so it was.

Trembling with excitement, Amelia entered. I don't know what she expected would happen. I never knew rightly what happened before. Of course, if it really was seventeen—these are wild words.

"Scones and butter and tea for two," I ordered.

"I thought you were Scotch," said Amelia.

"Hoots, lassie, ye dinna ken. Ah'm English. My name is Norval, and on the Grampian Hills my father fed his flock. At least he didn't. If he fed them any where, it was on Primrose Hill."

"Well, anyhow, they are called scons."

"When you had seventeen they were called scons."

"It wasn't seventeen, Teddy."

"Seventeen is merely a symbol denoting excess."

Really, I refuse to call them "scons."

In this relation there is a pretty little story about me, which I proceeded to tell to Amelia. It brings out the nobleness of my character. I figure very handsomely in this story. But it is in no spirit of self-satisfaction that I repeat it now; rather for the good it may do others.

Once upon a time there was in an A. B. C. shop a fair Scotch waitress. She was a newcomer, but in this shop they know my ways. One day I was not quite sure what to have, so I left it to her. I said, "I leave it to you, partner." At least, she took it upon herself to say:

"Scons or cut bread and butter with your honey?"

Now, I wanted scone. But, as she had said "scon," I couldn't correct her by saying, "Scone, please." I did not wish her to feel her Scotch inferiority. You appreciate, of course, my instinct? Nor could I bring myself to say "scon;" my English blood boiled at the idea. So I said, "Bread and butter, please;" and I didn't want it a bit.

Amelia says it was very nice of me.

I claim to have discovered scones and honey. There

is, of course, a story that somebody's wife was "in the parlour eating scones and honey." (Or perhaps I am confusing the Spider and the Fly with the Knave of Hearts' performance.) But toasted A. B. C. scones and honey is, I am sure, my own invention. I use the plural in a confident way; but the A. B. C. scone is, really, about the size and weight of the ancient *diskus*. If any-one will prove to me that he has eaten two of these toasted, with honey (total cost, 6d.), at a sitting, I will give a shilling to any charity he likes to name—as they say. This is genuine; no money returned. And I think I may add that, if this wager is taken up, kind friends would oblige by accepting this the only intimation.

Amelia has just ordered some blackberry jelly. I am ruinéd.

The beauty ot the A. B. C. is its catholicity. A man sat down next to me one morning—I was having my modest roll and butter for lunch—and ordered fried fish. "Fried fish off? Oh, well, then I'll have—let's see—a plate of porridge and an apple." After that he could have had a sparkling limado and a tin of butter drops had he wished.

"You couldn't do that at Princes', you know," I said to Amelia. "A plate of porridge, perhaps; a sparkling limado under another name, no doubt; but the butter drops, I fancy not. On second thoughts I should say that one could hardly rely on the porridge—for lunch."

"What is a sparkling limado?"

"It isn't the same as a sparking plug."

"Shall I ask for one?"

"Not while I'm here," I said firmly.

"Then *you* ask. You're afraid, I believe."

"No, I'm not."

"Then ask."

"Not now. I promise to ask for one some time, if that will do."

"Very well, then. Only mind you do."

Amelia then asked for and obtained a piece of iced madeira cake. *Gourmande!*

The A. B. C. pays, I believe, an excellent dividend. It also presents such *employées* as are in need of it with a wedding cake. So I hope they won't mind my saying that their tea cups are too thick. The idea, no doubt, is that in this way they are unbreakable. I feel sure that this is the idea, because I have so often heard the A. B. C. girls trying to break them. I could make other complaints, too; for my experience is great. I have had tea here often; lunch, at one time, invariably; and, for a period, breakfast. I don't know why. One could get a tin of butter drops as cheap anywhere else. The marble tops to the tables are polished just as well at the Carlton. The serving is no better than it is at the Savoy. . . . Frankly, I abhor the A. B. C. as I abhor nothing else. But it is an institution, a habit. . . .

It is a great joke to watch old ladies at the dépôts of the Aërated Bread Company—(called by the vulgar, I am told, A.B.C's.). They study the *menu* with such care;—as though they were about to order a six-course lunch. The "wine" is selected with the pains of a *connoisseur*. Number Sixty-three. A small milk. For *entrées* they fall back on eggs. I find that one generally falls back on eggs at A. B. C.'s. Personally, I fall back often on two poached eggs on toast. Sometimes on two scrambled eggs.

Scrambled eggs are the nearest approach to mystery, to romance, that one can make. The keynote of the A. B. C. is its obviousness. You may get there everything which is plainly something, and nothing which might be anything. You order a meal, and can say at once, "This is a plate of ham"—or a poached egg, or a sardine, or an apple, or porridge. There is nothing fancy, nothing made-up. Its plainness is almost a pose. . . .

Of course one might be in doubt for a moment about sparkling limado. . . .

I told Amelia my ideas and experiences of A. B. C.'s, and she said, "You think of nothing but your—" She answered, "Your thoughts turn only to—" What she implied was that my sole care was for—that I worshipped, in fact, my—Amelia is American and she speaks in a plain blunt way like Antony. But it is not true. I have a heart above my stomach; physiologically, anyhow.

An epicure, indeed! There's gratitude for you. No more luxury for Amelia. No more A. B. C.'s. . . .

Meanwhile there was this beastly sparkling limado

hanging over me. I worried about it all the way to South Kensington. Amelia tried to cheer me up by telling me about people who had been happy with an even more terrible ordeal before them. It was no good. I saw her safely home, and sadly walked back to my club.

CHAPTER VIII.

THE FINEST VIEW IN LONDON.

My club has the finest view in London. If I were to change my politics, my colour, my creed; if I were to lose my family or my favourite pipe; if circumstances compelled me to become a German spy—whate'er befel, I should insist on keeping my club. I might be forced to spend five years in Portland, you say? Then I should arrange to be a country member. The Committee might come to me on bended knees, and beseech me to consider myself blackballed. They might point out with tears in their eyes, and truth, that I joined as a married greengrocer with Conservative tendencies, and that I am now an Irish Nationalist, a bachelor, and a butcher. "My dear sirs," I should reply, "I came here because I know a good view when I see one; not as a butcher, but as a lover of London, I condescended to join this club. Go away."

But how to describe the view? Even were mine the necessary skill, yet I must see to it that there is a vagueness about the picture. My club must never reveal its identity. This is not an advertisement authorised by a secretary at a loss for new members. No; I must be cautious. . . Hist! . . .

Below lies the river. Is it the Severn? Is it the Yalu? Alas! it were useless to deny that this is the Thames.

Below lies the Thames. The heavy barges slide down it. They slide slowly under the bridge (Charing Cross Bridge, perhaps; perhaps another), and overhead the trains rattle and rattle unendingly. Sometimes a steamboat paddles importantly past, and then again a long string of barges.

(Two men are taking that barge up the river with oars. It is hard work. They are rowing at three to the minute. Steady, bow! Look, look! Can it be? Yes, it is! They are quickening to four! Now you have them, Cambridge.)

Opposite, between bridges, warehouses and wharfs. When the tide is high they come straight down into the water, and this of itself gives them an air of adventure. Strange things could happen over the river when the sun was set: things out of the run of our well-ordered lives. A body could be dropped from one of the lower windows there. It would hide fearfully a moment behind the moored barges; then, out into the tide, and away down to the sea. Nor anyone the wiser.

But there is romance there, too. What are the words it brings to one's mind? Ah, yes.

> "For ere she reach'd upon the tide
> The first house by the water side,
> Singing in her song she died,
>   The Lady of Shalott.
> A gleaming shape she floated by,
> A corse between the houses high,
>   Silent into Camelot.
> Out upon the wharf they came,
> Knight and burgher, lord and dame,
> And round the prow they read her name,
>   The Lady of Shalott." . .

But that was before I was elected.

Away on the left rise two modern palaces. Red and white, and gardens beneath them. We are in good company. Even to-day knights and burghers, lords and dames, lunch quite close to us.

Further round with the bend of the river is an older palace. Alas! a palace no longer. Certain minions of the Government work here now. I say "work." I think that will put you off the trail. You will begin to wonder what this wonderful Government building can be.

And overtopping all at the head of the river is St. Paul's. Yes, surely, it is St. Paul's—I must grant you that. When the sun is setting this is the finest view in London. A great artist has called it the finest view in England. I won't go so far as that with him. But, so far as London is concerned, I am behind him. He has my authority for his statement. This is the best view in London.

And to think that some people want to climb up monuments to get views.

CHAPTER IX.

FOR ONE NIGHT ONLY.

On the 29th of February, Edward the VIIth being on the throne and our relations with other countries continuing to be of a peaceful nature, I went to a masked ball. A feature of the evening—perhaps I should say "another feature of the evening"—was that the ladies were to ask the men for dances—a reversal of the customary etiquette, as, perhaps, my readers are aware. (I am confident of two readers, at least.)

I had talked to Amelia about this dance, and wondered if I should wear fancy dress as well. Amelia thought I had better not.

"What would you go as?" she asked.

"Port Arthur. Act I.: Provisioning for the Siege."

"Pig!"

"Act II.: The Surrender. I wish you were going to be there. The opportunity only comes on leap-year days, and I can't wait another four years. Mother wants me to go off this season."

"I'm sorry I shan't be there," said Amelia, with a smile. "Mother and I are going out somewhere. You must tell me all about it."

For One Night Only.

I happened to know one of the stewards, so I discussed with him the chances of getting a full programme

"That girl might be pretty," I said. "But that's the best of a masked ball—anybody might be pretty."

"But she really is," he said. "I'll introduce her to you."

A minute later: "May I have the pleasure?" said the domino.

I handed her my programme.

"I have taken 'five,'" she said.

"Oh, have six or seven, won't you?" I pleaded. "Five isn't very many."

"I meant number five," she said, coldly.

We *must* remember to be haughty, I thought to myself.

"The fact is," I said, "there are so many people here who want to dance with me. I have such a lot of friends here to-night, you know. I am afraid I can only square you a spare—I mean spare you a square one."

But she had already passed on. I looked at my programme, and wondered who she was. Five. My favourite waltz. That was practically a proposal, wasn't it? Anyhow, I think it is where one begins to hope.

I watched her steadily through four dances. Then suddenly it struck me. "But it can't be," I thought; "it's simply impossible. She said she was going out with Aunt Anne."

I worried about it a bit, and then I approached my friend the steward.

"Is there anyone here as Joan of Arc?" I asked.

"Hundreds."

"What I mean is, Is there anybody here who—who *says* she's Joan of Arc. She wouldn't be dancing."

"Oh, I see. Yes, I think there is."

Then that accounted for Aunt Anne; and she had, indeed, come out with her mother. Bless her! We were going to have some fun.

After number five was over we found a secluded corner.

"My programme," I said, pointedly, "is a desert. There," pointing to five, "is the one oasis. I have a premonition that I shall soon be thirsty again." I always talk like this at dances.

"Didn't you come with friends?" she asked.

"Oh, heaps, heaps. But when once your initials were there it seemed sacrilege to let another scan it."

"You are rather—well, progressive, aren't you, considering this is the first time we've met?"

"I'm not really much of a sprinter," I said, modestly; "but to-day being to-day—"

"Oh, do you believe in leap-year proposals?"

"As a pursuit?"

"Well, it does amount to that, I suppose," she said, with a smile.

"Oh, I didn't mean—"

"No, but really?"

"Isn't it rather a dangerous topic?" I suggested,

"Of course, it's quite safe with me, but you might put ideas into anybody else's head."

"Oh, indeed," she began, indignantly. "But why is it so safe with you?" she ended.

"There is another," I said. "Besides, we've only just met."

"Yes," she said, thoughtfully. . . .

Two hours later I pointed out, "You've had six dances with me."

"I can't enter into statistics," she said, carelessly. "They're always misleading, too."

"Still it is interesting," I suggested.

"Possibly, but not to me."

I wondered whether to keep up the farce of pretending that I didn't recognise her. She seemed very keen on it herself. She even talked in a silly, affected voice, not a bit like her own. I decided to play with her a little longer.

"You haven't told me your name yet," I murmured.

"No?"

"The initials on the programme I can't read," I went on.

"Can't you? Let me look." She took my programme. "Can't you really read that?" she said, and looked down.

I seized the programme, and examined them carefully. By Jove!

My name begins with a C. Amelia's initials are A. R and the initials on the programme were A. C.! Surely this was a sign on Leap Year night! The music had gone to my head. I looked into space, and said firmly :

"I do."

"Likewise I will," I added.

"You conjugate very well," said the girl.

"It's the 29th," I said, softly. "Go in and win. Don't be afraid."

She turned away.

"Oh you silly girl," I cried. "Did you really think I didn't know you? Take that thing off and let me see you. . . . There! Oh Lord!"

For it wasn't Amelia!

It was a perfect stranger.

Well hardly that, because we had had six dances together.

Apologies were useless.

"Anyhow, you're American," I said.

She admitted it.

"So I feel sure you will understand," I went on. "You must have thought me an awful bounder. But I'm not, really. You ask Amelia."

She began to laugh to herself.

"I think I ought to go back to mother," I said.

She held out her hand. . . . We had five more dances together. It turned out that she was engaged to a great friend of mine, so there was no danger. But I didn't quite see how I was to tell Amelia all about that dance. I had promised to, you remember.

CHAPTER X.

TWO IN HEARTS.

I LEFT it to her, partner. She looked at her hand again, and frowned. Amelia is but a beginner at Bridge.

It was she and I against her father and mother. Amelia's mother plays a stern, unrelenting game. (I would quote Lamb here, only it is done so often and one is a little tired of it. Men like Lamb have a lot to answer for.) She is also conspicuously unsuccessful. Amelia's father can place every card in the pack after three rounds, now that he is used to his wife's style of play. But trouble ensues from this habit of his.

"I meant you to lead the knave," he says casually, at the end of the game.

"My dear William," says his wife, "I cannot lead a card that I have not got in my hand. Of course I should have played the knave of trumps if I had had it."

"But, mother," says Amelia.

"I think, Amelia, you should give me credit for knowing what I have in my own hand. I confess I don't know what other people have in their hands, nor do I care to enquire how they get their information. Why Edward should have played the queen, and not the ace, just now, unless he knew that I had the king. . . . Of course I'm not suggesting—"

"Amelia," I said, "we are betrayed. *Conspuez* Zola."

"Honours?" says Amelia's father, looking up from his scoring. "I had the ace and ten. You must have had simple. Sixteen above."

"*We* had simple honours," says Amelia's mother. "I'm certain of it. I remember distinctly."

"They had the king and queen," he said. "Who had the knave?"

"I had the knave," said his wife indignantly. "Don't you go losing us our honours. It was a good thing I remembered. You were just going to give them sixteen."

Then Amelia's father smiles. He is always right, somehow.

Meanwhile I had left it to her. She went through her hand once more.

"May I play, partner?" she asked.

"Certainly not," I said. "You've got to make trumps."

"Anything I like?"

"Now don't be giving her a hint, Edward." It is unnecessary to indicate the speaker.

"Forward, Amelia."

"Well—say hearts."

Her father led. "She's only got two hearts," he chuckled.

"Oh, Amelia! Only two?"

"They're very determined," said Amelia.

"Two hearts with but a single thought. Little one, please."

Amelia threw on a small club. "Is it going to be all right?" she asked.

"They're such baby ones."

"One's almost grown up. He's just got his first little pair of knickerbockers."

"Amelia!" said her mother.

"It's all right, dear. It's no secret."

I took the trick and led a diamond. Amelia had the ace, queen. The *finesse* failed.

"Blow," I said. "Blow, blow."

"My dear Edward!" said Amelia's mother indignantly.

"Thou winter's wind. Shakespeare," I added. "Thou art not so unkind as man's ingratitude. As man's—let's see, you lead a spade, do you?—ingratitude. Thy tooth is—h'm, a spade—thy tooth—three there, and four's nine, and five in my own hand, fourteen—thy tooth is not so keen, so—there are fourteen spades at least in the pack, Amelia—thy tooth—well, we'll try a knave. Where had I got up to?"

"Thy tooth was not so keen," said Amelia.

"Oh yes. Thy—"

"If you can't play the game properly, we had better stop," said her mother.

"I'm sorry. It's nervousness. Amelia's little trump is just going into—going to take a trick, I mean."

It did. "That was a mistake," said Amelia's father.

"Pure accident," I admitted.

"I meant that you'll lose a trick by it."

"You haven't seen my hand. It's all palm. Couldn't take anything. Ace of diamonds, please."

They got three tricks, which took them out. The usual discussion followed.

"Why did you go hearts?" I asked, more in sorrow than in anger.

"Well, you said we wanted two in hearts to win, and I had two."

"Ah, of course. Well they got three, I'm afraid."

"Didn't we get more than three?" asked Amelia's mother.

"I know we got one," I said, "because I watched it carefully."

"Well, I took eight in my own hand, and you had three, if not four, William."

"And Amelia took two, and I took two," I added. "Why these recriminations? Anyhow, that's sixteen already. Anybody else got any?"

"Honours?" said Amelia's father.

"I had all five in my own hand," said his wife.

"Yes, it was very unfortunate," I pointed out. "She sat right over Amelia's four of trumps."

"Why ever didn't you double, and why ever didn't you lead trumps?"

"I called for trumps," said his wife stiffly.

"I am afraid I wasn't listening."

"And you always get angry if I don't return your lead, so I purposely didn't lead trumps."

"I never get angry," he said.

I thought it was time to intervene.

"I saw a very pretty little problem the other day," I began, pacifically.

"Yes?" said Amelia, to help me.

"A. and B. were partners against X. and Z."

"And you *knew* I was weak in clubs," went on Amelia's mother, argumentatively.

I coughed loudly.

"Lord A. and the Marquis of B.," I repeated, "were partners against the Duke of X. and—and Prince Z."

"What is this, Edward?" asked Amelia's mother. "A problem? How interesting! Do go on."

"Well, Viscount A. had practically nothing in his hand. An ace or two perhaps, but for a viscount—well, you know what they are. So he left it to his partner."

"The Marquis of B.?"

"Exactly. Well, he went no trumps. The score was twenty-four love in their favour. So the Earl of C.—"

"But who was he?" asked Amelia's mother. "You haven't mentioned him before."

I really didn't know. I was getting muddled with so many peers, and I had only begun the beastly problem to clear the air.

"Oh no—no, of course not," I stammered; "*he* was looking on, you know. He said, 'Well, you *are* a bally ass.'"

"Oh!"

"Yes. So X.—"

"The Duke of X., yes?"

I felt that I must have one commoner among them.

"He wasn't a duke. Just X. A member of the Victorian Order. And he—well, really, I've forgotten what happened now. I know it ended up—What should Viscount A. do? I think the answer was, Nothing."

I wiped my heated brow. Amelia telegraphed her sympathy across the table.

"Best problem I ever heard," said her father, "was this. Score twenty-four love. Dealer has ace, king, six, two of hearts, king and another diamond, five small clubs, and three spades. What did he go?"

We discussed it carefully.

"Obviously clubs or leave it," I said. "I think I should have left it, but I don't know."

"Hearts," snapped Amelia's mother. "Certainly hearts."

"Rather risky with only four."

"What do you say, Amelia?"

"I hardly like to say, father. What did you say, Teddy?"

"Leave it."

"Then I guess I'll leave it, too."

Two in Hearts.

"Hearts," persisted her mother, "I know I'm right."

"Well, what did he go?" I said at last.

Amelia's father rose with a smile, and made for the door.

"He didn't go anything. It was a misdeal. That hand had fourteen cards in it. Have you ever been caught like that before?"

CHAPTER XI.

EARL'S COURT.

WE sat down in the Queen's Court, and I took out my programme.

"Now, what shall we do first?" I said. "The placid waters of the lake are spoken of with enthusiasm in the programme, but that sounds more like an after-dinner amusement."

Amelia glanced up at the captive flying machine, which was rapidly whirling through space.

"I suppose we ought—" she began.

"The point of view is affected by gravitation," I remarked. "It says so here;" and I tapped my programme again.

"Oh, what does that mean?"

"I think it means that if you look over the side your 'point of view' is, in fact, affected by"—I thought for a moment. "'Point of view,'" I continued, "is a pleasant euphemism."

"I think I begin to understand," said Amelia, pensively. "You get all the fun of travelling by water without the discomfort of seeing a foreign country."

"The motion without the ocean, to put it epigrammatically," I suggested.

"And there is the water below to help the illusion. Oh, dear! I know it so well."

Really, it is very handsome of them to do it to the life. Coming down by the Underground you are reminded (by the pace and dirt) of the journey to Dover. Once there, you are whirled rapidly six times through space, until you feel like you feel when you land at Calais. After that it is a mere step to Venice by Night.

We were soon in Venice. "Venice in London," they call it. I wonder if they have a "London in Venice," to which weary Venetians take the family. "Why not?" says Amelia.

Why not?

Bassanio having paid at the turnstile, enters "London by Night." "This way for the omnibuses!" shouts a voice. Bassanio pays again, and the family climbs up. The omnibus proceeds to glide placidly over the smooth cobbles. The conductor points to the scene painting on the right. "Westminster Abbey," says he, off-handedly. Bassanio gazes in rapture at St. Paul's.

"Westminster Abbey, my dear," he says in Italian.

"Ah-h," says his wife; "wasn't that where Wordsworth lived?"

Bassanio thinks "No."

"Savarino, listen to what father's saying, dear. That's Westminster Abbey."

Savarino looks vacantly at the Tower of London.

"Oh, I have a pretty picture of that in my little geography-book at home," he says, as a well-brought-up child should.

A barrel-organ strikes up the old English air "Pansy Faces." Bassanio's face softens. His arm steals slowly round his wife's waist. They are back fifteen years now, when she was a simple country lass and he came a-courting her.

She looks up at him with a smile. The old, old melody is wafted over the cobbles. . . .

"Remember the conductor—thank you!" says the conductor in Italian. It is the only Italian he knows.

Bassanio wakes from his dream with a start. He hands the conductor the small Italian coin which one hands conductors in Italy. Then he leaps lightly into a mud-heap placed fortuitously there by the "London in Venice" County Council.

The memory of his courting days is still strong upon him. He turns back and helps his wife off the 'bus.

So we picture it.

After Venice came dinner. Absorbed as she was in the Venetian atmosphere, Amelia insisted on a real Italian dinner. She began with a sardine from Sardinia, and finished up with a Neapolitan ice from Naples. You see how strong in geography I am getting.

On the way she fell in with macaroni. Personally, I did not touch it; but when she had finished I told her how macaroni is made. First you—(but perhaps some of our gentle readers are in the middle of their macaroni at this moment; maybe they have been promised some for tea if they are good). Well, then, you—(Amelia says she'll never touch it again, and I'm a nasty, horrid person. But it isn't my fault; I didn't ask her to listen; I was merely soliloquising). After that all you have to do is—(but they do say that it's the same with everything. If you saw chocolate made, I'm told . . . you'd never eat it again. Of course, that sounds rather absurd).

So that's how they do it.

By the way, macaroni is not the same as Garibaldi, who is a man. It's a small point, but I mention it in passing. (P.S.—Amelia wishes to add that there is a biscuit called Garibaldi, so there! And I'm not so clever as I thought I was.)

We did not glide over the placid waters of the lake, as originally intended. Instead, we proceeded to float in mellowy darkness to a vault of shimmery blue. This is what the Capricians do at Capri. It is really very fine. Space and the uses of advertisement forbid further praise.

But the best of the evening was spent at the band. Surrounded by all the glories of the pyrotechnist's art (Amelia thought a pyrotechnist was a Spanish brigand), we sat and dreamed of wonderful things.

At least I did. But Amelia's first remark to me, as we walked out into the night, was—

"How do you know it's made like that?"

CHAPTER XII.

THE SHORTEST IN THE BOOK.

THIS is probably the shortest chapter in the book. It records how Amelia went into a shop of some magnificence to buy table linen for an American friend. She found some which pleased her. It was worked in the corner with three feathers.

Amelia liked the design.

"How much is this?" she asked the splendid shop-walker.

The man looked condescendingly at her.

"Exclusive for Marlborough House, ma'am," he said, in a cold voice.

Amelia went out and ordered something hot for lunch.

CHAPTER XIII.

WE CALL ON COUSIN NANCY.

NANCY is my cousin, and has no connection with the great American continent. Sometimes, as a reward for blameless conduct in the past, I take Amelia to see her. I make it quite plain that it was I who discovered Nancy, that Amelia is an outsider—not to say an interloper, and that Nancy and I are—well—!

This came off the first time, Amelia--I believe they call it "bridling."

"What are you doing to-morrow afternoon, Teddy?" she asked. She ought to have supposed that I would be working, but this never seems to strike her.

"I'm going to see Nancy," I said.

"Is that a play, or what?"

"A cousin."

"Oh!" said Amelia coldly.

"The dearest, prettiest thing in the world."

"Arthur and I," began Amelia, "thought of—" (I hadn't an idea who Arthur was).

"I rather hoped you would come with me," I said.

"I should think you'd get on very well by yourselves. You see, Arthur and I—"

"Yes, but how about Nancy and I—I mean, me?"

"Miss—"

"Nancy. Everyone calls her Nancy."

"I hate that sort of girl."

I thought it was time to reveal the ter-ruth.

"Please, she's only four," I said.

"Oh! . . . You pig."

"How old is Arthur?"

She held up her arm, and waggled a little ivory elephant that clung to her bangle.

"Arthur," she said. "The dear!" So the next day we called on Cousin Nancy.

Nancy is, as I have said, my cousin. However, the difference in our ages leads her to call me "uncle." It is her own idea, and certainly I fancy myself most as an uncle. I remember that at school half the fellows used to be uncles, and I was never even a stepfather. But, thanks to Nancy, I may now lord it with the rest.

Nancy wears her hair short, another whim. Evidently she wishes me to be the uncle of a real nephew.

She was in bed with a cold. In a blue dressing gown she was prepared to receive callers. We arrived in style.

"Please come in," she called.

"Oh, *how* do you do, Mrs. Jones?" I said effusively.

"*How* do you do?" said Nancy.

"I ventured, dear Mrs. Jones, to bring Mrs. Jenkins with me." I presented Amelia. "Mrs. Jones, Mrs. Jenkins."

We Call on Cousin Nancy.

"*How* do you do?" said Nancy, with a sweet smile.

There was a pause. I kicked Amelia gently.

"Charmin' weather we're havin'," said Amelia, Mrs. Jenkins.

"Yes," said Nancy, Mrs. Jones. "Would—would you like some tea?"

"Comin' along in my motor—"

"Would you like some tea?" asked Nancy, turning to me.

"I said to Lord Percy—" continued Mrs. Jenkins.

"Dear Mrs. Jones, we *should* like some, so much," I broke in. "You must excuse Mrs. Jenkins. This is the first time she has ever been out to tea, and she is nervous. She generally has an egg in the nursery. And how is your dear daughter Belinda?"

"Oh, she's very well. . . . Will you excuse me a minute while I speak to my maid?"

Nancy turned away to the bedpost, and began to whisper violently. We caught the word "tea." Amelia smiled across to me, and I sent a wireless message back that this was Clapham, and she wasn't to come siding about here with her motor cars and Lord Percies.

"My maid says she will bring tea up in a moment," said Nancy.

"Oh, thank you," I said. "Mrs. Jenkins, this is Belinda." Amelia shook a limp wax hand.

"Here is tea," said Nancy. She put her head on one side. "Sugar?"

"Nine lumps," I said.

"None for me," said Amelia. "Thank you, dear Mrs. Jones. Oh, this *is* delicious tea. Where *do* you get it from?"

"From the grocer. May I have your cup back?"

Then an awful thing happened. Losing my customary *sang froid* and *savoir faire*, I swallowed the cup. It was an unpardonable breach of manners. A thing never done in the best circles.

"I'm awfully sorry," I said, "but I've swallowed the cup."

"Oh!" said Nancy. This was a new situation.

"I don't know how I came to do it," I apologised. "It's a thing that has never happened before with me."

"I'm afraid, dear Mrs. Jones, that he's not used to small cups," put in Amelia. "He prefers the thick wooden ones."

"Not to swallow," I explained. "Dear Mrs. Jones, can you forgive me?"

Nancy regained her nerve.

"Good-bye, Mr. Jenkins," she said. "I hope you've had a nice time. I'll just ask my maid to clear away."

She whispered behind the bedpost again. When she had finished Mr. and Mrs. Jenkins had left, but Amelia and Teddy were there for any other game.

Before we went away I tried to persuade Nancy to return our call. I don't think she was keen.

"I can't. I've got a cold," she said.

"Oh, but surely that won't matter."

"I've got two colds," said Nancy.

"Oh!"

"And—and a sneeze."

When we were saying good-bye there was a slight accident. It happened in this way.

"Good-bye, Nancy dear," I said.

"Good-bye, uncle," she said, casually.

"Good-bye, Nancy," said Amelia.

"Good-bye, dawlin'," said Nancy.

I was jealous at this. It was *my* cousin, and I wasn't going to be cut out by Amelia. I leant over to kiss Nancy.

Amelia saw my movement. From the other side of the bed she leant over, too. . . .

Nancy doesn't like being kissed. She drew away her head suddenly. It didn't seem to make any difference, though . . .

"I'm awfully sorry," I said, realising what had happened. Amelia got up without answering, waving the red flag.

"It was quite a mistake," I went on. "Nancy—"

"Nancy, you darling," I said, all at once. "We aren't a bit sorry, are we?"

"I hope you've had a nice time," said Nancy.

"A glorious time," I said.

CHAPTER XIV.

THE CONFESSIONAL.

WAITING one day for a train to Kew, Amelia and I lingered at the bookstall. Amelia bought a *Woman's Life*, "for Maid and Wife"—which is poetry. It is recognised that a purchase of this sort gives you the right to turn over everything else on the stall. Together we glanced at the *Sketch*, and then, while Amelia looked through "Everybody's Book of Etiquette," I made for "The Complete Letter Writer." (You know the blue sixpenny series.)

"It isn't etiquette to eat soup with a knife," said Amelia. "It's not done in England."

"Not this season."

"You must take it with a spoon, half-way between the middle of it and the end."

"Which end?"

"The spoon end, of course."

"Not the handle. Well, I always do. I measure it with a compass. 'Dear madam, pardon the addresses of a perfect stranger, but ever since I sat behind you that day in church I have dared to worship you. I am a butcher in a fair way of business, and many times lately have I had the pleasure of serving you in my shop. I can give you testimonials as to my honesty and sobriety, and would write to your father first if you preferred it.' *Answer unfavourable to the above.* 'Sir!' '

"Are you fixing up a proposal, Teddy?"

"Well, I was thinking of it. Hallo, here's a confession-book; let's buy it." . . .

Later on, in Amelia's drawing-room, we went through it together.

Page 1 was for the owner of the book. The book was undoubtedly Amelia's.

"I will fill it in for you," I said.

Details as to name and age were soon done. Then came more interesting things.

"Your favourite hero in real life?" I read.

"Oh, that's easy. Teddy—"

"Spare my blushes. Besides, what would your mother say? I understand of course, and I think it is very nice of you. At the same time—"

"Teddy Roosevelt, I was about to say."

I had my revenge.

"Who is he?" I asked, carelessly; "an American?"

Amelia's outburst was suppressed with difficulty—and two cushions.

"Favourite poet? Longfellow," I suggested.

"Of course."

"Favourite hero in fiction? You had better fill that in yourself. I have only read one American novel; it was called 'Uncle Tom's Cabin,' or something like that. So I can't suggest a hero for you. My own novel, of which I am the hero, is not yet out."

"Most hated vices," broke in Amelia. "Conceit and self-advertisement."

In most confession-books one is asked one's favourite flower. If one is really witty one then replies "Cauliflower." This jest has a great reputation in the suburbs. In fact, one can be very funny in a confession-book if one tries. I hope you understand that I am giving particulars of Amelia's confessions solely in order that you may appreciate her character. Like a distinguished American, "I never try to be as funny as I can." I never—

"Most hated vice," repeated Amelia, "self-advertisement. Have you got that down? Now then."

Here follow a few:—

Favourite game. Lawn tennis. (In the suburbs they say "pheasant.")

Favourite animal. "Toddles." (Toddles is believed to be a dog. Outside he is mostly hair, and might be anything; but the Real Toddles, or Toddles from Within is, as I say, believed to be a dog.)

Favourite food. Candy.

Favourite drink. Soda-water. (Ugh!)

Favourite occupation. Seeing London. (A delicate compliment to me, as I am showing her London. Dear madam, pardon the addresses of a perfect stranger, but I am a butcher in a fair way of business . . .)

Favourite instrument. Banjo. (She plays rather well.)

Favourite waltz. "Waves of the Danube."

And so forth. When we had finished Amelia kindly allowed me to fill in a page for myself. I had her at the very start, just as she had had me. It was my r—revenge.

"Favourite heroine in real life, Amelia."

Amelia turned away. You know how they "turn away" in novels, in order to "cast their eyes on the ground."

"Amelia," I repeated. "Our cook. She made the most heavenly meringues. Ah! those were happy days."

Lower down I was asked my pet aversion. I have seven—five literary men, one politician, two cricketers, one newspaper, one policy, puns, tapioca pudding, whisky, all hairdressers, two more literary men, hockey, John Gilpin, Wordsworthians, one dramatic critic, and Essex. Some day, when I am asked, I shall write my Avowals, explaining these aversions. Until then I content myself with the single entry in Amelia's book—*Insects*.

"Your favourite hero in history, Teddy?"

The good English boy sucks the end of his pen, and scrawls "Nelson." This is the only hero he knows. The good American boy says "George Washington." The American girl, perhaps, William Lloyd Garrison. The English girl, some well-known divine or reformer, or Sir Philip Sidney. In any case, it is hard to pin one's hero down to the board. Yet, if there is a man to admire—

"Columbus," I said; "I owe him a good deal."

"Thank you," smiled Amelia.

"That sort of pretty speech comes quite natural to me on Fridays," I said. "To-day being a Thursday, it was rather forced. I saw it coming a long way back."

The last question was my ambition in life. Ladies aren't asked for theirs. It is assumed they have none. They are only supposed to weep. Or it may be that the question is deemed unnecessary, since all girls have the same ambition. I was once introduced to somebody, and by-and-by it came like this. (It has to come, you know.)

". . . But I adore acting. All my friends say I ought to have gone on the stage; only mother wouldn't let me. Eva Moore parts suit me best."

I replied:

"My little brother is going to be a sailor."

"I didn't know you had a brother."

"He is an allegory," I said.

Since then, I have revived my little brother several times with effect. His is a useful but uncertain life.

In Amelia's case it was Ethel Barrymore parts which suited her. I am inclined to agree.

Well, as I say, I had to name my ambition in life. I hesitated for a time. First I thought I would say, "To be famous;" then it struck me that this was not ambition, but destiny. (The effect of this sort of remark on Amelia is delightful.) For a moment I considered a Sandford and Merton observation.

Other ideas occurred; to be written down and crossed out. . . . I made rather a mess of the book.

Amelia was glancing over my shoulder all the time. I threw down the pen, and looked at her.

"I'll tell you later on," I said.

CHAPTER XV.

OUR PRIZE STORY.

I HAD dropped into tea, and Amelia's mother had left us to amuse ourselves, like dears, while she attended to something else. I had seen that Amelia had something on her mind, and at this it came out. Bringing out an evening paper, she began,

"Do you want to earn three guineas?"

I was somewhat astonished. It was not the way people usually opened conversations with me. I felt as Lasker would feel if his opponent started by castling his king, when the more usual method, I believe, is to advance the pawn. (But may be I have that wrong, for I am no expert at chess.) So I said to Amelia:

"May we have that again, please?"

"Well, it's half of three guineas, really."

"Ah! that sounds more life-like. One pound eleven and six."

Amelia gazed at me in admiration.

"As a boy I won a prize at the arithmetic for long division," I explained. "It was not a good prize, but my Auntie has it still."

"Oh, I see. Well, now we're going to win three guineas between us. It's for a prize story."

"All right. What sort of story?"

"It must reflect the romantic side of life. It must be of living human interest. It must teem"—she glanced at the paper in her hand—"I know it teems with something—oh, here it is. 'It must teem with living human interest.'"

"It's done that already," I interrupted.

"Oh, I beg its pardon. I meant 'with quiet humour.' You see it's quite simple. Now then, what shall we have for a plot?"

She drew her chair closer to mine. The only thing left for me to do was to draw my chair closer to hers.

"A plot," I said, reflectively.

Most of my stories have a way of avoiding anything that approximates to a plot. They do this of their own intention, not regarding the wishes of the author. Often have I longed, regretfully, in the retrospect, for a plot. Why am I so different from others? Why did I never have a plot; a plot to which I could have retired when old age was near. "Of all sad words of tongue or pen . . ." And so on. Then I take myself in hand. "Come, come," I say to myself, "a truce to idle longings. The past cannot be altered. But there is no reason why you should not have a plot in the future. Be firm with your next story. Insist that it shall at least hint at some reference to a plan, to an arrangement." . . .

But now I see that I cannot plot. I am a harmless, mild-mannered person. There is nothing "strong" about my work; nothing that calls for any violent display of emotion on the part of my puppets. I doubt if there could be an illegitimate canary (even) in my stories. . . .

Forgive this personal interlude. I only introduce it to explain why, when for the third time I said to Amelia, "H'm, yes, a plot, quite so," I was no nearer to one than I am—well, than I am now!

"Well, have you got one?"

"No; but I don't see that there's any hurry for it. Let's settle the hero first, and then we can see what is likely to happen to him."

"Right O!" said Amelia. "First then, he must be clean shaven." I have a neat moustache. That's a woman all over.

I took out a pencil. "'Hero,' I jotted down on my cuff, "'has slight moustache.'"

"Teddy! *I* said clean shaven."

"'Hero,'" I corrected, "'has a moustache like a walrus.' You'd better be careful," I said, looking up, "or he shall have a beard as well."

"Teddy!" said Amelia sternly.

"Do you really mean it?"

"I think you're very rude."

"Then how's this? 'Hero, who had had a neat moustache, which was justly the admiration of the ladies, had lost it in a railway accident a few days before this story opens.'"

Amelia laughed. "Have it your own way. But anyhow, his name is Jack."

Mine's Edward. This story isn't going a bit as it ought to.

"He was at Cornell," went on Amelia. (Amelia's brother was at Cornell! Cornell! Cornell! Rah! Rah! Rah! At least I think that was it.)

"You're in England now," I protested. "As a delicate compliment to me, anyhow, the hero ought to be an Englishman."

"Right O! Oxford."

"Cambridge."

"Compromise, and say Durham."

"What a beastly man he's going to be."

"Oh, well, then—Edinburgh."

"Sorry; can't get it on my cuff. There's only just room enough for Durham. You've spoilt his life. I hope you're satisfied now."

"It doesn't matter much," said Amelia, "because his adventures happened afterwards."

"My dear Amelia," I said, "if you have written the story, why should I take half the money?"

"Oh, but I haven't. I've only got an idea, and you must work it up. Besides, you must correct me if I go wrong anywhere. You know I'm American."

"Proceed."

"Well, Jack, after serving in the Boer War, where he

won a medal with two clasps, embraced the profession of a—"

"There's too much clasping and embracing about Jack for me," I put in. "I don't think he's going to be a nice man at all."

"It was only just at first. Please don't interrupt. Afterwards be became a solicitor."

"Oh, I see."

"He then fell in love with a beautiful but poor maiden."

"Such things have been known to happen in England, as well as in America."

"And Jack, though well dressed and so on, depended chiefly on his aunt for his money."

"We call them uncles in England. . . . Oh, I see! I beg your pardon."

Amelia thus went on to explain that Jack's aunt was really younger than he was, which is of course possible, though confusing. And she was in love with the man with whom the girl whom Jack loved was in love. Taken quickly, that is even more confusing still. But possible. Quite possible. And the man with whom the girl whom Jack loved was in love was in love with the girl who was in love with Jack. The difficulties of this situation are entirely due to Amelia's absurd diffidence in giving names to her characters.

"This isn't a story," I interrupted. "It's a trial in tact. And the right answer is, 'Jack commits *hara kiri*.'"

"No, really. What do you think of it?"

I had one or two phrases running in my head.

"The subject," I said, "is a trifle thin. Likewise it is much too smart. The plot is hackneyed, not to say *vieux jeux;* there is too much of the religious element; the climax is unduly prolonged; the dialogue is not true to life; the murder in the fifth chapter is a trifle strained; the—"

"I suppose that's what they say of your work?"

"It is," I confessed.

Amelia smiled.

"It's a good plot," I went on, "but the country isn't ripe for it. More spade work is necessary."

"But do let's do it," pleaded Amelia. "I should like to win a prize so much."

So we did it. We made Jack speak in the Scots tongue. "Hoots ava, I'm no what ye'd call doited the noo," were his opening words, for he was gleg at the up tak'. Everybody else was a peer of the realm.

We sent it under Amelia's name, and it got a prize.

You needn't believe this.

CHAPTER XVI.

TWO AT THE TOWER.

AMELIA hadn't been to the Tower since she was six, nor I since I was eight. We went (it appears) in the same year, and our united age is now four hundred and thirty-seven. Now, tell me: How many horses are there in the stable?

I beg your pardon. I was quite carried away by the thought of a breakfast-table problem in real life.

Well, anyhow, we hadn't been over the Tower of London since we were quite small. But as I have already told you Amelia's age, I shall not dwell upon it again.

One begins by crossing the Moat. Some soldiers were playing football in it, but we would rather have seen water there. Certainly one of them shaped well at outside left, but this doesn't altogether compensate. Oh, for the days when one could plunge noiselessly in and swim across to the succour of one's lady! (After removing one's doublet, pardie.) I have no historical backing for such incidents, but I supposed they occurred.

Amelia thinks not. Amelia says what really happened was that she waved one lily hand from the dungeon keep, and murmured, "Eftsoons, he cometh not, Sir Guy." She implies, in fact, that I funked the affair. Ha, indeed!

But that was years ago. Yesterday we crossed the Moat on dry land, and proceeded through an array of Beefeaters to the Armoury. At the entrance to this we found an ordinary policeman! Amelia begs to lodge a formal protest. This is not doing the thing in style.

In the Armoury we were struck by the number of presents made to Henry VIII. by admiring friends, and in particular by the Emperor Maximilian.

"I didn't know he was so popular," I said. "It seems that I have misjudged him."

"Silly," said Amelia, "they're wedding presents, of course. If you got married six times you'd have a lot of presents."

Of course.

Among the presents to the bridegroom we noticed a fine set of fluted armour, bearing the Nuremburg stamp, richly *repoussé*, and displaying the Burgundian cross *ragulé*, etc., etc.

"Maximilian to bride, a combed morion."

And so on.

But poor Max must have got tired of it all.

We imagine him in his garden retreat when a courier bursts into the presence.

"Sire, his Majesty King Henry the Eighth thought that you might have forgotten that he is getting married to-morrow."

"What, *again?*"

"Yes, please your Majesty."

"I say, look here, this can't go on. Tell him I shall bring an action against him if he does it again. He's ruining me."

However, being a kind-hearted man, he fetched down a helmet from the box-room. You may now see it in the Armoury on the left-hand side as you go in.

But if Anne Boleyn ever saw Henry wearing it—well, Amelia is sure that she welcomed her fate.

In this room also is a "collar for prisoners." Personally, both for neatness and comfort, I prefer the ordinary up-and-down sort. But fashions change.

If only these were the days of armour how much more interesting shopping would be. "Two suits of chain mail for the summer, please."

In boys' books the hero is always presented with the most beautiful chain mail, which he wears under his vest. It is somewhat cold at first, and a little bit rough on his mother, who had told him always to wear flannel next to his skin. This mail is very finely wrought (in gold, I fancy), and it is a dying gift from his uncle, who got it from a Jew. The dying uncle told him to wear it night and day, and that is why he wears it under his vest—to simplify the problem of undressing without removing it. The other reason is that, when the villain finds him in bed, and stabs him three times quickly, with the words, "Ha! so is my lord avenged!" then your hero sits up, and says, "Yah! never touched me!" After this the villain is his faithful slave for ever after, and no wonder. A hero whom nothing can perforate is worth serving.

"But, really, it must be splendid," I said to Amelia, "to have a mare Swallow between your knees, and to feel absolutely fire-and-burglar proof up above, and to go dashing about the country all along o' the Black Prince and sich."

"You'd probably fall off," said Amelia; "and think of me, all alone; and anyhow, you promised to play croquet to-morrow afternoon. So, you see, the Black Prince will have to worry along without you. It can't be done at the price."

"One's country first, Amelia, please. If the Black Prince wants me to fight the Wars of the Roses for him, I can hardly plead croquet as an excuse."

"No; but you might tell him that you had been kept in for history, and couldn't get off. He would quite understand."

I find I have forgotten to mention Henry the Heighth's Harquebus. There is nothing in it, except the name.

Leaving the Armoury, the intelligent visitor may proceed to the Beauchamp Tower. Inside there is an elaborate piece of sculpture—a memorial to the four brothers Dudley. There is a wreath of roses for the first (Ambrose), oak-leaves for Robert, gilly-flowers for Guildford. So far we see that the designer has shown a pretty wit. But, alas! we find "Honeysuckle for Henry!"

Lovers in London.

Oh, Henry!

And he stood on the top of Beauchamp Tower, he did, and sang, "I'll be your honey honey-suckle. . . ."

And she, the jailer's daughter Beatrice, stood below and listened, and wondered that an Earl should woo her.

And when he died (killed at the siege of St. Quentin, 1558, as Amelia will tell you) she went and told his eldest brother John. He was head of the family, and had a right to know.

John, so it happened, was engaged upon a piece of amateur sculpture. Surrounding a bear and a lion (John fancied himself most at bears), he had designed to put four wreaths for his four brothers.

He wasn't altogether a bad sort, John, but a trifle dull. So when, after much thought, he had decided on roses for Ambrose, oak-leaves for Robert ("Robur an Oak," said John, and was proud), gilly-flowers for Guildford, he was fairly baffled by Henry.

Then came Beatrice.

"Honeysuckle for Henry. Oh, Henry!"

CHAPTER XVII.

ENGLAND *v.* AMERICA.

I HAVE an aunt who lives at Chiswick. (You mustn't think I'm boasting.) Hither came at noon Amelia and I. The International Croquet Tournament takes place at Chiswick now and then. England *v.* America. One Amelia represents America. Modesty prevents me from naming the English champion.

Once, though, I left the honour of the old country in the hands of Nancy. (I hope you haven't forgotten Nancy.) The result was excellent.

Nancy plays left-handed, with something of a golf-action; as she leans forward to make her stroke there is a foot or so of handle projecting above her neck. With her feet slightly apart she brings the mallet-head well over her shoulders; there is a look of determination on her face. "See me hit *him* in the eye," you can hear her say. . . . .

Thud!

She has missed the ball, as the turf will show.

Amelia laughed unkindly. Nancy looked up at her calmly.

"I sometimes do that often," she explained

Another effort, and the ball cleared a hoop ten yards away. "Good gracious, dawlin'," is her only comment. It gave her confidence, however, and she got going with black. Her method (an infallible one) is to chivy the ball through all the hoops at the end of the mallet. The game, played this way, resembles hockey. Nancy went round three times with black, scoring forty odd goals. She was on her fourth round before Amelia grasped the idea. Then she called Nancy's attention to a hoop that had been left in the cold.

"Won't you go through that one?" she suggested.

Nancy sat down on the grass, and looked at Amelia in surprise.

"I should think it's your turn now," she said with scorn for one who knew so little of the game.

Amelia took a futile shot with red.

"Your turn, Nancy," she said, brightly.

Nancy rose, and surveyed the field.

"I think I'll go with red this time," she said. "It hasn't done much lately."

Poor Amelia! Red took a few hoops with the air of a *connoisseur*. Amelia followed with yellow. Yellow happened to be in position—a pure oversight. The blood of all the Gibson girls was up. Yellow was going to do a hoop.

"Won't you play with red, dawlin'?" came Nancy's voice.

So England won.

After lunch we went out on to the lawn. Amelia

sat down in a deck chair, while I selected a mallet. By the time I had found one which looked as though it would do justice to my style of play, Amelia was asleep.

"Coward," I said; "America's frightened. America was in for a licking this afternoon."

Amelia opened one eye.

"Don't," she said; "I'm changing presidents, and I must be kept quiet. You're too energetic."

"I can go to sleep if you like," I said. "No one is better at sleeping in the afternoon than I am. But I'm fighting against it."

"I don't want to fight, but by—"

"Look here, if you'll just begin then you can go to sleep while my turn is on."

America agreed to this, and when I had got the four balls going, she retired to her chair.

"2.25 p.m." I called out, "Red doing the third hoop."

Amelia snored delicately.

"2.30 p.m. Grand passage. Weather brilliant. Red making the fifth hoop."

Amelia sighed.

"2.40 p.m. Wind dropped. Red ball drifting towards the stick."

"May the best boat win," murmured Amelia.

"2.45 p.m. Wind shifted a point. It *would* do it. Red ball rounded the stick, and beating up to the seventh hoop. The men are splendid."

Then I missed.

"Regrettable incident," I reported. "Yellow ball ambushed behind a wire entanglement. It's your turn, Amelia."

Amelia came out of her retirement and looked round.

"Where's black?"

"Oh, black. Well you see that beautiful bed there, with the hymantifilums in it?" (Hymantifilums is all the botany I know, and I don't really know that.)

"Yes."

"Well, black's behind that."

"What's he doing there?"

"Just resting. He's been out of an engagement for some time."

"I don't see how he got there," said Amelia suspiciously.

"He must have jumped the bed. Naughty boy! How dare he?"

"Then that's the way he's coming back."

"Oh, but think of Aunt Ethel's hymantifilums. Let me implore you to think of them before it is too late."

Amelia thought so much of them that she brought her ball round to the front of the bed, and took a shot from there. It hit red.

"The charm of croquet," I said, "is its uncertainty. The same applies to cricket, if we are to believe the special correspondents of the *Mail*."

"Now then," said Amelia.

"Don't be bloodthirsty."

"Where would you like red to go?"

"Through the eighth hoop," I answered promptly. "It's rather a long shot from here, but you might do it. Try."

"No, I've got a better future for red than that."

"Red really wants to be a sailor," I said; "but, as you say, he's rather young to decide."

"How about *that* corner of the lawn?" she meditated.

"No, not *that* corner of the lawn," I pleaded. "We speak for those who cannot speak for themselves."

"The other corner is certainly farther."

"Yes, the other corner's father all right. He hasn't a mother, poor lad. Pity the poor step-orphan."

So Amelia laughed and spared him. She also did five hoops, and wired yellow.

"Is yellow supposed to be wired?" I asked scornfully.

"Theoretically it is wired."

"An ounce of practice is worth a pound of theory," I moralised. "Look out."

"If you do hit, it will be a foul stroke."

"A follow-on stroke," I corrected.

I hit as hard as I could, twisted the mallet slightly, and heaved. There is nothing in the rules about that. Yellow and black dashed into the laurels. The hoop itself soared over into the next garden. A beautiful shot. If I had been allowed to go on I could have done the hole in three. . . .

"I don't know," I said, "but I think it must be tea-time."

CHAPTER XVIII.

MY COUNTRY HOUSE.

WHEN I am tired out by a week's hard work I run down to my Country House on the Sunday. Last week Amelia came with me, and we spent the afternoon sitting out by the lake. She didn't know at first that she was in my grounds. No, the silly thing must actually mistake it for St. James's Park!

We have tried all the parks, but we cling to St. James's. Indeed, I have now appropriated it, as you see. Battersea for its river, and Regent's for flowers; Kensington Gardens for its children, and Hyde Park for its grown-ups; Finsbury Park for them as likes it, and Victoria Park for those who know how to get there; the Green Park, too, for Piccadilly.

But St. James's for us.

I was somewhat nervous when Amelia came down. I had had to discharge one of my keepers that morning, and the thing had worried me a bit. Also I thought the grass wanted cutting. (Our boy had hurt his hock, and couldn't pull the mower.)

"I hope you like it," I said diffidently, as I brought her in. "I am afraid you aren't seeing it at its best. The autumn, when the leaves are turning; or the spring, when the buds are shooting; or the winter, when the snow is on the ground. In fact, this is really the worst time."

"I must come again in the autumn."

"I'm afraid you won't see it at its best in the autumn," I said. The spring, when the buds are shooting; or the summer, when the flowers are blooming; or the — "

"I think it's very nice," said Amelia. "Has it been in the family long?"

"Only a few weeks. I throw it open to the public on Sundays, you observe. That man there without a collar, for instance, he isn't one of the guests. Oh, you mustn't run away with that idea."

"I suppose," said Amelia, doubtfully, "you must almost keep a gardener to look after it?"

"He drops in every other morning and does a bit of weeding. The lawns aren't cut, because the boy has strained his fetlock. I mean—the pony has a headache. Gardeners and things are a great nuisance."

Amelia's father has a gardener in America of whom he is very proud. (I don't mean that he is proud of having one, but proud of having this particular one. Not proud of him *quâ* gardener, as they say.)

Amelia's father prattles with him pleasantly about Hymantifilums and fertilisers, and Mrs. Simkins and aphides. The gardener, not to be outdone, retaliates with a remark as to the evil effects of a maritime influence on the conifers. He has seen better days, and could, if necessary, add a word of French.

I have said that Amelia's father is proud of him. He is; prouder, indeed, than he is of Amelia or her brother. I believe that he would be more pleased if the man planted a tulip the right way up (inadvertently) than if his daughter married the most confirmed Duke.

"He's spoiling the man," said Amelia.

"I'm always careful with my underlings," I said; "at least, until last night."

"What happened then?"

"I killed a gardener's wife."

"Badly?"

"Don't joke about it. It's very sad. I didn't exactly kill her, but—"

It was like this. The day before I wrote a story. One of the characters was a gardener named Searle. He didn't come in much, but he had to come in a little. I fancy he opened the gate to the hero as the latter came back from the wars. One always calls gardeners Mister. So he was Mr. Searle.

I sent it to be typed. It came back that night, and I had a good many corrections to make. One sentence caught my eye. "'And glad it is I am to see you, maister,' said Mrs. Searle." (Mark the 'maister'; this is called local colour.) *Mrs.* Searle! Without thinking, I picked up a pen and ran a line through the "s"; and I put a little "d" in the margin—all as neat as could be. Then, suddenly, I realised what I had done. I had killed the gardener's wife!

"For one short hour, Amelia, that noble woman had lived and loved. She had made that interesting, and now historic, remark to my hero; and she had called him 'maister.' She may even have made other observations. A noble life was hers. . . . And think of Mr. Searle. Married for an hour, and now a bachelor again. Or is it a widower? No, I think a bachelor. Poor, poor man. Yes, I am a murderer!"

"Cheer up, Teddy."

"But think of the possibilities of Mrs. Searle. Think of the power for good she might have been. Ah, well . . . You know, Amelia, I think Mrs. Searle was one of the most finely drawn of all my characters. I am proud of that woman."

It is not only gardeners who worry me. I have a keeper who is supposed to feed the ducks. Does he ever remember this? No. The minnows in the lake are supposed to be preserved. But what do we see to-day? Hundreds of little boys fishing. Then take the sparrows. How can I let the shooting if they won't look after the sparrows?

"A landowner's life is a hard one. I sometimes wish that I were poor, that I had to eke out my existence on a paltry three thousand a year."

"So do I," said Amelia. "Being a great heiress bores me frightfully. I want to be loved for myself alone."

Right O. She shall. That hundred pounds of hers shall be settled on herself exclusively. . . .

"Good-bye, Sir Charles," said Amelia, as she got up to go. "Charmin' old place this of yours."

"Good-bye, dear lady."

"Say, I guess Poppa would just like to buy it. I'll send him right along to fix it up. How much would you be wanting?"

"My dear, dear lady!"

"Only a million? Guess Poppa would pay more than that to please me. Guess I—hallo! there's our bus. Shriek, Teddy, and wave your hat. We just can't miss it. Have you got tuppence? Because I haven't."

CHAPTER XIX.

LORD'S AND A LADY.

"I PLAYED cricket once," said Amelia.

"In Amurrika?" I asked.

"Yes; it was fun."

"But I thought they only played base-ball in Borseton," I objected.

"Oh no, they do lots more. They drink iced water, and eat popcorn, and say Momma. Oh, and marry real dukes. There are a heap of things you have to learn yet."

"Very well, I'll learn 'em, and write a book about America. But I shall leave out that bit about the dukes. It isn't giving a chap a fair chance."

Amelia's original remark had followed a suggestion of mine that we should look in at Lord's for an hour. "Looking in" at Lord's sounds so much better than "going" there. It implies that one is a member of the M.C.C. Which one isn't.

So we hailed a hansom. To leap into a hansom was the work of a minute. (If this seems unusually quick, it must be remembered that Amelia comes from America, where they do things fast.) In a little while we were on the ground.

Kent was batting. If I were writing a novel I shouldn't dare to say Kent was batting, for fear of discovering the identity of my hero. I should remark that Loamshire was at the wickets, owing to the fact that the Downshire captain had lost the toss. This is very subtle.

But I cannot deceive you. Kent really was batting.

Bosanquet was bowling. His name might have been Smith or Jones or Robinson. But it wasn't. It wasn't even Hogbin. It was Bosanquet, and he was bowling "googlies." You see how honest I am with you.

As I had undertaken to explain to Amelia the sights of London, my duty now was evident.

"These are 'googlies,'" I said perfunctorily.

"Who is?"

"There. That's a 'googly' now."

"Oh, I see. We call them umpires in the States. Isn't it strange?"

"Goo-oh-ell-ee-ess-googlies," I said. "It's the name of that particular kind of ball."

"You mean when it pitches half-way and bounces twice?"

"Well, now and then," I admitted.

Apart from this, Amelia knows all about the game, so I said nothing more. But there was an old gentleman sitting behind us who insisted on explaining everything in detail to the lady with him. We listened (we couldn't help listening) with interest at first, but soon grew tired. He fairly leapt at anything that came his way.

"'L.b.w., bowled Trott,'" he read out from his card. "Now, do you know what that means? When the batsman—impedes with his leg—a ball which—otherwise—would have struck the wicket—he is out. L.b.w., leg before wicket—that is to say—his leg—is in front of the wicket—and so—so—impedes the ball."

He spoke in puffs, being in difficulty with his breath. Later on he noticed one of the eleven in the pavilion wearing a Band of Brothers blazer.

"You see—now that he is out—he puts on—a jersey—to prevent himself catching cold. They got very hot—at the wicket—and so they have—these jerseys. Some are red—some are blue—or any colour. When they are batting—they wear pads—to protect themselves from the ball. Some of the balls are very swift—and could give them a good hard blow. These athletics—are a great thing—for the youth of England. You know—we have a saying that—Waterloo—"

"I beg to move that the question be now put," said Amelia to me. [Cries of "Gag, gag!"]

"I'm glad," she went on, "that you aren't always explaining things."

"It *is* nice of me," I admitted, "and is not to be attributed to ignorance. As an ardent follower of Kent, may I say, 'Blow,'" I added, as my pet batsman was caught.

"It was a jolly good catch."

"A child could have caught 'it," I said bitterly. "The old gentleman behind us could have caught it in his mouth. 'Twas ever thus from childhood's hour; I never loved a dear gazelle—and oh! the difference to me."

"Did 'ums! Did the nasty deep-extra-cover catch the horrid ball, then? Come and examine the pitch."

The innings being over, we gathered round the wicket, and speculated as to which end we should put Amelia on. She herself thought the nursery end, as the wind would help her swerve. But, as I pointed out, the wicket was badly cut up that end, and she could take advantage of it by bowling from the pavilion. Besides, the ball couldn't be hit out of the ground so easily from that wicket.

"But, really, I am jolly good," she said.

"I once made seven myself," I put in. "Don't think I'm boasting, but facts are facts."

"Oh, but I'm a bowler."

"I also bowl. I bowl very fast, and compared with me, James B. King is a slow leg-breaker. So is Kotze."

"Let's take a team to America," suggested Amelia.

"Right O. I guess I'll ask Charles B. Fry. We'll play matches against Borse-ton."

"You seem to think Boston is the only place in America."

"I don't, really," I said. "There's Noo York as well. We'll play Noo York, if you're good."

"If you make fun of me you shan't go on to bowl."

"I'm very sorry," I said. "Beneath a poor but honest face and abominable manners I hide a kindly heart. So forgive me, there's a dear, and let me open the attack."

"Very well. And you shall report for the *Daily Mail.*"

So it was agreed, and I entered upon my reporting duties at once. This was my telegram for that afternoon:—

LORD'S.

Weather ripping.
Amelia and I both scored very fast.
There was only one maiden the whole day.
Only one worth mentioning.
And she looked simply sweet.
She took tea with me afterwards.
It ought to be a good match.
But you never can tell.

CHAPTER XX.

EARLY IN THE MORNING.

It was ten o'clock as I sat down by the water next morning, in the gardens of my country house. (After all, ten o'clock is not so very early in the morning.) There was a mist, which showed the hot day to come, and I considered, without remorse, the hard fate of millions of workers around me.

There is something delightfully wicked about a wasted morning. The morning, one is told, is for work. The afternoon, if you can afford it, for recreation perhaps; more probably for work. The evening for social pleasures, possibly; but, of course, for work, if you want to be Lord Mayor. But anyhow—this is the point anyhow—the morning for work.

Theoretically, the morning is my busiest time. Breakfast over at nine, and then four hours' solid work till lunch time. I have pictured the scene to myself again and again. It is nothing to my imagination. But actually—well, Lords' is not far off, and Jessop is sixty not out, and—and—

Once there, you feel you are living riotously. You are the very dickens of a fellow. There is nothing you will not dare after this. You see, opening before you, the life of crime and adventure. You run away to sea, and don't care a pin for the motion; you rob your kind master's till (that comes before really); and finally, after a series of breathless escapes, you come to an unromantic end, such as is depicted by Hogarth in the Fourth Stage of Cruelty.

But it was worth it! Worth it a thousand times.

I have stolen this morning (as many other mornings), but I am not going to Lord's to-day. For one thing, I went yesterday; and, for another, Amelia wouldn't be there. She may not be here, but she won't be there.

Also she was here the other day. . . .

I am really saving money now.

If I were working in my rooms, I should probably be wanting to buy a box of nibs or some blotting paper. Or else I should be writing stories which would have to be typed. . . .

I spotted Amelia on the other side of the water. If only a wild bull would attack her, I could plunge in, and swim across to her rescue. Why is there no wild bull handy? As it is, I must take the prosaic (but drier) course of walking round.

She didn't see me. I sat on the end of her seat, and still she didn't see me.

"A beautiful morning," I said; "oughtn't you to be doing needlework? Or what is it girls do in the morning?"

Early in the Morning.

Amelia gave a start as I began to speak, but didn't look round.

"Oh, good morning," she said.

"Won't you look at me and make sure it is me? I might be someone else."

Amelia smiled, and continued to look over the water.

"'His Ship in Sight,' by Marcus Stone. Note the *chiaroscuro* on the water. Or is it a brigantine?"

It turned out to be one of the wild birds for which St. James's Park is so famous.

"As a matter of fact, I'm not who you think I am. He's at home working hard. Good boy!"

Amelia looked round.

"I wanted to talk to you, Teddy," she said.

"It was very nice of you to call on me here."

"Yes, I thought I should find you at home. Now I'm going to be serious."

"Serious?" I said in dismay. "You'll spoil everything."

"Yes, really serious."

Well, anyhow, it shall have a chapter to itself.

CHAPTER XXI.

SHOWING THAT ST. JAMES'S PARK HAS ITS MOMENTS.

"NOW then," she began, "I'm going to talk like a mother and a father and an uncle all in one."

"Very well. I'll listen like a son and a nephew."

"Please be serious, Teddy. What do you do?"

"I don't do. I am."

"What am you then?"

"A nauthor, a rising nauthor."

"Late—rising, I expect. You write stories in magazines, don't you?"

"I think you misjudge me," I said; "I write stories in exercise-books. Then I pin the pages together and send them to be typed. After that the typed copy goes to a magazine accompanied by a polite note. The polite note points out that I am theirs faithfully. By-and-bye the typed copy returns. It is accompanied by another polite note which intimates that, on the contrary, the honour is theirs."

"But you have had things accepted, haven't you?"

"Certainly. There was one only last winter."

"You do nothing else but write stories?"

"And things. I was once 'Our Military Expert' in an evening paper. I gossiped about *échelons*."

"What I'm thinking, Teddy, is that you don't work hard enough. Now for instance—this morning—why aren't you writing something?"

"The duties of a host," I began.

"Teddy, I'm not playing now."

"Well, you see, *Punch* came out last night, so this is always a slack day with us. And the editor of the *Times* gave me a holiday as well."

"Of course, if you make a joke of everything —"

"I'm not making a joke of it, I'm being very bitter and sarcastic."

Amelia sniffed.

"I'm soured," I said; "I've drained the cup to the dregs. I've—"

"Isn't it a pretty view?" said Amelia.

"I do take the whole thing very seriously," I went on. "You mustn't think—"

"Oh, don't let's worry about it," said Amelia, pleasantly. "It's nothing to do with me. I wonder what the time is."

"Of course, if—"

"Oh, don't keep on! I'm sure you work very hard. What do you say the time is?"

I glanced at her as I took my watch out.

"Don't be angry with me," I said.

"Angry! My dear boy, what have I got to be angry about?"

"Nothing. Absolutely nothing."

"I'm glad you think so."

"Well, don't you think so?"

"I don't want to discuss the question."

I got a glimpse with the left eye. She was looking straight in front of her, and was really very angry. We surveyed the water for a while. At last,—

"This is the first quarrel we've had," I said. I couldn't have made a more tactless remark if I had tried. It deserved, and got, no answer. I tried again.

"It was my— I mean your fault," I said.

Amelia leant back in her chair.

"You shouldn't have talked so much like my uncle," I said. "I always get angry with him when he talks like that."

I turned round and looked at her.

"Don't be an uncle to me," I implored.

Amelia put up her parasol.

"I say, don't let's be cross," I pleaded. "Say you're sorry I've been so disagreeable, or I shall go straight home and commit *banzai*. You wouldn't like it to be said of a nephew of yours that he went straight home and committed *banzai*, would you?" . . .

"She's very disagreeable, and I shan't play with her any more. I shall go and talk to a duck instead." . . .

A duck waddled up out of the water.

"Go away," I said nervously. "I was only joking. I'm not going to talk to anybody. Don't stop to thank me. Go away."

We sat in silence for ten minutes. . . .

"By the way," said Amelia, "I can't go to the British Museum to-morrow, after all."

"No? Had you arranged to go with somebody, then?"

"Ridiculous though it may sound, I had arranged to go with you."

"Surely not. I've got an engagement to-morrow. You must have been going with somebody else."

"Oh yes, you're quite right. I was going with a man called— but I won't tell you his name. He used to be a dear friend of mine. Something like you in looks, only he happened to be a gentleman."

"Poor man. I know that sort. And the extraordinary thing is that I was going to the British Museum with somebody very much like yourself, only certainly not so pretty. No. She has a perfectly sweet mouth, and she's always smiling and playing silly tricks like that with it. Of course that spoils her. Otherwise. . . . But I won't insult her by calling her a real lady. . . .

"She was a dear, though. We used to have perfectly ripping times together. We used to go to the Zoo, and the Tower, and silly places like that. Did your man ever take you to the Zoo? You can have awful fun there, you know. . . .

"And we used to have teas at places like the A.B.C. You can play there, too, rather well. Did your man— oh, but he was a real gentleman! He probably took you to the Carlton. . . .

"And then we used to play in the parks. I used to meet her there in the mornings sometimes. Quite by accident, she thought. But it wasn't really an accident, you know, because I was there every morning—just on the chance. I used to work every night till about three to make up. Of course I didn't let her know, because she would have said I was ruining my health, or my eyesight, or something. . . . And seeing her was really working, because she was the heroine of the play I was writing. Somehow she seemed to be the heroine of all the things I was writing. I think editors must have got a bit tired of it. . . ." I looked over the water again.

"Was this girl you were going to the British Museum with—was she very nice?" said Amelia, after a pause.

"Simply sweet."

"I think she's a beast."

"No, no, you don't know her as well as I do."

"Well, you aren't going there with her now."

"No?"

"No. You're going to try and forgive her; and, to show that you do, you're going to take her down into the country to-morrow. She's a little—a little tired of London."

"And how's she going to show she has forgiven me?"

"By being really nice to you to-morrow. You know, she can be awfully nice when she tries."

"Don't I know it? Oh, don't I know it?"

"Will you meet her at Victoria to-morrow at half-past nine? Will Victoria do?"

"Victoria is the one station."

"All right. And be very nice and jolly to her, and we won't be serious any more. I think I'll go home by myself. You stay here. Good-bye—dear."

CHAPTER XXII.

THE MORNING.

WHAT follows, then, has really no place in the book, seeing that we were no longer in London. It is an interlude in the country. But its immense importance to two people in the world justifies its inclusion—(as they say of the twelfth man in the 'Varsity Match).

At nine twenty-five I was at Victoria. At nine thirty-five Amelia appeared. At nine forty—but no. Let us dissemble. We don't want you to have any clue to the spot chosen for our interlude. If you knew what time the train started, you might swarm down in your millions and vulgarise the place. At nine something, then, we got into an empty carriage.

"Alas! there's nobody to say good-bye to us," said Amelia, as the train moved off amid handkerchief-wavings and sobs.

"The last time I was on the line a woman got in at Clapham Junction, and her daughter saw her off, and said, 'Now, mind you write, dear, as soon as you get to London, and let us know you've arrived safely.'"

"I've never been to Clapham. Did she write?"

"Alas! at that breathlessly exciting point the story

ends. Of course, your not having been to Clapham—I say, you are looking ripping. I don't know if I may just mention it."

"I never expected you'd be in time."

"Ah! but you didn't see my breakfast. Somehow it always seems to be Friday in my rooms. Never mind; wait till lunch."

"Shall we have lunch at an inn? What fun!"

We got out at the little station. It is a mile or more from our village, and really belongs to another one. We bought chocolates at the "grocer and draper."

The day was hot and cloudless.

I should like to describe the day more fully, but I think that gives you the impression. Hot and cloudless, and the smell of flowers, and the hum of bees, and I pointing out places of interest with the end of my cigarette to Amelia answering, "You don't say," with her mouth full of chocolates.

This pointing out of places of interest is a terrible ordeal for the stranger. The host must know that he is boring his visitor, and yet he has no mercy. "I'll just take you round after breakfast, and show you the country," he says. "That's where Sir Thomas lives—you know—the soap man. This road used to be private property, and then we made a row about it, and Sir Thomas . . . You see that building there—what would you say that was? A hospital? No. Everyone guesses hospital. Well, I'll tell you. It's . . ." And so on, *ad nauseam.*

"There," said I, "I chased butterflies as a lad."

"Oh, really!" said Amelia.

"There we used to buy sweets. There was a particular kind of chocolate cream, and you got two for a penny, on the understanding that every fifth one had a threepenny bit inside it. We never seemed to strike the fifth one somehow. It seems incredible to the trained mathematician."

"Horrible gambler!"

"True. You see this lovely house here? The man who used to live there is now selling matches in the streets!" I announced this in a hushed voice.

"How terrible!" said Amelia. "Wax ones, or wooden ones with pink heads?"

We reached the village, and climbed up the hill to the common. Under a clump of firs we sat, and looked down upon the little church, the inn, the vicarage, the few shops. We looked at the wall of wooded hills all round us, the village in the valley below us.

"London isn't bad," said Amelia at last. "Only this is better."

"But it doesn't do to think of it when you are in London. Yes, this is where I retire to."

"And that's where you'll go to church every Sunday."

"Yes, you'll see me walking up the hill after the service, talking some of the way perhaps with the Vicar, and arranging to sing at his next concert on behalf of the cricket nets. And I compliment him on his sermon

—on the gentle, unassertive voice in which he delivered it. Then I wander up here to get an appetite for lunch. Perhaps I meet the blacksmith, and congratulate him on his wonderful bowling the day before. . . . And so home. That's my house, I think."

"It's much too big for you."

"Is it? I wonder."

Below us the Vicar turned out of his house, and set off down the road.

"Why, there he is," said Amelia. "And—and there are you! But you've grown a beard!"

"That's the first thing I should do in the country."

"He's telling you about the concert."

"Yes."

"But he isn't asking you to sing."

"Isn't he, indeed?"

"No; you misunderstood him. He's saying would you mind *not* singing at the concert for the cricket nets, because they want the nets rather badly."

A lady joined the two men. "I feared as much," said Amelia. "You're married."

"Why not?"

"And you've brought her to live down here. Poor thing! She used to play Bridge all Sunday in town, and go to dances every day, and now she's eating her heart out in the dull, dull country."

"Not a bit," I said. "We run up once every month

to town for the night. We have the two front seats in the upper circle at His Majesty's. And we always go to the dance at the schools. Yes, and I'm teaching her bezique."

"Poor, poor thing!"

The elderly lady shook hands with the bearded ruffian, and entered a shop.

"It isn't my wife," I said. "It's a friend of the Vicar's, and she's very keen on Church matters. She knitted the last lot of hassocks. Being a churchwarden myself, I am bound to be polite to her. It is now my lunch-time. Will you come with me?"

We lunched at the "Blue Lion." The sign left no doubt as to the blueness, but was speculative as to the lion.

"Here's the 'Blue Lion,'" I said, as we came up to it.

"It isn't a lion. It's a spaniel. No, it's not a spaniel, it's a jagu-are."

"My dear Amelia," I said, "your knowledge of botany is slender. It's either a lion or a cauliflower. And this is the Blue Lion Inn."

"It's nothing like a lion."

"Don't be obstinate. Have you ever seen a blue lion?"

"I've seen a ——"

"You've never seen a blue lion, so you can't say that it isn't one."

"I've never seen a purple cow," said Amelia; 'I

never want to see one. But I can tell you, anyhow, I'd rather see than be one."

We entered. It appeared that the inn was really called the "Bull."

"Not the 'Jagu-are,'" I pointed out to Amelia.

CHAPTER XXIII.

THE AFTERNOON.

WE had an excellent lunch in a room decorated with a portrait of King Edward, a fiscal almanac, and a broken piano. I carved. It was really a round of beef we learned afterwards, but I carved it as though it were steak. We ate it under the impression that it was mutton. Amelia said it tasted like veal. We were very hungry.

We earned a reputation with the landlord as a keen judge of horseflesh. [This is a new paragraph.] When once you have grasped the elementary rule that horses are measured by hands, not feet, it is an easy matter.

"And how many hands might she be? Really? . . . Fifty pounds! I should think not, indeed—I should want at least sixty if she were mine. I must come down one afternoon and take her out. . . . No, I'm afraid I can't now. We have to look over a house."

We strolled down past the church.

"Somebody told a story, I'm afraid," said Amelia.

"Somebody didn't. We're going to look over a house now. There, that one with creepers all over it."

"How do you know it's empty?"

"'Cos I've been here before. Rent thirty pounds a year. Excellent *pied-à-terre*, comprising large kitchen garden and spacious summerhouse. *Pied-à-terre* is good, isn't it?"

"Excellent. I don't know how you think of those things."

"I am indeed a one."

We entered the house, opened the windows, and sat down on the stairs.

"Now then," said Amelia, "do you know how to look over a house?"

"Are there any particular rules? The ordinary way of keeping the eyes open I know."

"I'm afraid you don't know anything about it. The three things to go for first are the ceilings, the kitchen, and the rates."

"Let's go for the ceilings first," I said, and I began to take off my coat.

"Teddy, stop, or I shall scream."

"I'm not frightened," I said, rolling up my sleeves.

Amelia explained that all that was necessary was to see that the ceilings were in good repair.

"Oh!" I said, disappointedly. "Well, consider that done. What's the next thing?"

"The next thing is the kitchen."

"The kitchen, of course."

"Yes, we must see what sort of range there is. What would be the good of a spacious summerhouse if the bacon wasn't cooked properly?"

"What, indeed? All the same I've cooked bacon without a range."

"There are other things besides bacon."

"Yes, there's fish."

"And the third thing," said Amelia, "is the rates."

"We shall have to ask someone that, shan't we? We'll ask at the 'Bull.'"

We examined some of the ceilings. They seemed good ceilings, as ceilings go.

"I think we pass the ceilings," I said. They really were very good ceilings.

"Then come on to the kitchen."

The kitchen looked like most kitchens. I don't know much about them, though. Amelia certified that it was good.

"I suppose," I said, "that we may as well see how many bedrooms there are, or doesn't that matter so long as the sink is an excellent one?"

We counted the bedrooms. Four. It was a jolly little *pied-à-terre.* (I nearly called it a house!) We then did the garden. While I counted the fruit trees, Amelia inspected the roof—an important matter she says. I am afraid I could never come house-hunting alone. I should always go for the wrong thing.

The summerhouse was chiefly cobwebs. There was no stabling, but then think of the mare at the "Bull" waiting to be taken out! Having seen all we could, we got out into the road again, and continued our walk.

"By Jove!" I said, suddenly.

"What's happened?"

"You're a pretty house-hunter, you are!"

"Am I?" said Amelia, looking down.

"Yes, you are. What about the bathroom?"

"Oh, the bathroom?"

"Yes. The three things to go for first, let me tell you, are the bathroom, the number of apple trees, and the distance from the tobacconist. Thanks to my foresight, we know one of those three. The others—blow the ceilings!"

"There's gratitude, after all I've done for him. I shall go back to the inn, and have tea by myself. You can come, too, if you like. In fact, you had better come, because I have no money."

We had an excellent tea. (I always seem to be referring to meals.) We found the landlord in the stables.

"Yes," he was saying, "I wouldn't take fifty pounds for her."

"I should think not, indeed."

"The parson, he offered forty—"

"The bounder!" I put in.

"But I said fifty or nothing I said."

"I should have had the nothing," said Amelia. "*How* many hands did you say she was?"

"By the way, what are the rates," I asked casually.

"The what?"

"R-a-t-s, rates."

"Oh! She'll do her eleven mile in the hower, she will."

"Eleven? No!"

"Eleven mile in the hower. Now, Squire Morton's place, how far away would you say that was? Ten mile? Ten and a 'arf?"

"Oh, that's a good eleven miles," I said firmly.

"There you are then! I took her over there last Sunday. Ten o'clock we left 'ere, and it wanted two minutes of eleven as I drove up to his door."

"Well, really! By the way, how much are the rates here?"

"The rates?"

"Yes, I'm thinking of taking a house here. Are they very high?"

"High? Ah! that they are. Why when I first came 'ere . . ."

We left him, and climbed on to the common again. The evening sun shone on a gravel pit near us until it gleamed like gold. Three dark fir trees stood sentinel over it. They had the treasure to guard. . . .

I heard Amelia's voice at my side.

CHAPTER XXIV.

THE END AND THE BEGINNING.

'IT'S been a glorious day," she said; "glorious! I don't think I shall try to thank you. You will understand."

"Yes, I think I understand. It was just what I wanted to say to you."

"And now we have to go back to London. Oh, well ——"

"We've had some good times in London, though. Don't be hard on the place."

Amelia was silent.

"There was the Zoo," I went on, "that was the first place we went to. Do you remember the polar bear? And Charles? And there was the Abbey, and the jolly tea afterwards. And the Tower, and ——"

"Of course I remember them all."

"But you'll forget 'em all when you go back to America."

"Shall I?"

"You will, won't you?"

"You say I will."

"America is such a big place, and there are such a lot of people, and ——"

"There are several millions," put in Amelia.

"That's it," I said.

I looked at the sentinels over the pit of gold. Lucky trees with such a treasure to guard. Yet there was something better than gold—or gravel.

"Don't go," I whispered. "I want you."

She looked over the valley to the hills. Beyond the hills, only a little way beyond, was London.

"I've shown you London," I said. "Let me show you the world. It's such a big world, you know. It would take years to see it properly."

"It would take more than years."

"Yes, it would be a lifetime. Perhaps more than that. . . . Oh, I know I'm a very bad showman, but my heart's in the work. And this would be my first place. If you will give me a trial, I will serve your ladyship faithfully. Oh, not your ladyship—your Majesty."

"Well," said Amelia, talking quickly, "you have a very good character, and you look honest and obliging, and so if you'll sign an agreement, I'll take you for a month on trial. Oh, Teddy, not for a month, for ever—for ever, my darling."

Teddy signed the agreement.

* * * *

"Do you remember calling on Cousin Nancy?" I asked.

The End and the Beginning.

"Dear, I remember every little thing we ever did together."

"Do you remember saying good-bye to her?"

"Let's see," said Amelia, "it was something like this, wasn't it?"

*   *   *   *

We walked to the station in the dusk, hand in hand.

"Anyhow, the ceilings are all right," I pointed out. "You said so yourself. And the ceilings are the most important part."

"And there were eleven apple trees, you said."

"And the sink was in a class by itself."

"What did he say the rates were?"

"Oh, blow the rates. . . ."

"She was not fair to look upon," I said. "I'm glad she's only the person who does the hassocks."

"And you won't grow a beard, dear?"

"Never! You noticed my moustache, didn't you?

We found an empty carriage.

"I love you very much," whispered Amelia.

"Do you?"

"Yes. I'm not marrying you for your title, or your ancient mansions, or your future as a statesman."

"I'm afraid they'll think you are," I said. "The statesman part, I mean. America and England having just entered into a treaty—"

"Please I'm annexed," said Amelia.

THE END.

BRADBURY, AGNEW & CO., LD., PRINTERS
LONDON AND TONBRIDGE.

Milton Keynes UK
Ingram Content Group UK Ltd.
UKHW021535010324
438759UK00008BA/808

ESUS SPOKE THES
FTED UP HIS EYES
N, AND SAID: "FA
OUR HAS COME.
OUR SON, THAT Y
LSO MAY GLORIFY YOU, AS
OU HAVE GIVEN HIM AUTHOR-
Y OVER ALL FLESH, THAT HE
HOULD GIVE ETERNAL LIFE TO
S MANY AS YOU HAVE GIV-
N HIM. AND THIS IS ETERNAL
FE, THAT THEY MAY KNOW
OU, THE ONLY TRUE GOD,
ND JESUS CHRIST WHOM YOU
AVE SENT. I HAVE GLORIFIED
OU ON THE EARTH. I HAVE
NISHED THE WORK WHICH
OU HAVE GIVEN ME TO DO.
ND NOW, O FATHER, GLORI-
Y ME TOGETHER WITH YOUR-
ELF, WITH THE GLORY WHICH

The *Real* Lord's Prayer

Christ's glory and grace in John 17

Ian S McNaughton

DayOne

First printed 2012

ISBN 978–1–84625–296–9

British Library Cataloguing in Publication Data available

Published by Day One Publications
Ryelands Road, Leominster, HR6 8NZ
☎ 01568 613 740 FAX 01568 611 473
email—sales@dayone.co.uk
web site—www.dayone.co.uk
North America—email—usasales@dayone.co.uk

Cover design by Wayne McMaster
Printed by TJ International Ltd

Sound theology, helpful exegetical comment and pointed contemporary application make this a very useful book. With the Lord's prayer in John 17 as our starting point, we are taken on a wide-ranging journey through the Scriptures and enabled to see how Christ is the heart and centre of all God's revelation.

Dr Jonathan Bayes, Carey Outreach Ministries / Grace Baptist Mission, Bible Teacher in Asia

No more sublime—and yet no more practical—chapter is found in all Scripture. Every time we return to it we find insights we had not found before. Each occasion we hear a sermon on this prayer of our Lord our hearts are warmed and our minds are turned heavenwards. Here is a treatment of this chapter which is searching and encouraging. It caused me to give thanks anew to God for such a faithful High Priest who ever lives to pray in this way for a sinner like me and never wearies of it. Where would we be without our compassionate, prayerful Saviour?

Revd Geoff Thomas, Pastor since 1965 of Alfred Place Baptist Church, Aberystwyth, Wales

I have been really blessed reading this thorough treatment of the passage! It is deeply theological, but also of real help devotionally. It certainly fulfils Ian's aims and I am sure it will be helpful to those who read it!

Revd Dr Andrew Christofides, Pastor of St Mellons Baptist Church, Cardiff, Wales

Ian writes as a pastor with an eye to explaining and applying our Lord's words to a wide range of theological issues. His approach to 'Jesus's Great Prayer' is also unmistakeably devotional; yet what strikes me most is his clarity. Clarity is at a very high premium in Christian literature, and a Bible teacher who cares about clear description and application will always do us good. Throughout there is a rigorous engagement with

Reformed teaching, and if I had to highlight one particular doctrine, it would be the doctrine of the Holy Trinity. Ian carefully draws the reader's attention to the Trinitarian significance of God the Son in profound communication with God the Father. The great truths of our faith should not be locked up in a drawer for safe-keeping; they should be proclaimed and made to work in all we do for God. I commend this commentary to all who want to delve into a gospel chapter which has, at times, rightly been described as 'the Holy of Holies'.

Pastor John Griffith, Fittleworth Evangelical Free Church, West Sussex, UK

Ian McNaughton has provided an excellent doctrinal and practical exposition of the awesome High-Priestly prayer of our Lord. In application he addresses relevant contemporary issues clearly.

Erroll Hulse, author, conference speaker, and editor of* Reformation Today, *UK

In this work Ian McNaughton gives us a thorough and perceptive analysis of John 17. In doing so he brings out the many facets of this jewel of truth and with it gives helpful outlines of doctrines, including Jesus as our High Priest, assurance of salvation, sanctification, the worship of God and the place of preaching. The work is enriched with apt quotations from divines past and present. The whole study is made relevant for today with his selective interaction with the alternative contemporary views. The book will prove useful for both pastors and lay people, especially with the questions for further study and thought at the conclusion of each chapter.

John J. Murray, Interim-Moderator of Partick Free Church (Continuing), Glasgow, Scotland, and author of several books, the latest of which is* Catch the Vision *(Evangelical Press)

Among the many things that make Jesus the great Saviour that he is, none is more central to our faith than the fact that he is our Great High Priest. He bridges the gulf between a holy God in heaven and his people here on earth. There is a once-for-all aspect to his Priesthood in that he not only made atonement for his people's sins, but also offered himself as the perfect sacrifice God required. But there is also an ongoing aspect to his Priestly work. In the language of the book of Hebrews, 'he ever lives to make intercession for his people'. If we want a glimpse of what that intercession looks like, we find it in the prayer he prayed on the eve of his crucifixion. This book provides a helpful insight into what that prayer entails.

Revd Mark G. Johnston, Senior Pastor, Proclamation Presbyterian Church, Bryn Mawr, PA, USA

Some excellent quotations, and very helpful points and notes. The teaching is clear, simple to understand and profound, covering many important doctrines. May God use and bless this work for the extension of his kingdom, so that people will indeed know the only true God, and Jesus Christ whom he sent.

Roop Ram, missionary and church planter, India

Ian McNaughton expounds in a clear and relevant manner the profound and remarkable prayer of the Lord Jesus recorded in John 17. As we know, it is a prayer rich with insights into the relationship that exists between the Father and the Son, and their eternal purpose to bless sinners eventually in their presence for ever. As he explains the details of the prayer, the author deals with several crucial doctrines connected to the Saviour's Person and Work. The author helps us to understand how the Lord Jesus engages in his High-Priestly work, and what are the issues about which he intercedes. This book should increase one's gratitude for and delight in the Lord Jesus.

Malcolm Maclean, Minister of Greyfriars Free Church of Scotland, Inverness, Scotland

The seventeenth chapter of the Gospel of John has always been highly valued by the

Lord's people, as it provides an extraordinary insight into the relationship between the Father and the Son. The 'High-Priestly prayer' of Jesus Christ recorded in that chapter surely takes us as close to the heart of that relationship as is possible this side of eternity. Ian McNaughton's able exposition of the chapter addresses the breadth of issues which arise from that prayer and helps us in our understanding of the theology which underlies it and its practical implications for Christian living today.

Robert Strivens, Principal of London Theological Seminary, UK

To the 'Tuesday Nighters' at West Worthing Evangelical Church
Thanks to all the regulars for their support and encouragement
Soli Deo Gloria

Contents

Preface

Church history is full of those who have fallen in love with John 17. For example, English theologian John Owen regarded it as 'the blessed spring of our holiness',[1] and it is reckoned that Scottish Reformer John Knox was converted to the evangelical faith through this chapter. It was, he declared, 'the place where I cast my first anchor'.[2] On his deathbed he had it read to him as comfort for his soul. Older theologians distinguished this special prayer of our Lord from the Lord's Prayer in Matthew and Luke's Gospels by calling it 'The Lord's Great Prayer'; this title also declared the greatness of Jesus Christ's Person and of the covenant of redemption fulfilled by him.

Current popular books such as Dan Brown's *The Da Vinci Code* have challenged the Bible's view of Jesus Christ that has been held for nearly two thousand years. However, unless one believes in the Jesus Christ of the Bible there is no other historical Jesus to be found; all alternative profiles of him are, at best, sincere attempts to understand the mystery of God's Son incarnate. Evangelical Christians believe that the New Testament is a reliable historical document made up of eyewitness accounts from the contemporaries of Jesus Christ and those who researched his life shortly after his death and resurrection. The New Testament can therefore be trusted to deliver to us the truth about the life, work, death and character of Jesus Christ (Luke 1:1–4; John 1:14–18; Gal. 1:18–24; 2 Peter 1:16–21; 1 John 1:1–4). The Fourth Gospel is John's testimony concerning Jesus's historical self-disclosure as the Christ and the Son of God, and along with the rest of Scripture is the foundation on which faith rests; it is not the product of faith but the story that produces faith.

This Bible study on John 17 endeavours to present a high view of

Christ and finds support in other portions of Holy Writ to illuminate the Saviour's Person and Work. It recognizes his equality with the Father and his faithfulness to his Messianic mission. The mystery of his place in the Trinity was revealed to the apostles just before Christ was arrested and crucified, yet this aspect of divine revelation has almost been lost sight of in Western Christianity, partly due to the use by the ancient church of extra-biblical terminology in its defence of our Saviour's eternal nature and in its explanation of what the Bible is really saying. I seek to bring the doctrine of the Trinity to the fore in this work.

My study also presents a high view of Holy Scripture and sees a dignity in the redeemed and adopted people of God that the world fails to recognize. The great truths and doctrines of the Christian faith are again under attack in the Western world to such a degree that they are even in danger of being lost in the churches. I hope that this book will bring before the reader some of the essentials of the faith; if it has moved off that pathway, I alone am responsible. My intention is to speak the 'whole counsel of God' (Acts 20:27) and to include issues and topics that are mostly now forgotten or ignored among evangelicals. These include the impeccability of Christ, his pre-existence and unconditional election. Added to these I reinforce the importance of holding to Bible inerrancy and infallibility (I use both terms here deliberately). I have also mentioned the subjects of prayers for the dead and antinomianism, and I highlight the issues around the Sonship and the prophetic ministry of our Saviour that are being challenged by Islam in its evangelization of the West. However, the main topic is, of course, the High Priesthood of Jesus Christ, the only Head of the church, a topic which is relevant to the church in every age.

I would like to acknowledge my thanks to the friends who have read my book in manuscript form and offered advice and encouragement. Their support was invaluable to me and I am greatly indebted to them.

Loving thanks must also go to my dear wife, Violet, for her support and patience through all my labours.

Ian McNaughton,
Worthing

Notes

1 **John Owen,** *The Works of John Owen*, vol. iii (London: Banner of Truth, 1972), p. 50.
2 Cited at www.victorshepherd.on.ca/Heritage/johnknox.htm; accessed February 2012.

Part 1. Background

A good High Priest is come,
Supplying Aaron's place,
And taking up his room,
Dispensing life and grace,
The law by Aaron's priesthood came,
But grace and truth by Jesus' name.
(John Cennick, 1718–1755)

Setting the scene

The High-Priestly prayer of Jesus Christ is a monologue directed by God the Son to God the Father and into which readers 'intrude'. In doing so, they stand on holy ground, because John 17 is one of the most wonderful and exciting portions in the whole of Scripture. It is spiritually profound, reaching depths we cannot plumb and heights we will never scale. It is the longest prayer of Jesus given to us—indeed, it is the longest prayer recorded in the New Testament. We have many sermons, parables and conversations of Jesus recorded for us, but few prayers. Often in the Gospels we are told that Jesus was in the act of prayer, but apart from here and his prayer in Gethsemane in Matthew 26:39, we are not told the content of his intercessions. Thus, we have something almost unique here in John 17. The prayer marks the end of Jesus's earthly ministry and looks forward to the spread of the gospel throughout the world by the apostles and their successors.

The Gospels are the key to understanding who Jesus Christ was, and the Fourth Gospel makes a special contribution to this knowledge. This is especially relevant today in the face of the rejection of the gospel by the new rationalism, which constantly highlights the 'truth of science' as its source of authority, and the Islamic religion now firmly ensconced in Western society. Rationalism robustly rejects the supernatural and denies the resurrection of Jesus from the dead on the third day. Islam also denies Christ's resurrection as well as his Messianic credentials, thus robbing Christ of his rightful glory. It disavows Christ's divinity by questioning the accuracy of the Scriptures and the historic veracity of the essential matters of his Person and Work. In the light of these challenges, Christians must declare with all their energy the truth about Jesus Christ.

As John 17 takes us to the very heart of the Christian faith and demonstrates who Jesus Christ really is, we will, in this study, examine some of Islam's claims about Jesus Christ and the Christian religion and show that they are spurious in the light of the Scriptures themselves. Jesus Christ is the citadel of Christianity; without him there is no gospel. Minimize his Person and Work and there is no Saviour. For example, in John 17, the unique relationship between Jesus Christ and God the Father is revealed. No hymnwriter declares the mystery of the Godhead better than Charles Wesley:

Veiled in flesh the Godhead see,
Hail the incarnate Deity. ('Hark! The Herald Angels Sing', 1739)

Does God have a Son? John 17 leaves us with the clear answer that he does. Yet growing propaganda from Islam declares that God (Allah) can have no Son.

Before we look at this special prayer, we must endeavour to set John 17 into the context of the New Testament's teaching on Christ's Priesthood and the doctrine of prayer, as these topics come to the fore in this profound chapter, along with the deity and eternal Sonship of Jesus Christ our Lord.

The Gospel of John

This Fourth Gospel, having its own particular character, reveals events that are not recorded in the three Synoptic Gospels; thus it is often set apart from them. This is so because John appears to have written separately from the others, was an eyewitness of all that Jesus Christ did and said, and because he deals mainly with the last few weeks of the Saviour's earthly life. The three other Gospels contain a longer history while presenting the same general view of the life and teachings of Jesus. These facts have made John's Gospel the object of intense scrutiny and have given rise to suggestions that it is a second-century document, which would mean that it could not have been written by a disciple such as John the brother of James. It is not within the scope of this work to deal with the question of the authorship of John's Gospel;[1] however, evangelical Christians hold to a date of authorship between AD 80–98. Although the name of John never occurs in the Gospel itself, the traditional view holds that the author was the apostle John, the son of Zebedee. He calls himself the disciple 'whom Jesus loved' (e.g. John 20:2; 21:20) and he deliberately withholds his identity. What is sure is that the writer was an eyewitness of Christ's glory (1:14) and that he wrote so that 'you may believe that Jesus is the Christ, the Son of God' (20:30–31; see also 19:35).

Chapter 17 in context

John 12:36 marks the point of completion of Jesus's public ministry: 'These things Jesus spoke, and departed, and was hidden from them.' Now he needed to spend time with his disciples in order that they might receive final teaching and insight into his Person and mission before he was crucified. The whole purpose of the Scriptures, to which these disciples contributed, is to reveal both what Jesus Christ did and who he was (John 1:29; Col. 1:14–18; Heb. 1:3; Rev. 1:1–16). Without the Bible, we are blind and know nothing. Jesus taught his disciples all that the Father had told him, and in chapter 17 he would express this fact. However, there were some last things to be said and prayers to be made. His earthly ministry of signs and wonders was over (12:37), so now he prepared for the greatest sign of his Messianic claim, namely his resurrection from the dead. This would bring justification to all who believed in him and would declare him to be the Son of God (Rom. 4:23–25).

In chapters 13–17 we have what is called 'the final discourse'. Chapter 13 opens with these words: 'Jesus knew that His hour had come that He should depart from this world to the Father' (13:1). Before his anticipated death he engaged in a final moment of private teaching with the men whom the Father had given to him as his apostles, knowing that he would soon be glorified in heaven with his Father.

We are reminded in chapter 13 of the fervent love Jesus had for those whom the Father had given him: 'having loved His own who were in the world, He loved them to the end' (13:1). This most tender and affectionate statement is a fitting introduction to all that would be said by the Saviour before he hung on the cross as Substitute and Redeemer (15:13). He would command them to 'love one another' (13:34), for they needed to put on Christ and take up their cross daily and follow him. The phrase 'having loved His own' describes the objects of his love as *belonging* to him. This theme will continually come to the fore in our study.

Christ's prayer in John 17

In this remarkable prayer Jesus Christ prays for his church: it is a family prayer. He does not pray for the world but for the apostles and all the people of God, prefacing his intercessions by revealing something about his relationship with God his Father. He uses the word 'Father' six times, twice with preceding adjectives—'Holy Father' (v. 11) and 'righteous Father' (v. 25)—and four times without (vv. 1, 5, 21, 24). In the Holy Trinity God is Father to Christ in an eternal and unique relationship. It is a Fatherhood that is exclusively Trinitarian. The word 'world' (*kosmos*) is used eighteen times in Christ's prayer, and the personal pronouns 'they', 'them' and 'those', referring to the disciples, at least twenty-five times. The topics covered are varied and profound. They include the Son's divinity and pre-existence, the incarnation, the impeccability of Jesus Christ, the finished work of Christ, unconditional election, salvation, adoption, Christian discipleship and perseverance, antinomianism, sanctification, the unity of the body of Christ, true ecumenism and the love of Christ for his church.

Jesus's prayer reveals both his deity and humanity. It is full of references to his eternal union with the Father in the Godhead but also gives insight into his Messianic role as the Son of Man. There has been much controversy about the two natures of Christ. The issue was settled theologically in AD 325 with the Creed of Nicaea, which declared the Son to be 'of one substance with the Father'.[2] The doctrine was strengthened at the Council of Chalcedon in AD 451, when Christ was recognized to be 'in two natures, without confusion, without change, without division, without separation'.[3] Thus he was understood as being 100 per cent divine and 100 per cent human without confusion of substance. Throughout history, many groups have challenged this teaching, such as the Gnostic philosophers in the post-apostolic days of the early church, some of whose work is known to us in the Gospels of Thomas and Judas. Today, such groups include the Jehovah's Witnesses, who believe that Christ is a created super-being. Gnostic ideas have also been popularized this century through the writings of author Dan Brown, especially in his book *The Da Vinci Code*, and they are increasingly being used by both liberal Christian scholars and Islamic writers to bring into question the Bible's record of the historical Jesus.

However, a true understanding of the High-Priestly prayer in John 17 is dependent upon our awareness of the two natures of Jesus Christ. This doctrine is, of course, foolishness to the Gentiles and an obstacle to the Jews (1 Cor. 1:23). Christians believe that Jesus Christ is 'the image of the invisible God' (Col. 1:15), not only because he is a man made in the image of God (Gen. 1:26–27; 1 Cor. 11:7), but also because he is in his very nature God; as the Epistle to the Hebrews puts it, he is 'the brightness of [God's] glory and the express image of [God's] person' (Heb. 1:3).

The historical Jesus

Who was Jesus Christ? The Bible holds the answer to this question. All four New Testament Gospels reveal the historical Jesus. They were written in order that the world would know who Jesus Christ really was and is, and what he came to earth to achieve. Ancient historians such as the Jewish Josephus (AD 37–*c.* 100) and the Roman Tacitus (AD 56–117) both acknowledged in their writings the historical existence of Jesus of Nazareth,[4] but the Bible does more; it records Jesus's works of power, his atonement and his God-Man nature (John 1:14). Christ's Messianic office is revealed to us in the use of various wonderful titles and names given to him in the opening chapter of John's Gospel. He is called:

- The Word (vv. 1, 14)
- The Light (vv. 5, 7)
- Jesus Christ (v. 17)
- The only begotten Son (v. 18)
- The LORD (v. 23)
- The Lamb of God (vv. 29, 36)
- The Son of God (vv. 34, 49)
- Rabbi (v. 38)
- Jesus of Nazareth (v. 45)
- The Christ (v. 41)
- The King of Israel (v. 49)
- The Son of Man (v. 51)

The New Testament was given in order that we might believe (John 20:30–31) and is a reliable historical document made up of eyewitness accounts from those who knew Jesus Christ or who researched his life shortly after his death (Luke 1:1–4; 4:22; John 1:14; 1 Cor. 15:3; Gal. 1:18–19 (Paul spoke to eyewitnesses); 2 Peter 1:16–21; 1 John 1:1–4). This gives us confidence in accepting its evidence. The eyewitnesses were chosen and were with Christ from the beginning. They were promised the Holy Spirit to assist them to write clearly and truthfully (2 Peter 1:20–21) in the fulfilment of their task, so that what we read about Jesus Christ is what God means the world to know and believe in regard to him and his saving work (John 3:16; 14:26; 15:16, 26–27; 16:13–15; 17:18; 20:21–22, 30–31).

There is no historical Jesus other than the Jesus of the Holy Scriptures, and all attempts at finding another are doomed to failure.[5] Some may not believe in the Jesus revealed in the pages of the New Testament—that is their choice; but there is *no other Jesus* (2 Cor. 11:4). History records no Christ other than the one presented to us in the New Testament (Acts 4:12).

Jesus Christ is at history's centre, and John 17 is an important part of the evidence for our understanding of him.

Gethsemane

John 17 is known as the High-Priestly prayer of our Lord Jesus Christ. It is a prayer made in the shadow of the cross and, like Christ's time of prayer in Gethsemane (Matt. 26:36–46; Mark 14:32–42; Luke 22:40–46), it admits us to Christ's very heart and mind, showing us the love and affection he has for his church as he speaks to God his Father about those he came to save. In Gethsemane, he makes prayers of *oblation*, submitting himself to the will of the Father; however, in the upper room among his followers he engages in prayers of *intercession*. Gethsemane points to the cross, while John 17 looks to post-crucifixion realities, the eternal victories of Christ's obedience; thus in John 17 we find Jesus Christ in earnest supplication on behalf of his redeemed people. Here, also, is the promise of his future priestly ministry of intercession in heaven (Rom. 8:34).

The Saviour's payers of oblation in the garden of tears were, of course, grounded in his union with the other members of the Godhead; so, while every word and phrase reveals his perfect human nature, his prayers are still an example to all who aspire to pray well because they were rooted in relationship—that of the eternal Trinity. We learn from this that all who pray well do so on the basis of fellowship with God the Father, through God Son, in the power of God the Holy Spirit, because prayer is the highest activity of the human soul and is rooted in a spiritually redeemed relationship. Without this connection, all attempts at prayer lack knowledge and faith (1 John 1:3; 1 Peter 2:5—prayer being a spiritual sacrifice).

Jesus our High Priest

The high priest was the chief priest of the Hebrew people, especially of the ancient Levitical priesthood traditionally traced from Aaron. The chief priest could perform all the duties of the priesthood but he alone could represent all Israel as the mediator before God on *Yom Kippur*, the Day of Atonement. No other priest was to take this honour and responsibility upon himself (Heb. 5:4). Moses established this institution in Israel after the exodus, having received special instructions (revelation) to do so. These he relayed to the people in the Book of Numbers. The office of high priest, first conferred on Aaron, was normally hereditary and for life, but ever since the destruction of the Second Temple in Jerusalem in AD 70 there have been no Jewish high priests or national sacrifices.

The Epistle to the Hebrews argues for Christ's superiority over Aaron in the sight of God (Heb. 5:5–6). It is important to note that the Aaronic priesthood was a type of the greater office yet to come in the Person and Work of Jesus Christ (Heb. 7:11–12). The typology was partly seen in the holy garments that were especially designed for high-priestly office and worn throughout the year. Worthy of note for our study of the High-Priestly office of Jesus Christ are the 'two onyx stones' and the 'breastplate of judgment' allotted to the high priest as part of his official apparel:

> Then you shall take two onyx stones and engrave on them the names of the sons of Israel: six of their names on one stone and six names on the other stone, in order of their birth ... And you shall put the two stones on the shoulders of the ephod as memorial stones for the sons of Israel. So Aaron shall bear their names before the LORD on his

two shoulders as a memorial ... You shall make the breastplate of judgment ... And you shall put settings of stones in it, four rows of stones ... They shall be set in gold settings. And the stones shall have the names of the sons of Israel, twelve according to their names ... they shall be according to the twelve tribes. (Exod. 28:9–21)

These precious gems constantly reminded the high priest of his duty to care for the children of Israel. The two onyx stones, engraved with the names of the tribes of Israel, symbolized his intercessory work. He was to represent the people before the Lord. The names of the twelve tribes of Israel were also written on his two shoulders, so that he could lift them up to the Lord (Jehovah) as he stood before him in the Holy of Holies. In addition, the high priest wore a breastplate that was bedecked with twelve stones, one for each of the tribes of Israel. This breastplate rested close to his heart and typified Jesus's love for the Israel of God:

So Aaron shall bear the names of the sons of Israel on the breastplate of judgment over his heart, when he goes into the holy place, as a memorial before the LORD continually ... and they shall be over Aaron's heart when he goes in before the LORD. So Aaron shall bear the judgment of the children of Israel over his heart before the LORD continually. (Exod. 28:29–30)

It was the high priest's duty to make atonement on *Yom Kippur*, by burning incense and sprinkling sacrificial animal blood to propitiate his own sins and those of the people of Israel. On this special occasion he wore only white linen garments, symbolizing his cleanness after making atonement for himself. Here again we see the Antitype, Jesus Christ, who did no sin and was himself 'HOLINESS TO THE LORD' (Exod. 28:36); Christ, having been made like his brethren, has become a faithful High Priest after the order of Melchizedek, king of Salem and priest of God (Heb. 7:1, 17). As High Priest Christ made propitiation for the sins of his people, and because he himself suffered and was tested, he can help those who are tested and tempted (Heb. 4:14–16; 1 John 2:2). Through suffering, death and obedience Jesus made a perfect sacrifice once for all, and has made all Old Testament sacrifices obsolete.

In the Old Testament model the high priest could not mourn the dead, had to avoid defilement incurred by proximity to the dead, and could marry only a virgin (Lev. 21:10–14). The blood of Jesus Christ bought his bride, the church, and she will be presented as a chaste virgin to him at the great marriage supper of the Lamb. It was the apostle Paul's desire that his ministry would secure the elect's spiritual purity in order that the saints might be presented as a holy bride to their Saviour (see Rom. 7:4; 2 Cor. 11:2; Phil. 1:6). The multitude in heaven sing,

> 'Let us be glad and rejoice and give Him glory, for the marriage of the Lamb has come, and His wife has made herself ready.' And to her it was granted to be arrayed in fine linen, clean and bright, for the fine linen is the righteous acts of the saints. Then he said to me, 'Write: "Blessed are those who are called to the marriage supper of the Lamb!"'
>
> (Rev. 19:7–9)

The children of God may rejoice when pondering the precious truth that the Great High Priest bears them on his shoulders and close to his heart. His strength can never fail. No load is too heavy for him to bear.

The Epistle to the Hebrews

Both John 17 and the Book of Hebrews present Jesus Christ as the High Priest of the people of God, and although Protestantism has rightly rejected the idea of the continuation of the office of the sacramental priesthood, believing instead in the doctrine of the priesthood of all believers, the topic of Jesus Christ's Priesthood is not irrelevant or uninteresting; rather, it is of utmost importance. In the Old Testament dispensation, men and women could only approach God via a mediator, and the same is still true today. God-given priesthood is as relevant to the

New Testament period as it was to the Old. Without a high priest, Israel of old would have been left without atoning sacrifices for sin and with uncleanness, to face the just wrath of a holy God alone. Thus the high priest of Israel made atonement once a year alone in the presence of God for them (Heb. 9:7). Under the new covenant, we still need a mediator to stand in our place and offer sacrifice. This Jesus Christ did once for all when he died at Calvary, offering himself to God as an atoning sacrifice for our sins (Heb. 7:24–27; 9:24). Christ's Priesthood is greater than that of Israel's great high priest, Aaron; indeed, it completely replaces the Old Testament priesthood. In the Book of Hebrews, the writer proves that Jesus Christ is the Great High Priest of Israel because he fulfils the duties of a priest (5:1, 7), he meets the qualifications of priesthood (5:1–2, 4–6) and he is without the infirmities of Aaron and his posterity (5:2–3). The Saviour Jesus Christ is proclaimed in the New Testament to be the only Mediator between God and mankind because he has made atonement, being 'a faithful High Priest ... to make propitiation for the sins of the people'.

In both Hebrews and John, Jesus is seen as the author of sanctification, for he is the one 'who sanctifies' and his sacrificial death achieves the goal of a sanctified elect (John 17:19; Heb. 10:10; 2:11). It is his blood that cleanses the sinful conscience, setting it apart unto God and his service (Heb. 9:13–14). The Saviour was willing to be separated from the community of God's people—by being condemned and treated as a law-breaker—in order to make atonement for his people's sins (Heb. 13:12). Christ's death—his substitutionary atonement for sinners—was necessary in order to consecrate a people unto God. His death was not purposed to bring riches, prosperity or happiness, but to save his people from their sins (10:10–14). This High-Priestly work of Jesus allows sinners to approach heaven with the assurance of acceptance with God through him (4:14–16; 10:19–25). Now, Christ 'always lives to make intercession for them' (Heb. 2:17; 7:25).

The incense in the tabernacle consisted of various spices blended together (Exod. 30:34–35), and it was the proper blending of these that made the perfume so fragrant and refreshing. So with Christ's prayers, they include all the elements necessary to render them sweet and fragrant before our Father in heaven.

The Lord's Prayer

The Lord Jesus taught us to pray, 'Our Father in heaven …' (Matt. 6:9). When Christians pray, they are to approach God Almighty as their Father as well as their Creator. He has given them life and he keeps them close to his heart. Because of this relationship, when they pray Christians must start with God and look to him alone. He must be the object of their prayers. We are not to pray to angels or 'saints'; we must not ask them to hear us, or think that they can answers us. If there were any value or good reason to pray to 'saints' or angels, Jesus Christ would surely have taught us to do so. After all, he was asked to 'teach us to pray' (Luke 11:1), and in response he prayed to the Father. Thus, all prayer should be to the Father, through the Son, by the aid of the Holy Spirit.

Prayer is the human soul reaching out in faith to God, and it does so with the aspiration that it will be received graciously. The prayer of John 17 is both Christ's human nature reaching out to God his Father and his divine nature enjoying unbroken fellowship with the Father and Holy Spirit through the unity of the divine essence. For the Saviour, prayer was made without sin, but for sinners, sending acceptable prayer to the throne of grace is a challenge, as it requires not only the correct content but also the correct attitude of heart and mind. When teaching on prayer, Jesus Christ said to his disciples, 'Do not use vain repetitions … For your Father knows the things you have need of before you ask Him' (Matt. 6:7–8). Jesus Christ's words are not a barrier to urgent cries from the redeemed saints of God; rather, he is denouncing the use of repetitive mutterings made in the vain attempt to gain merit or atone for sin. Such effort is superstitious and lacks the Holy Spirit. The attitude of boldness and earnestness, combined with a dogged persistence, is taught in the Parable of the Friend at Midnight (Luke 11:5–8). In this parable, the intercessor asks his neighbour for help in time of need. He gets what he wants because of his persistence, even though his neighbour is at first reluctant to help him. This persistence, which comes from a sense of duty, respect and love for his weary guest, wins through in the end and teaches us that lifeless prayers are useless; our supplications must come from the heart and be energized through the boldness of faith. The Father is waiting for such prayers and is ready to help in time of need (Heb. 4:14–16).

Prayer and the Christian

In the Lord's Prayer Jesus says that we should pray 'Our Father', not 'Our Maker', 'Our Master', 'Our Redeemer' or even 'Our Sovereign Lord'. Why is this? All these terms would be acceptable, but 'Our Father' is best, for it signifies a loving relationship. God has not left us to guess what his Fatherhood entails. He revealed the full meaning of this relationship finally through our Lord Jesus Christ and the New Testament Scriptures.

Why does God accept prayer? The answer lies in the sinner's justification and adoption. Jesus describes the disciples as 'the men whom You have given me' (John 17:6), but are we all given to Christ? Are we all the children of God?

In the Bible, three kinds of Fatherhood are described. Firstly, there is a Fatherhood that is exclusively Trinitarian: the Fatherhood of the Father, the First Person of the Trinity, in relation to the Son, the Second Person. Secondly, there is a universal Fatherhood of God, because creatively and providentially he gives to all people 'life, breath and all things' (Acts 17:25). We are his offspring since he is the Father of spirits and the Father of lights (Acts 17:29; Heb. 12:9; James 1:17–18). Thirdly, and more fully, the term 'Father' as applied to God and the title 'sons of God' as applied to men are about redemption and adoption.[6]

When we pray 'Our Father', we acknowledge God as our heavenly Parent. However, it must be remembered that the Bible differentiates between the children of God and the children of the devil. Jesus said to the Jews who sought to kill him, 'You are of your father the devil' (John 8:44), while the apostle John wrote, 'In this the children of God and the children of the devil are manifest ...' (1 John 3:10). Here two origins and two families are juxtaposed: one belongs to creation and the other to the realm of salvation. Thus, it is only believers who can truly pray the Lord's Prayer. As John Murray says, 'To substitute the message of God's universal fatherhood for that which is constituted by redemption and adoption is to annul the Gospel ... In a word, it is to deprive the Gospel of its redemptive meaning. And it encourages men in the delusion that our creature-hood is the guarantee of adoption into God's family.'[7] Sinners are so fallen, so lost, so undone, that they are no longer like Adam before the fall, and no longer God's children. How does God deal with this problem? James M. Boice has the answer: 'God has dealt with the problem of alienation through adoption.'[8] J. I. Packer says, 'The revelation to the believer that God is his Father is in a sense the climax of the Bible.'[9]

The phrase 'Our Father' is not only a term of sonship, but also a family term. The Father is not 'mine', or 'yours', but 'ours'. God is the Father of a great worldwide family called the church. Christ is our Brother—'He is not ashamed to call them brethren' (Heb. 2: 11)—and this is because of adoption. 'By adoption the redeemed become the sons and daughters of the Almighty; they are introduced and given the privileges of God's family.'[10] In adoption, God take us into fellowship with himself and with his family; there he establishes us as his children and heirs. This results in a special closeness, affection and generosity, for these are at the heart of the relationship. 'To be right with God the judge is a great thing, but to be loved and cared for by God the Father is a greater.'[11]

The key, then, to powerful and effective prayer is located in adoption, the sinner having been accepted in Christ Jesus through faith in his work of reconciliation.

By you my prayers acceptance gain,
Although with sin defiled;
Satan accuses me in vain
Since I am God's own child.

(John Newton, 'How Sweet the Name of Jesus Sounds', 1779)[12]

Prayer is not only an exercise of grace, but it is also a response to our relationship and standing with God the Father as his adopted children. The simple cry of the believer is true prayer as the Christian goes to God just as a child goes to his or her father when in need. This comes from the Holy Spirit (Gal. 4:6). Because God is their Father in heaven, the people of God are enabled to fulfil their duty in prayer by approaching the Father 'with reverence, love and gratitude'.[13] Adoption is, then, the ground of the sinner's acceptance in prayer. It allows him or her to approach God as Father without fear, instead expecting a welcome. It is because of Christians' adoption that their affections are stirred, their dignity is found and their voices are heard. The doctrine of adoption is a wonderful topic and it is closely related to that of the Fatherhood of God.

Prayer and worship

God is worshipped because he is the eternal, immortal and invisible Creator of the universe and Redeemer of the church (through the atoning blood of Jesus Christ). Christians therefore worship him because of his greatness and because of his grace, while the spirit of true worship brings them before him with awe and joy. Prayer, praise and preaching are the three main elements in public Christian worship. Gathered on the Lord's Day, local churches worship God through praise using psalms, hymns and spiritual songs, and prayers of adoration, confession and supplication. Then they are called to respond in faith and obedience to the preached Word of God, which reveals God's mind and will.

Prayer is a vital part of our worship of God and therefore the call to prayer is essential in our worship services. According to John Bunyan, prayer 'is a sincere, sensible, affectionate pouring out of the heart or soul to God, through Christ, in the strength and assistance of the Holy Spirit, for such things as God has promised, or according to his Word, for the good of the church, with submission in faith to the will of God'.[14] According to the Lord's Prayer, four elements are necessary in prayer: adoration, thanksgiving, confession and supplication.

ADORATION

When he taught his disciples to pray, 'Hallowed be Your name' (Luke 11:2), Jesus Christ demonstrated that we must worship God through our prayers. 'Hallowed' comes from the Greek word meaning 'holy' (*hagios*). We must treat God as the epitome and quintessence of holiness. He is apart from us, for he is Spirit and eternally light and life. Thus we are to remember his otherness and praise him for such, and also because he is the most holy, valuable, glorious Being in the entire universe. To devalue God is to devalue everything. The psalmist's call to worship, 'Oh, magnify the LORD with me, and let us exalt His name together' (Ps. 34:3), is to be ours too. This is a blow to Satan, because such praise gives God his rightful place of honour and majesty, which Satan seeks for himself. To begin worship with humble yet intense reverence dethrones the pride resident in our hearts and, at the same time, lifts our redeemed souls towards the Father in heaven in the strength of the Holy Spirit. To start our prayers with praise and adoration is to recognize the glory, beauty and lovingkindness of God and expresses the hope we, the people of God, find in Jesus Christ his Son. This sense of hope and joy is expressed by the palmist thus: 'I will bless the LORD at all times; His praise shall continually be in my mouth' (Ps. 34:1).

THANKSGIVING

The apostle Paul sees thanksgiving as an indispensable element of believing prayer: 'Continue earnestly in prayer, being vigilant in it with thanksgiving' (Col. 4:2). Delight in God is evidence of a thankful heart. Thanksgiving is often the missing element in our prayers today. We ask much, but do we also return thanks? In a society that abounds in material comforts of which our ancestors could only dream, are we thankful for our many blessings? Even in New Testament times, the Lord's people were not good at thanksgiving. We know this because of what Paul wrote to the church in Thessalonica: 'in everything give thanks; for this is the will of God in Christ Jesus for you' (1 Thes. 5:18). Thankfulness should characterize the Christian life in every circumstance; not thanks *for* everything, but thanks *in* everything. Paul emphatically states that this is the will of God. We find an Old Testament example of this when Job lost his children and his health, and yet blessed the name of God in spite of his personal tragedies, not because of them (Job 1:21). Nothing speaks more powerfully of walking with God than continual thankfulness. Giving thanks should be the Christian's native emotion; if Romans 8:28 is true, the people of God should be able to praise the Lord at *all* times, in *all* circumstances, and *in everything*, just as long as in doing so we do not excuse sin. Laziness in this aspect of prayer is inexcusable; Paul wrote that Timothy should stir up the 'gift of God' which was in him (2 Tim. 1:6), which is likened to a fire that burns and lives in those who believe (see NIV). It can be quenched: 'Do not quench the Spirit' (1 Thes. 5:19). There is a need for the people of God to respond well to the light of the gospel in their souls and the joy of Christ in their hearts.

Paul's prayer in Ephesians 3 closes with a soul-inspiring doxology. The preceding requests have been vast, bold and seemingly impossible. Nevertheless, God is able to do more than we can ask or think, so thanksgiving and adoration are obligatory: 'Now to Him who is able to do exceedingly abundantly above all that we ask or think, according to the power that works in us, to Him be glory in the church by Christ Jesus to all generations, forever and ever. Amen' (Eph. 3:20).

CONFESSION

Confession and sorrow for sin are principal parts of real prayer. Charles Spurgeon said, 'If there is no prayer, you may be quite sure the soul is dead.'[15] Christians say 'sorry' and acknowledge their sins to their High Priest, Jesus Christ, in heaven when they come before the throne of grace, believing that they are promised forgiveness through his atoning blood—not just once, but always—when they repent (1 John 1:8–9). Jesus calls on us to pray, 'Forgive us our sins' (Luke 11:4), because sin is a barrier to fellowship with the Father through the Son and forfeits our privilege of forgiveness from God (Ps. 66:18). Remembering that God is all-knowing, worshippers must approach him with a penitent heart, trusting in Christ's blood for mercy (Luke 18:9–14, esp. v. 13). This will enable them to offer powerful prayers before God (John 9:31; James 5:16).

SUPPLICATION

Prayer is a weapon more powerful than the sword, the bomb or even the pen. Martin Luther said, 'This little word Father, lisped forth in prayer by a child of God, exceeds the eloquence of Demosthenes, Cicero and all others so famed orators in the world.'[16] The Bible, from Genesis to Revelation, teaches us about effective and powerful prayer that prevails with God and moves his hand. It teaches us that prayer is at the forefront of the work of God. It is not a supplement to God's work; it *is* God's work, and is an essential part of every spiritual ministry. Whatever work is done for God must first begin with prayer and then be carried out in prayer (Acts 13:1–3). The Methodist Samuel Chadwick said, 'Prayer is the mightiest force in the universe of God.'[17] Tertullian said, 'We knock at heaven and the merciful heart of God flies open ... this holy violence we offer to Him in prayer is very pleasing to Him.'[18] The disciples were told by Jesus that 'The kingdom of heaven suffers violence, and the violent take it by force' (Matt. 11:12; 'forceful men lay hold of it', NIV[19]), understanding that Jesus was speaking about prayer. Prayers of supplication are full of urgent cries because they come from the heart and will not accept 'no' for an answer (1 Sam. 1; Luke 11:5–12; 18:1–8).

Worship is not a passive but an active endeavour; thus it requires time, spiritual energy and a heart that seeks after and desires God. All this is seen in abundance in Jesus's great prayer of John 17, as we shall see in the rest of this book.

FOR FURTHER STUDY

1. In what way is the Gospel of John different from the Synoptic Gospels?
2. What are the differences and similarities between the Old Testament and New Testament priesthoods?
3. Who were the eyewitnesses who confirmed the truth of the life and miracles of Jesus?
4. What are the main differences between the Lord's Prayer (Luke 11) and Jesus's great prayer in John 17?

TO THINK ABOUT AND DISCUSS

1. Why is it that not all people are God's redeemed children?
2. Why is there a need to resist the trend to question the accuracy of the New Testament record about Jesus Christ?
3. What is the Holy Spirit's role in the prayer life of Christians?
4. What are the most important elements when Christians pray?

Notes

1. See the Bibliography for commentaries that deal with the issues involved in dating this Gospel.
2. **Henry Bettenson,** *Documents of the Christian Church* (Oxford: Oxford University Press, 1974), p. 25.
3. Ibid., p. 51.
4. **Josephus,** *The Antiquities of the Jews*, and **Cornelius Tacitus,** *Annals*, Book 15, both mention Christ as a man convicted by Pontius Pilate during Tiberius's reign.
5. See **Scot McKnight,** 'The Jesus We Will Never Know', in *Christianity Today*, April 2010, for a frank admission that the search for the historical Jesus using historical studies has been futile: 'the historical Jesus game has run its course and it cannot deliver us the original Jesus' (p. 26).
6. **John Murray,** *Redemption Accomplished and Applied* (London: Banner of Truth, 1961), pp. 135–136.
7. Ibid.
8. **James M. Boice,** *Foundations of the Christian faith* (Leicester: IVP, 1986), p. 442.
9. **J. I. Packer,** 'Adoption', in *Knowing God* (London: Hodder & Stoughton, 1973), p. 225.
10. **Murray,** *Redemption*, pp. 132–133.
11. **Packer,** 'Adoption', p. 231.
12. Hymn 299, *Praise!* (Darlington: Praise Trust, 2000).
13. **Thomas Manton,** *Works*, vol. i (Edinburgh: Banner of Truth, 1993), p. 48.
14. **John Bunyan,** *Prayer* (London: Banner of Truth, 1965), p. 13. His text was 1 Cor. 14:15. In the work Bunyan sets himself the task of 'showing [his readers] the very heart of prayer'. The 'Publisher's Foreword' to this edition says, 'Although shaped in some fashion by the historical context this is nevertheless a deeply spiritual work by a man to whom prayer was a real grappling of the soul with Almighty God.'
15. **C. H. Spurgeon,** 'What Is it to Win a Soul?' ch. 1 in *The Soul-Winner*; available at The Spurgeon Archive, www.spurgeon.org/misc/soulwinr.htm#toc; accessed February 2012.
16. Cited in **William Gurnall,** *The Christian in Complete Armour,* vol. ii (Edinburgh: Banner of Truth, 1995), p. 297.
17. **Samuel Chadwick,** *The Path of Prayer* (London: Hodder & Stoughton, 1968), p. 45.
18. Cited in **Gurnall,** *The Christian in Complete Armour*, vol. ii, p. 297.
19. Holy Bible, New International Version Copyright © 1973, 1978, 1984 (International Bible Society). Henceforth, all references to the NIV are to this edition.

Part 2. Concerning himself: the Lord and his Father (17:1–5)

This union of two natures in Christ's one Person is doubtless one of the greatest mysteries of the Christian religion.
(J. C. Ryle, *Expository Thoughts on the Gospels*)

Chapter 2

The High Priest's relationship: the Son of the Father (v. 1)

Jesus spoke these words, lifted up His eyes to heaven, and said: 'Father, the hour has come. Glorify Your Son, that Your Son also may glorify You.'

In order to save us, Jesus Christ took on human nature in the womb of the Virgin Mary, becoming perfect man while remaining perfect God (Gal. 4:4–5). His was the union of the divine nature with our humanity, yet without sin's pollution and guilt. When reading Christ's prayer of intercession, then, we walk on holy ground and draw close to the heart of the Saviour. This prayer is deeply reflective and reaches depths the human mind cannot plumb and heights it will never reach. We are, as it were, eavesdropping on Jesus Christ, God manifested in the flesh, in prayerful communion with his Father. Thus we must stand in awe.

The Son speaking

Jesus spoke these words.

Where did Jesus pray—was he in the upper room or somewhere else? In John 13–14 Jesus and his disciples were in the upper room, but in 14:31 we read Jesus saying, 'Arise, let us go from here.' Because of this, it is possible that Jesus's speech in the next three chapters was delivered as he and the apostles went on their way to Mount Olivet. On the other hand, David Brown, in his *Discourses and Sayings of Our Lord*, thinks that Jesus and his disciples stayed in the upper room until 18:1.[1]

It is as part of the Last Supper discourse (from 13:12) with his apostles and Judas Iscariot, during which Christ institutes the Lord's Supper, that he begins his special prayer. It is made prior to his sacrifice of himself at Calvary and is the prayer of the High Priest of God (Heb. 2:17) whose duty it is to intercede for the people of God as well as to mediate between them and their Holy Father. Christ did not need to make personal confession of sin, for he was 'holy, harmless, undefiled, [and] separate from sinners' (Heb. 7:26) and possessed a conscious realization of his perfect obedience to his Father (John 17:4). The inability to sin, which was innate in Jesus Christ the Son of God, equipped him to be the spotless Lamb of God.

The Son praying

Jesus ... lifted up His eyes to heaven.

We find Jesus in the same posture as when praying for Lazarus (11:41). This mode of prayer indicates inward cleanness, purity of heart, and utter sincerity of soul. Mostly it identifies a unique relationship between the Father and his Son. No other person prays this way in the New Testament except the Pharisee in the Parable of the Pharisee and the Tax Collector who was condemned as being proud and in spiritual darkness (Luke 18:9–14).

Note the different posture when Jesus was in the garden of Gethsemane: there he 'fell on His face, and prayed' (Matt. 26:39). Why the difference? In Gethsemane, he travailed in prayer as the Redeemer of souls under the greatness of our sin laid on him, and so his posture was humble; in John 17, however, he prayed as the eternal, spotless Son of God with no sin to bar his communion with God. The praying Jesus had a perfect relationship with the Father—they were one (John 17:21), united in mind and heart. However, the children of fallen Adam ought to humble themselves before God when they pray (1 Peter 5:6–7).

Jesus... said: 'Father ...'

As discussed in the previous chapter, Jesus, when teaching the Lord's Prayer, exhorted us to pray, 'Our Father ...' This reminds believers of their adoption (Gal. 4:5). Jesus's relationship with the Father is different. In John 8:28, 38 he uses the phrase 'My Father', for he is the Son by eternal generation; Christians are sons only by adoption (1 John 3:1–2), being grafted into the living and true Vine (John 15:1–4).

At the Fall, Adam lost not only the rights and the footing of a child, but also the heart and the spirit of a child; now all Adam's posterity are lost and ruined sinners standing in need of Christ's procured forgiveness.[2] How does God deal with this loss of fellowship? He does so through justification and adoption. Through justification God reckons sinners righteous; through adoption God takes them into his family and establishes them as his children and heirs (Gal. 4:5–6). We must grasp that to be saved from the consequences and guilt of our sin is the greatest privilege we can know. Loved with an everlasting love, the redeemed have a relationship of sonship with God the Father. Erroll Hulse says, 'The superlative privileges of adoption are immense: firstly, intimate filial relationship with our Father gives us intimate fellowship with Him. Secondly, chastening is the act of a loving father. These are privileges beyond measure (Heb. 12:4–12).'[3] The apostle John wrote, 'Beloved, now we are children of God' (1 John 3:2a): those born again are not what they once were, namely lost and under the condemnation of a broken law; rather, they are now accepted in Christ and welcomed into the family of God (John 1:12–13). Packer suggests that 'Adoption is the highest privilege that the Gospel offers; higher than justification ... because of the richer relationship with God it involves'.[4]

Father, the hour has come.

This 'hour' (*hora*) is the God-appointed moment for Christ's sacrificial atoning death. Earlier he said to Mary his mother, 'My hour has not yet come' (2:4; see also 7:6), but now he acknowledges that the time has come for him to depart from this world (13:1). The set time of his death is near and the Seed of the woman is about to bruise the head of the serpent (Gen. 3:15). The cross, with its shame, pain, insult and death, is imminent, and the predestined hour for him to fulfil his work as Mediator and Saviour has come (8:20; 12:23; 13:1).

It is clear that this 'hour' did not take Christ unawares; he knew all about it. In fact, it was for this very hour that he had come into the world. His prayer acknowledged that he was ready to die and to stand in the place of death as Substitute and Redeemer. He was ready to obey and to lay down his life for his friends (15:13). This was the predetermined hour for fulfilling prophecy (Isa. 53), the hour for the new covenant to be ratified and sealed by his blood (Mark 14:24), and the hour of his triumph—for three days after his burial he would rise again from the dead (20:1; Heb. 10:12).

The Son longing

Glorify Your Son, that Your Son also may glorify You.

The phrase 'Your Son' indicates once more the deity of Jesus Christ. Christ's humanity and divinity are to be seen in unity. His divinity is important, as it was only as God that his sacrifice had infinite value. His humanity is also important, as only as a sinless man could he achieve atonement for fallen sinners. Just as our offspring carry our likeness, so God's only Son is of the same essence as the Father, co-equal and eternally with him. The uniqueness of their relationship in the Trinity is emphasized by the apostle John's exclusive use of the Greek word *huios* ('Son') in reference to Jesus, compared with his use of *tekna* ('little children', similar to the Scottish 'bairns') for those brought into the kingdom of God through adoption (1:12; 11:52; 1 John 3:1–2).

The word translated as 'glorify' (from the root *doxa*) 'refers to a visible and powerful manifestation of God'.[5] Christ does not say 'Glorify Me' but rather 'Glorify Your Son'. His death would ultimately be for the Father's glory. Jesus had already spoken of this (13:31), and now the apostles and their successors were to know that 'whatever you ask in My name, that I will do, *that the Father may be glorified in the Son*' (14:13, emphasis added).

The plan for Christ to be glorified was integral to the covenant of redemption, which also included the giving of the Holy Spirit, who was to come as the 'Helper' or 'Comforter' to the church (14:16–18; 15:26). Before this point, 'the Holy Spirit was not yet given, because Jesus was not yet glorified' (7:39). Now was the moment: 'The hour has come that the Son of Man should be glorified' (12:23). Jesus now looked to his Father to carry him through the violent and atoning experience of the cross to a triumphant completion of his work. This would show that he was indeed God's Son and the Saviour of the world.

Christ's crucifixion was planned from eternity and was not an afterthought because the Jews rejected their Messiah. This was made clear when the two disciples on the road to Emmaus were told, 'Ought not the Christ to have suffered these things and to enter into His glory?' (Luke 24:26). His ascension was a vital moment in the transition from the old to the new covenant era. This watershed marked the start of the dispensation of the Holy Spirit. Having said this, we must not fall into the trap of Modalistic Monarchianism, a doctrine first set forth by Sabellius (c. AD 220) which taught that the Father, Son and Holy Spirit are not three distinct personalities but three different modes or temporary manifestations (phases) of the one true God. Thus the Son's longing was that glory would come to the Father alone.

To God be the glory, great things he has done,
So loved he the world that he gave us his Son. (Fanny Crosby, 1875)

FOR FURTHER STUDY

1. Which texts prove the believer's adoption?
2. Why is the doctrine of adoption so comforting for the believer?
3. Why is Modal Monarchianism wrong? Which Scripture texts back up your answer?
4. What was the watershed that marked the start of the dispensation of the Holy Spirit?

TO THINK ABOUT AND DISCUSS

1. On what basis does God answer prayer?
2. How can we be confident that God hears our prayers?
3. How can believers bring glory to the Father?

Notes

1 **David Brown,** *Discourses and Sayings of Our Lord* (London: Banner of Truth, 1967), p. 438.

2 See **R. A. Webb,** *The Reformed Doctrine of Adoption* (Grand Rapids, MI: Eerdmans, 1947), pp. 21–27.

3 **Erroll Hulse,** 'Recovering the Doctrine of Adoption', in *Reformation Today,* 105, 1988, p. 12.

4 **J. I. Packer,** 'Adoption', in *Knowing God* (London: Hodder & Stoughton, 1973), pp. 230–231.

5 **Herman N. Ridderbos,** *The Gospel of John* (Cambridge: Eerdmans, 1997), p. 52.

Chapter 3

The High Priest's right: the Son of authority (v. 2)

You have given Him authority over all flesh, that He should give eternal life to as many as You have given Him.

In this verse we learn about the authority that our Saviour possesses as the Son of Man, which extends 'over all flesh' and involves the granting of eternal life 'to as many as [the Father has] given Him'. We also learn about the doctrines of unconditional election and the believer's adoption into the family of God, both of which are meant to encourage the saints to love and obey God more (1 John 4:10–11).

The Son's dominion

You have given Him authority over all flesh.

'Authority' (*exousian*) is also used in 1:12: 'as many as received Him, to them he gave the right [*exousian*] to become children of God'. Christ's authority extends over all creation and is emphasized by the apostle Paul in the Epistle to the Colossians, where he speaks of Christ's nature thus:

> He is the image of the invisible God, the firstborn over all creation. For by Him all things were created that are in heaven and that are on earth, visible and invisible, whether thrones or dominions or principalities or powers. All things were created through Him and for Him. And He is before all things, and in Him all things consist. And He is the head of the body, the church, who is the beginning, the firstborn from the dead, that in all things He may have the preeminence. (Col. 1:15–18)

Christ is 'the image [*eikon*] of the invisible God'. This oxymoron declares that in Jesus Christ the nature and being of God exist, and have done so throughout all eternity. What God is, Christ has revealed in visible form. The Son represents God and manifests his nature and likeness to the world. The phrase 'the firstborn over all creation' does not refer to Christ being the first of all created beings; that would contradict the fact that 'all things were created ... for him'. What is meant is that the Son of God existed as God's only begotten Son through all eternity past and now is the Redeemer of the church and its resurrected Saviour (Rev. 1:5). Paul, led by the Holy Spirit, speaks about Jesus Christ using exalted and extraordinary language in a way that reveals Christ's true identity and proclaims Christ's Lordship over all creation. Jesus Christ is not man deified or God humanized; rather he is indissolubly divine and human, and has never ceased to be the eternal God. His eternal Sonship and pre-existence are revealed here just as in other portions of the New Testament (e.g. John 1:1; 8:58; 2 Cor. 8:9; Phil. 2:6–7; Heb. 1:2; 10:5–9; Rev. 1:17).

The idea of 'given' or delegated authority in John 17:2a does not mean that Jesus is inferior in nature to the Father. It is his Messianic office, not his substance, that is in view. This verse has reference to the incarnate Christ who has the authority to change hearts, to admit people into his kingdom and power to execute judgement at his second coming (John 5:26–30). The Son longs to bring the Father glory, and that will be achieved when he himself is glorified through giving 'eternal life to as many as You have given Him' (17:2b). Contrast this with Pilate's perceived authority: 'Do You not know that I have power to crucify You, and power to release You?' Jesus replied, 'You could have no power at all against Me unless it had been given you from above' (John 19:10–11). Pontius Pilate's delegated authority was realized in his judicial office as Procurator of Judea (AD 26–36) and is here juxtaposed with Christ's innate right to it as the only begotten Son of God from heaven above (Matt. 28:18).

Jesus's authority is 'over all flesh'. In John 1:14 'flesh' (*sarkos*) speaks of the sinless human nature of Christ which, because of the fall, was subject to weakness, pain, death and so on; in John 3:6 the same word is used to describe fallen human nature as a vehicle of sinful desire and disobedience. In John 17:2 it is a Hebraism for 'all people' (those fallen in Adam)—Jews and Gentiles alike (see Rom. 3:23). Jesus Christ has authority over everyone without exception (John 1:12; 5:27–30). The Son's dominion entails power and authority that belong to him by divine right.

The Son's gift

You have given [the Son] authority ... that He should give eternal life.

Man's life here on earth is temporary and like a candle: while it burns it gives out light, but it will soon burn out and vanish from view. Those who are in Christ, however, will never die, because the life our Saviour promises is everlasting (5:26–29). In the New Testament eternal life is contrasted with the wages of sin; the latter is eternal death, but the former, the gift of God, is eternal life through Jesus Christ (Rom. 6:23). Jesus Christ gives this life to those who believe in him because 'in him [is] life' (John 1:4; 3:16b). He gives what he himself possesses and is free to impart to those who believe his gospel. So not only are *authority* and *right* unique to Jesus Christ, but also he alone possesses what fallen human beings must receive to have eternal life: 'In Him was life, and the life was the light of men' (1:4). Life dwells in him just as it dwells in the Father, and he gives it freely to all who trust in him. Authority, affection, fellowship and honour are implied in Christ's relationship with his Father and these are extended to all God's adopted children. The gift of eternal life establishes our sonship and seals our eternal adoption: 'As many as received Him, to them He gave the right to become children of God' (1:12). Here again we see the apostle John's use of the Greek word *tekna*, 'little children', for those brought into the kingdom of God (see also 11:52). Christian sonship has to do with the 'now' as well as the 'not yet': it has to do with our present *dignity* as God's children and our future *destiny* as God's heirs and Christ's joint heirs.

The apostle John was thrilled to reflect on the doctrine of sonship: 'Behold what manner of love the Father has bestowed on us, that we should be called children of God!' (1 John 3:1). The word 'behold' is often employed in the Bible when God wants to tell us something wonderful: 'Behold! The Lamb of God' (John 1:29); 'Behold, how good and how pleasant it is for brethren to dwell together in unity!' (Ps. 133:1). Thus John is telling us of something wonderful regarding the justified sinner. Christian adoption is a gift given to believers in order that they may be designated 'children of God'. John uses the Greek word *tekna*, meaning 'little children', deliberately. It comes from the root *tiktein*, which means 'to give birth to'. This emphasizes family origin, with God as the Father of all who believe. It is only those who have been 'born of him' (John 3:3–8) who are truly the children of God.

The Son's charge

[The Son] should give eternal life to as many as You have given Him.

Eternal life is given to those who believe in Jesus Christ. This happens in time, but Jesus speaks in this verse of the eternal decree of unconditional election. Throughout the history of redemption, election has characterized God's saving activity. He chose and called Abraham, making an everlasting covenant with him and his offspring (Gen. 12:1–7; Neh. 9:7). He chose Israel from among the nations of the world to be his special covenant people (Deut. 7:6–7; Isa. 41:8; 44:1). The New Testament makes it clear that God has his elect in the Gentile nations also (Eph. 1:4–5; 2 Thes. 2:13; 1 Peter 1:1–2). Those given to Jesus by the Father are drawn to him for salvation (John 6:44, 65; 10:27–28).

Three things must be understood about the election of God lest we think that it is cruel, unjust or indefensible: the love of God, the chain of salvation and man's responsibility.

THE LOVE OF GOD

The source of election is the love of God; it is a sovereign act of his mercy. The Fall in Adam rendered all humanity 'dead in trespasses and sins' (Eph. 2:1; Rom. 5:17–21); the loss of the original righteousness of Adam's posterity alienated them for all time from the God who loved and created them. Nevertheless, God found a way to undo what Adam had done in the Garden of Eden.

The doctrine of election maintains that God has chosen some from all of fallen humanity to be the objects of his eternal love. We read in the Epistle to the Romans, '… that the purpose of God according to election might stand … it was said to [Rebecca], "The older shall serve the younger." As it is written, "Jacob I have loved, but Esau I have hated"' (Rom. 9:11–13; see also vv. 14–26; 11:7). Thus we see that this doctrine is based on the very nature of God himself, which is love (1 John 4:8). In his prayer in John 17 Jesus says that there is a cohort that the Father has given to the Son: 'the men whom You have given Me out of the world' (v. 6). Christ repeats this truth several times in his prayer, as if to emphasize continually the importance of God's gift to Christ (see vv. 9, 11–12, 24). Repetitions in the Bible indicate emphasis and are of great importance. In the verses cited above from John 17, Jesus is primarily referring to his apostles (vv. 6–19), but he also refers to the total blood-bought church (vv. 20–26), those who are 'elect according to the foreknowledge of God the Father, in sanctification of the Spirit, for obedience and sprinkling of the blood of Jesus Christ' (1 Peter 1:2).

Election has to do with God looking into himself and writing down in the Lamb's Book of Life the names of those he has chosen. Stephen Charnock says, 'God knows everything not by viewing the things, but by viewing himself: his own essence is the mirror and book wherein he beholds all things that he ordains, disposes and executes: and so he knows all things in the first and original cause.'[1] When God looks into himself, he sees all things and knows all things. Therefore he is not looking at man's decisions but at his own; 'the Spirit searches all things, yes, the deep things of God' (1 Cor. 2:10). God's knowledge of himself is perfect and comprehensive. There is nothing that he does not know completely, whether past, present or future. Thus we read, 'He chose us in Him before the foundation of the world ... having predestined us to adoption as sons ... according to the good pleasure of His will' (Eph. 1:4–5). This good pleasure 'He purposed in Himself' (Eph. 1:9); salvation is not 'of the will of the flesh, nor of the will of man, but of God' (John 1:13).

In Ephesians 1:4–9 we see

- The election of God: 'He chose us in Him before the foundation of the world' (v. 4)
- The sovereignty of God: 'according to the good pleasure of His will' (v. 5)
- The love of God: 'which He purposed in Himself' [who is love] (v. 9)

Election is the Father's idea, and the number of the elect is not known to us. 'The Lord knows those who are His' (2 Tim. 2:19; see also John 6:39, 44).

THE CHAIN OF SALVATION

It is biblical to say that those who have been given to Christ by the Father (election) are those who are saved through Christ's atoning work on the cross. Election in and of itself does not save; it is merely one 'link' in the 'chain of salvation'. Election to salvation takes place in Christ as a part of God's purpose for the human race, but it does not stand alone, nor is it an end in itself. In John 15 Jesus said, 'You did not choose Me, but I chose you and appointed you *that you should go and bear fruit*' (v. 16, emphasis added). An effectual call (see below) comes through the proclamation of the gospel of Jesus Christ to the lost sinner but a believing response of faith and repentance on the sinner's part is required. The elect choose Christ because he first chose and called them to himself, but they first need to hear the powerful, irresistible call of grace in the gospel. We must remember that salvation 'is not of [ourselves]; it is the gift of God' (Eph. 2:8). Romans 8:28–30 unfolds this:

> And we know that all things work together for good to those who love God, to those who are the called according to His purpose. For whom He foreknew, He also predestined to be conformed to the image of His Son, that He might be the firstborn among many brethren. Moreover whom He predestined, these He also called; whom He called, these He also justified; and whom He justified, these He also glorified.

Here Paul places the doctrines of election and predestination in a pastoral setting. He calls the saved 'God's elect' (Rom. 8:33) and he lists the process of the 'chain of salvation', sometimes known as the *ordo salutis*,[2] for his readers' encouragement. This chain takes us from the foreknowledge God has in himself to the glorification of the believer at death.

Why is it that we can 'know that all things work together for good to those who love God'? It is because those Paul is speaking about are foreknown by God: 'For whom He foreknew [*proegno*—we get 'prognosis' from this word] He also predestined to be conformed to the image of His Son' (v. 29). 'Foreknew'—'known beforehand'—expresses the relationship Jehovah had with Israel and also with the elect: 'elect according to the *foreknowledge* of God the Father' (1 Peter 1:2, emphasis added). Foreknowledge refers to God's knowledge of and love for his elect before they were even born. It was not that God's knowledge of future events determined his choice; rather he chose out of a heart full of love and sovereign grace 'according to His purpose' (Rom. 8:28). This is very personal. Romans 8:29 does not say '*what* he foreknew' but '*whom* he foreknew'. This reminds us of the prophet Jeremiah's words: 'Yes, I have loved you with an everlasting love; Therefore with lovingkindness I have drawn you' (Jer. 31:3).

Some believe that God's 'foreknowledge' refers to the fact that, in his omniscient wisdom, God knew who would respond to Christ by faith. This, however, makes God's choice dependent on man's will, not the divine will. However, according to both views it is God alone who saves, as people can never earn salvation through works (Eph. 2:8–10).

To 'predestine' means to mark out beforehand, to establish one's boundary or limits in advance. God has a fixed and ultimate destiny planned from eternity that will bring the elect into conformity to the likeness of his Son (Phil. 1:6). Note how the words 'predestined', 'called', 'justified' and 'glorified' (Rom. 8:28–30) are in the past tense. That is because, from God's eternal perspective, this process has already been completed. We have already been glorified because God sees us as righteous in Jesus through faith alone. However, we must still undergo the process of being conformed to the image of God's Son through faith and repentance (for justification) and obedience (for sanctification). Predestination is the means by which that destiny is realized: God bringing to pass all the necessary events and measures to save and keep his elect people. God marks out beforehand the way they shall take. Even Christ's path to the cross was planned beforehand: 'Herod and Pontius Pilate ... were gathered together to do whatever [God's] hand and [God's] purpose determined [*proorizo*] before to be done' (Acts 4:27–28). The same verb is used of those chosen in Christ before the foundation of the world: 'whom He foreknew, he also predestined [*proorizo*] to be conformed to the image of His Son' (Rom. 8:29).

The effectual call of God

Romans 8:30—'Moreover whom He predestined, these He also called'—

speaks of the call which supplies all the spiritual light and power necessary to convince sinners of their need to accept Jesus as their Saviour and Lord (James 1:18; 1 Peter 1:23). It is effectual through the Holy Spirit's work of regeneration and as a result the sinner is made willing in 'the day of [God's] power' (Ps. 110:3a).

There are two calls in the Bible: the universal call, which is general and outward; and the effectual call, which is inward and powerful. When the elect hear this latter call, it is accompanied by God's grace to bring them to conversion. The truth of a universal call is found in the statement 'For many are called, but few are chosen' (Matt. 22:14). Here we have calling and election side by side in Holy Writ, yet not resulting in salvation for all. The effectual call is God's command to respond believingly to the gospel (1 Cor. 1:26–29). This powerful call is the initiatory act in the chain of salvation; by it, people are summoned to faith in Christ and to repentance of their sins.

- The effectual call is the call to *come out of darkness and into light*: 'But you are a chosen generation, a royal priesthood, a holy nation, His own special people, that you may proclaim the praises of Him who called you out of darkness into His marvelous light; who once were not a people but are now the people of God, who had not obtained mercy but now have obtained mercy' (1 Peter 2:9–10).
- The effectual call is the call to *a new relationship as children of God*: 'But may the God of all grace, who called us to His eternal glory by Christ Jesus, after you have suffered a while, perfect, establish, strengthen, and settle you. To Him be the glory and the dominion forever and ever. Amen' (1 Peter 5:10–11).
- The effectual call is the call to *the 'fight of faith'*: 'Fight the good fight of faith, lay hold on eternal life, to which you were also called and have confessed the good confession in the presence of many witnesses' (1 Tim. 6:12).

- The effectual call is the call to *holy living*: 'For God did not call us to uncleanness, but in holiness' (1 Thes. 4:7).

The elect were chosen in Christ before the beginning of the world and are called by the grace and power of God to receive Christ as Saviour, in order that they may be justified by faith alone: 'whom He called, these He also justified' (Rom. 8:30). These are not abstract ideas; they are pragmatically glorious. The effectual call is *subjective*—we feel it, we respond to it, we hear it. It comes to us when we hear the gospel in the power of the Holy Spirit. Election, however, is *objective*—God makes the choice, and it is God's will that matters. Election is God's sovereign choice in eternity past. Our salvation is all of God. The prophet Jonah could say, 'Salvation is of the LORD' (Jonah 2:9), and New Testament believers must agree.

MAN'S RESPONSIBILITY

The goal of election is clearly stated thus: 'For whom He foreknew, He also predestined to be *conformed to the image of His Son*' (Rom. 8:29, emphasis added). Here, human responsibility is put alongside God's divine sovereignty. The doctrine of election does not diminish man's responsibility; the Scriptures call all believers to be watchful, careful and earnest in the things of God: 'Be even more diligent to make your call and election sure' (2 Peter 1:10).

Becoming a Christian means becoming 'alive to God in Christ Jesus our Lord' (Rom. 6:11; Eph. 2:1, 5) and being called to 'be [a] partaker of the divine nature' (2 Peter 1:4). This does not mean that Christians become gods; the essence of deity is not transferable to them. Conversion results in being grafted into the Branch, the True Vine, and being given divine grace (John 15:4; Eph. 2:8–9). Dignity and joy belong to believers, for theirs is a high and holy calling: they are the children of God. By the world's reckoning, they are foolish and thoughtless, but in God's sight, they are special and holy: 'you ... once were not a people but are now the people of God, who had not obtained mercy but now have obtained mercy' (1 Peter 2:9–10).

Through faith, the elect know God and possess eternal life. They are new creatures, with a new knowledge and a new and special relationship with God through Jesus Christ. As members of Christ's Body, their lives are now hidden with Christ in God (Col. 3:3). This being so, believers are to live, grow and bear spiritual fruit as evidence that they really are born again and dwell in Christ (John 15:1–8). Fruit is expected from them because of the new life of God within their souls. It is not enough to say that we are Christians; we need to show it by being salt and by letting our light shine (Matt. 5:16).

The apostle Peter reveals the processes and graces involved as believers walk the road of Christian discipleship:

> Giving all diligence, add to your faith virtue, to virtue knowledge, to knowledge self-control, to self-control perseverance, to perseverance godliness, to godliness brotherly kindness, and to brotherly kindness love. For if these things are yours and abound, you will be neither barren nor unfruitful in the knowledge of our Lord Jesus Christ … Therefore, brethren, be even more diligent to make your call and election sure, for if you do these things you will never stumble. (2 Peter 1:5–8, 10)

Some have difficulty when they try to reconcile the doctrines of divine sovereignty (election) with human responsibility (free will). However, we must not attribute to fallen humanity a free will which can stop God reaching the lost he has planned to save. Men and women lost their free will in Eden and are only 'free' now to follow their fallen and corrupt nature as it leads them in rebellion against God. It is best to remember C. H. Spurgeon's thought: 'There will be no doubt about his having chosen *you*, when you shall feel no doubt about having chosen *him*.'[3]

FOR FURTHER STUDY

1. What blessings and glory are yet to come for believers following their adoption?
2. Which texts express the doctrine of election, and what are their implications?
3. Write out the *ordo salutis*, attaching biblical references for each step.

TO THINK ABOUT AND DISCUSS

1. What does 1 John 3:1–3 say about the Christian's standing and dignity in God's sight?
2. Man's free will or God's sovereignty: which decides our election? Give reasons for your answer.
3. Using 2 Peter 1:5–11, consider the implications of a person claiming that he or she is a born-again Christian.

Notes

1 **Stephen Charnock,** *The Attributes of God*, vol. ii (London: Parsons Edition, 1815), p. 74; quoted by **Errol Hulse,** 'Psalm 139 and the Omniscience of God', www.reformation-today.org/articles/187Psalm_139_and_the_Omniscience_of_God.pdf; accessed March 2012.

2 *Ordo salutis:* the order of salvation or the way we are brought to salvation by the Holy Spirit and kept there. It involves effectual calling, regeneration, faith and repentance, justification, adoption, sanctification, perseverance and glorification.

3 **C. H. Spurgeon,** 'His Name: The Counsellor', sermon preached on 26 September 1858; no. 215 in *The New Park Street Pulpit* and available at The Spurgeon Archive, www.spurgeon.org/sermons/0215.htm; accessed February 2012.

Chapter 4

The High Priest's redemption: The Son of life (v. 3)

And this is eternal life, that they may know You, the only true God, and Jesus Christ whom You have sent.

This is the only place in the New Testament where our Lord calls himself 'Jesus Christ'; by doing so he speaks of his commission as Messiah. The Son was 'sent' from heaven to earth to become the Redeemer (John 3:17, 34; 5:36–37; 8:18) and he was very conscious of this commission. He was sent as Prophet (to speak God's words), as Priest (to mediate between God and sinners) and as King (to rule God's kingdom, the church). He knew *who* he was and *what* his purpose was. This is clearly seen in his 'I am' statements in John's Gospel, especially in these words: 'Do you say of Him whom the Father sanctified and sent into the world, "You are blaspheming", because I said, "I am the Son of God?"' (10:36; see also 9:5; 10:9–11; 11:25). The Jews present on that occasion were very conscious of Jesus's claim to be the promised Anointed One, so they tried to kill him (10:37–39).

The Son's goal

That they may know You.

How can sinners reach heaven? This verse tells us that it is only through the Son, Jesus Christ. The Son's goal is to give eternal life to those the Father has given him, that 'they may know You, the only true God'. Sinners obtain eternal life through knowing God 'and Jesus Christ'. Paul writes that there is only 'one Mediator between God and men, the Man Jesus Christ' (1 Tim. 2:5; see also Acts 4:12; John 14:6). Those given to the Son are those who will believe; those who believe are those who have been given to the Son. Eternal life is not reached through a casual knowledge gleaned from a religious upbringing, or an intellectual knowledge gained by academic study, but by faith alone in Jesus Christ. There is an experience to know and a relationship to find.

God is incomprehensible, yet we must not despair; knowing God is not impossible *in Christ*. Jesus said, 'He who has seen Me has seen the Father' (John 14:9). When conversion is experienced, the sinner's mind is fully engaged and active, but the Son wants sinners to know the Father by spiritual experience; it is not sufficient to know facts about God. There must be a new birth (John 3:3).

For example, I could tell you things about my father by describing his physical features and his likes and dislikes, and by discussing his family tree. Would that mean that you *knew* him? You might feel that you knew something about him after our talk, but only if you were introduced to him and met him face-to-face would you feel you actually knew him. Similarly, knowing God means meeting him and talking with him face-to-face in the spiritual realm, and this is possible only through the Son of God, Jesus Christ. Jesus Christ tells us that it is not enough to know God's *name*; we must know him and his Son *personally*. Thus, to seek God without Jesus Christ is to fail, because Jesus Christ is the only Mediator who can bring us into communion with God. It is only in Christ that sinners can gain access to God's love, mercy, forgiveness and peace.

Those who know God are called the friends of God. Such people have found that their purpose and destiny rest in Christ. This is recognized by Question 1 in the Westminster Shorter Catechism:

Q: What is the chief end of man?

A: Man's chief end is to glorify God, and to enjoy him for ever.

There are many religions and cults in the world and it has been estimated that about 7,000 religions seek God. However, Christianity teaches that there is only one way to God, and John 17:3 makes this clear. The knowledge of both Father and Son is necessary for salvation. Many religions reject Jesus Christ and his Messianic claim, but those who would be saved must not do this, for Jesus alone introduces sinners to the Father through their repentance of sins and faith in him (John 3:36; 14:1, 6; Acts 4:12). Many people have head-knowledge about God but they are not saved. Even the devil possesses such head-knowledge but he is destined to remain unsaved.

More than speculation is envisaged in this knowledge of God in John 17:3. We need an understanding of the truth that seals our knowledge of God and our salvation for all eternity. Thus, to gain eternal life there has to be:

BELIEVING KNOWLEDGE

The Bible describes the relationship of believers with God as that of children with their father. Therefore, when we believe and trust all that God says to us in and through his Word, the Bible, we become like little children. This involves humbly accepting the truth about ourselves as sinners, about God as holy and merciful, and about his love in Christ, being assured that the gospel's promises are to be trusted (2 Cor. 1:20). Jesus said, 'Whoever does not receive the kingdom of God as a little child will by no means enter it' (Mark 10:14). Those who cannot trust the Bible and its message about Jesus Christ and the way of salvation will never know God or receive forgiveness for their sins.

PERSONAL KNOWLEDGE

When we trust God's Word, the Holy Spirit seals our relationship with an inner witness so that we enjoy illumination and do not depend on speculation or misinformation. It is vital to grasp that without the inner working of the Holy Spirit in our souls we remain in spiritual darkness (1 Cor. 2:14; Titus 3:5). This world is full of ideas that are not related to the truth as it is in Jesus Christ. Two thousand years ago Paul called this 'philosophy and empty deceit, according to the tradition of men' (Col. 2:8). Philosophy has failed to understand the reason for man's existence and to answer satisfactorily the big moral and spiritual questions that have haunted mankind over thousands of years. The knowledge that will satisfy the human soul comes to us only through Jesus Christ, God's Son. The Holy Spirit unlocks the power of the gospel when we believe it personally: 'when the Helper comes, whom I shall send to you from the Father, the Spirit of truth who proceeds from the Father, He will testify of Me' (John 15:26).

SAVING KNOWLEDGE

Forgiveness and peace with God are the fruits of saving faith. The life of God in the soul is ours when we believe the gospel. What ultimately matters in the great scheme of things is not how much we know about religion, or about God or Jesus Christ, but whether we have believed unto salvation through faith alone. It is whether we are *in Christ* and are children of the living God by justification unto adoption. This 'big picture' needs to be grasped. Life's goal and end is God himself. Bishop Augustine of Hippo said, 'Our hearts are restless until they find their rest in [God].'[1] The human soul is unsettled until it finds rest through grasping that in Jesus Christ alone is peace with God granted. All religions seek God as their final goal and resting place; however, it is in Christ alone that this salvation becomes a reality.

In Christ alone my hope is found;
He is my light, my strength, my song;

This cornerstone, this solid ground,
Firm through the fiercest drought and storm.
What heights of love, what depths of peace,
When fears are stilled, when strivings cease!
My comforter, my all in all—
Here in the love of Christ I stand. (Keith Getty and Stuart Townend, 2001)

THIS IS NOT EXCLUSIVISM

The knowledge of God is not reserved for an exclusive band of initiated followers. There are sects and cults which tell us that *they* are 'the kingdom of God' and which seek to draw others into a system and a philosophy contrary to the true way of salvation. Evangelical Christians recognize the existence of the Christian family and the brotherhood of all the redeemed. All true Christians belong in God's family and to Christ. No single group, sect or cult has a monopoly on the throne of grace, the Holy Spirit's gifts, or the knowledge and the will of God. There is no such exclusivism in the New Testament. Neither has any believer more right to God's grace and love than another because God is '*Our* Father' (Matt. 6:9, emphasis added). All God's people are adopted into his family by grace alone, through faith alone, and in Christ alone. Evangelical Christianity does not promote a cultic experience but a saving knowledge of God that is freely offered to all. In Jesus Christ alone our hope is found. There was a time when knowledge of God was exclusive: it started with Abraham and continued through Moses; but now in these last days God has spoken to all by his Son (Heb. 1:1–2).

THIS IS NOT GNOSTICISM

Gnosticism was a perversion of early Christianity, a synchronism of Judaism, Christianity and heathen speculative thought. It was similar to today's New Age Movement, which has 'absorbed all possible religious ideas ... to generalise and harmonise them'.[2] Gnosticism was associated with rites, mysteries and the teaching of magic, and it claimed to have a deeper knowledge of divine spiritual realities than could be obtained by adhering to the teachings of Jesus Christ alone. It also made a distinction between Jesus the Man and the Christ who came from God. Gnostics denied the incarnation: that Jesus is the Christ, and that Jesus Christ is both God and Man. This is not what we are offered in Christ, which is peace with God by faith alone (Rom. 5:1). The knowledge of God is not an intellectual experience (although the mind is not dormant, but is always active and learning). It is rather a spiritual experience in the soul and the gift of eternal life (John 3:3). The Son wants us to know the Father, 'that they may know You, the only true God, and Jesus Christ whom You have sent.'

FOR FURTHER STUDY

1. Where do we find evidence of the threefold offices of Jesus Christ in the New Testament?
2. How does Jesus's prayer help us to see him as God's Messiah and Saviour of the World?
3. Which cults require extra-biblical sources to support their theology? What about the Jehovah Witnesses?

TO THINK ABOUT AND DISCUSS

1. Why is it that Gnostic ideas are growing in acceptance in the West?
2. Read John 14:1–2 (NKJV). What are the implications of these verses in today's multi-faith environment, especially the words 'believe also in Me'?
3. Describe your conversion experience to others and back it up with Scripture references.

Notes

1 **Augustine of Hippo,** *Confessions*, Book 1, Ch. 1; available at www.leaderu.com/cyber/books/augconfessions/bk1.html; accessed February 2012.

2 **Louis Berkhof,** *The History of Christian Doctrines* (London: Banner of Truth, 1969), p. 46.

The High Priest's rest: The Son of obedience (v. 4)

I have glorified You on the earth. I have finished the work which You have given Me to do.

These words remind us of the penultimate saying of Jesus from the cross as recorded in John 19:30: 'It is finished!' (In the Greek, only one word is used: *teleio*, 'finished', 'completed'.) His death on the cross as a substitute for sinners was a once-and-for-all-time event (Heb. 9:28a; 10:12, 14); as he anticipates this moment while praying, Jesus brings it before his Father in heaven as if it has already been achieved. He speaks in the past tense because his life and soon the crucifixion will fulfil the plan of redemption. The communion table, with its bread and wine, is a visualization of the way Jesus achieved his goal. His body was broken and his blood poured out for elect sinners at Calvary.

The Son's joy

I have glorified You on the earth.

The glorifying of God through the works of the Son did not add to the Father's essential glory but showed to the world the Father's love, goodness, truth and patience, as well as the plan of salvation. These divine attributes declare the majestic glory of the Father.

Here Jesus uses the word *doxazo* ('to bestow glory on'). The Saviour, by his life and his resurrection, bestowed glory on his Father.

Seven sayings of Christ from the cross

1. Cry of forgiveness (Luke 23:34)
2. Cry of mercy (Luke 23:43)
3. Cry of thoughtfulness (John 19:27)
4. Cry of desertion (Matt. 27:46)
5. Cry of thirst (John 19:28)
6. Cry of completion (John 19:30)
7. Cry of trust (Luke 23:46)

In John 8:50 Jesus said, 'I do not seek My own glory', and he told the apostles that he would answer their prayers so that 'the Father may be glorified in the Son' (14:13). This makes clear that it was Christ's commission to represent to the world the beauty of the holiness and greatness of God. Christ had opened his High-Priestly prayer with the words, 'Father ... glorify Your Son, that Your Son also may glorify You' (v. 1). This was Christ's mission and consuming purpose, and he was delighted and thankful to be able to say to his Father that he had achieved this goal.

What a great ambition Jesus had! Christians are to emulate their Saviour by dedicating their lives to bringing glory to the Father and the Son in the strength of the Holy Spirit (1 Cor. 10:31). Christian ambition and zeal need to be governed by this goal. The apostle Peter wrote, 'If anyone speaks, let him speak as the oracles of God. If anyone ministers, let him do it as with the ability which God supplies, that in all things God may be glorified through Jesus Christ, to whom belong the glory and the dominion forever and ever. Amen' (1 Peter 4:11).

The Son's faithfulness

I have finished the work.

By 'work' Christ includes his perfect keeping of the Moral and Ceremonial Laws. He obeyed the Father's will without sin and there was nothing in him that allowed Satan to deceive him, influence him or overcome him. Christ fulfilled a Prophetic ministry as Teacher, revealing the mind of God especially to the apostles (v. 6). His Priestly ministry as Mediator revealed the heart of God. His Kingly authority over all creation was demonstrated through his miracles of healing and power.

As noted above, Jesus Christ let nothing hinder his ambition to do God's will and bring glory to the Father (Heb. 12:2). This was his meat and drink (John 4:34). He let nothing distract him from this goal because he had come for that very purpose (John 4:34; 6:38; Ps. 40:7–8; Heb. 10:5–7; Matt. 26:39). He would do nothing independently, without the Father; and likewise believers can do nothing without their Saviour (John 15:5). He was not independent in his actions or selfish in his ambitions, but faithfully discharged his duties, no matter the cost to himself. He knew that the Father had sent him and that he had a Messianic mission to fulfil. He was faithful to the end in preaching, teaching and in the performance of works of power. Whatever people said or thought about him was secondary to his ordained and recognized commission and the approval of the Father (John 17:3a; 11:42). The wicked temptations of Satan did not stop him finishing the work. Neither did the opposition he encountered from the religious Jews. The prospect of the shame and agonies of the cross did not keep him from completing what was assigned to him (Heb. 12:2). His work was not half-done or only 90 per cent achieved, but rather was fully completed. It was finished and faithfully discharged. *He* was not finished, but his work was!

Jesus, my great High Priest
offered his blood and died;
My guilty conscience seeks
No sacrifice besides;

His powerful blood did once atone,
and now it pleads before the throne.

(Isaac Watts, 'Join All the Glorious Names', 1709)

At the Fall Adam asserted his independence by deciding to disobey God, but the last Adam (1 Cor. 15:45) did nothing by himself; he and the Father always worked together in unity, harmony and equality. Jesus saw everything from God's perspective and accepted it as good, right, just and loving.

Christians are called to cooperate with Christ's Spirit and serve as God's fellow workers in his kingdom (1 Cor. 3:9). The aim of bringing glory to God and Christ should regulate Christian living, wherever Christians are called to live and work in Jesus's name. This includes at home with loved ones, in the workplace with colleagues, as well as in the local church (Col. 3:18–24). Christians are to bring glory to the Father by completing works of faith and love (1 Cor. 15:58; Col. 4:17). This is the way of the cross and the path of servanthood which reflects Christ's ministry of suffering and teaching. He was able to say, 'I have finished the work which You have given Me to do', and we must aspire to do the same.

The Son's incarnation

The work which You have given Me to do.

There could be no saving work without Christ's incarnation. Nowhere is this better explained than in Philippians 2:

Let this mind be in you which was also in Christ Jesus, who, being in the form of God, did not consider it robbery to be equal with God, but made Himself of no reputation, taking the form of a bondservant, and coming in the likeness of men. And being found in appearance as a man, He humbled Himself and became obedient to the point of death, even the death of the cross. Therefore God also has highly exalted Him and given Him the name which is above every name. (Phil. 2:5–9)

Four important truths about the incarnate Christ are found in these verses from Philippians.

WHAT JESUS WAS

Paul tells us that before Jesus became a man he was in the 'form of God' (v. 6). The word 'form' (*morphe*[1]) stands in contrast to 'appearance' (v. 8). It means 'the inner essential and abiding nature of a person or thing',[2] that is, the specific character or essence of a thing or individual. An example that helps us to understand what the New Testament means here is to think of steel and why steel *is* steel—the material that we use for knives, forks, cars and cookers. Steel is not brass or aluminium because of its *form*. This does not mean *shape* but character and constitution; it is that quality which distinguishes steel from all other materials and makes it what it is. Similarly, Paul explains, Jesus was in *the form of God*: Jesus had those qualities that distinguished him from all others and which constituted him God; without them he would not be God. This is the Bible's message about Jesus Christ. He is 'the image of the invisible God' (Col. 1:15)—he is God. He is all that God is, possessing all the qualities of deity. Jesus himself said, 'He who has seen Me has seen the Father' (John 14:9). The Word Incarnate has always been God by nature. All the divine attributes were and are his eternally (John 1:1–3; 8:58; 17:24; 2 Cor. 4:4; Col. 2:6; Heb. 1:4). The words and phrases the Bible uses to describe Jesus Christ are intended to prove what Paul here conveys: that whatever God is in uncreated eternity—infinite, incomprehensible, all-holy, all-blessed—so is Jesus Christ, who is his only Son. Thus, the Bible says, Jesus Christ is 'the brightness of [God's] glory and the express image of [God's] person' (Heb. 1:3).

WHAT JESUS THOUGHT

Christ 'did not consider it robbery to be equal with God'. Our Saviour knew that his equality with God detracted nothing from the Father's own infinite glory. When Peter said of Jesus 'You are the Christ, the Son of the living God', Jesus did not correct him but rather confirmed Peter's words, saying, 'Flesh and blood has not revealed this to you, but My Father who is in heaven' (Matt. 16:16–17). Similarly, when Doubting Thomas confessed Christ as his 'Lord and ... God' (John 20:28), the Saviour accepted this statement without rebuke, even though Thomas, a Jew, believed in the existence of only one God. Jesus could say in John 14:1, 'You believe in God, believe *also* in me' (emphasis added). When the dying thief hung on the cross, Jesus opened the gate of life to him and assured him that he would be with him in Paradise *that very day* (Luke 23:43). By saying this, he did not think he was robbing God by assuming the right to open the gate of forgiveness and eternal life for this sinner. God the Son 'did not consider equality with God something to be grasped' (NIV), because this equality was already his from all eternity. Nor was he robbing God of his glory when he took the divine name 'I am' to himself (John 6:35; 8:28).

WHAT JESUS DID

By making 'Himself of no reputation, taking the form of a bondservant', the Word veiled his deity with his humanity but retained the essential qualities of the Godhead. It was William Tyndale who translated the Greek as 'but made Himself of no reputation', but others have preferred the phrasing 'He emptied Himself'. The idea of Jesus emptying himself begs the question, 'Of what did he empty himself?' Not his divinity, nor his existence 'in the form of God'. This issue has given rise to much debate, including the error known as the Kenosis theory.[3] Paul's meaning is that Christ made himself of no standing; he gave up the glory and riches of heaven on our account, but he did not rid himself of his deity.[4]

'Great is the mystery of godliness: God was manifested in the flesh ...' (1 Tim. 3:16). Our Saviour stooped so low that he had to borrow a stable to be born in, a house to sleep in, a boat to preach from, an ass to ride on to get into Jerusalem, a room in which to hold the Last Supper and a tomb to be buried in after his crucifixion. He came to this earth deliberately as a man without land, money or political power. His work was utterly full of self-sacrificial love.

Down from his glory,
Ever-living story,
My God and Saviour came,
And Jesus was his name.
Born in a manger
To his own a stranger,
A man of sorrows, tears and agony.

What condescension,
Bringing us redemption,
That in the dead of night,
Not one faint hope in sight,
God, gracious, tender,
Laid aside his splendour,
Stooping to woo, to win, to save my soul.

(William E. Booth-Clibborn, 1893–1969)

He took 'the form of a bondservant', that is, all the characteristics, marks, qualities and attributes of a servant. The NIV reads, '[He] made himself nothing, taking the very nature of a servant'. He did this because he had come to serve and not to rule; he said, 'I am among you as the One who serves' (Luke 22:27). Jesus took to himself the qualities that belong to a servant in order to make the atonement.

WHAT JESUS BECAME

The Bible says that Christ came in the likeness of man: 'And being found in appearance as a man, He humbled Himself and became obedient to the point of death, even the death of the cross.' This describes the incarnation, with its virgin conception and birth, which is spoken about in other portions of Scripture:

- 'Behold, the virgin shall conceive and bear a Son, and shall call His name Immanuel' (Isa. 7:14).
- 'When the fullness of the time had come, God sent forth His Son, born of a woman, born under the law, to redeem those who were under the law, that we might receive the adoption as sons' (Gal. 4:4).

The Scriptures teach us that the Son of God came into the world to take flesh and blood, body and soul, 'in the likeness of sinful flesh' (Rom. 8:3). His humanity was real and complete, yet without the stain of Adam's first sin (Heb. 4:15). He remained God but became Man. Thus, he was God and Man in one: one Person with two natures.

The word translated as 'appearance' in verse 8, *schema*, means the 'outward (changeable) fashion (form)'.[5] Paul was saying that Christ looked like a man because he *was* a man, while all the time he was 'in the form of God' (v. 6). If we think of an apple tree, we see that it has a *form* (its inner nature) that remains the same all year round, but its appearance changes with the seasons. During the year it buds, blooms, is covered in leaves, bears fruit and is picked clean. In the autumn, the leaves fall off and the tree looks different from how it did in the springtime with its blossom and leaves. Similarly, when Jesus became Man he appeared to the Jews and all who saw him as a man—which he was; he had brothers and sisters, and he got hungry, thirsty, weary and so on. So in his 'appearance' he was recognized as a *Homo sapien*.

Thus the divinity of Christ Jesus is spelled out for us in these verses. He looked like a humble servant but he was, by very nature, the Lord of

Glory. He was in 'the form of God' but in 'appearance' a Man. Even so, John was able to say, 'The Word became flesh and dwelt among us, and we beheld His glory ... full of grace and truth' (John 1:14).

Having declared who Jesus Christ really was and is, Paul tells us why Christ left heaven. It was all because of his role as Messiah of the Jews and Saviour of the world that 'He humbled Himself and became obedient to the point of death, even the death of the cross' (v. 8). As the Lamb of God Christ gave himself as a sacrifice for the salvation of lost sinners. The purpose of the incarnation is thus clearly seen in this verse. Christ was born to die: 'The Son of God became the Son of Man that we, the sons of men, might become the sons of God.'[6]

FOR FURTHER STUDY

1. The *logos* (Word) was the pre-existent Christ. Read what the Christian commentators say about John 1:1–14.
2. Read John 1 and note all the names and titles given to Jesus in that chapter.
3. Where else in the New Testament do we find references to the incarnation?

TO THINK ABOUT AND DISCUSS

1. Why is it critical for Christians to uphold the doctrine of the incarnation?
2. Jehovah's Witnesses consider Jesus Christ to be a created being. What does the Bible say on this issue, and which passages could you use, from both the Old and New Testaments, when discussing it with Jehovah's Witnesses?

Notes

1 '*Morphe* (form), implying essential character as well as outline. It suggests unchangeableness as contrasted with *schema* (figure, fashion). In Phil. 2:6 the reference is to the pre-incarnate Christ with divine attributes'; from **Alexander Souter,** *A Pocket Lexicon to the NT* (Oxford: Oxford University Press, 1960).

2 **William Hendriksen,** *A Commentary on the Epistle to the Philippians* (London: Banner of Truth, 1963), p. 104.

3 The Kenosis theory states that Jesus gave up some of his divine attributes—omniscience, omnipresence and omnipotence—while he was a man here on earth. It is claimed that Christ did this voluntarily so that he could function as a man in order to fulfil the work of redemption. This view was first introduced in the late 1800s in Germany by Gottfried Thomasius (1802–1875), a Lutheran theologian. See **Matt Slick,** 'Kenosis', Christian Apologetics and Research Ministry (CARM), at http://carm.org/kenosis (accessed January 2012).

4 For a full discussion see **Hendricksen,** *Philippians*, pp. 102–110.

5 **Souter,** *A Pocket Lexicon*.

6 This quote is often attributed to **Athanasius, Archbishop of Alexandria,** but his actual words were, 'For He was made man that we might be made God.' Easily misunderstood, because of the patristic doctrine of 'divinization', Athanasius's words have not fared well in the later Western world. The quote here sounds more like **Augustine,** who says, 'He alone became the Son of man, in order that we might become through Him sons of God' (*A Treatise against Two Letters of the Pelagians*, 4:6). Thanks go to **Dr Nick Needham** for this comment.

The High Priest's righteousness: the Son of eternity (v. 5)

And now, O Father, glorify Me together with Yourself, with the glory which I had with You before the world was.

The Saviour here refers back to the promise made to him by the Father in the covenant of redemption, agreed before the world was created. Now, at the fulfilment of his duties and responsibilities as the Surety of that covenant, Christ asks for his promised reward.[1] John Owen says that Jesus expected that the promises given to him in the covenant would be made good and fulfilled, 'being made unto him and being confirmed with the "oath of God"' (see Heb. 7:20; 12:2).[2]

This request pulls aside the veil of Christ's Person and sheds light upon his deity; thus Ryle says of Christ's words, 'These things are very deep and beyond man's understanding.'[3] Jesus's appointed time of death had arrived. He could have glorified himself, but he would do nothing independently of the Father. Here we see the unity of the Father and the Son. Jesus was not a solo agent but part of a team, always working with the Father and the Holy Spirit in perfect Trinitarian unity and endeavour. While on earth he testified to his divinity, not only by the miracles he performed but also by declaring, 'I can of Myself do nothing. As I hear, I judge; and My judgment is righteous, because I do not seek My own will but the will of the Father who sent Me' (John 5:30); 'For I have come down from heaven, not to do My own will, but the will of Him who sent Me' (6:38; see also 5:19–21; 8:28).

Three truths from this verse demonstrate that Jesus Christ is the Son of God:

His divine equality with the Father

O Father, glorify Me together with Yourself.

If he were not equal with the Father, Jesus would here be speaking blasphemously (10:36). Here is a reaffirmation of the truth stated in the opening words of John's Gospel: 'In the beginning was the Word, and the Word was with God, and the Word was God' (1:1). At the incarnation, the Word assumed human nature but remained God, being the Son from all eternity by nature, not by creation or inheritance. He was always the only begotten Son. Manton helps us understand this:

> He did not lose his Godhead though he took flesh; he was still the eternal Son of the Father. He was still co-equal with his Father; the fullness of the Godhead dwelt in him; his flesh was taken into the fellowship of the divine nature as soon as it began to have a being in the womb of the virgin, the highest dignity a creature is capable of. The person of the Son was truly communicated to the nature of man, the nature of man truly communicated to the person of the Son. He that was the Son of man was truly the Son of God, he that was truly the Son of God was truly the Son of man; and by virtue of this union there was a communion higher than all other communions; the fullness of grace was subjectively and inherently in his human nature (Ps. 45:7; John 3:34).[4]

Isaiah the prophet saw the glory of Jesus when he 'saw the Lord [*adonai*] sitting on a throne, high and lifted up, and the train of His robe filled the temple' (Isa. 6:1). The apostle John (12:41) recognized that this revelation was a vision of the glory of the incarnate Word (*logos*). Isaiah saw Jesus Christ the Messiah, yet in Isaiah 6:5 he says it was the Lord Jehovah, 'The LORD of hosts', who was before him. Herman Ridderbos, commenting on John 12:41, says,

The Evangelist does not mean that Isaiah already foresaw Jesus' (later) glory, but that the glory of God as the prophet foresaw it in his vision was no other than that which the Son of God had with the Father before the world was and that was to be manifested before the eyes of all in the incarnation of the Word (1:14, 18).[5]

Isaiah prophesied that Christ's glory would be seen (Isa. 40:5), and it is seen by the elect (John 17:24)—by those who believe in him (John 11:40)—and will be revealed to the world at the end of time. The Father's plan is to dignify his Son before all creation (Rom. 8:19–23; Phil. 2:9–11).

Jesus is God and Man in one Person. Two men, both from Alexandria, dominated the incarnation debate in the fourth-century church: Arius (c. 250–336), a presbyter, and Athanasius (c. 296–373), a deacon. Two words were involved: *homoousia* ('*same* nature') and *homoiousia* ('*similar* nature'). The presence or otherwise of the letter 'i' in the middle of those words is the difference, in theology, between Christ being acknowledged as creature or the Creator. R. A. Finlayson wrote, 'These two words scarcely differ as to sound and sight, but a chasm stretches between them as vast as between infinitude and infinity.'[6] The debate was resolved a century later at the Fourth Ecumenical Council of Chalcedon in AD 451. Christians believe that the 'Lord Jesus Christ is complete in Godhead and complete in manhood ... of one substance [*homoousia*] with the Father' (the Creed of Chalcedon).[7] To be *the* Son of God and to be *a* son of God are two very different things. The former is to be the Son by nature while the latter is to be a son by grace.

His pre-existence

The glory which I had with You before the world was.

The glory and equality of Jesus with God the Father preceded the creation and the incarnation. Thus the Bible speaks of the 'Trinitarian Son' who:

- descended from heaven (John 3:13)
- came from the Father into the world (16:28)
- ascended back to heaven (16:7, 28b; Acts 1:9–11)

Proof of Christ's pre-existence is found in the opening prologue of John's Gospel: 'In the beginning was the Word, and the Word was with God, and the Word was God. He was in the beginning with God. All things were made through Him, and without Him nothing was made that was made' (John 1:1–3). The phrase 'in the beginning' represents the life of Christ in eternity, before the heavens and the earth were created, and brings light to us concerning the true character of the Son of God and his place in the Godhead. The Word was the genesis of all things; Christ himself was not created but was the Creator of all things (v. 3; Gen. 1:1; Col. 1:16–17). The 'Word was with God' (John 1:1), face-to-face with God (*pros ton theon*), and was a distinct Person in his own right. 'The Word' is no longer referred to thus in the rest of the Gospel of John; instead the narrative speaks of the incarnation of the Word and the historical Person of Jesus Christ as being one and the same (v. 14). 'The Word was God' (John 1:1) is a clear statement concerning the deity of Jesus Christ. This is confirmed by the sentence structure: 'in order to place all the emphasis on Christ's full deity the predicate in the original precedes the subject [*kai theos en o logos*].'[8]

The writer to the Hebrews also speaks of the pre-incarnation existence of Jesus: 'Inasmuch then as the children have partaken of flesh and blood, He Himself likewise shared in the same, that through death He might destroy him who had the power of death, that is, the devil' (Heb. 2:14). Reflecting on this verse John Brown said,

The language of the inspired writer seems obviously intended to suggest the idea of the pre-existence of the Deliverer of men before He became a man. He does not say, what he might have said, 'Inasmuch as the children were partakers of flesh and blood, He also was a partaker of flesh and blood.' He intentionally changes the expression, so as to convey the important truth, that He was a possessor of another nature than the human. 'He was a man; but He was—He existed—before He was man; He became man: He voluntarily assumed human nature into personal union with that divine nature of which from eternity He was the possessor.'[9]

The New Testament is clear that there was not a time when Christ did not exist. Jesus himself stated this (John 8:58). Paul expresses his wonder at this truth thus: 'And without controversy great is the mystery of godliness: God was manifested in the flesh, justified in the Spirit, seen by angels, preached among the Gentiles, believed on in the world, received up in glory' (1 Tim. 3:16). The Son was sent forth, having existed eternally with the Father and the Holy Spirit.

His impeccability

The glory which I had with You.

Jesus was perfect man, true God and one Christ This begs a question that is often asked: Was it possible for Jesus Christ to sin?

In both the Old and the New Testaments Jesus is called Immanuel, 'God with us'. Isaiah 7:14 points to the virgin's son whose name is 'Immanuel'; in Matthew 1:23 Christ is irrefutably seen to be the fulfilment of this prophecy. So could Jesus have sinned—that is, transgressed the laws of God—while he was on earth as the God-Man? All Christians believe in the sinlessness of Jesus Christ, but not all are convinced that he *could not* sin. All Christians say that he *did not* sin, but some say that he *could* have done so; if this were not the case, they say, his genuine humanity would be in question.

This concerns the doctrine of the impeccability of Christ. 'Impeccable' comes from the Latin word *impeccabilis*, meaning incapable of sinning. The doctrine teaches that Christ could not sin—that he had no ability to sin—and that this was not due to regeneration or sanctification.

Why is this question relevant to Christians? Firstly, because Christ's impeccability establishes without question the incarnate Word's essential deity and equality with the Father and the Holy Spirit. Secondly, it also clarifies for us those qualifications required for the Messiah in order to undo the consequences of the Fall and restore the promise of Paradise for the blood-bought saints of God. Jesus Christ was able to finish the work of redemption, being the second man and the last Adam (1 Cor. 15:45).

Thirdly, the question has relevance to the heavenly sitting of Christ at the right hand of God (his Session), where he is actively engaged in the continuation of his mediatorial work as our High Priest, and to our understanding of his willingness to meet sinners at the place of prayer (Heb. 4:14–16). 'Christ is a royal priest (Zach. 6:13), not Aaronic, but Melchisedekan, and his intercession is a perpetual holding up of his own righteousness [to the Father] on behalf of his own people by a perpetual pleading.'[10] Thus, the impeccable Christ now ascended to heaven acts as God's righteous Viceroy on behalf of all the people of God. Fourthly, Christ's being the last Adam and unable to sin guarantees that there will be no second Fall or ruination of the perfection of the new heavens and the new earth at the end of the age (Rev. 21:1), because the redeemed will be like him, that is, not predisposed to sin and disobedience (1 John 3:2).

As revealed by the angel Gabriel, the incarnation guaranteed the sinlessness of Jesus Christ: 'And the angel answered and said to [Mary], "The Holy Spirit will come upon you, and the power of the Highest will overshadow you; therefore, also, that Holy One who is to be born will be called the Son of God"' (Luke 1:35). The apostle John affirmed this holy sinlessness to be true when he wrote, 'And the Word became flesh and dwelt among us, and we beheld His glory, the glory as of the only begotten of the Father, full of grace and truth' (John 1:14). Gabriel and John were both witnesses to a sinless Son and a sinless Person. There is no doubt that the canon of the New Testament asserts that Jesus Christ was sinless and did no sin. He was born without sin and lived without fault. Having no blemish he could truly be seen as the 'Lamb of God who takes away the sin of the world' (John 1:29). Spurgeon said, 'The prying eyes of the prince of this world could find nothing in him, and the still more accurate search of the all-seeing eye of God found no fault in him.'[11] The texts below all testify to his unique sinlessness:

- 'For He made Him who knew no sin to be sin for us, that we might become the righteousness of God in Him' (2 Cor. 5:21)
- 'For we do not have a High Priest who cannot sympathize with our weaknesses, but was in all points tempted as we are, yet without sin' (Heb. 4:15)
- 'For such a High Priest was fitting for us, who is holy, harmless, undefiled, separate from sinners, and has become higher than the heavens' (Heb. 7:26)
- '[He] committed no sin, nor was deceit found in His mouth' (1 Peter 2:22)
- 'And you know that He was manifested to take away our sins, and in Him there is no sin' (1 John 3:5)

'Immanuel' means 'God with us'; thus the human nature of Jesus Christ does not exist separately from his divine nature. Immediately the human nature of Christ was conceived in the virgin's womb, it was inseparably joined with the divine nature for ever. Louis Berkhof states, 'In the incarnation he did not change into a human person; neither did he adopt a human person. He simply assumed, in addition to his divine nature, a human nature which did not develop into an independent personality.'[12] As a result, the New Testament can say, 'For in Him dwells all the fullness of the Godhead bodily' (Col. 2:9); in other words, Christ did not cease to be what he already always was (John 1:1) but became indissolubly divine and human. Proof of this can be seen in the Book of Acts, where Paul speaks of 'the church of God which [Christ] purchased with His own blood' (Acts 20:28). Here 'blood' speaks of Christ's human nature and 'God' his divine nature (see 1 Cor. 2:8).

Our Lord and Saviour was eternal God and perfect Man; but was he sinless because he lived a sinless life, or did he live a sinless life because he was impeccable? The latter is surely the case because Jesus taught,

> You will know them by their fruits. Do men gather grapes from thorn bushes or figs from thistles? Even so, every good tree bears good fruit, but a bad tree bears bad fruit. A good tree cannot bear bad fruit, nor can a bad tree bear good fruit. Every tree that does not bear good fruit is cut down and thrown into the fire. Therefore by their fruits you will know them. (Matt. 7:16–20)

His sinless life was the result of the union of the divine and human natures. It was also a witness to his Messianic office. As God the Christ, he could not change; neither could he change as the God-Man. Satan changed and Adam changed, but not the last Adam: 'Jesus Christ is the same yesterday, today, and forever' (Heb. 13:8). The promised Messiah is called, in Isaiah 9:6, 'mighty God' (*El Gabor*; see also 10:21). Can the 'Mighty God' sin? If not, it would be wrong to assume that Immanuel could, given that he is 'God … manifested in the flesh' (1 Tim. 3:16). The Messiah came into the world to do the Father's will and 'those things that please Him' (John 8:29; see also Ps. 40:6–8; Heb. 10:7). It was impossible for Christ not to do the Father's will, and therefore impossible for him to sin, because sin is the transgression of the Law. His baptism declared that he had come to 'fulfill all righteousness' (Matt. 3:15), indicating a flawless humanity.

Perhaps the greatest proof that Christ could not sin is seen in his temptations in the wilderness. This incident is recorded in all Synoptic Gospels (Matt. 4:1–11; Mark 1:12–13; Luke 4:1–13) and gives rise to the question, How could the temptations of Jesus be real if he was not able to sin? We remember that Satan sought to provoke Jesus to sin three times, and each time Jesus rebuffed Satan, quoting the Holy Scriptures. There were three attempts and three failures. Were they real? Did they trouble our Saviour? We must agree that they were real and concede that they troubled Jesus, but we do not believe the theory that unless Christ could have sinned, these challenges by the Tempter were a sham. When, for example, gold is tried, it is to prove its quality and purity. It is gold *before* it is tested, but the fire proves it to be what it already was. Similarly, an invincible army can be attacked, but it cannot be defeated. Jesus's victory over Satan demonstrated his invincibility and impeccability and gave Satan a shock from which he did not immediately recover. Satan had never before failed in such a task. Adam and Eve sinned when put to the test, and every son of Adam after the Fall had succumbed to Satan's temptations; but when he came up against Jesus Christ, he got the greatest shock imaginable to discover that God had indeed sent his Son into the world to save sinners.

Hebrews 4 is helpful here: 'Seeing then that we have a great High Priest who has passed through the heavens, Jesus the Son of God, let us hold fast our confession. For we do not have a High Priest who cannot sympathize with our weaknesses, but was in all points tempted as we are, yet without sin' (Heb. 4:14–15). He 'was in all points tempted as we are, yet without sin'; he took the full force of Satan's temptations and experienced them to the ultimate degree, but without succumbing to their power or attraction. As a result of this combat with Satan, Jesus Christ can fully understand and sympathize with fallen sinners when the enemy tempts them. This gives us great incentive to 'come boldly to the throne of grace, that we may obtain mercy and find grace to help in time of need' (v. 16). We believe that Jesus Christ could not lie, change, nor transgress the precepts of God, because he was impeccable God and impeccable Man.

Thus Jesus was 'not able to sin', *non posse peccare*, as theologians often describe it. This will be the condition of humanity in the final state of glory. Adam, before the Fall, was 'able not to sin', *posse non peccare*; after the Fall he was 'not able not to sin', *non posse non peccare*, because the Fall rendered him guilty and dead in trespasses and sins (Gen. 2:17; Rom. 5:12; 6:23; Eph. 2:1). As the second Man and the last Adam (1 Cor. 15:45, 47–49) Jesus Christ obtained so great a salvation for us that we will be like him, sharing his perfect humanity at the last (1 John 3:2). This means that heaven will be safe from the defilement of sin and saved from the disaster that befell the first Paradise in the Garden in Eden. At the resurrection the redeemed will be very much more than 'able not to sin', *posse non peccare* (as Adam was), because they will bear the image of the heavenly Man:

> The first man was of the earth, made of dust; the second Man is the Lord from heaven. As was the man of dust, so also are those who are made of dust; and as is the heavenly Man, so also are those who are heavenly. And as we have borne the image of the man of dust, we shall also bear the image of the heavenly Man. (1 Cor. 15:47–49)

FOR FURTHER STUDY

1. Which Old Testament texts speak of Christ's pre-existence and deity?
2. Which Scriptures speak about the Saviour's impeccability, that is, the impossibility that he *could* have sinned as the Son of Man? Are there any portions of Scripture that speak of the possibility that Jesus Christ *could* have sinned as the Son of Man?

TO THINK ABOUT AND DISCUSS

1. In what ways was Jesus equal with God (see John 1:1–14; John 5:18)?
2. Why is it that Christ could not sin, and what are the implications of that?
3. Why is it that some cannot accept that Jesus was not able to sin?

Notes

1 'The suretyship of Christ is a branch of his mediatorial office … The Greek word for "surety" *egguov* is used but once throughout the whole New Testament (Heb. 7:22 [see also Gen. 43:9]) and there of Christ; where he is said to be made, or become, "the Surety of a better testament", or covenant … Christ, as a Surety, drew nigh to his Father on the behalf of the elect, struck hands with him, and gave him firm security for them, and put himself in their place and stead, and engaged to perform everything for them that should be required of him': **John Gill,** 'Of Christ, the Surety of the Covenant', in *A Body of Doctrinal Divinity*, Book 2, Ch. 12; www.sermonindex.net/modules/articles/index.php?view=article&aid=25260; accessed March 2012.

2 **John Owen,** *The Works of John Owen* (London: Banner of Truth, 1972), vol. xviii, p. 94.

3 **J. C. Ryle,** *Expository Thoughts on the Gospels: John*, vol. iii (London: James Clarke & Co., 1969), p. 188.

4 **Thomas Manton,** *An Exposition of John 17* (Wilmington, DE: Sovereign Grace, 1972), p. 89.

5 **Herman N. Ridderbos,** *The Gospel of John* (Cambridge: Eerdmans, 1997), p. 445.

6 **R. A. Finlayson,** *The Story of Theology* (London: Tyndale Press, 1969), p. 23.

7 **Henry Bettenson,** *Documents of the Christian Church* (Oxford: Oxford University Press, 1974), p. 51.

8 **William Hendriksen,** *The Gospel of John* (London: Banner of Truth, 1969), p. 71.

9 **John Brown,** *Hebrews* (London: Banner of Truth, 1972), p. 123.

10 **R. L. Dabney,** *Systematic Theology* (Edinburgh: Banner of Truth, 1996), p. 549.

11 **C. H. Spurgeon,** 'The Sin Offering', sermon preached on Leviticus 4:3 on 10 March 1867; quoted at Shout for Joy, http://techlinkonline.net/ps100/2012/01/the-sin-offering-part-1/.

12 **Louis Berkhof,** *A Summary of Christian Doctrine* (London: Banner of Truth, 1968), p. 87.

Part 3. Concerning men: the Lord and his disciples (vv. 6–19)

In loving Christ the Father loved us; in choosing Christ as head of the church, the members were included in that election, for head and body cannot be severed.
(Thomas Manton, *An Exposition of John 17*)

The general acts of Jesus Christ as high priest of the church are two—namely *oblation* and *intercession*. These the nature of the office generally doth require, and these are constantly assigned unto him in the Scripture.
(John Owen, *The Works of John Owen*, vol. xviii)

Qualifications of discipleship (vv. 6–8)

I have manifested Your name to the men whom You have given Me out of the world. They were Yours, You gave them to Me, and they have kept Your word. Now they have known that all things which You have given Me are from You. For I have given to them the words which You have given Me; and they have received them, and have known surely that I came forth from You; and they have believed that You sent Me.

Jesus now prays for his disciples, and as he intercedes for them, he gives us a picture of a true disciple and those things that qualify someone to be such. A clear definition is given so that there will not be any confusion as to who his followers really are. Four qualifications are found in these verses.

A willingness to learn from Christ (v. 6)

I have manifested Your name to the men whom You have given me.

The Twelve sat at Jesus's feet, and so should all believers. The teachings of Jesus Christ are set out in the Gospels and the Epistles of the New Testament and they are there for our learning and salvation (John 20:30–31). Through his teaching Jesus 'manifested' or 'revealed' what had before been hidden or unknown. The Greek word translated 'manifested' (from the verb *ephanidzo*) is used around eighteen times in John's Gospel (see, for example, 21:1; compare Col. 1:26; 4:4; Titus 1:3). Discipleship necessitates knowledge, and true Christian disciples must learn from their Master. This task was at the very core of Christ's Prophetic work and at the heart of his teaching. It is not for the disciples to think that they know more than their Master does. Christ's mission was to manifest God's name, that is, to reveal what God is like. Not just any concept of God will do; what Christ revealed was a picture of the Father that was realistic, revealing his whole character to prevent an inadequate and distorted view of his Father. Likewise, Christians must guard against views of God that are built on imagination and are symptoms of fallen spiritual blindness. Christ's ministry was a revelation of truth and light accompanied by the divine power of the Holy Spirit (John 6:63) and it was undertaken to explain who God is and who his incarnate Son is (14:9). A hunger for this knowledge marks out the true disciple from the false. As students of theology, Christ's apostles, during their three years with the Saviour, received a right and comprehensive knowledge of the Father (14:9b). Ignorance of God and the Scriptures will not bring glory to Jesus or achieve his goal of glorifying the Father (17:4a).

A willingness to leave the world behind (v. 6)

The men whom You have given me out of the world ... have kept Your word.

The apostles belonged to the Father by right of creation and to the Son by right of redemption (15:16). The Father had ordained from all eternity that they become disciples of his Son (6:37, 39). The Greek noun which is translated here as 'men', *anthropos*, is a generic term for 'a human being'. Though all the apostles were men, women were to be Christ's disciples also (see, for example, Rom. 16:1–2). Christ's disciples are called out of the world from among the mass of humanity to embrace a true Christian lifestyle which will bring them into conflict with the world's ideas and practices (15:18–19). This conflict is to be expected, and the apostle Paul speaks of it, noting that 'all who desire to live godly in Christ Jesus will suffer persecution' (2 Tim. 3:12). This is a theme that Jesus will return to later in his prayer (e.g. v. 9) and one which the apostle John speaks boldly about in his later epistles. Christians are to 'let [their] light ... shine' and to take up their cross daily and follow Christ Jesus (Matt. 5:16; Luke 9:23).

Obedience to the Word of God and the teachings of Jesus is the outward evidence that there is inward grace in the soul. Jesus declared obedience to be a mark of true discipleship (John 14:21–24). 'Practical obedience', says J. C. Ryle, 'is the first great test of genuine discipleship'; he further points out that the apostles were weak in faith, slender in knowledge and faint in heart, yet they would keep God's Word and persevere to the end.[1]

ANTINOMIANISM

The issue of living for Jesus Christ daily with an obedient eye to his commandments is often dealt with in a controversial way when it is asked just which commandments we are talking about. Historically and theologically this has bothered the church. The word 'antinomianism' (from *anti*, 'against', and *nomos*, 'law') is used to describe the rejection of the Moral Law (the Ten Commandments) as a relevant part of the Christian experience—that is, the contention that the Moral Law has no place in the life of believers and does not bind them as rules for Christian living. This charge was laid by Christ himself at the Gnostic sect of the Nicolaitans in the Book of the Revelation; he commended the Ephesian church for rejecting that sect and its teachings: 'But this you have, that you hate the deeds of the Nicolaitans, which I also hate' (Rev. 2:6). It is clear that antinomianism had infected this local church for some time.

The burden of Christ's prayer in John 17 focuses on the need for obedience in the life of the disciples of Christ. His request in verse 17 that the Father 'sanctify' them includes the idea of definitive sanctification, but it is made in the light of the need for progressive sanctification, which requires obedient living. Paul, Peter and James all have things to say to the saints to counter the influence of antinomianism in their lives. Paul, in the Epistle to the Romans, concludes his defence of justification by faith alone by refuting suggestions that justification leaves room for a type of living that is contrary to the Moral Law of God: 'What shall we say then? Shall we continue in sin that grace may abound? Certainly not! How shall we who died to sin live any longer in it?' (Rom. 6:1–2). Likewise, Peter and James both forthrightly condemn those who live antinomian lifestyles:

> For when they speak great swelling words of emptiness, they allure through the lusts of the flesh, through lewdness, the ones who have actually escaped from those who live in error ... For if, after they have escaped the pollutions of the world through the knowledge of the Lord and Saviour Jesus Christ, they are again entangled in them and overcome, the latter end is worse for them than the beginning. For it would have been better for them not to have known the way of righteousness, than having known it, to turn from the holy commandment delivered to them. But it has happened to them according to the true proverb: 'A dog returns to his own vomit' and, 'a sow, having washed, to her wallowing in the mire'. (2 Peter 2:18–22)

> If anyone among you thinks he is religious, and does not bridle his tongue but deceives his own heart, this one's religion is useless. Pure and undefiled religion before God and the Father is this: to visit orphans and widows in their trouble, and to keep oneself unspotted from the world. (James 1:26–27)

Martin Luther (1483–1546) first used the word 'antinomianism' in his controversy with his colleague John Agricola, when Agricola exaggerated Luther's emphasis on Christian freedom to the extent of denying the lawful responsibilities of believers.[2] It is said that while Luther was at dinner, a letter from Agricola was handed to him which claimed that the Law should not be preached in the churches because we are not justified by it. Luther replied, 'Such seducers are come already among our people while we live; what will be done after we are gone?' Agricola was a bold man who, although he vacillated between orthodoxy and heresy, nevertheless persistently maintained, in opposition to Luther in his Commentary to the Galatians, that the Law was not to be preached for the purpose of bringing sinners to repentance. Luther's successor, Melanchthon (1497–1560), regarded antinomianism as a monster 'that lurked and lay hid in the church of his times'. John Calvin (1509–1564) believed that the Moral Law instructs us in holiness and demands obedience, stating that it is 'like a whip to the flesh and is a constant stimulus'; thus, the Moral Law leads the believer to Christ for mercy. Calvin specifically spoke against antinomianism: 'Some skilful persons ... discard the whole Law of Moses, and do away with both tables, imagining it unchristian to adhere to a doctrine which contains the ministration of death. Far from our thoughts be this profane notion.' He maintained that the Law 'ought to have a better and more excellent effect on the righteous', for it contains 'a perfect pattern of righteousness' and a 'rule of life'. He concluded his section in his *Institutes* on antinomianism by saying, 'The law has lost none of its authority, but must always receive from us the same respect and obedience.'[3]

It is therefore not enough to 'feel' saved or to claim that one is saved; rather, one has to show love for God and grace in dealings with others. This is the evidence of the new birth and true conversion. Professing believers who live contrary to the commandments and precepts of the Bible must not complain when they are regarded as unsaved by their fellow Christians and the world. The Saviour made this plain when he said, 'You will know them by their fruits' (Matt. 7:16–20).

A willingness to believe in Christ's divine mission (v. 7)

Now they have known that all things which You have given Me are from You.

Faith in Jesus Christ is the gift of God (Eph. 2:8; 2 Thes. 3:2) and is essential to eternal life (John 3:36; Heb. 11:6). In this verse Jesus teaches that faith (1) must have knowledge ('they have known'); (2) needs conviction ('all things which You have given Me'); and (3) requires trust (that these things 'are from You'). Christ is sending his disciples into the world to preach the gospel (Mark 16:15), but before he does so he imparts grace into their hearts and communicates assurance by his Spirit (Rom. 5:5; Gal. 4:6). In the three years they were with him the apostles learned that he was from God (John 1:14). His words were from God the Father and his grace was the result of being filled with the Holy Spirit at his baptism (Luke 3:22).

DEUTERONOMY 18, JESUS CHRIST AND ISLAM

The apostles believed in Jesus's divine mission as God's Prophet and Holy Servant. This is evidenced by Peter's confession in response to Jesus's question, 'But who do you say that I am?' Peter answered, 'You are the Christ, the Son of the living God' (Matt. 16:15–16). The true identity of Jesus was revealed to Peter and the others by the Spirit of God: 'Jesus answered and said to him, "Blessed are you, Simon Bar-Jonah, for flesh and blood has not revealed this to you, but My Father who is in heaven"' (Matt. 16:17).

Jesus's office as Prophet was first described by Moses in Deuteronomy 18:15–19, when he spoke about the Messiah to come: 'I will raise up for them a Prophet like you from among their brethren, and will put My words in His mouth, and He shall speak to them all that I command Him. And it shall be that whoever will not hear My words, which He speaks in My name, I will require it of him' (Deut. 18:18–19). However, Islam claims that Muhammad is the prophet foretold in these verses. This is an attempt to undermine the faith of God's elect. Muslims argue tenaciously that because Jesus's name is not given in the text of Deuteronomy 18, and because the prophet is to be *like Moses*, who did not die for the sins of

Israel or rise again on the third day, this prophecy cannot be speaking about Jesus Christ but must rather point to another prophet.[4] Muslims also make the following assertions to confuse untaught Christians and take the mind away from the truth as it is in Jesus:

- Jesus had a miraculous birth; Moses did not.
- Jesus was not married; Moses was.
- Jesus was rejected by the Jews; Moses was not.
- Jesus was crucified; Moses was not.
- Moses was a ruler over God's people and so was Muhammad.
- Moses brought God's laws to his people as Muhammad did.

These ideas will startle most Christians and challenge their knowledge of the Bible, but they are just a random group of thoughts taken utterly out of the context of the rest of the Old Testament. What do the Scriptures say in answer to these wicked assertions? In what way does Deuteronomy 18 speak about Jesus Christ? How do we answer Muslims? Firstly, we can show that:

- Jesus was especially chosen by God, as was Moses (both their early lives are recorded in the Bible, but Muhammad is not given this honour or even named).
- Jesus was sent to the elect Israel as God's chosen leader, as was Moses.
- Jesus was the architect of redemption and deliverance from bondage, as was Moses, who planned the Passover meal as well as the exodus from Egypt.
- Jesus believed in one God; Moses was also monotheistic.
- Jesus is the Good Shepherd who gave his life for the sheep; Moses was a shepherd in Midian for forty years.
- Jesus gave to the apostles God's words (John 17:8); Moses gave God's laws to Israel (Exod. 20).

Secondly, the Muslim claim that Muhammad is the prophet spoken of in Deuteronomy really rests on Muslims proving that Ishmael, from whom Arabs claim their ancestry, was a Jew! Deuteronomy 18:18 says, 'I will raise up for them a Prophet *like you from among their brethren*' (emphasis added). For the prophet of Islam to be the one foretold here, he would need to be a Jew; but Muhammad was an Arab. Both the Old and New Testaments make it clear that the Messiah and the Prophet to whom Moses referred would be:

- *From the family of Jacob, the elect grandson of Abraham, and not from his son Ishmael:* 'I see Him, but not now; I behold Him, but not near; a Star shall come out of Jacob; a Scepter shall rise out of Israel' (Num. 24:17); 'For they are not all Israel who are of Israel, nor are they all children because they are the seed of Abraham; but, "In Isaac your seed shall be called"' (Rom. 9:6b–7; see also Gen. 21:12; Heb. 11:18); 'For it is written that Abraham had two sons: the one by a bondwoman, the other by a freewoman. But he who was of the bondwoman was born according to the flesh, and he of the freewoman through promise ... Now we, brethren, as Isaac was, are children of promise. But, as he who was born according to the flesh then persecuted him who was born according to the Spirit, even so it is now' (Gal. 4:22–23; 28–29).
- *From the house of King David:* 'And I will pour on the house of David and on the inhabitants of Jerusalem the Spirit of grace and supplication; then they will look on Me whom they pierced. Yes, they will mourn for Him as one mourns for his only son, and grieve for Him as one grieves for a firstborn' (Zech. 12:10); 'I, Jesus, have sent My angel to testify to you these things in the churches. I am the Root and the Offspring of David, the Bright and Morning Star' (Rev. 22:16).
- *Born in Bethlehem:* 'But you, Bethlehem Ephrathah, though you are little among the thousands of Judah, yet out of you shall come forth to Me the One to be Ruler in Israel, whose goings forth are from of old, from everlasting' (Micah 5:2); 'Now after Jesus was born in Bethlehem of Judea in the days of Herod the king, behold, wise men

from the East came to Jerusalem, saying, "Where is He who has been born King of the Jews? For we have seen His star in the East and have come to worship Him"' (Matt. 2:1).

- *God's Son:* 'For unto us a Child is born, unto us a Son is given, and the government will be upon His shoulder, and His name will be called Wonderful, Counselor, Mighty God [*El Gibor*], Everlasting Father, Prince of Peace' (Isa. 9:6; compare with 10:20–21: 'And it shall come to pass in that day that the remnant of Israel ... will return, the remnant of Jacob, to the Mighty God [*El Gibor*]); '"Behold, the days are coming," says the LORD, "that I will raise to David a Branch of righteousness; a King shall reign and prosper, and execute judgment and righteousness in the earth. In His days Judah will be saved, and Israel will dwell safely; now this is His name by which He will be called: THE LORD OUR RIGHTEOUSNESS [*Yahweh Tsidkenu*]"' (Jer. 23:5–6).

Thirdly, Islam regards the Bible as having many discrepancies; thus Muslims do not trust the Word of God and therefore cannot trust their own conclusions made from it. It is not possible to prove that they are correct if the Bible, as they claim, is untrustworthy. However, the Scriptures say that 'Philip found Nathanael and said to him, "We have found Him of whom Moses in the law, and also the prophets, wrote—Jesus of Nazareth, the son of Joseph"' (John 1:45).

Fourthly, the Epistle to the Hebrews was written to prove the exclusive greatness of Jesus Christ; he is therein revealed to be the rightful heir to the title Messiah, the one who is greater than Moses:

> Christ Jesus [was] faithful to Him who appointed Him, as Moses also was faithful in all His house. For this One has been counted worthy of more glory than Moses ... And Moses indeed was faithful in all His house as a servant ... but Christ as a Son over His own house, whose house we are if we hold fast the confidence and the rejoicing of the hope firm to the end.
> (Heb. 3:1b–6)

Fifthly, Jesus spoke of Moses as a witness to himself:

Then He said to them, 'O foolish ones, and slow of heart to believe in all that the prophets have spoken! Ought not the Christ to have suffered these things and to enter into His glory?' And beginning at Moses and all the Prophets, He expounded to them in all the Scriptures the things concerning Himself. (Luke 24:25–27)

And He said to them, 'Why are you troubled? And why do doubts arise in your hearts? Behold My hands and My feet, that it is I Myself. Handle Me and see, for a spirit does not have flesh and bones as you see I have' ... Then He said to them, 'These are the words which I spoke to you while I was still with you, that all things must be fulfilled which were written in the Law of Moses and the Prophets and the Psalms concerning Me.' (Luke 24:38–39, 44)

A willingness to believe in Christ's gospel (v. 8)

For I have given to them the words which You have given Me; and they have received them, and have known surely that I came forth from You; and they have believed that You sent Me.

By 'the words which You have given Me' we understand the teachings and the doctrines of the Christian faith. The disciples believed that Jesus Christ was sent by God as the only Mediator between God and humanity, and that he had given to them the words of eternal life.

They ... have known surely that I came forth from You.

Simon Peter was willing to believe that Jesus was the promised Messiah and Saviour; he said, 'Lord, to whom shall we go? You have the words of eternal life. Also we have come to believe and know that You are the Christ, the Son of the living God' (John 6:68–69). He accepted that Jesus's task as Prophet and Teacher was to reveal the Father to the world. He and the other apostles received and accepted as valid all that Jesus taught, which was the whole counsel of God—whether it was about hell and heaven, and Jesus's corrections and rejection of the doctrines of the Pharisees and Sadducees. However, although the apostles received it, they did not understood it all until after Pentecost (John 14:26; Acts 1:8). Saving faith embraces the whole gospel and recognizes Jesus Christ as its object.

And they have believed that You sent Me.

Faith in Jesus Christ, as defined by the Bible, is not a step into the dark but is 'knowledge passing into conviction and it is conviction passing into confidence'.[5] With saving faith, knowledge comes first, conviction follows, and trust, which motivates the will, is also present. This is why it is essential for pastors and ministers to preach the Word of God so that the gospel, which is the power of God for salvation, will be heard and believed (Rom. 1:16; 10:14b). The elect must believe unto salvation because God will not believe for them! Before people can fully trust in Jesus Christ, they need gospel knowledge; when conviction is added, their hearts respond to the gospel. Knowledge satisfies the reason and conviction satisfies judgement. Reason and judgement then move the will to acceptance. Thus there is a need not only to preach the gospel but also to tackle the issues that hinder faith in the unbelieving heart.

They have received [My words], and have known surely that I came forth from You; and they have believed that You sent Me.

These words speak of Christ's eternal generation and his essential unity with the Father. The Creed of Nicaea states that he was 'begotten not made, of one substance with the Father ... who for us men and our salvation came down and was made flesh, and became man'.[6] Christ was always God but he took on body and soul at the incarnation, and through the virgin birth he was made man without the imputation of Adam's sin. This meant that Jesus Christ was holy, sinless and undefiled—and he remained so. He was impeccable. His words in John 12 leave us in no doubt that his ministry and authority came from his union with the Father in the Godhead:

> If anyone hears My words and does not believe, I do not judge him; for I did not come to judge the world but to save the world. He who rejects Me, and does not receive My words, has that which judges him—the word that I have spoken will judge him in the last day. For I have not spoken on My own authority; but the Father who sent Me gave Me a command, what I should say and what I should speak. (John 12:47–49)

FOR FURTHER STUDY

1. Study Luke 1:1–4; John 1:14–18; 2 Peter 1:16–21; 1 John 1:1–4; and Galatians 1:18–24. What do they tell us about the reliability of the New Testament?
2. Which Old Testament prophecies speak clearly about Jesus Christ as Messiah, and what characteristics does he possess that make this clear?
3. Why is it that Christians claim that the Bible (Old and New Testaments) has *never* been changed?
4. Study Deuteronomy 18:18–19 in the light of the New Testament.
5. What is antinomianism, and how is it to be recognized?

TO THINK ABOUT AND DISCUSS

1. What are the marks of the true disciple of Jesus Christ?
2. Why must believers not set the teaching of the Old Testament against that of the New Testament, and vice versa?
3. Why is it that the unbelieving world can see only the human side of Jesus Christ?
4. What threat does Islam pose to the Christian church, especially in the West (see John 14:6)?

Notes

1 **J. C. Ryle,** *Expository Thoughts on the Gospels: John*, vol. iii (London: James Clarke & Co., 1969), pp. 190–202.

2 **K. M. Campbell,** 'The Antinomian Controversies of the 17th Century', in *Living the Christian Life,* Westminster Conference Papers, 1974, p. 61. I am grateful to K. M. Campbell for what follows.

3 **John Calvin,** *Calvin's Institutes* (Grand Rapids, MI: Associated Publishers & Authors, 1970), 12:7:12 to 12:8:3.

4 **Ahmed Deedat,** *What the Bible Says about Muhammad* (Birmingham: Islamic Propagation Centre International, 1989*).* See **F. S. Copleston,** *Christ Or Mohammed* ([n. p.]: 1989), pp. 147–164, for the strange claims made regarding Muhammad.

5 **John Murray,** *Redemption Accomplished and Applied* (London: Banner of Truth, 1961), p. 111.

6 **Henry Bettenson,** *Documents of the Christian Church* (Oxford: Oxford University Press, 1974), p. 25.

Chapter 8

The disciples' relationship to Christ (vv. 9–11a)

I pray for them. I do not pray for the world but for those whom You have given Me, for they are Yours. And all Mine are Yours, and Yours are Mine, and I am glorified in them. Now I am no longer in the world, but these are in the world, and I come to You.

Loving election (v. 9)

I pray for them. I do not pray for the world but for those whom You have given Me, for they are Yours.

This part of Christ's prayer has proved difficult for some. G. Campbell Morgan, a former minister of Westminster Chapel, London, wrote, 'I read that verse for years and did not like it.'[1] Was this because it seemed impossible to reconcile Jesus's expression 'I do not pray for the world' with the following Bible texts? 'For God so loved the world that He gave His only begotten Son, that whoever believes in Him should not perish but have everlasting life' (John 3:16); 'God was in Christ reconciling the world to Himself, not imputing their trespasses to them, and has committed to us the word of reconciliation' (2 Cor. 5:19).

The answer to this seeming paradox is found in the doctrine of election. This special intercession in John 17 reveals Jesus's love for his church. He prays for them because they are his sheep. He shows special concern for their safety and well-being, for he will die for their sins. The High Priest of Israel made intercession on behalf of the ancient people of God and Christ fulfils the type as he prays for the new Israel of God (see Rom. 8:34b; Gal. 6:16; Heb. 7:25; 9:24). We need to challenge the idea that Jesus was being unloving or unjust here. It needs to be remembered that human nature is fallen in Adam and is now therefore morally corrupt (Eph. 2:1); thus it always inclines towards sinfulness. Paul calls this inclination the 'old nature', and he laments that the good he would do he does not do because of his fallen nature in Adam (Rom. 7:19; see also Gal. 5:19–21; Eph. 4:24). Fallen human nature will always choose according to its unrighteous character unless controlled by the Spirit of God. Thus it is not unjust for God to elect some, since no one deserves to be saved (Rom. 3:23). Election must be seen as a gracious act of mercy and love on God's part. It is unconditional, unmerited, and an expression of the eternal, sovereign will of God (Acts 13:48; Rom. 9:11). The elect are God's children and the Father charges the Son with their preservation: 'those whom You have given Me'.

Christ prays out of a fervent love for his disciples, but he does *not* pray for the world! This is because his intercession is on behalf of those who belong to the Father and have been given to Christ for his glory (v. 10). They are Christ's by right of redemption and are his inheritance (15:16).

Loving adoption (v. 10)

And all Mine are Yours, and Yours are Mine, and I am glorified in them.

In this verse Christ speaks of God's children beloved by Father and Son alike. All whom the Father elects Christ redeems; all whom Christ redeems the Father adopts. The ownership of these disciples is constantly raised by Christ and it highlights once again the truth of adoption; although the disciples are given to Christ, they are never deserted or forgotten by the Father, because of their adoption. In Galatians 3:26–4:7 Paul conceives of a real change of status in the sinner after conversion. When saved, sinners are adopted as children of God. Paul sees adoption as having to do with the formal translation of the sinner from the kingdom of Satan to the kingdom of God. It is a legal action, taking place outside of us, in which God the Father gives us new status in his family. Thus God, on the basis of the imputed righteousness of Christ, accepts us as his children and heirs. This is why the old theologians linked adoption with justification in the *ordo salutis*.

But when the fullness of the time had come, God sent forth His Son, born of a woman, born under the law, to redeem those who were under the law, that we might receive the adoption as sons. And because you are sons, God has sent forth the Spirit of His Son into your hearts, crying out, 'Abba, Father!' Therefore you are no longer a slave but a son, and if a son, then an heir of God through Christ. (Gal. 4:4–7)

The word translated here as 'adoption', *huiothesia*, is also found three times in Romans (8:15; 8:23; 9:4) and once in Ephesians (1:5). These verses in Galatians speak of redemption, assurance, freedom and inheritance, and they tell us that all these are to do with what we now have in Christ our Saviour. How wonderful to know that there is more than these four blessings! 'Having justified us God could still have left us on a much inferior level of status and privilege. Instead, He took us into His own family, giving us the status of daughters and sons.'[2]

Loving consecration (v. 11a)

Now I am no longer in the world, but these are in the world, and I come to You.

Christ anticipates his death and departure from this fallen world. He prays for his disciples because he is leaving but they will remain in a hostile world after his death (Matt. 10:16). They are weak, small in number and will shortly be persecuted; thus his prayers are essential for their victory and eternal safety. His coming ascension into heaven will usher in what is known as Christ's Session: the heavenly sitting of Christ at the right hand of God, where he is actively engaged in the continuation of his mediatorial work as our High Priest (Rom. 8:34; Heb. 7:25; 9:24).

'World' (*kosmos*) is used nineteen times in John 17. Seven times it refers to the planet (earth) or the universe (vv. 5, 11–13, 15, 24) and twelve times it refers to sinful humanity (vv. 6, 9, 14, 16, 18, 21, 23, 25). When in verse 9 Jesus says, 'I do not pray for the world', he means, 'I do not pray for sinful mankind'. Jesus has a special interest in and concern for the believer's safety and spiritual well-being. Jesus prays in order that 'all things [might] work together for good to those who love God, to those who are the called according to His purpose' (Rom. 8:28).

These are in the world.

This world is fallen and cursed by sin. It is doomed and it will be destroyed by fire ('fervent heat', as Peter describes it in 2 Peter 3:10–12). The Christian's relationship with the world is not the same as the non-Christian's. This is because the Christian's union with Jesus Christ changes his or her attitude towards this fallen world (2 Cor. 5:17). This world is not the Christian's home; Christians are just passing through. Abraham and Sarah understood this while they lived as nomads in the Near East so long ago. The Epistle to the Hebrews tells us that they, like others among God's people down the centuries, understood that they were strangers and pilgrims; they desired 'a better, that is, a heavenly country. Therefore God is not ashamed to be called their God, for He has prepared a city for them' (Heb. 11:13–16).

Christ's disciples are called to a life of pilgrimage and to reject philosophies, attitudes and methods which are contrary to the Holy Spirit and the world view of the Bible. Having presented their bodies as living sacrifices (Rom. 12:1) it is necessary for them to 'walk by faith, not by sight' (2 Cor. 5:7) and to keep themselves in the grace of God. Once separated to Christ by faith—sanctified and transferred into the kingdom of Christ—they are to speak out and lead others to an understanding of the Christian world view. Christians are not to hide or hibernate. Theirs is not a calling to a monastic vocation or a hermit's existence (see John 17:14–18). Jesus Christ is concerned that his disciples reach out into the world with his message so that it testifies that he was sent from God (vv. 20–21).

I come to You.

Jesus will soon go to the Father in heaven. He will do so through death by crucifixion, burial, rising again on the third day and ascension into glory. This is what was planned and agreed among the three Persons of the Godhead in the Council of Eternity before the foundation of the world. The Messiah will take the form of a Servant in order to become the Saviour of the world.

His crucifixion

The Old Testament foretold that God would redeem his people through his Suffering Servant (Ps. 22:1, 7–8; Isa. 1:27). Crucifixion was the most terrible torture ever devised. The word comes from the Latin *crucifīgere* which means 'to fix to a cross'. The method was invented by the ancient Phoenicians and was made even more brutal by the Romans, who added a cross member to the initial vertical stake. Crucifixion was an everyday event in the Roman Empire, but it was not common in Palestine when Pilate was governor. It was a barbaric mode of capital punishment as it allowed no mercy but rather was designed to inflict maximum pain and suffering. The Romans used it as a punishment for slaves; their own citizens were exempt. The Emperor Constantine I abolished it in AD 315.

This method of Christ's death was of man's devising, but it was also in fulfilment of Old Testament prophecy. This is seen from Psalm 22, where we read 'all My bones are out of joint' (v. 14) and 'they pierced My hands and My feet' (v. 16). This psalm reads like a contemporary eyewitness narrative, yet it was part of the Jewish Old Testament canon written around a thousand years before the time of Christ (compare Matt. 27:39, 43–46).

Our Saviour was certified dead after the Roman soldiers, using a spear, punctured his heart and ruptured the pericardium (the membrane that encloses the heart) and 'immediately blood and water came out' (John 19:34). On the cross, breathing would have been very difficult indeed, and the heart of Jesus had to work harder and would eventually have produced 'water', that is, a clear fluid containing no red or white blood cells.

In the plan and purpose of God, Jesus Christ's crucifixion achieved atonement for sin and reconciliation between God and fallen mankind, so that all sinners who repent and believe find peace with God. 'Jesus our Lord … was delivered up because of our offenses, and was raised because of our justification' (Rom. 4:24–25); 'Christ also has loved us and given Himself for us, an offering and a sacrifice to God for a sweet-smelling aroma' (Eph. 5:2; see also 2:14–18). Calvin points out that 'Sin is the cause of enmity between God and us; and, until it is removed, we shall not be restored to the Divine favor. It has been blotted out by the death of Christ, in which he offered himself to the Father as an expiatory victim.'[3]

The death of Christ reconciled sinners to God: 'You, who once were alienated and enemies in your mind by wicked works, yet now He has reconciled in the body of His flesh through death, to present you holy, and blameless, and above reproach in His sight' (Col. 1:21–22). These verses speak of man's depravity, so when Paul talks of being reconciled to God he is preaching the gospel. Reconciliation means a resolution of problems and a restoration of friendship between those who are out of fellowship. Propitiating reconciliation is rooted in Christ's death. It was the Father who sent the Son to Calvary; there the Son was judged, sentenced and punished on our account to establish peace between us, believing sinners, and God. The ultimate aim of reconciliation is the removal of God's wrath and the presentation of believers as 'holy, and blameless, and above reproach in His sight' (see also Rom. 3:25; 1 John 2:1–2).

His burial

The Gospels give us the facts regarding Christ's burial. His body was placed in a new tomb owned by a rich men called Joseph of Arimathea. Here Christ lay until the third day. A guard was placed by the Romans at the tomb with the agreement of the Jewish hierarchy so that the body would not be stolen. The significance of his burial is threefold:

- It was the fulfilment of Old Testament prophecy. In Psalm 16:10 King David said, 'For You will not leave my soul in Sheol, nor will You allow Your Holy One to see corruption', yet David himself was buried but did not rise from the dead. These words were quoted by the apostle Peter on the Day of Pentecost (Acts 2:31) as proof that Jesus Christ was the promised and awaited Messiah of the Jews.
- It proves that the Romans soldiers had certified Jesus as dead when they took him down from the cross. They were used to this procedure and were sure that he was deceased.
- Jesus's followers took careful note of the location of the tomb where he was buried. It was definitely this tomb they visited on the Sunday morning, but it was empty; thus they became eyewitnesses to Christ's resurrection.

His resurrection

The resurrection receives special attention in all four Gospels (Matthew 28; Mark 16; Luke 24; and John 20). This is because the resurrection of Jesus Christ lies at the very heart of the Christian faith; take it away and all that is left of Christianity is another religion whose founder is dead and buried and whose teachings can be superseded in the years to come. However, all honest readers of the Bible must agree that Scripture teaches without reservation or contradiction that Jesus Christ rose from the dead on the third day, and that that day was the first day of the week (Sunday).

The Jews, Romans and Christians at the time all agreed that (1) Jesus Christ was dead when taken from the cross; (2) he was buried in a new tomb; (3) on the third day his body was missing from the tomb; and (4) his body was not removed by the Jews or the Romans. Where had the body gone? When the women arrived at the tomb early on Sunday morning to continue their burial preparations on Jesus's body, expecting to find the corpse where they had laid it two days before, they found the stone rolled away and the tomb vacant (Luke 24:1–3). The Bible states that an angel of God had removed the stone (Matt. 28:2). A short time later, the risen Saviour appeared to Mary Magdalene. This was the first of at least ten resurrection appearances Jesus made over a forty-day period before he ascended into heaven to the Father (Acts 1:9).

Christians believe that their faith is rooted in historical fact and not fiction. The Bible proclaims the fact of Christ's resurrection, but it does not attempt to describe the process. It simply tells us what happened and expects us to believe it. Those who reject the truth of Christ's resurrection reject the testimony of the Holy Scriptures, seeing it as unreliable, and they charge its writers (the apostles and prophets) with fraud and deceit. One thing is clear, however: the Bible never doubts the resurrection of God's Son from the dead.

Resurrection is the triumph of Jesus Christ over 'the last enemy' (1 Cor. 15:26). Because of this, believers can be confident that they will rise as he did on the last day. Christ has defeated Satan, who had the power of death. This power was taken from him at the cross (Col. 2:14; Heb. 2:14–15). The traditional Christian definition of 'resurrection' is that 'The bodies of the unjust shall, by the power of Christ, be raised to dishonour; the bodies of the just, by his Spirit, unto honour, and be made conformable to his own glorious body.'[4] When the resurrection day arrives, believers will be given bodies like that of the risen Saviour; these new bodies will be perfect, fitted for a spiritual existence and with the power of an endless life (1 Cor. 15:50–55). Here is the solution to death and its humiliation.

Those who believe the words 'I am the resurrection and the life' (John 11:25) will share in Christ's everlasting victory. As A. W. Pink puts it,

> Then shall be fulfilled that mystical word, 'I say to you that many will come from east and west, and sit down with Abraham, Isaac, and Jacob in the kingdom of heaven' (Matt. 8:11). As the Lord Jesus declared, 'I lay down My life for the [OT] sheep. And other [NT] sheep I have which are not of this fold; them also I must bring, and they will hear My voice; and there will be one flock and one shepherd' (John 10:15–16). Then it shall be that Christ will 'gather together in one the children of God who were scattered abroad' (John 11:52)—not only among all nations, but through all dispensations.[5]

Christians must oppose all attempts to deny, invalidate or rewrite the resurrection accounts as found in the Gospels. Such attempts are common today, with, for example, increasing amounts of literature being produced by Islamic sources to discredit the four historical accounts in the Gospels. One such effort is centred on the New Testament phrase 'the sign of the prophet Jonah'.

THE SIGN OF JONAH

The phrase 'the sign of the prophet Jonah' is found in Matthew 12:39–40 and Luke 11:29–32 (compare John 2:18–19). It is part of the repeated narrative of our Lord carrying out his teaching ministry with the apostles. The fact that it is repeated in the Gospels signifies its importance in the plan of redemption and to the gospel message. It lays emphasis on the time Christ would be in the tomb before he arose bodily at his resurrection, and on the resurrection as a sign that tells the world that Jesus Christ is Lord.

Sign of repentance

In Luke 11:29–32 the 'sign of the prophet Jonah' is a call to repentance:

> And while the crowds were thickly gathered together, He began to say, 'This is an evil generation. It seeks a sign, and no sign will be given to it except the sign of Jonah the prophet. For as Jonah became a sign to the Ninevites, so also the Son of Man will be to this generation. The queen of the South will rise up in the judgment with the men of this generation and condemn them, for she came from the ends of the earth to hear the wisdom of Solomon; and indeed a greater than Solomon is here. The men of Nineveh will rise up in the judgment with this generation and condemn it, for they repented at the preaching of Jonah; and indeed a greater than Jonah is here.

Jesus says that the Queen of Sheba and the Ninevites will put the unbelieving Jews to shame on the Day of Judgement. She heard wisdom from Solomon's lips and believed, but they had heard someone greater than Solomon and refused to believe. Likewise, the Gentile nation of Nineveh was moved to repentance when the prophet Jonah preached, but the Pharisees refused to do likewise, even when the preacher was the Son of God. A man sent from God preaching faith and repentance was a sign from God. This principle still holds true today. God expects us to listen and respond well to the gospel message. We do so by accepting it and repenting of our sins. The sign of Jonah will also be a sign to unbelieving Israel. This reminder of the repentance of the Gentiles before the very Word of God (as preached by Jonah) is a reminder to them of God's grace in the gospel. The population of Nineveh received his Word with repentance and faith, and so must the true Israel.

Sign of resurrection

In John 2:18–22, Christ's resurrection (the event the 'sign of Jonah' is about) is a call to believe: 'So the Jews answered and said to Him, "What sign do You show to us, since You do these things?" Jesus answered and said to them, "Destroy this temple, and in three days I will raise it up"' (vv. 18–19).

Here the Jews are looking for a sign of legitimization. They want to see a miracle; they want Jesus to authenticate with signs and wonders his claim as the Prophet of God and Reformer of Israel. This desire of the Jews was a constant theme throughout Christ's ministry (Matt. 12:38–39; 16:1–4; Luke 11:29–30). It had its roots in their history, because every prophet of renown was able to prove by works of power that God was with him (Moses, Elijah, Elisha, etc.). Moses said that the true Messiah would be recognized by his works (Deut. 18:15–22).

The cleansing of the temple (John 2:13–17) had been a startling act by which the Jews discerned the Messianic claim of Jesus; accordingly they sought a sign. Jesus's response—'Destroy this temple, and in three days I will raise it up'—meant that there would be a sign, and they would have to believe in it. The second temple in Jerusalem, according to the Jewish historian Josephus, was begun in the eighteenth year of Herod the Great (c.20 BC) but it was not completed until AD 66. However, Jesus's words were actually a reference to his own resurrection. They may have had a secondary reference to the temple, for it was destroyed in AD 70, but we know that it was definitely a reference to his future resurrection because the Holy Spirit has told us so in John 2:21: 'But He was speaking of the temple of His body. Therefore, when He had risen from the dead, His disciples remembered that He had said this to them; and they believed the Scripture and the word which Jesus had said.'

Sign of rest

In Matthew 12:39–40 the 'sign of the prophet Jonah' is a call to enter into rest:

> But He answered and said to them, 'An evil and adulterous generation seeks after a sign, and no sign will be given to it except the sign of the prophet Jonah. For as Jonah

was three days and three nights in the belly of the great fish, so will the Son of Man be three days and three nights in the heart of the earth. (Matt. 12:39–40)

The sign here is about the time period Jonah spent in the belly of the great fish. It typified the three days in the tomb. The resurrection of Jesus from the dead was a sign to the world that Jesus Christ is the Lord of glory.

The seventh day (Sabbath) was given to the Jews as a sign that reminded Israel of its covenantal requirements: 'The children of Israel shall keep the Sabbath, to observe the Sabbath throughout their generations as a perpetual covenant. It is a sign between Me and the children of Israel forever; for in six days the LORD made the heavens and the earth, and on the seventh day He rested and was refreshed' (Exod. 31:16–17). The Sabbath was a memorial to the covenant between God and Israel, serving as a weekly reminder of their special relationship with him. No one doubts this. God said through Ezekiel, 'I ... gave [Israel] my Sabbaths, to be a sign between them and Me' (Ezek. 20:112). Matthew makes it clear that the sign the Jews were to receive was the resurrection of Christ from the dead.

The sign of Jonah points prophetically to Christ's resurrection on the first day of the week. Thus, keeping the first day of the week (Sunday, the Lord's Day) holy proclaims that there is a new covenant between God and sinners. Sunday is the one special day on which the people of God are called to gather together for public worship. Every Lord's Day-Sabbath is a signpost to the historic resurrection of Jesus Christ after three days in the tomb and on the first day of the week. Just as the primeval creation Sabbath was given by God to the unbelieving world as a sign (Gen. 2:2–3; Exod. 20:8–11), so is the Christian Lord's Day-Sabbath (Rev. 1:10). Jesus rose from the dead on the first day of the week and that is *the* sign proclaiming his glory and Messianic mission. We cannot see him in his resurrected and glorified body, for he is in heaven; nor were we at the empty tomb that first resurrection morning; but the eyewitnesses were and have recorded it for us in the New Testament. However, the weekly Christian Sabbath, every first day of the week, points fifty-two times a year to his triumph over death and Satan. Without a weekly Christian Lord's Day-Sabbath the resurrection would be so marginalized that it would hardly be noticed after two thousand years. However, God has seen to it that it is still remembered, and not only by the church but also by the world, through this weekly event. If the churches should stop meeting on the first day of the week, the powerful witness—the sign of the resurrection—of the Christian Lord's Day-Sabbath would be lost to the world. If it were not for the Christian Lord's Day-Sabbath there would be little public and visible appearance of serving, worshipping and reverencing the Supreme and Invisible Being.[6] As Christians attend church Lord's Day by Lord's Day, they bear witness to the empty tomb and proclaim to unbelieving Jews and Gentiles alike that Jesus Christ is Lord and Messiah.

The following God-given signs are operative today so that we might believe in Jesus Christ his Son:

- Men sent from God preaching faith in Jesus Christ and repentance towards God. God expects all people to listen and respond well to the gospel declaration.
- The resurrection—the ultimate sign of Jesus's Lordship. Peter's confession of Jesus's Messianic role was a turning point in the apostles' understanding of who Jesus was (Matt. 16:16). From that point on, Jesus spoke to them of his death and resurrection (Matt. 17:9, 22–23; 20:17–19).
- The weekly Christian Lord's Day-Sabbath. This is God's sign to the world about the resurrection of Jesus Christ from the dead. Many disregard the importance of this one day in seven because they have failed to appreciate its significance and connection with the powerful resurrection of our Saviour.

The sign of Jonah and Islam

Muslims refuse to accept that Jesus was in the tomb for three days and nights and endeavour to interpret the biblical texts concerning the sign in a way that contradicts the New Testament's testimony to his resurrection on the third day. They put their own ideas onto the New Testament text and make out that Jesus swooned on the cross, was mistaken for dead and, in the cold of the new tomb, revived and later fled to Syria (there is nothing new in this idea; it has been around for centuries). They challenge the resurrection using the phrase 'the sign of the prophet Jonah', ignoring the obvious meaning of Christ's words and spinning them out of all proportion. One Islamic writer asks,

> A fish swallows Jonah. Was he dead or alive when swallowed? ... Surely dead men don't cry and don't pray! ... Was he dead or alive for three days and nights? Alive! Alive! Alive! is the unanimous answer from the Jew, the Christian and the Muslim! If Jonah was alive for three days and three nights, then Jesus also ought to have been ... Jesus is *supposed* to be in the tomb on the night of Friday ... You will no doubt note that the *grand total* is *one* day and *two* nights, and *not* three days and three nights ... is this not the mightiest hoax in history?[7]

How should we reply to this attack? We need to think about the Jewish use of time. If Jesus was actually in the new tomb only for one day and two nights (from Friday evening until Sunday morning), how do we explain the statement 'three days and three nights'? Three things are pertinent:

- In first-century Palestine, when counting a time period, the Jews took any part of the day to mean the whole day. For example, Jesus's first appearance to the apostles and the women on resurrection day (Sunday) was followed by a second appearance 'after eight days' (John 20:19, 26). This, in Jewish parlance, meant one week later (what we would count as seven days later).

- '[St] Augustine finds this particular sign instructive and clarificatory for understanding the nature of signs. Augustine reads the sign of Jonah as a part which signifies a whole, namely the resurrection of Christ. He tells us that this is a particular example of a kind of sign, called a *synecdoche*, in which the part can either be read for the whole, or the whole for the part.'[8]
- John Gilchrist says, 'Furthermore we must also note that the figure of speech, as used in Hebrew, always had the same number of days and nights. Moses fasted forty days and forty nights (Exod. 24:18). Jonah was in the [fish] three days and three nights (Jonah 1:17). Job's friends sat with him seven days and seven nights (Job 2:13). We can see that no Jew would have spoken of "seven days and six nights" or "three days and two nights", even if this was the period he was describing. The colloquialism always spoke of an equal number of days and nights and, if a Jew wished to speak of a period of three days which covered only two nights, he would have to speak of three days and three nights. A fine example of this is found in the Book of Esther where the queen said that no one was to eat or drink for three days, night or day (Esth. 4:16) but on the third day, when only two nights had passed, she went into the king's chamber and the fast was ended. So we see quite plainly that "three days and three nights", in Jewish terminology, did not necessarily imply a full period of three actual days and three actual nights but was simply a colloquialism used to cover any part of the first and third days.'[9]

Thus, when Jesus told the Jews he would be three days and three nights in the earth, they took this to mean that the fulfilment of the prophecy could be expected after only two nights. Note that on the day *after* his crucifixion, that is, after only one night (Friday), they went to Pilate and said, 'Sir, we remember, while He was still alive, how that deceiver said, "After three days I will rise." Therefore command that the tomb be made secure until the third day' (Matt. 27:63–64). The Jewish hierarchy clearly feared that his body might shortly go missing.

His ascension

The ascension of the risen Saviour into the heavens is recorded in Mark 16:19–20 and Luke 24:50–53, and the Book of Acts continues where they leave off. Ascension Day fixes this event in history in the Christian calendar.

> Now when He had spoken these things, while they watched, He was taken up, and a cloud received Him out of their sight. And while they looked steadfastly toward heaven as He went up, behold, two men stood by them in white apparel, who also said, 'Men of Galilee, why do you stand gazing up into heaven? This same Jesus, who was taken up from you into heaven, will so come in like manner as you saw Him go into heaven.'
>
> (Acts 1:9–11)

All that is recorded about the church and its early history in the Book of Acts, and all that the church does for the glory of God, is grounded on the doctrine of the ascension of Jesus into heaven to sit at the right hand of the Father (Heb. 1:3). Jesus is no longer on earth but is glorified in heaven, and this has great implications for the church and the world. Jesus Christ's ascension was a historical event visible to the apostles that took place forty days after his resurrection. It reassures believers that the work of Jesus Christ is complete and acceptable to God the Father, and that he succeeded in the task of reconciling sinners to God. Because of this, Christ is deserving of exaltation. Ascension Day was Christ's Coronation Day. 'Lift up your heads, O you gates! And be lifted up, you everlasting doors! And the King of glory shall come in' (Ps. 24:7). Christ has entered heaven to reign over his enemies, being crowned with glory and honour (Heb. 2:9). He governs and reigns as King (1 Tim. 6:15), and rules over angels

(1 Peter 3:22), the church (Eph. 1:22) and the world (Heb. 2:6–8). Paul said, 'For [Christ] must reign till He has put all enemies under His feet' (1 Cor. 15:25).

THE ASCENSION GAVE THE CHURCH ITS AUTHORITY

Jesus Christ did not rise from the dead to start a new life experience all over again (reincarnation); no, he rose that he might ascend to glory, into the true tabernacle, the Holy of Holies, heaven itself, and sit at God's right hand (Heb. 1:3; 8:1–2; 9:12, 24). The enthroned Christ is the Head of the church for all ages:

> He raised Him from the dead and seated Him at His right hand in the heavenly places, far above all principality and power and might and dominion, and every name that is named, not only in this age but also in that which is to come. And He put all things under His feet, and gave Him to be head over all things to the church. (Eph. 1:20–22)

The ascension is the necessary sequel to the resurrection and it has ushered in a new dispensation with a new order and authority (Matt. 28:18–20; 1 Tim. 3:15). 'When he ascended on high, He led captivity captive' (Eph. 4:8a).

> Jesus! The Name high over all,
> In hell, or earth, or sky;
> Angels and men before it fall,
> And devils fear and fly. (Charles Wesley, 1749)

THE ASCENSION SECURED THE CHURCH ITS VICTORY

The Epistle to the Hebrews tells us that Christ's work as Mediator and High Priest took him into heaven itself, where he presented himself and his shed blood to the Father as an atoning sacrifice for sin (Heb. 8:1–2: 9:11–12, 24). His human nature has been glorified, not deified. He has crowned human nature with glory and lifted it above that of the angels and archangels. Following the ascension, redeemed human nature has been united to the divine and has been dignified for ever. The risen Christ is seated in heaven, and it will not be long before all the redeemed sit there too (Rev. 3:21; 5:6). His ascension opened the door through which transformed and redeemed humanity can enter heaven. The resurrection vanquished death, while the ascension transferred Christ's humanity to heaven. Now the dead in Christ can enter heaven, having been washed in his blood (Rev. 1:5; 5:9; 7:14). In heaven Jesus Christ continues his High-Priestly office, praying for the redeemed: 'Christ ... is also risen, who is even at the right hand of God, who also makes intercession for us' (Rom. 8:34). On the Day of Judgement the ascended Christ Jesus will sit on the 'great white throne' as Lord of all creation and will judge the nations (Rev. 20:11; Acts 10:42; 17:31).

THE ASCENSION EQUIPPED THE CHURCH FOR ITS MINISTRY

The outpouring of the Holy Spirit at Pentecost was not possible until the Saviour ascended to heaven; in fact, it was to the church's advantage that Jesus returned to his Father in heaven. Jesus said that he needed to go away before the Holy Spirit descended on the church and gave gifts to his people: 'Nevertheless I tell you the truth. It is to your advantage that I go away; for if I do not go away, the Helper will not come to you; but if I depart, I will send Him to you' (John 16:7).

Apostolic teaching (the New Testament canon) would not be in our hands as the Word of God if Jesus Christ had not ascended into heaven (John 15:26–27; 16:13–15; 17:20): 'But the Helper, the Holy Spirit, whom the Father will send in My name, He will teach you all things, and bring to your remembrance all things that I said to you' (John 14:26); 'Therefore He says: "When He ascended on high, He led captivity captive, and gave gifts to men." ... And He Himself gave some to be apostles, some prophets, some evangelists, and some pastors and teachers, for the equipping of the saints for the work of ministry, for the edifying of the body of Christ' (Eph. 4:8, 11–12).

Since the ascension of Christ Jesus, the church has had a duty to evangelize and continue the work he started on earth:

> And Jesus came and spoke to them, saying, 'All authority has been given to Me in heaven and on earth. Go therefore and make disciples of all the nations, baptizing them in the name of the Father and of the Son and of the Holy Spirit, teaching them to observe all things that I have commanded you; and lo, I am with you always, even to the end of the age.' Amen. (Matt. 28:18–20)

Jesus Christ is now enthroned in bodily form in heaven; therefore, Christians may pray in his name and expect a sympathetic response: 'I go to My Father. And whatever you ask in My name, that I will do, that the Father may be glorified in the Son. If you ask anything in My name, I will do it' (John 14:12–14).

Praying in Jesus's name allows the church to continue his ministry on earth until he returns (John 14:3). Christ's exaltation began at his resurrection and was fully accomplished when he sat at God's right hand: 'His exaltation answered his humiliation, his death was answered by his resurrection, his going into the grave by his ascending to heaven, and his lying in the grave by his sitting at God's right hand.'[10] The ascension brought glory to Christ. By it, he exalted human nature and took it into the realms of glory previously forbidden to it. At the resurrection of the body, believers will share in the glory of Christ (but not his essential nature as God), being united with his divine Person and given immortality, power, knowledge and grace, and being made free from all infirmities (Rev. 22:3–5).

FOR FURTHER STUDY

1. Which New Testament verses speak about the believer's election?
2. The ascension was the exaltation of Jesus's human nature. Think about the ascension (see Ps. 24:7; John 14:2; Acts 1:9) and list its benefits to the church.
3. What were the events that made up Jesus Christ's earthly ministry?
4. What do Muslims say about the resurrection of Jesus, and why?

TO THINK ABOUT AND DISCUSS

1. What do you think the risen Christ prays for you?
2. What signs has God given to the world so that it might believe in Jesus Christ?
3. Why do so many believers find the doctrine of election difficult to accept? Why do they feel that it is not helpful to evangelism? What is the biblical response to these attitudes?
4. Why must believers be able to answer the claims of Islam?
5. Why is so little made of the ascension in evangelical churches?

Notes

1 **G. Campbell Morgan,** *The Gospel According to John* (London: Marshall, Morgan & Scott, 1934), p. 273.

2 **J. M. Boice,** *Foundations of the Christian Faith* (Leicester: IVP, 1986), p. 443.

3 **John Calvin** on Eph. 2:16, *Commentary* in *John Calvin Collection* (CD-Rom; Christian Library series; Rio, WI: AGES Library, 2007).

4 Westminster Confession of Faith, 32:3, and The London Baptist Confession of Faith 1689, 31:3; at www.reformed.org/documents/wcf_with_proofs/ and www.grace.org.uk/faith/bc1689/1689bc01.html; both accessed February 2012.

5 **A. W. Pink,** *An Exposition of Hebrews* (Grand Rapids, MI: Baker, 1979), p. 891.

6 **Jonathan Edwards,** 'The Perpetuity and Change of the Sabbath', *Works*, vol. ii (Edinburgh: Banner of Truth, 1974), p. 101.

7 **Ahmed Deedat,** 'What Was the Sign of Jonah?', at www.islamworld.net/jonah.html; accessed March 2012.

8 **Chad Pecknold,** 'Reading the Sign of Jonah: A Commentary on Our Biblical Reasoning', *The Journal of Scriptural Reasoning*, 3/1 (June 2003), at etext.virginia.edu/journals/ssr/issues/volume3/number1/ssr03-01-e05.html.

9 **John Gilchrist,** 'What Indeed Was the Sign of Jonah?', at http://answering-islam.org/Gilchrist/jonah.html; accessed March 2012.

10 **Thomas Manton,** *An Exposition of John 17* (Wilmington, DE: Sovereign Grace, 1972), p. 91.

Christ's intercession for his disciples (1) (vv. 11b–16)

Holy Father, keep through Your name those whom You have given Me, that they may be one as We are. While I was with them in the world, I kept them in Your name. Those whom You gave Me I have kept; and none of them is lost except the son of perdition, that the Scripture might be fulfilled. But now I come to You, and these things I speak in the world, that they may have My joy fulfilled in themselves. I have given them Your word; and the world has hated them because they are not of the world, just as I am not of the world. I do not pray that You should take them out of the world, but that You should keep them from the evil one. They are not of the world, just as I am not of the world.

Verse 11 begins the main section of Christ's prayer. It contains the bulk of his intercession for the disciples and thus for his church. Jesus's prayer is that they will be 'kept', and this keeping is the theme through to verse 16. He prays to the One who is the 'Holy Father' (v. 11b). This title is unique to God the Father and is found in the New Testament only here. For others to take this title to themselves would be blasphemy. Nor should this title be used by believers for the pope or any other prelate.

Christ anticipates his death and departure from this fallen world; he knows that he is soon to die. His prayers for those the Father has given him can be summarized as follows: he prays for their unity (vv. 11, 21), safety (v. 12), joy (v. 13), perseverance (vv. 14–15), sanctification (v. 17) and glorification (vv. 23–24). These things do not belong to those who are of the world but only to those who believe in Christ Jesus and follow him. Jesus was of course concerned that his disciples would reach out to the world in order that the world might believe that the Father had sent him and know that he was from God (see vv. 21, 23). However, the Saviour does not pray for the world's security, joy, sanctification or glorification. He makes intercession only with regard to 'those whom You have given Me' (v. 9): those given to Christ in order that he might protect them, keep them and bring them safely to glory. This was his responsibility and his appointed Mediatorial role.

Kept from division: their continuing unity (v. 11b)

Holy Father, keep through Your name those whom You have given Me, that they may be one as We are.

Christ prays that the disciples may be kept from division. The redeemed are mystically united to Christ and to one another because of the new birth and so possess a unity that is from God through conversion. This is so vital for the life of the body of Christ and for the church's witness to the world that it comes first in Christ's list of prayer points (he also returns to it in vv. 20–23). From the context, we see that he prays that they will be united in their stand against the world. Christians are *in* the world (v. 11) but are not *of* the world (vv. 14, 16). They have been called out of the world (v. 6) and called to witness to the world (v. 18). The unity of the church does not rest on colour or nationality, but on grace and truth (v. 17; see also 1:14).

Unity is defined for us by the Saviour: 'that they may be one as We are'. He speaks of the unity between the Father and the Son, which is expressed among believers when they walk:

IN THE SPIRIT

Father and Son share the divine nature. There is a mystical and spiritual union between them (and the Holy Spirit), as they have had mutual relations within the one essence from all eternity. Believers are likewise one; being born again of the Spirit of God (John 3:3) they too partake of the divine nature (2 Peter 1:4; John 1:12–13), although they always remain sinners saved by grace. Paul calls their particular union the 'unity of the Spirit' (Eph. 4:3). Thus the unity Christ prays for is the work of God and not men or women. It exists because the redeemed are united with one Father, partake of one Spirit, and are redeemed by the one sacrifice of Christ. This unity is not created by bringing delegates together. Jesus is not praying for denominations but for 'those whom You have given Me', that is, individuals saved by grace alone through faith alone. The unity of believers is not voluntary, something which Christians can take or leave, but inevitable, because 'there is one body and one Spirit ... one Lord ... one God and Father of all ....' (Eph. 4:4–6).

IN THE TRUTH

Jesus taught the apostles what the Father had given him to say (v. 8; 7:16; 12:49); thus he and the Father are one in truth. True unity is based on the understanding and acceptance of the truth of God's Word (1 John 5:20); thus Paul also calls this unity the 'unity of the faith' (Eph. 4:13). This faith became known in early Christianity as 'the apostles' doctrine' (Acts 2:42). The apostles received it from the Saviour, and they in turn wrote the Gospels and Epistles so that the church might be set free by the truth (John 8:32). Agreement about the content and message of the gospel is a requirement of organic unity. When truth as defined by the Bible itself is missing, visible unity is impossible (Amos 3:3).

IN LOVE

Jesus said, 'I ... abide in [the Father's] love' (15:9–10), so the unity between the Father and the Son is not only spiritual and grounded in truth, but also shared through love. Strong love for one another and for all people should mark out the children of God (15:12, 17; Gal. 6:10). The pagan world of the early church stood amazed at the power of the love expressed in the lives of the believers because they were ready even to die for one another. This amity and affection for fellow Christians has its source in the new birth and stands in direct contrast to the prohibition not to love the world (1 John 2:15; John 17:9; compare Acts 4:32; 1 John 4:7–8). This love is not like that which is experienced between friends in a public house or on the sports field, but is a self-sacrificing grace seen when one is kind and patient even with those one dislikes or regards as enemies.

IN FAITH

Jesus claimed that he did nothing independently of the Father and that he had finished the work he had been given to do (v. 4; 4:34). The New Testament makes it clear that the Father and Son (with the Holy Spirit) were active in creation and redemption (Col. 1:16; Heb. 1:2), and will act together on the Day of Judgement. The Son's mission on earth was in harmony with the Father's will, so the people of God must tell the lost about the Saviour and work together for the advancement of the Kingdom of God (1 Cor. 3:9).

This theme of Christian unity is prominent in the Epistle to the Ephesians:

> With all lowliness and gentleness, with longsuffering, [bear] with one another in love, endeavoring to keep the unity of the Spirit in the bond of peace. There is one body and one Spirit, just as you were called in one hope of your calling; one Lord, one faith, one baptism; one God and Father of all, who is above all, and through all, and in you all.
>
> (Eph. 4:2–6)

These words of Paul's are not exhortations but declarations. He does not say, 'Let us be united in one body'; rather he declares that, as a result of their conversion, all believers are already joined in a mystical unity that transcends visible and denominational unity. The term 'one body' (v. 4) refers to the whole universal church consisting of Jews and Gentiles who have come to faith in Christ. All believers are members of the invisible and mystical body of Christ because they are 'in Christ' (Eph. 1:3–4; 1 Cor. 10:17). The term 'one Spirit' expresses unity as a statement of fact; the Third Person of the Trinity indwells believers and is the cause of their unity (1 Cor. 12:13; Eph. 2:18). Believers, being born again, have become the children of God. They have 'one hope'—the same aspirations; they all look forward to the same inheritance in Christ. Their future is bright and exciting, as they will all see Christ in glory and partake in heavenly and eternal blessings. Thus the inward effectual call of the gospel brings people, through faith and repentance, into fellowship with God and imparts the guarantee of the Holy Spirit in their hearts, which produces hope (Eph. 1:14). Hope includes both expectation and desire. There is a Trinitarian emphasis in Paul's words:

- 'One Lord' (v. 5): we belong to Christ and he is our King. 'Our reason is subject to his teaching, our consciences to his commands, our hearts and lives to his control.'[1]
- 'One faith': the faith is that objective truth that we call the gospel as found in the Bible and expressed in the creeds and confessions of the Protestant churches since the Reformation. It could also mean faith in the subjective sense of personally believing the promises of God and Christ. It is the latter that makes us friends with other believers right away, but it is the former that is essential to the unity of the local churches.
- 'One baptism': baptism is performed in the name of the Trinity (Matt. 28:19); all Christian converts make the same profession and accept the same Saviour. The reference is to baptism by water. Paul is saying that Christ is the one Lord in whom we believed in order to

be baptized. This rules out other contenders who would challenge Jesus Christ's place as the Lord of the people of God.

- 'One God and Father of all': the emphasis here is on God's Fatherhood. God is our Father in heaven (Matt. 6:9). All Christians acknowledge this and all churches hold to it. We are brothers and sisters in the same family, and we share in the privileges of that great, universal household.

Thus the unity Paul speaks of is founded on the doctrine of the Trinity: one God and Father, one Lord, and one Holy Spirit. Denying the Trinity excludes someone from salvation. Our union does not centre on mere opinion, as in politics, for example, but it is something spiritual, mystical and sustained by the Holy Spirit in us. The life in the people of God is not natural or intellectual, but spiritual—the life of God in the soul. Paul is saying that it is a common life. There is mystical fellowship, divine love and a shared creed. This is what Jesus was praying for in John 17:11: 'that they may be one as We are'.

Unity is what believers are born with, and they have a duty to keep it alive and to preserve it. They are bound by the Holy Spirit to work hard not to upset it or hinder it: 'And do not grieve the Holy Spirit of God, by whom you were sealed for the day of redemption. Let all bitterness, wrath, anger, clamor, and evil speaking be put away from you, with all malice. And be kind to one another, tenderhearted, forgiving one another, even as God in Christ forgave you' (Eph. 4:30–32).

Kept from falling: their continuing perseverance (v. 12)

While I was with them in the world, I kept them in Your name. Those whom You gave Me I have kept; and none of them is lost except the son of perdition, that the Scripture might be fulfilled.

Because of Jesus's pending departure from the world, he is conscious that his protection for the disciples must continue. Christians owe their security and perseverance to the power of their Saviour; they cannot keep themselves from evil because diligence in holiness is a gift of God's grace. Christ's first use in this verse of the words 'I kept' is the Greek word *tereo* and can also be translated 'I preserved'; the idea is of the owner of an object demonstrating watchful care over his possession to secure its preservation. What the Father has given to Christ he has kept safe from evil. Believers need daily grace so as to persevere and fight the good fight of faith. They are to use all the means of grace to strengthen themselves and to keep themselves separate from the world's ways and passions. The means of grace include the reading of the Scriptures, the ordinances of baptism and the Lord's Supper, and Christian fellowship, prayer and public worship. Christians are kept by the power of God as they partake of the grace of God by faith (1 Peter 1:5).

In verse 11 Christ asked that his disciples might be preserved in their faith and union with him. Assurance of salvation is a blessed knowledge but it often evades true believers. Here Jesus assures all who read his High-Priestly prayer that 'all Mine are [the Father's], and [the Father's] are Mine' (v. 10); that is, all those who are in Christ belong to the Father and are held safe in the Father's hand. On this basis he asks the Father to continue keeping them safe. 'My Father, who has given them to Me, is greater than all; and no one is able to snatch them out of My Father's hand' (John 10:29).

The Bible speaks of a twofold assurance: objective and subjective. Objective assurance has been defined as 'the certain and undoubting conviction that Christ is all he professes to be, and will do all he promises. It is generally agreed that this [objective] assurance is of the essence of faith.' Subjective assurance 'consists in a sense of security and safety … that the individual believer has had his sins pardoned and his soul saved'.[2] When thinking about assurance it is necessary to make a distinction between it and faith. Faith is not belief that we have been saved but trust in Christ *in order* to be saved. For Calvin, faith was more than the assent of the mind, and always involved both knowledge and confidence[3] (see Heb. 11:1). True faith includes trust and carries with it a sense of security with feelings of safety, gratitude and joy.

Those whom You gave Me I have kept; and none of them is lost …

The New Testament gives us a picture of Christ as the Good Shepherd, faithfully fulfilling the task of looking after his flock (John 10:1–18). The verb translated here as 'I have kept' (*phulasso*) is another Greek verb meaning 'I guard, I protect'. The picture is of a shepherd guarding his flock of sheep and faithfully watching for the straying, weary or ill ones, in order to protect them from danger. The 'Lord is faithful'; he guards us from the evil one (2 Thes. 3:3). Christians are therefore called to believe that what they have committed to Christ by faith he is able to keep until the Day of Judgement (2 Tim. 1:12; see also Jude 24). The Saviour's love is seen as he protects those the Father gave to him; they are precious to him (John 13:1). Christ is like the strong man in Luke 11:21 who protects the goods that are his because he loves them. The elect are dear to him and he has promised never to leave them nor forsake them (Matt. 28:20; Heb. 13:5–6; 1 Peter 5:7; Jude 24). Trust in the Saviour's love and power to save are essential for a healthy and happy Christianity (Ps. 62:8).

Except the son of perdition.

Here Christ speaks of Judas Iscariot. Jesus does not say, 'I have kept everybody except Judas', as if he were unable to keep Judas safe. No; this loss is defined by the next phrase: 'that the Scripture might be fulfilled'. Jesus did not *lose* Judas, for he was *not his* to lose (remember that Jesus prays for 'those whom You *have given Me*', emphasis added; see vv. 2, 6, 9, 11, 24). Yes, Judas was one of the Twelve, but Jesus knew that he was 'a devil' (John 6:70–71; see also 13:18). The word translated as 'devil' (*diabolos*) can also be translated as 'slanderer' or 'false accuser'. Judas was a servant and instrument of the devil who falsely accused Jesus before the chief priests.

The phrase 'son of perdition' means 'the one destined to perdition/destruction'; it is similar to 'son of death', the literal translation of the Hebrew in 2 Samuel 12:5, meaning 'one appointed to die'; and also to the phrase 'son of hell' (Matt. 23:15), meaning 'one deserving of hell'. 'Son of perdition' is a very strong phrase and is used of the antichrist, who is ordained to face, and is worthy of, utter destruction (2 Thes. 2:3).

That the Scripture might be fulfilled.

This phrase refers back to John 13:18, where Jesus quotes from Psalm 41:9, the prophecy which was fulfilled in Judas Iscariot (Matt. 26:14–16). Some think that prophecy should be blamed for the sins of Judas Iscariot, but he was not compelled to sin; he did so of his own accord. Judas was worthy of hell because of his sinfulness (John 12:4, 6; 13:2, 26–27; 18:1–5; Matt. 27:3–10). We must resist the modern temptation to be sorry for Judas Iscariot. The apostle Peter, referring to both Psalm 69:25 and Psalm 109:8 in his speech to the apostles in Acts 1:20, says that the Scriptures were fulfilled when Judas was removed from the office of apostle.

Kept from sadness: their continuing joy (v. 13)

But now I come to You, and these things I speak in the world, that they may have My joy fulfilled in themselves.

Jesus is the Author and Object of the Christian's joy and affection. Johann Sebastian Bach wrote 'Jesu, Joy of Man's Desiring', believing that in Jesus Christ fullness of joy is found.[4] Joy, as described in Christ's prayer, is deeper and more profound than a mere sense of happiness, which is a temporary impression. The joy of which Jesus speaks is more permanent, liberating and spiritual. J. C. Ryle says that Jesus prays 'in order that [the disciples] may be cheered and comforted and feel the joy which Christ gives in their hearts'.[5] Christian joy is a permanent delight in the Person and salvation of Christ, while happiness is rooted in the self and is dependent upon circumstances, being only transitory and fleeting. Jesus speaks of 'My joy' as he is the fountain from which true joy springs and the source from which it flows. Christian joy is part of the fruit of the Spirit (Gal. 5:22) and the birthright of all who believe (Acts 13:52; 1 Thes. 1:6). Joy ought to be the Christian's constant, normal condition and a source of inner spiritual strength (Neh. 8:10). When Christ is the object of faith, he is the believer's altogether lovely One, the Lover of the soul (S. of S. 5:16). The nature of joy is personal and comforting. When Christians remember that Christ loved them and gave himself for them (Gal. 2:20), there ought to be an inward sense of comfort imparted to their souls.

Christian joy flows from the believer's sweet love for Christ. 'Jesus Christ, whom [you have] not seen you love. Though now you do not see Him, yet believing, you rejoice with joy inexpressible and full of glory, receiving the end of your faith—the salvation of your souls' (1 Peter 1:7–9). 'A bundle of myrrh is my beloved to me' (S. of S. 1:13). C. H. Spurgeon comments on this latter verse:

Myrrh may well be chosen as the type of Jesus on account of its preciousness, its perfume, its pleasantness, its healing, preserving, disinfecting qualities, and its connection with sacrifice. There is enough in Christ for all my necessities; let me not be slow to avail myself of him. The emblem suggests the idea of distinguishing, discriminating grace. From before the foundation of the world, he was set apart for his people; and he gives forth his perfume only to those who understand how to enter into communion with him, to have close dealings with him. Oh! blessed people whom the Lord hath admitted into his secrets, and for whom he sets himself apart. Oh! choice and happy who are thus made to say, 'A bundle of myrrh is my well-beloved unto me.'[6]

Paul spoke about personal Christian joy when he wrote his Epistle to the Philippians: 'Rejoice in the Lord always. Again I will say, rejoice! Let your gentleness be known to all men. The Lord is at hand' (Phil. 4:4–5). Christian joy has an aspect and quality that make it impervious to outside forces and providential circumstances. Paul was writing from a Roman prison, yet he could exhort the believers to 'Rejoice in the Lord always', showing that Christians are to rejoice in the Saviour's personal love, no matter what. They are to love him for himself and not for what he gives them. In the New King James translation of Philippians, the noun 'joy' and the verb 'rejoice' are found some fifteen times. The Greek words used by Paul are *chairo* ('to rejoice') and *chara*, 'joy'. The former, *chairo*, means to rejoice when there are grounds for doing so or when it is the occasion to do so (Phil. 1:18; 2:28–29; 3:1; 4:4, 10). Trusting in Christ's Priestly intercession (Rom. 8:34) gives us ample grounds for giving thanks, no matter what our circumstances may be. The verb *chairo*, strengthened by the prefix *sun*, is used in the Parable of the Lost Sheep to describe the joy experienced by the shepherd who found the one sheep missing from the flock (Luke 15:6–7). Paul uses the same verb in Philippians 2:17–18, showing that Christians ought to find in Christ's arms the comfort and peace that renew his joy in them, which, in turn, brings courage to their souls when struggling with dark providences and personal pain.

Christian joy in the Person and Work of Jesus Christ is of the essence of true faith, but it must be protected from injury and looked after. In Philippians 4, Paul gives advice on how it can be maintained. He recommends that as Christians we should:

LIVE SO YOU CAN ALWAYS REJOICE

Paul finds it necessary to address two woman, Euodia and Syntyche, who belong to the fellowship at Philippi. He tells them to 'be of the same mind in the Lord' (4:2). We do not know the problem between them but it must have been causing injury to the church and may have threatened a split among the church families. It is evident that the problem was not doctrinal or moral; perhaps it was personality-driven and both ladies were to be blamed, with neither humble nor spiritual enough to see this. Our joy in Christ will be injured when we are out of fellowship with our co-workers and fellow believers in the local church, so it is necessary to be ready to act when it comes to forgiving faults and forgetting injuries. Nothing saps the believer's joy more than conflict with his or her brothers and sisters in the Lord.

BELIEVE SO THAT YOU WILL ALWAYS REJOICE

Euodia and Syntyche's names were in 'the Book of Life' (4:3). This book is a record of all the names of the elect of God redeemed by the blood of Christ. It was compiled 'before the foundation of the world' (Rev. 13:8; 17:8). As the people of God reflect on this, it surely prompts praise to God for mercy shown and justification received by faith alone. In Luke 10 we read that, when 'the seventy returned with joy' (v. 17), having cast out demons, the Lord Jesus told them not to make their achievements the cause for their joy, for there was something more wonderful than this: the fact that their 'names are written in heaven' (v. 20). These names will never be removed or forgotten, for the redeemed are God's adopted children. When the people of God stop looking at themselves, start remembering the truth about electing love and believe the promises of the Bible, then they will be filled with Christ's joy. If we are saved, there is good reason to be joyful (2 Cor. 1:20).

REACT SO THAT YOU WILL ALWAYS REJOICE

Paul wanted every Christian in Philippi to exercise the gentleness that was found in Christ Jesus their Lord because of their mystical union with him. The Greek word translated as 'gentleness' (v. 5) is *epieikes*, and, says William Hendriksen in his commentary on Philippians, it needs eleven other words to define it properly! The word is an adjective-noun and means 'big-heartedness'. The sense is conveyed by words like forbearance, geniality, reasonableness, charitableness, mildness, magnanimity, generosity and the like. 'Gentleness' is a beautiful grace, and it is an essential quality when working with others.[7] The lack of it may have been the reason why Euodia and Syntyche were not getting along. Were they reacting badly to each other's company or activity? Our joy in Christ will be maintained when we stop looking at the speck in our neighbour's eye and pay proper attention to the plank in our own (Matt. 7:3).

TRUST SO THAT YOU WILL ALWAYS REJOICE

Christian joy is not to be controlled by the fickleness of the weather or the political mood in the land. The believer's joy in the Lord is based only on who God is and what he has done for the soul's eternal benefit. Thus trust in Christ's promises is essential in order not to lose heart. Philippians 4:6–7 are two of the most comforting of all New Testament verses: 'Be anxious for nothing, but in everything by prayer and supplication, with thanksgiving, let your requests be made known to God; and the peace of God, which surpasses all understanding, will guard your hearts and minds through Christ Jesus.'

The joy in Christ which belongs to the redeemed is succinctly summed up in these words of the psalmist: 'Bless the LORD, O my soul; and all that is within me, bless His holy name!' (Ps. 103:1). Here the psalmist encourages himself to praise God, come what may. The Christian life is victorious when Christians believe that 'all things work together for good' (Rom 8:28) and when they 'Trust in Him at all times' (Ps. 63:8). If we know his joy in us, we are much more forbearing towards others and freer from worry. Fretting often depresses the spirit and kills hope. Christ's disciples must not lose sight of the big picture. When Christians *fully* trust their Saviour, things are put into eternal perspective and they see that there is good reason to 'rejoice always'.

Kept from evil: their continuing protection (vv. 14–16)

I have given them Your word; and the world has hated them because they are not of the world, just as I am not of the world. I do not pray that You should take them out of the world, but that You should keep them from the evil one. They are not of the world, just as I am not of the world.

The importance of the Holy Scriptures in the protection of the elect is seen here. The sixty-six books of the Bible are special, reliable, infallible and inerrant,[8] and they are didactic, intended to be a bulwark against all error and spiritual wickedness (Ps. 119:89, 105, 160). Christ could have said, 'I have given them the Holy Spirit' (see 20:22), but he preferred to speak of the importance and power of the Word of God. He could have given the disciples money, political power or an army of soldiers (or angels) to protect and support them, but he would rather give them 'Your word'. Thus he intends us to realize that the Holy Scriptures are of the utmost importance and must not be neglected or consigned to a secondary place in the church's life or outreach. Of all that Christ could have given his people, and of all that he did give them, God's Word was the most important; it would sanctify them (v. 17) and save those who would believe its message (20:30–31). The sixty-six books of the Bible are Christ's gift to the world, and especially to those who believe. 'The word of God is living and powerful, and sharper than any two-edged sword, piercing even to the division of soul and spirit, and of joints and marrow, and is a discerner of the thoughts and intents of the heart' (Heb. 4:12).

KEPT IN THE WORLD

The world has hated them because they are not of the world, just as I am not of the world.

The thought of the world hating the apostles may have come as a shock to them, but they were not to fear, for the Saviour was interceding on their behalf. Their ministry was not over; in fact, it was just beginning (v. 20; see Acts 1:8). God's power alone keeps believers from falling and protects them from evil (1 Peter 1:5). Jesus would never have prayed this way if it were within the individual Christian's own power to keep him- or herself from evil. That Christ prays for believers is a most precious thought, and that he prays that they be kept from Satan's power is a most welcome doctrine and is part of the Priestly ministry of the Saviour (14:16). God watches over believers outwardly as well as inwardly. His providence is on their side and he is able to keep them from temptation and deliver them from evil (Matt. 6:13). Nor will he let temptations become overwhelming (1 Cor. 10:13), because he provides armour for the Christian's protection (Eph. 6:10–18). All this is necessary because Satan 'walks about like a roaring lion, seeking whom he may devour' (1 Peter 5:8).

God's providence

God's providence orders times, circumstances and events to keep believers from harm. In eternity, we will see that there were situations through which God kept us, in answer to the prayers of Christ; situations that would otherwise have resulted in disaster. Christians owe their Saviour so much for his prayers. In eternity, those prayers will prove to be the cornerstone of their persevering grace.

There are some things we just cannot explain. In the book *When Heaven Is Silent*, Ronald Dunn tells the story of how he escaped death when a man with a gun robbed him in a motel car park. The robber pushed him over and shot him. The bullet missed and struck the pavement just beside his head. Later Ronald said that God must have been protecting him that day. Yet, not long before, intruders had fatally shot two of his friends in their own home. Why did God not protect them? The question haunted him.[9] This has to do with the mystery of providence. Providence can be defined as the foresight, intervention, prudent management and benevolent care of God. He knows the end from the beginning and all things are under his care and ordered by his sovereign will (2 Tim. 1:9). 'And we know that all things work together for good to those who love God, to those who are the called according to His purpose' (Rom. 8:28).

Christ's Session

Christ's Session refers to the heavenly seating of Christ at the right hand of God, where, as our ascended High Priest, he is actively engaged in the continuation of his mediatorial work on behalf of the people of God, ever living to make 'intercession for us' (Rom. 8:34). There is some confusion about the role of the Holy Spirit in this regard because of Romans 8:26–27:

> The Spirit also helps in our weaknesses. For we do not know what we should pray for as we ought, but the Spirit Himself makes intercession for us with groanings which cannot be uttered. Now He who searches the hearts knows what the mind of the Spirit is, because He makes intercession for the saints according to the will of God.

Are both Christ and the Holy Spirit praying for us? Is there dual intercession? G. S. Wakefield gives a helpful solution:

> The Holy Spirit cannot make intercession to himself or he would be less than God; nor can he interpose in heaven on our behalf, for that is the priestly office of Christ. He works in us, stirring us up to pray, and he makes us able to pray. Thus it is by the strength and assistance of the Holy Spirit that we are enabled, albeit groaningly, to approach God through Christ. He is the Spirit of Christ, the legacy of the Lord now in Glory, [and our hearts turn] to him who pleads before the throne.[10]

The Holy Spirit has come among the church as *another* Helper (*parakletos*) who takes our prayers and deposits them with Christ; Christ then brings them to the Father.

Perseverance

I do not pray that You should take them out of the world.

Christians bear a constant testimony against the world's opinions and practices. The more boldly this is undertaken, the more believers will find that they are hated for righteousness' sake; so they must put on the whole armour of God and walk by faith, being obedient to the light of Scripture. Christ now requests that the Father not 'take them out of the world'. In other words, he is praying that they will receive the Father's divine protection from evil and from Satan himself. The Saviour sends believers (not the holy angels) into the world with the gospel in their hearts and on their lips, so that the lost may hear of gospel mercy freely offered to the children of Adam's fallen race (Rom. 1:16–17). 'World' here is the representation of the power of unbelief and the expression of hostility to God. Believers are to live and work in the midst of unbelievers, bringing them the good news of atoning blood.

We owe much to this prayer and are deeply indebted to Christ our Saviour for his intercessions. The Great High Priest of the church remembers the weaknesses and needs of fallen human men and women. The Saviour wants his disciples to stay in the world for at least four reasons:

- So that they will witness personally to Christ's saving and keeping grace. Through their lives of faith and perseverance in a hostile world they will bring glory to God. Christ will one day glorify them but, until that day, they will bring the Son glory through lives of love and obedience. The world will see that Christians have been kept safe by God's faithfulness (Jude 24–25; Ps. 143:1).
- So that they will become mighty evangelists and teachers, filled with

the Holy Spirit, as Jesus had prophesied (Luke 3:16; John 7:39; Acts 1:8; 2:1–4). They will teach the gospel of Jesus Christ to others (John 17:21). It was very important that they 'make disciples', as their apostolic ministry would be the foundation on which the church was built, Jesus Christ being the chief cornerstone (Eph. 2:20–22).

- So that the gospel can be preached to all nations, starting at Jerusalem (Matt. 28:19–20). The apostles were now in receipt of God's Word and Christ's gospel, so for them to leave the world now would mean that the gospel message would not go into the entire world, which would leave it in darkness and without the light of life.
- So that the New Testament Scriptures would be written by 'holy men … moved by the Holy Spirit' (2 Tim. 3:16; 2 Peter 1:20–21). The world cannot know the gospel of Jesus Christ without the Bible's eyewitness testimonies to his Person and Work, or the plan of redemption without the Epistles and the rest of the New Testament (John 17:20; 1:14; Luke 1:1–4; 2 Peter 1:16; 1 Cor. 15; Phil. 3:20–21). Through the Word of God truth will be spread, faith given and salvation found (John 17:17; Rom. 10:13–14).

Without the strength of God in the soul as a result of the intercessions of their Saviour, God's chosen messengers would become weary and even despair of life itself, longing for death. Saints such as Job, Moses, Elijah and Jonah all found themselves in this state at one time or another. The patriarch Job experienced deep sorrow and despair after the sudden and shocking bereavement of his ten children, and this, coupled with a serious personal debilitating disease, made him pray that God would end his life (Job 6:8–9; 3:11; 7:15). Moses, under great stress, complained to God about the burden of his leadership ministry and asked for death (Num. 11:14–15). Elijah, in fear of Queen Jezebel, ran from the land of Israel in painful dejection and unbelief, desiring that God would end his life for him (1 Kings 19:4). The prophet Jonah, who was offended and angry because of the kindness of God's providence to the Gentile people of Nineveh, wanted to die. He prayed for death because he could not face the prospect of justifying his actions to the backslidden people of Israel: 'Therefore now, O LORD, please take my life from me, for it is better for me to die than to live!' (Jonah 4:3). That none of these men took their own lives can be attributed to the prayers of their Saviour Jesus Christ, Israel's eternal High Priest (Rom. 8:34).

The doctrine of perseverance or eternal security is often discussed among believers. The question is raised, Can one be saved and then lost? Is it possible to accept Christ as Saviour and *not* get to heaven? Several Scriptures indicate clearly that the power of God keeps believers from falling into apostasy (see below) when they are 'in Christ': God 'is able to keep [us] from stumbling' (Jude 24); believers are 'kept by the power of God through faith' (1 Peter 1:5); God 'knows how to deliver the godly out of temptations' (2 Peter 2:9). Paul was personally convinced of his eternal spiritual safety in Christ, saying, 'I know whom I have believed and am persuaded that He is able to keep what I have committed to Him until that Day' (2 Tim. 1:12). This assurance was the product of the work of the Holy Spirit and the promise of the prophetic Word in his heart: 'And I will make an everlasting covenant with them, that I will not turn away from doing them good; but I will put My fear in their hearts so that they will not depart from Me' (Jer. 32:40; see also Isa. 55:3; Ezek. 16:60; 37:26; Rom. 8:35–39).

Hebrews 6:4–8 may appear to contradict the doctrine of perseverance and eternal security; however, on closer examination this is not so.

> For it is impossible for those who were once enlightened, and have tasted the heavenly gift, and have become partakers of the Holy Spirit, and have tasted the good word of God and the powers of the age to come, if they fall away, to renew them again to repentance, since they crucify again for themselves the Son of God, and put Him to an open shame.

The thought that these verses might speak of genuine Christians falling from grace and being eternally lost would be shocking! Is this supposed falling away possible, when the Saviour and Good Shepherd, who gave his life for the sheep, asserted that 'I give them eternal life, and they shall never perish; neither shall anyone snatch them out of My hand. My Father, who has given them to Me, is greater than all; and no one is able to snatch them out of My Father's hand' (John 10:28–29)?

The difficulty raised by these verses in Hebrews is removed when it is realized that the author was speaking about a cohort who were never regenerate but who had tasted something of the power of God in times of revival. This is made clear when we notice the contrast that is made between those he speaks of in verse 9—'But, beloved, we are confident of better things concerning you'—and those described in verses 4–6—'those who were once enlightened … if they fall away'. Two different groups of people are in the writer's mind: the genuine believer and the mere professing believer. This is made even clearer by the illustration given in verses 7–8, which speaks of God's kindness in sending rain to all, whether regenerate or not. However, fruitfulness is seen only in genuine believers who, like the land drinking in the rain, bring forth a good crop and are blessed by God.

PROTECTED FROM SATAN

You should keep them from the evil one.

That Satan is the wicked fallen ruler of the world is taught plainly by the Lord Jesus Christ. The identification by Jesus of Satan as the 'ruler of this world' (e.g. John 12:31) portrays Satan as a real being with power and dominion in the earthly realm. Writing in his first epistle John calls Satan the 'wicked one' (1 John 2:13; 3:12; 5:18). In this epistle Satan (the fallen angel) and this fallen world are juxtaposed because they will suffer the same eternal end (2 Peter 3:12; Rev. 20:10). The Bible calls Satan 'the prince of the power of the air, the spirit who now works in the sons of disobedience' (Eph. 2:2), 'the power of darkness' (Col. 1:13) and 'your adversary' (1 Peter 5:8). He can assume the form of an angel of light (2 Cor. 11:14) and can hinder the plans of the servants of Christ (1 Thes. 2:18). He is presumptuous, proud and powerful (Matt 4:5–6; John 13:2). Satan is real, and we cannot keep ourselves from his influence unless we are in Christ. Satan will be defeated when Christians resist him and draw near to God by faith (James 4:7–8a).

However, because of the Person and Work of Christ, this wicked one is 'cast out' and his defeat is at hand (John 12:31–32; 16:11). Because of the impeccable holiness of Christ the devil has 'nothing in [Christ]' (John 14:30): he has no point of contact with him and is powerless over him. Because of the righteous judgement of God 'the ruler of this world is judged' (John 16:11).

Colossians 2:15 alludes to the defeat of Satan and Christ's victory on the cross over the powers that opposed him and that were against 'those whom You gave Me' (John 17:12): 'Having disarmed principalities and powers, He made a public spectacle of them, triumphing over them in it.' Christ 'disarmed principalities and powers', that is, he stripped them of their power. These dark powers gathered against him as he hung on the cross. They thought victory was theirs as they watched him die, but he turned the tables on them and they were defeated, disarmed and stripped of their power to accuse us and to control us because of Christ's resurrection. There was no doubt that Satan and his cohorts came together to attack the soul of Christ when he was enduring the judgement for our sins. They fiercely assaulted him for three hours while he hung on the cross; nevertheless, he triumphed over them making 'a public spectacle of them'. Many think that Paul is here using the imagery of the Roman victory parade. The Roman army marched with their captives chained behind them as trophies, putting them on show as defeated foes and making a public spectacle of them before the emperor and the citizens of Rome. Colossians 2:15 speaks, then, of the resurrection of Christ, when he broke the chains of death and hell and made captivity captive. Let us grasp the triumph of Christ over the devil.[11]

Apostasy

Apostasy should not be confused with backsliding. A true believer may wander very far from Christ by wilfully sinning and so losing his or her (direct) fellowship with God. He or she may even reach the point of losing all assurance of salvation and no longer being recognized as a Christian by others. However, such a person can be restored to full fellowship through repentance of the folly and the confession and forsaking of all sinfulness (1 John 1:9). Apostasy, however, is more like the unpardonable sin described in Mark 3:29. That was the sin of attributing the miracles of the Lord Jesus to the prince of the demons. Jesus's miracles were performed in the power of the Holy Spirit. To attribute them to the devil is tantamount to blaspheming the Holy Spirit. It implies that the Holy Spirit is the devil. Jesus said that such a sin could never be forgiven, neither in this age nor in the age to come. Apostasy is also similar to the 'sin leading to death' described by John: 'If anyone sees his brother sinning a sin which does not lead to death, he will ask, and He will give him life for those who commit sin not leading to death. There is sin leading to death. I do not say that he should pray about that' (1 John 5:16). John was writing about people who had professed to be believers and had participated in the activities of local churches but had imbibed the false teaching of the Gnostics and spitefully left the Christian fellowship. Their deliberate departure indicated that they had never truly been born again (1 John 2:19). By openly denying that Jesus is the Christ (1 John 2:22) they had committed the sin leading to death, and it was useless to pray for their recovery (see Lev. 10:1–2; Num. 16:30–31; 1 Chr. 10:13–14; Ps. 19:13; 1 Cor. 3:17).

Perseverance and watchfulness are clearly described by the New Testament authors as the responsibility of every Christian. There are warnings not to 'receive the grace of God in vain' (2 Cor. 6:1). The elect of God are to 'make [their] call and election sure' (2 Peter 1:10), knowing that 'it is God who works in [them] both to will and to do for His good pleasure' (Phil. 2:13). Therefore, believers are to 'work out [their] own salvation with fear and trembling' (Phil. 2:12), fully trusting in the sufficiency of the grace of God to keep them and to present them faultless in Christ's presence (Jude 24).

They are not of the world, just as I am not of the world.

The phrase 'They are not of the world' repeats the words used in verse 14. Jesus is conscious that Christians are pilgrims and strangers (1 Peter 2:11) in a fallen world, and he now confirms that the servants will suffer the same rejection as their Lord. Christian discipleship entails the exercise of daily faith and separation from the world.

FOR FURTHER STUDY

1. What are the implications of the following texts concerning the perseverance of the saints: 2 Thessalonians 3:3; 2 Timothy 1:12; 1 Peter 1:5; 2 Peter 2:9; Jude 24?
2. Why did the Saviour not want his disciples taken out of the world (John 17:15)?
3. That Satan is the ruler of this world is taught plainly by the Lord Jesus (John 12:31; 14:30; 16:11). What are the implications of this for believers and for the unsaved?
4. How is unity defined by Jesus?
5. What is apostasy, and what are its signs?

TO THINK ABOUT AND DISCUSS

1. Why is it that affliction does not 'kill' Christian joy? (See John 16:22–24; Acts 20:23–24; Rom. 14:17; Col. 1:11; 1 Thes. 1:6; 1 Peter 1:8.)
2. In what way does God the Father 'keep [Christians] from the evil one', in answer to Christ's prayer (v. 15)?
3. What does Jesus mean by separation from the world (John 17:11–16; see also 8:23; 15:19; 1 John 2:14–17)?
4. Can a Christian be saved and then lost? Use Scripture to support your answer.
5. What are the implications of Christ's Session?

Notes

1 **Charles Hodge,** *The Epistle to the Ephesians* (London: Banner of Truth, 1964), p. 206.
2 **Louis Berkhof,** *Systematic Theology* (London: Banner of Truth, 1971), pp. 507–509.
3 See John Calvin, *Calvin's Institutes* (Grand Rapids, MI: Associated Publishers & Authors Inc., 1970), 3:2:6, 8.
4 'Jesu, Joy of Man's Desiring' is the English title of the tenth movement of the cantata *Herz und Mund und Tat und Leben*.
5 **J. C. Ryle,** *Expository Thoughts on the Gospels: John*, vol. iii (London: James Clarke & Co., 1969), p. 215.
6 **C. H. Spurgeon,** *Morning and Evening* (McLean, VA: Macdonald Publishing, [n.d.]), 13 April, p. 208.
7 **William Hendriksen,** *Commentary on Philippians* (London: Banner of Truth, 1963), p. 193.
8 I have used 'infallibility' and 'inerrancy' as interchangeable and synonymous concepts.
9 **Ronald Dunn,** *When Heaven is Silent* (Milton Keynes: Nelson Word, 1994), pp. 59–61.
10 **G. S. Wakefield,** *Puritan Devotion* (London: Epworth Press, 1957), p. 80.
11 See my *Opening Up Colossians and Philemon* (Leominster: Day One, 2006).

Christ's intercession for his disciples (2) (vv. 17–19)

Sanctify them by Your truth. Your word is truth. As You sent Me into the world, I also have sent them into the world. And for their sakes I sanctify Myself, that they also may be sanctified by the truth.

Kept from the flesh: their sanctification

In verse 14 Christ said that he had given his disciples God's Word. He now returns to that thought in verse 17 and connects the Scriptures with the sanctification of the saints, both definitively and progressively. Jesus prays not only that 'those whom You gave Me' (v. 12) will start the Christian life, but also that they will continue to grow in grace. He then makes a memorable statement about the Bible: 'Your word is truth.' Somc look for truth in the autonomy of human reason or through human experience; many consider that objective truth is impossible and are content to rely on non-biblical evidence and rational deduction alone. Such world views are contrary to the words of Jesus Christ, who taught that truth is not found in human reason or human experience, but in divine wisdom

Jesus prays for separation from the world to a life of holiness and wise service. A correct view of biblical sanctification is necessary in order to understand the way of holiness; justification and sanctification are to be distinguished. Holiness is an idea that terrifies, repels and bewilders the mind of the unregenerate, but it is rejoiced in by those who know God (Phil. 1:21–23). Church history shows the need to be right about the meaning of sanctification as many have fallen into views of salvation that place works before faith, believing that their works are accepted as meritorious acts by God and justify them in God's sight. Islam, for example, teaches that a surplus of good deeds is required to achieve an everlasting existence in Paradise.[1] This is a path also taken by cults and all other false religions but it is 'a different gospel' (Gal. 1:6–9). A clear distinction between justification and sanctification is made in the New Testament, but if the two become entangled, so that works and love are regarded as having merit before God for salvation, none can be saved, for the Bible clearly says that 'we are all like an unclean thing, and all our righteousnesses are like filthy rags' (Isa. 64:6; see also Matt. 5:20). The Bible teaches that sanctification is the fruit of justification and is distinct from it (see diagram); it also teaches that salvation is by grace alone, through faith alone, in Christ alone (Rom. 3:28; 5:1; Eph. 2:8–9). Sanctification follows justification in the *ordo salutis* as it is a work of God in the soul. J. C. Ryle's words are helpful:

> Election is always to sanctification. Those whom God chooses out of humanity, He chooses not only that they be saved but that they may bear fruit, and fruit that can be seen. All other election besides this is a mere vain delusion, a miserable invention of man. It was the faith and hope and love exhibited in the lives of the Thessalonians which made Paul say, 'I know your election of God' (1 Thes. 1:4). Where there is no visible fruit of sanctification, we may be sure there is no election.[2]

The nature of sanctification

In these verses of John 17 Jesus prays that the people of God will be separated from the world to God, first through conversion and thereafter by consecration. The former is known as definitive sanctification and the latter is called progressive sanctification. Christ has in mind his disciples' progress in holiness. Through salvation and calling, they are set apart for the work of apostleship and, like all the saints, they are chosen to be holy through the work of the Spirit of God in the soul. This is the goal of their election (Eph. 1:4; 2 Thes. 2:13; 1 Peter 1:2). They are called out of the

What is sanctification?

'Sanctification is the work of God's free grace, whereby we are renewed in the whole man after the image of God and are enabled more and more to die unto sin and to live unto righteousness.'

(Westminster Shorter Catechism, Q. 35)

JUSTIFICATION	SANCTIFICATION
1. Is an objective change of relationship	1. Is a subjective change of character
2. Is perfect the moment one believes	2. Is never perfect until heaven
3. Admits no growth	3. Is a progressive and continuous work of the Holy Spirit within
4. Is by faith only	4. Is progressed by obedience
5. Is not our own but is imputed to the believer	5. Is a personal righteousness imparted to the believer
6. Is the gift of God's free grace	6. Is the result of one's union with Christ

world into fellowship with Christ and to his service. The Saviour needs disciples who, having left the old life behind, are enthusiastic for spiritual life and holiness. They are to go into the world with the gospel, possessing a willingness to live under the Lordship of Christ Jesus and having rejected those attitudes and aspirations which are contrary to holiness (John 14:15; Matt. 5:27–30; 5:43–48; 7:1–6).

The word sanctify (*hagiadzo*) has the fundamental idea of setting apart for holy use, separation from the world, and thus consecration and devotion in the service of God. It is used in the New Testament to describe being separated from an ordinary purpose to a sacred purpose and thus being exclusively and entirely God's. The New Testament speaks of (progressive) sanctification that brings to completeness the work of God's grace. Conversion brings an inner change in the heart of believers as they partake of the divine nature (Ezek. 36:26; 2 Cor. 5:17; 1 Peter 2:10; 2 Peter 1:4), while progressive sanctification continues the work of God the Holy Spirit in the heart until death. Believers are purged from the corruption of sin and the world little by little. 'They are not only accounted holy, but made holy ... it is not only the expulsion of sin but the infusion of grace'[3] (see 1 Cor. 6:11; 2 Tim. 2:12). This is a work of God's grace and carries believers higher and further in order to make them more Christlike (John 17:19; 1 Thes. 4:3–5; 5:23). Sanctification is a process that never reaches perfection in this life (Prov. 20:9; Phil. 1:6; 1 John 1:8), but it would seem to be complete at the very moment of death or immediately after death as far as the soul is concerned (Heb. 12:23; Rev. 14:5; 21:27).

The need for sanctification

Although judicial wrath does not dwell on believers because they are justified by faith (Rom. 5:1; 8:1), new Christians need to go on to maturity and grow in grace. Holiness is important to God, which is why he gave the Ten Commandments (the Moral Law). He has bestowed his Spirit upon his people and provided the Holy Scriptures in order that Christians will walk in holiness all the days of their lives. God's aim is the elimination of the power of sin so that believers are victorious over the sins of the flesh and mind (Rom. 6:22; 1 Thes. 2:13; 1 Tim. 2:15; Heb. 4:14; 1 Peter 1:2). The Scriptures clearly teach that without holiness heaven cannot be entered (1 Peter 1:15–16; Heb. 12:14); thus both conversion and growth in holiness are to be sought. Believers are to pray to be more Christlike and less worldly; this is because 'sin does not change its character as sin because the person in whom it dwells (and by whom it is committed) is a believer'.[4] Christians are cleansed by degrees and clothed with God's image and likeness as they await the Second Coming (1 Thes. 5:23).

Indwelling sin involves conflict in the hearts of the people of God. The more conscious they are of the sin that remains, the sharper will be their hatred of it. Murray points out further that there is a great difference between remaining sin and reigning sin: 'it is one thing for sin to remain in us; it is another for us to live in sin.'[5] Charles Spurgeon concurs:

Beware of light thoughts of sin. At the time of conversion, the conscience is so tender, that we are afraid of the slightest sin. Young converts have a holy timidity, a godly fear lest they should offend against God. But alas! very soon the fine bloom upon these first ripe fruits is removed by the rough handling of the surrounding world: the sensitive plant of young piety turns into a willow in after life, too pliable, too easily yielding. It is sadly true, that even a Christian may grow by degrees so callous, that the sin which once startled him does not alarm him in the least. By degrees men get familiar with sin. At first a little sin startles us; but soon we say, 'is it not a little one?' Then there comes another, larger, and then another, until by degrees we begin to regard sin as but a little ill; and then follows an unholy presumption: 'We have not fallen into open sin. True, we tripped a little, but we stood upright in the main. We may have uttered one unholy word, but as for the most of our conversation, it has been consistent.' So we throw a cloak over sin; we call it by dainty names. Christian, beware how thou thinkest lightly of sin. Take heed lest thou fall by little and little. Sin, a *little* thing? Is it not a poison? Who knows its deadliness? Sin, a little thing? Do not the little foxes spoil the grapes? Doth not the tiny coral insect build a rock which wrecks a navy? Do not little strokes fell lofty oaks? Will not continual droppings wear away stones? Sin, a little thing? It girded the Redeemer's head with thorns, and pierced his heart! It made him suffer anguish, bitterness, and woe. Could you weigh the least sin in the scales of eternity, you would fly from it as from a serpent, and abhor the least appearance of evil. Look upon all sin as that which crucified the Saviour, and you will see it to be 'exceeding sinful'.[6]

The means of sanctification

Together with the Holy Spirit, the Bible is the means of sanctification. If Bible truth is neglected or resisted, the process of continued sanctification will be hindered and ultimately stopped. There is an important distinction to be made between the natural revelation and the Word of God. Natural revelation displayed through creation tells us much about God but it is not this truth that sanctifies the saints of God (Rom. 1:18, 25). Nor are the general facts of history the means of greater personal holiness. We may well believe that the Prince of Wales married Lady Diana Spencer in 1981 and that they had two sons, Prince William and Prince Harry, but it does not make the slightest difference to the soul's eternal well-being. However, if the Bible is read and believed to be God's revelation, it will work to the good of the soul. Bible truth is the great and effective instrument by which the Holy Spirit carries forward the process of inward sanctification. This means that the Word of God must not be neglected but must be read, studied on a regular basis and believed. Truth transforms the fallen nature and makes it more Christlike; hence Jesus's prayer, 'Sanctify them by *Your truth. You word is truth*' (John 17:17, emphasis added; see also 2 Thes. 2:13; Titus 1:1).

THE BIBLE AND TRUTH

What is truth? This question was asked by Pontius Pilate in the Praetorium when Jesus stood before him (John 18:38). Pilate did not receive a reply from Christ because his question was meant rhetorically, but the concept of truth is one which today draws much controversy. Helpfully, the Lord Jesus clears up any misunderstanding as to what *truth* really is. He says it is God's Word: 'Your word is truth.' By 'Your word' he means the sixty-six books of the Old and New Testaments, but not the apocryphal books; they form no part of the canon of Holy Scripture and have no authority in the church. The Bible's canon is complete and no addition can be—nor needs to be—made to it (2 Tim.

3:16; Gal. 1:8–9; see also 1 Cor. 13:10). Evangelical Christians believe that 'There are no fresh truths of revelation to be discovered either in nature or in church history and tradition which are not to be found in Scripture.'[7] Church tradition has no authority over God's Word, nor does it hold equal status as a source of God's revelation to humanity; this would in effect result in the subordination of Scripture to tradition. Scripture is the final authority and standard beyond which there is no appeal.

The Bible's authority rests on God himself. He is the Source and Originator of Holy Scripture; thus it has power to command and to require submission. Christianity is a religion of revelation. God speaks to us by his Son (Heb. 1:1–2). Holy Scripture did not originate in the minds or imaginations of people but was supernaturally given through holy men who were inspired by the Holy Spirit when the canon was in formation (2 Peter 1:19–21; 2 Tim. 3:16–17). This revelation is ultimately about God, his ways and his will for fallen humanity (John 17:6, 8, 14). The Bible is wholly true, and whatever the Bible says, whether that teaching has to do with doctrine, history, science, geography, geology or any other discipline, is accurate, correct and contains no errors. The entire truthfulness of Scripture is for most Christians an acceptable doctrine.

Truth is timeless and dependable, so what we read in the Scriptures is meant to be trusted. One evangelical statement of faith puts it this way:

> God has revealed himself in the Bible, which consists of the Old and New Testaments alone. Every word was inspired by God through human authors, so that the Bible as originally given is in its entirety the Word of God, without error and fully reliable in fact and doctrine. The Bible alone speaks with final authority and is always sufficient for all matters of belief and practice.[8]

The truths of the Fall of Adam into sin (Gen. 3) and the bodily resurrection of Jesus Christ (John 20; 1 Cor. 15), like all Christian doctrines, have powerful and continued implications today. Without the doctrine of sin there would be no need for the gospel; and without the resurrection of Jesus Christ from the dead there would be no hope for lost sinners of mankind. Truths like these sanctify those who believe them, and fit them for heaven.

The Bible is revelation from God given to us through inspiration of the Spirit, and it is by listening to the voice of God in the Scriptures that we learn why we must repent of our sins and how we can live well. Do we make our own rules? If we listen to the voices of our sinful hearts we might think we ought to; but Christians believe that God has revealed his will for mankind in the Ten Commandments (Exod. 20:1–17) and through all the pages of Holy Scripture.

The Bible is:

- Authoritative: this arises from its divine authorship by the God who cannot lie (Titus 1:2).
- Accurate: this originates from its infallibility, being inspired by the Holy Spirit of God (2 Tim. 3:16).
- Authentic: this flows from its inerrancy; it is totally trustworthy, dependable and without error (John 17:17).

God's Word is revelation

In John 17:17 Jesus identifies Holy Scripture as something distinct from himself that is true and whose message is trustworthy and timeless (Ps. 100:5). It is not just *a witness* to the truth; it is the *very message of God* to a lost world and it can be understood by all people.

The words of the Father were passed on by Christ to the apostles, who received them and kept them:

They have kept Your word. Now they have known that all things which You have given Me are from You. For I have given to them the words which You have given Me; and they have received them ... I have given them Your word; and the world has hated them because they are not of the world, just as I am not of the world. (John 17:6–8, 14)

The Bible comes to us because of divine inspiration—'holy men of God spoke as they were moved [or 'carried along', NIV) by the Holy Spirit' (2 Peter 1:21); it is transmitted to us by divine inspiration—'All Scripture is given by inspiration of God' (2 Tim. 3:16); it is preserved by divine intervention (providence, Ps. 119:89); and it is understood because of divine regeneration (John 3:3, 7; 6:45; 1 Cor. 2:14). Peter used the Greek word translated as 'moved' (*phero*), which indicates that the 'holy men' expressed the mind of God in words provided by him; they did not act according to their own imaginations or ideas. Truth comes from God, not from our minds or imaginations. When the canon of Scripture was in formation the writers were supernaturally motivated by the Holy Spirit. The Spirit both inspired its writers and now enlightens its readers. This revelation of truth is ultimately about God and his Son (John 1:1: 17:8, 14, 17). What the Bible says, God says, because God cannot lie (Titus 1:2).

It must be rigorously maintained that the Scriptures are clear, and able to be understood by 'the learned' and 'the unlearned'; if this were not so, professional scholars could claim that they alone, through historical–critical methods, could understand the Scriptures properly. This is the doctrine of biblical perspicuity, which has been expressed thus:

All things in Scripture are not alike plain in themselves, nor alike clear unto all; yet those things which are necessary to be known, believed, and observed for salvation are so clearly propounded, and opened in some place of Scripture or other, that not only the learned, but the unlearned, in a due use of the ordinary means, may attain unto a sufficient understanding of them.[9]

To contend that every word of the Bible is inspired, says J. C. Ryle, 'is the only safe and tenable view that can be adopted',[10] and this statement must be held as being still true some 130 years after it was first written. To deny this is not only to detract from the Bible's value as the perfect rule of faith and practice, but also to deny its value as a weapon against error and a source of spiritual comfort to the dying. Ultimately, the denial of the inerrancy of the Bible (see below) leads to the loss of the gospel. If Bible truth can be changed because of the latest results of biblical scholarship or archaeology, it has been put on the same level as physics, geology, astronomy and so on, and this removes its special status as the Book of God.

God's Word is inerrant

The doctrine of inerrancy states that the Bible, in its entirety, is free from all falsehood, fraud and deceit,[11] and it is an evangelical and Reformed distinctive. This needs to be re-emphasized as some theologians today regard those who hold to this position as outdated. They use the terms 'traditionalist' and 'fundamentalist' in this context as terms of disdain and reproach. A battle for the Bible's credibility is going on today.[12] This attack comes also from both secular and theistic evolutionists, who both reckon that 'scientific truth' contradicts biblical truth. Their attitude is not new; what is new, however, is the growing acceptance by many within the evangelical and Reformed camp of accepting neo-Darwinism as a tool to modify and recalibrate the theological understanding of the creation account as revealed in the Book of Genesis and other portions of Scripture, which declare that the universe was created in six twenty-four-hour days (Gen. 1–2; Exod. 20:11; Heb. 11:3). Such support undermines the testimony of faithful churches and pastors to the inerrancy of Holy Scripture.

What the writers of Scripture received is not to be replaced by other teachings or regarded as partly true; rather it must be believed to be inerrant and unchanging revelation. Biblical inerrancy must be insisted upon, for Christ teaches, 'Your Word is truth'. To regard any parts of the Scriptures as errant will lead to the loss of the very truths which are taught in this chapter and will open the door for their revision by enemies of the truth and Christianity. We are not called upon to explain every difficulty found in Holy Writ, but simply to trust it as given and obey it as God requires. God's Word is revelation, and through inspiration it tells us what God is (1 John 4:8) and why he sent his only Son into the world (John 3:16). Jesus Christ wants us to take the Word of God seriously, recognizing its inerrancy, authority and sufficiency (Matt. 24:35; Rom. 1:16; 2 Tim. 3:16–17).

In John 17 Jesus Christ prays as the church's High Priest and as God's final Prophet. What he says is to be accepted as God's own voice to all people—all truth and nothing but the truth; he promised that the Holy Spirit would guide our understanding (John 16:13). The truth that Jesus Christ brings is to be received as reliable, dependable and unchanging. It is given to us in our own language through translation, but it remains the Word of God as long as the translation is accurate and rooted in the original autographs. If the Bible is only partly inspired and partly trustworthy, who is to determine which part is the authentic Word of God? To reject the Bible as inerrantly reliable leaves one depending on the options of philosophy or mysticism in the search for the knowledge of God. However, these are man-made answers to man's greatest questions. We are faced with a choice: either to accept the mind of God or to accept the minds of men and women; it is a choice between revealed religion and human enlightenment. Evangelical and Reformed Christians insist that the Bible is wholly true and reveals what God wants us to hear and believe, and we need not be afraid to cross the gap between revelation and faith because that way leads to the promise of heavenly comfort (Luke 16:31).

The challenge of Islam

Many Muslims work with the Bible text not because they feel that it speaks to them about their faith, but in order to reconstruct the church's doctrines, especially about our Lord Jesus Christ's deity and resurrection. But what are we to make of Islam's claim that the Bible has been changed? On the strength of the Koran, Muslims maintain that the Bible does not contain the actual words of Jesus, but rather the words of others about him (suras 2:75; 2:78–79), and assert, on the other hand, that the Koran is a miraculous document, with no errors or changes since its origin. This latter claim about the Koran cannot be upheld as extant copies show that it has been changed over time.[13] Their claim that the New Testament has been changed is without proof as the New Testament relies on some 5,300 Greek, ancient Syriac, Latin and Coptic manuscripts (as well as others, including Patristic quotations) to ascertain its original autographs. Bruce Metzger notes, 'The textual critic of the New Testament is embraced by the wealth of his material.'[14] Muslim authors fail to give the Bible its rightful place as the Word of God. A reading of the Old and New Testaments will easily correct such Muslim claims. 'Islamic creed is in fact aimed at denying Christianity, especially the finality of Christ, and asserting the supremacy of Islam.'[15]

THE HOLY SPIRIT

When sanctifying the elect God deals with them as those made in his image, having rational minds and sensitive consciences, though with fallen wills. He has given us his Word to enlighten our minds and give understanding (Eph. 1:18). His truth, accompanied by the grace of the Holy Spirit, purifies the heart because the Holy Spirit is the Spirit of truth and holiness (John 16:13). The Holy Spirit is the agent of sanctification, working through God's Word to give light and guidance (2 Cor. 3:17–18; 1 John 2:27). Both the Word and the Spirit are necessary for inner growth, while the Bible's precepts and promises must be embraced (believed) and obeyed for God's people to progress in holiness. The Bible must be read and the redeemed must play a conscious part in their own sanctification and not be passive or rebellious if holiness is to progress: 'Therefore, my beloved, as you have always obeyed, not as in my presence only, but now much more in my absence, work out your own salvation with fear and trembling; for it is God who works in you both to will and to do for His good pleasure' (Phil. 2:12–13); 'Therefore, having these promises, beloved, let us cleanse ourselves from all filthiness of the flesh and spirit, perfecting holiness in the fear of God' (2 Cor. 7:1).

The Holy Spirit works in the inner life, urging believers to walk in paths of holiness; hence Peter's words: 'you have purified your souls in obeying the truth through the Spirit' (1 Peter 1:22). The Holy Spirit, Bible truth and repentance resulting in obedience lead to purification. We need to hide God's Word in our hearts so that we do not sin against him (Ps. 119:11). This will result in the inner witness of the Holy Spirit bringing assurance of the truth to our souls: 'When He, the Spirit of truth, has come, He will guide you into all truth; for He will not speak on His own authority, but whatever He hears He will speak; and He will tell you things to come' (John 16:13); 'But the anointing which you have received from Him abides in you, and you do not need that anyone teach you; but as the same anointing teaches you concerning all things, and is true, and is not a lie, and just as it has taught you, you will abide in Him' (1 John 2:27).

There is a self-authenticating authority of Scripture that comes from the Holy Spirit. This is recognized in two great Protestant confessions of faith: 'The authority of the Holy Scripture, for which it ought to be believed, and obeyed, depends not upon the testimony of any man, or Church; but wholly upon God (who is truth itself), the author thereof; and therefore it is to be received, because it is the Word of God.'[16]

It is the Holy Spirit who communes with the believer as the Comforter (*parakletos*, John 14:16, 26; 15:26). He brings to remembrance the words of Christ and sheds abroad the love of God in the Christian's heart. He bears witness that we are the sons of God, seals us, is a guarantee, anoints us, adopts us, strengthens us, and grants us the spirit of supplication (Gal. 4:6; Eph. 1:13; 2:18; 3:16; 6:18).

THE CONSCIENCE

According to Calvin, the conscience is placed over us as a sentinel, to observe and spy out all the secrets of our fallen hearts.[17] It differs from intellect; those who sin stand convicted in their consciences before God. Conscience is another method of revelation which bears witness to God himself in our hearts (Rom. 2:14–15).[18] So our consciences approve when we do well, but when we go against them we feel guilty—unless the conscience has become suppressed or damaged. According to Thomas Watson, the conscience is the 'book of the heart'; he says 'The notion of deity is engraved on every man's heart.' 'If there were no Bible to tell us there is a God, yet conscience might.'[19] The Greeks in Athens built an altar 'TO THE UNKNOWN GOD' (Acts 17:23); this was because they knew that Deity should be worshipped. They had an innate (inborn) knowledge of the Creator in the soul which was not completely erased by the Fall. Because of this sense of the divine in the souls of all people (often called the *sensus divinitatis*), the preacher knows that when he brings God's Word to his hearers, they have the capacity to receive it, leaving them without excuse (Rom. 1:18–2:16). The preacher needs to preach to this sense of God in the soul of mankind and to take account of sin's intellectual effects as he engages with his hearers' consciences. It is the preacher's task to teach such knowledge in the work of evangelism. Paul said to Timothy, 'Do the work of an evangelist' (2 Tim. 4:5). To the people of God conscience says, 'Let us draw near with a true heart, in full assurance of faith, having our hearts sprinkled from an evil conscience' (Heb. 10:22). Only the Holy Spirit is above our conscience. He brings to mind the most helpful things when we need them. Paul said, 'I myself always strive to have a conscience without offense toward God and men' (Acts 24:16; see also 25:8, 10–11).

The reason for sanctification

As You sent Me into the world ...

Verse 18 continues with the theme of sanctification. Now Jesus thinks about his commission from the Father. Jesus was 'sent' into the world from heaven, so we see once again that the Son existed before the world was created and before his incarnation (v. 5). He did not *become* the Son; he was the One who was always in the bosom of the Father (1:18) and 'whom the Father sanctified and sent into the world' (10:36). Christ's coming into a lost world accomplished love's goal to redeem what was lost at the Fall, while the love of God was the ground of the atonement and the explanation why Jesus Christ was sent into the world.

This begs the question raised by Anselm of Canterbury (c.1033–1109) in his great work *Cur Deus Homo* ('Why God Became Man'): Was it necessary that the blood of the Son of God, the Lord of glory, be shed in order to make atonement for sin, or was another way possible for Almighty God? Could not the consequences and effects of the Fall simply be reversed by the word of God's power? Could God have saved us without the atonement? Anselm understood that

> God cannot deal with sin except as a holy God sees it to be. If it is not punished, or adequate satisfaction made for it, it is unjustly forgiven ... Satisfaction can only be offered by God Himself, yet it must be offered in human nature, or it would not be a satisfaction for man. Hence the necessity for the Redeemer being both God and Man.[20]

The Old and New Testaments teach the absolute necessity of the atonement through the shed blood of Jesus Christ, who was sent into the world for this very purpose. Salvation flows from the free and sovereign grace of God and requires the blood of holy sacrifice (Exod. 12:13; Eph. 2:8–9). This absolute moral necessity is the great motivating factor in the redemption of a world lost and ruined by the Fall.[21]

THE GREAT COMMISSION

... I also have sent them into the world.

Christ links sanctification with the Great Commission. Christ's disciples were sent into the world as 'lambs among wolves' and were to expect trouble, persecution and even death (Luke 10:3; see also Isa. 40:11). As he prays, he knows what privations await 'those whom You gave Me', yet he does not hesitate to send them as his messengers and evangelists because the servant is not greater than his Master. Christ has work for them to do. The Father sent the Son, so now the Son, as King and Lord of the church, sends the disciples into the world that they, like their Saviour, may fulfil the calling of God. It is God's love and compassion for a fallen world that motivate Christ to send his followers as evangelists seeking the lost (Matt. 28:19–20; John 3:16). Their effectiveness in the task of teaching and evangelism will be dependent, in part, on holy living, constant consecration to Jesus Christ and obedience to the call of ministry (John 4:38; 20:21; see also Rom. 12:1–2; 1 Cor. 3:9). Christ's witnesses must be holy in an unholy world. He sends them into his vineyard of service and action. He sends them, knowing the dangers that await them; yet they will have dignity as his ambassadors, speaking in his name (2 Cor. 5:20). He sends them into the world with his promise not to abandon them:

And Jesus came and spoke to them, saying, 'All authority has been given to Me in heaven and on earth. Go therefore and make disciples of all the nations, baptizing them in the name of the Father and of the Son and of the Holy Spirit, teaching them to observe all things that I have commanded you; and lo, I am with you always, even to the end of the age.' Amen.

(Matt. 28:18–20)

And for their sakes I sanctify Myself, that they also may be sanctified by the truth.

Again we find that the Father and Son are united in the work of salvation, and to this end Christ sanctifies himself, setting himself apart through the incarnation and the office of High Priest in order to offer himself as a sacrifice for sin (Acts 3:14–15; Heb. 1:2; 9:24–28; 1 Peter 3:18;). Jesus was always holy and did not need to be made so by atoning sacrifice, as Israel's priests of old did (Heb. 5:3). His act of consecration was twofold: firstly, he came from heaven and was made man, taking human nature, yet remaining without sin; and, secondly, he went to the cross as an atoning sacrifice and substitute for sinners, that they might gain eternal life (John 1:29; 6:54; 10:11; 15:13; 1 John 2:1–2). Christ engaged in this High-Priestly work as part of his ministry as Mediator between God and humanity (John 14:6; Acts 4:12; 10:43; 16:31; 1 Tim. 2:5–6). This fulfilled the prophecies of the Word of God which foretold the Christ's sufferings (Ps. 22; Isa. 53:4; Dan. 9:26). His concern was not for himself, so he gave himself utterly to the work of redemption as the Lamb of God, achieving not only justification but also sanctification for his people (John 2:29; Eph. 5:2; Titus 2:14; 1 Peter 2:24; 1 John 2:1–2). It was more important for Jesus to die than to live.

Jesus, my great High Priest,
Offered his blood and died;
My guilty conscience seeks
No sacrifice beside:
His powerful blood did once atone
And now it pleads before the throne.

(Isaac Watts, 'Join All the Glorious Names', 1709)

FOR FURTHER STUDY

1. What are the differences between justification and sanctification?
2. What do Philippians 3:21; Romans 8:29; 2 Corinthians 7:1; Ephesians 5:25–27; and 1 Peter 1:13–16 tell us about holiness?
3. What is inerrancy, and why must Christians regard the Holy Scriptures as inerrant?
4. What are the implications of John 15:3 with regard to sanctification?
5. What is the role of the Holy Spirit in sanctification?

TO THINK ABOUT AND DISCUSS

1. What should Christians believe when providence appears to go against them?
2. Can a distinction be made between 'infallible' and 'inerrant' with regard to the Bible?
3. Muslims claim that the Bible has been changed. What is the evidence that this claim is utterly untrue?

Notes

1 **I. A. Ibrahim,** *A Brief Illustrated Guide to Understanding Islam* (Houston: Darussalam, 1997), p. 41.

2 **J. C. Ryle,** *Expository Thoughts on the Gospels: John*, vol. iii (London: James Clarke & Co., 1969), [n.p.].

3 **Thomas Manton,** An *Exposition of John 17* (Wilmington, DE: Sovereign Grace, 1972), p. 289.

4 **John Murray,** *Redemption Accomplished and Applied* (London: Banner of Truth, 1961), p. 144.

5 Ibid., p. 145.

6 **C. H. Spurgeon,** *Morning and Evening* (McLean, VA: Macdonald Publishing, [n.d.]), 11 March, p. 142.

7 **D. B. Knox,** *The 39 Articles* (London: Hodder & Stoughton, 1967), p. 22.

8 'Basis of Faith', FIEC (Fellowship of Evangelical Churches), at www.fiec.org.uk. Accessed February 2012.

9 'Of the Holy Scripture', Westminster Confession of Faith, 1:7, and the 1689 Baptist Confession of Faith, 1:7; at www.reformed.org/documents/wcf_with_proofs/ and www.grace.org.uk/faith/bc1689/1689bc01.html; both accessed February 2012.

10 **J. C. Ryle,** *The Old Paths* (Edinburgh: Banner of Truth, 1999), p. 21.

11 See **N. L. Geisler,** (ed.), *Inerrancy* (Grand Rapids, MI: Zondervan, 1982).

12 Two recent books demonstrate the move away from the evangelical position: **Peter Enns,** *Inspiration & Incarnation* (Grand Rapids, MI: Baker Academic, 2005); **A. T. B. McGowan,** *The Divine Spiration of Scripture* (Nottingham: Apollos, 2007).

13 **Patrick Sookhdeo,** *The Challenge of Islam to the Church and Its Mission* (Pewsey: Isaac Publishing, 2009), p. 20.

14 **Bruce Metzger**, *The Text of the New Testament* (Oxford: Clarendon Press, 1968), pp. 34, 36–92.

15 **Sookhdeo,** *The Challenge of Islam*, p. 55.

16 'Of the Holy Scriptures', Westminster Confession of Faith, 1:4; at www.reformed.org/documents/wcf_with_proofs/; compare ch. 1 of the 1689 Baptist Confession of Faith, at www.grace.org.uk/faith/bc1689/1689bc01.html; both accessed February 2012.

17 See **John Calvin,** *Calvin's Institutes* (Grand Rapids, MI: Associated Publishers & Authors Inc., 1970), 4:10:3.

18 See **John Murray,** *The Epistle of Paul to the Romans*, vol. i (London: Marshall, Morgan & Scott, 1960), p. 75, n. 29.

19 **Thomas Watson,** *A Body of Divinity* (London: Banner of Truth, 1970), pp. 55, 41.

20 Quoted in **R. A. Finlayson,** 'Anselm and the Doctrine of the Atonement', in *The Story of Theology* (London: Tyndale Press, 1969), p. 38.

21 See **Murray,** *Redemption*, pp. 11–18.

Part 4. Concerning the church: the Lord and his people (vv. 20–26)

God needs the Church to be the Church
The world needs the Church to be the Church
The Church needs the Church to be the Church
(Author unknown)

The High Priest and his flock (vv. 20–22)

I do not pray for these alone, but also for those who will believe in Me through their word; that they all may be one, as You, Father, are in Me, and I in You; that they also may be one in Us, that the world may believe that You sent Me. And the glory which You gave Me I have given them, that they may be one just as We are one.

Verses 20–26 (we will look at vv. 23–26 in the next chapter) are extremely important and require that we understand them aright. Referring specifically to the words 'that they may be one just as We are one', D Martyn Lloyd-Jones said, 'Here we have what is undoubtedly one of the most exalted statements to be found anywhere in the whole of the Scriptures.'[1] This being so, these verses deserve our closest attention. Speaking about the nature of Christian unity, Lloyd-Jones goes on to say,

Now whatever may be said of these verses we are examining in Chapter 17, it is quite obvious that this statement [vv. 20–22] is not to be handled lightly, and glibly, and loosely, as if its meaning were perfectly clear and self-evident. Our Lord is dealing here with the mystical union which subsists between the three Persons of the blessed Trinity. It is the highest mystery of the Christian faith. And yet this is the term, the verse [v. 22] that is being banded about as if its meaning were obvious, and indeed as if it had but one meaning, namely some external organizational unity. Everything about the statement indicates the exact opposite. It is concerned about a unity of essence. That is the whole mystery of the Trinity. Now this is the way in which our Lord Himself defines this unity which already obtains among his people and which he prays God to preserve and keep after his return to glory.[2]

One shepherd (v. 20)

I do not pray for these alone, but also for those who will believe in me through their word.

This section of Christ's great prayer expresses the heart of Jesus as he looks to the future and the spread of Christianity around the world. The church would begin in Jerusalem but it would soon spread into Asia Minor and Europe, and then throughout the whole globe. Those who believed through the apostles' teaching and were added to the church (daily) (Acts 2:41; 4:4) are regarded as Christ's redeemed ones and part of his Body. They will bear witness to Jesus Christ's Lordship as Head of the universal church, and they will display a united testimony that Jesus Christ has been sent from the Father into this fallen world in order to be its Saviour.

Although this is the last section of Christ's prayer, it is closely connected to what has gone before, but now Christ concentrates specifically on the glorification of his people.

THE SHEPHERD'S PRAYERS

I do not pray for these alone.

It is worthy of note that no prayer for the dead is included in this High-Priestly intercession; that is because prayer can only be made for the living and for those yet to be born; the destiny of the dead is fixed in heaven or hell. Prayers for the dead assume that the subjects of prayer are not yet in heaven but are worthy of redemption and dwell in so-called Purgatory, where they are enduring temporal pains and an unspecified time of improvement in order to satisfy divine justice (making atonement) before being allowed into heaven. This unspecified time could be thousands of years! Yet the sixty-six books of the Bible give no warrant to believe in Purgatory or to pray for departed souls. The Epistles of the New Testament teach that there can be no change of character or destiny after death. The Gospel of Luke records Jesus himself teaching this in the Parable of the Rich Man and Lazarus (Luke 16:19–31).

This story is not a parable as normally understood by the term, but rather is to be regarded as an account of true history.[3] From it, we learn that people cannot get to heaven simply because they are wealthy or upstanding figures in society. Neither did the neglect of the poor by the rich man determine his destiny; rather it was the rich man's arrogance born of pride and unbelief that led to his omission from heaven and his eternal imprisonment in hell.[4] What is saddest of all in this narrative is that the rich man showed that he had not changed and was still as arrogant and unrepentant in hell as when on earth.

In John 17 Jesus prays only for the living and for those who will live in the future and—not for the dead. If it were desirable or important to pray for the dead, surely the Saviour would have taught us to do so and we would have an example of this type of intercession in the New Testament. Yet no such example is found. Hence we conclude that to pray for departed souls is at best superstition and at worst a denial of the gospel, which urges all people to respond believingly when they have the opportunity (John 3:14–15; Heb. 3:7–8, 15).[5] The Roman Catholic Church holds to praying for the dead and finds its authority for doing so in the Apocryphal book 2 Maccabees, where Judas Maccabeus prays for his men killed in battle: 'They turned to prayer, beseeching that the sin which had been committed might be wholly blotted out ... For if he were not expecting that those who had fallen would rise again, it would have been superfluous and foolish to pray for the dead ... Therefore he made atonement for the dead, that they might be delivered from their sin'

(12:42, 44–45). This contradicts the Bible, which teaches that there can be no change of character or destiny after death: 'It is appointed for men to die once, but after this the judgment' (Heb. 9:27).

The early Reformed churches were so conscious of this error of Rome that no prayers or exhortations were made at the graveside, lest 'some superstitious person think that singing and the reading of the living may profit the dead'.[6]

THE SHEPHERD'S PEOPLE

I ... pray ... also for those who will believe in Me.

Jesus has already prayed for the unity of the apostles (v. 11); now his concern is for the elect Jews and Gentiles who will make up the full complement of the redeemed church. His prayer is for all those who will hear the gospel after he has ascended into heaven. Jesus had said, 'Other sheep I have which are not of this fold; them also I must bring, and they will hear My voice; and there will be one flock and one shepherd' (John 10:16). Here the expression 'this fold' denotes the Jewish nation, while 'other sheep' speaks of all the elect chosen from before the foundation of the world out of the Gentile nations. Together they make up the 'one flock' who will believe in Jesus through the Bible's message.

Salvation is granted to those who trust believingly in Christ ('in Me') alone; he must be the object of faith for justification. There is no other way of salvation given by God to us, and it is by grace alone through faith alone (Eph. 2:8–9). Those who are right with God are those who hear his voice and follow him (John 10:3).

Christ intercedes for all God's people (Luke 22:31–32; Rom. 8:34; Heb. 7:25; 9:24)—the universal church; his prayers are not restricted to any one denomination, group or nationality in particular. This fact evokes praise and worship from the hearts of believers. Every believer reading John 17:20 can say, 'Jesus prayed for me some two thousand years ago!

Hallelujah!', and responds with love for the Saviour. Reflecting on this love, Charles Spurgeon wrote,

> Believers love Jesus with a deeper affection than they dare to give to any other being. They would sooner lose father and mother than part with Christ. Men have laboured to divide the faithful from their Master, but their attempts have been fruitless in every age. This is no every-day attachment which the world's power may at length dissolve. Neither man nor devil has found a key which opens this lock. Never has the craft of Satan been more at fault than when he has exercised it in seeking to rend in sunder this union of two divinely welded hearts. It is written, and nothing can blot out the sentence, 'The upright love thee' [S. of S. 1:4, KJV].[7]

THE SHEPHERD'S PILLARS

Through their word.

The apostles are Christ's chosen pillars on whom the church is founded (Gal. 2:9) and it is through their preaching and teaching that many after them will come to faith. This was their main role and has special reference to the New Testament Gospels and Epistles. The apostles were inspired by the Holy Spirit to write down the story of Jesus's life and grace in order that future generations would believe (John 1:14; 20:30–31; 2 Tim. 3:16). The apostles' teaching as found in the Bible is the church's message to the world. For Protestants, the 'apostolic succession' is preaching the faith of the apostles and prophets (Acts 2:42; Eph. 2:20; 4:11). The marks of the church are (1) the correct preaching and teaching of the gospel; (2) the correct administration of the two ordinances of baptism and the Lord's Supper; and (3) the correct administration of church discipline. The Word of God is normative and the keeping of its precepts and principles incumbent upon church leaders. Because the apostles are the foundation of the church (Eph. 2:20) we need to listen to 'their word'.

Today, copies of the Bible autographs are held in universities and libraries all around the world. Jesus was praying for these to be providentially and miraculously preserved so that the Christian faith would circumnavigate the globe. They have been translated into many languages and other tongues, as it is fitting to take the Word of God to our contemporaries so that they 'will believe in Me through their word'. Where there is an absence of Bible preaching there is a dearth of conversions; however, where one finds the Bible, there one finds the church.

Jesus's prayer at this point gives the people of God reason to preach and to be engaged in evangelism: it is the words of the apostles and prophets that bring faith to many. If faith comes by hearing the Word preached, preachers and missionaries must 'go and tell' (Rom. 10:14–17). God could have converted the Ethiopian eunuch without Philip (Acts 8:26–39) and the Roman centurion Cornelius without Peter (Acts 10); but he has ordained that the salvation of souls should come through the communication of the gospel from the lips of believers and the reading and hearing of the Bible. The gospel is found in the Word of God, and when it is believed and trusted it brings salvation; so let us pray that faith and trust will be found in the hearts of many unto salvation. 'For I am not ashamed of the gospel of Christ, for it is the power of God to salvation for everyone who believes, for the Jew first and also for the Greek. For in it the righteousness of God is revealed from faith to faith; as it is written, "The just shall live by faith"' (Rom. 1:16–17).

'It pleased God through the foolishness of the message preached to save those who believe' (1 Cor. 1:21; see also 2:4–5). Preaching is a timeless link between God and man, and is the medium that God uses to speak to his people. A man sent from God speaks for God. Many today have a low view of preaching, regarding it as merely a man giving some opinions and comments, even displaying personal prejudice. However, the Bible views preaching as a man speaking to God's people on God's behalf: 'How shall they preach unless they are sent?' (Rom. 10:15). Preaching is God's chief way of announcing his will to us: 'How shall they hear without a preacher?' (Rom. 10:14). Sadly, some people leave services of public worship before the sermon; this is because they regard the sermon as an option and not as the high point of the service. Yet preaching is the Lord's messenger speaking the Lord's message (Hag. 1:13). Therefore, the authority of the preacher is not in himself: he is merely the herald (from the Greek *kerux*, 'a herald' and *kerosso*, 'I proclaim' or 'I preach'). In times past the herald was of considerable importance. He was the monarch's messenger, the one through whom the monarch made known his will and laws. Likewise, the preacher is God's messenger and by means of him God reveals himself in the present through his Word. Preaching is thus a high and fearful task, for it is not about one man's opinions or ideas but a faithful reporting of God's mind as revealed in the whole Bible. It is a divine calling. Without close attention to God's Word, services can degenerate into a liturgical routine. Some traditions make the Eucharist or the Mass the focal point of Christian worship, and give no place to hearing the Word of God. This the Protestant Reformers rejected; they never set preaching and worship in opposition. They put the sermon in the place of the Mass and the pulpit in the place of the altar. Spurgeon said, 'True preaching is an act of faith, and is owned by the Holy Spirit as the means of working spiritual miracles.'[8] 'How beautiful are the feet of those who preach the gospel of peace, who bring glad tidings of good things!' (Rom. 10:15b).

Apostolic preaching is more than presenting a few thoughts that have occurred to the preacher through the week! Nor is it giving a little piece of advice. Bernard Lord Manning put it this way: preaching is 'a manifestation of the Incarnate Word, from the written Word, by the Spoken Word'.[9] It is not a lecture, for its aim is not simply to inform the mind but rather to convey the truths of Scripture and to motivate the will; or, as Charles Simeon said, to 'humble the penitent, to exalt the Saviour and to promote holiness'.[10] The preacher's task is to teach what the biblical text says and to explain it in the power of the Holy Spirit so that it is understood. Preaching is meant to feed the flock of God. It is not to be a series of short stories about one's private life loosely joined together by a few texts, but a discourse that feeds the soul with the meat and milk of the Word. It is like the sacred manna on which Israel fed in the wilderness: not cheese and biscuits but a main meal; not a 'P.S.' but the main letter. Preaching, therefore, is:

- directed to the mind, for hearing the Word of God is an action of the mind and we must apply our minds to it so that our souls are fed;
- directed to the conscience, for it is here that conviction of sin takes place and the peace of God for the forgiveness of sins is felt. Preaching calls for a response. Herbert Carson remarked, 'To view a congregation as being merely passive recipients of the spoken word is to put a sermon in the same category as a lecture or an after-dinner speech.'[11]

'He who has an ear, let him hear what the Spirit says to the churches' (Rev. 3:22). One cannot be neutral before God's Word. To detach ourselves or switch off will only harm us. God's house is the place to hear God's Word. Go there, not to criticize or to sleep, but to draw near and hear (Eccles. 5:1). We are not to apply what we hear to our neighbours, but we are to accept it for ourselves. A right attitude is important. If we come to worship in order to glorify God through praise and to humble ourselves before him in prayer, surely we will look forward with a true heart to hearing his Word. God expects us to respond well to him and to faithful preaching. Our response will glorify God if we recognize his Lordship over us and the beauty of his love for us.

One flock (v. 21)

I ... pray ... that they all may be one, as You, Father, are in Me, and I in You; that they also may be one in Us, that the world may believe that You sent Me.

Jesus now prays that all who believe in him will be party to spiritual harmony and he returns to the theme of verse 11: 'that they may be one as We are'. He does so with an eye to the mystical and eternal unity of the Father and Son. The unity of the churches is uppermost in the Lord's prayers, so much so that he repeats the petition 'that they may be one' with slight variation four times in verses 21–23. The pronoun 'they', used twice here, must be defined as the context demands, that is, 'those who will believe in Me through their word' (v. 20). His prayer has regard, therefore, to those who accept the gospel, are justified by faith and who are now the adopted children of God. Thus we can conclude that he is thinking about a unity of faith. This unity equates with the harmony shared by God the Father and Jesus Christ the Son. Unity of faith is to be seen in local churches: 'And they continued steadfastly in the apostles' doctrine and fellowship, in the breaking of bread, and in prayers' (Acts 2:42).

The apostle Paul, in his epistle to the Ephesians, tells us that the gifts to the churches of pastors and teachers are 'for the equipping of the saints … *till we all come to the unity of the faith*' (Eph. 4:12–13, emphasis added). This ministry will bring the saints to perfection (John 17:23).

THE EXAMPLE OF UNITY

That they all may be one, as You, Father, are in Me, and I in You.

Jesus illustrates the unity envisaged using the relationship of the Father with the Son in the Godhead. However, he makes a distinction between the essential and divine unity that exists between him and the Father, and our unity. He does not say, 'Let *us* all be one', but 'Let *them* be one': not 'as You, Father, are in *us*, and *we* in You', but 'as You, Father, are in *Me*, and *I* in You'. There is an eternal world of difference between Christ's Sonship and that of those adopted through faith into the family of God, and the Saviour clearly distinguishes these realities. This is emphasized by the apostle John's exclusive use of the Greek word *huois* (son) for Jesus and *tekna* (children) for the converted (John 1:12; 11:52; 1 John 3:1–2). Christ's Sonship is through eternal generation, while those who believe are God's children by grace through adoption (Gal. 4:4–5). The redeemed are united mystically to Christ and to one another because of the new birth and so possess a spiritual unity that is from God through conversion. Christ's prayer is, therefore, that the people of God will follow the *pattern* of unity that imitates the work of Father and Son and expresses the love between them.

There is no Sabellianism here, that is, the confounding of the Persons in the Trinity. Neither is there Arianism—that is, the dividing of the natures of the Persons of the Trinity. Jesus says not only that the Father is in him, but also that he is in the Father: they are united in one, sharing the same essence, experiencing prefect love and doing the same works. Thus Jesus prays that the spiritual union believers have will resemble in truth, love and good works the mystical union he has with the Father.

THE SECRET OF UNITY

That they also may be one in Us.

Unity is an intrinsic part of the grace of God in salvation. This is seen in the fact that all who are his are 'in [Him]' and abide in him and he in them. This is dependent on Jesus's words abiding in those who profess the Christian faith (15:1–7). The unity of which the Saviour prays is found only where and when people are found 'in Us'. It is therefore dependent on the free grace of God; it cannot be known outside of union with Christ and the Father, as it is only through Jesus Christ that such a variety and diversity of individual people can be included in spiritual unity. Outside of union with the Son, there cannot be unity of the type imagined here for it is based upon faith and truth, not on race, nationality or allegiance to a denomination or an assembly. Jesus is praying about something deeper and more miraculous than visible unity. He refers to that which is found alone among the regenerate and is expressed in love and kindness, but not at the absence of truth as defined in the Bible. Unity is not an option but a reality of Christianity, whether or not it is always properly expressed among the members of a congregation or those in a denomination.

Jesus's unity has to be kept 'in the bond of peace' (Eph. 4:3); thus where people are unregenerate, true unity cannot be found; and where people are quarrelling and judging one another, unity breaks down (Matt. 7:1–5; Eph. 4:2). Christ's plan for his saints is that they walk in the Spirit, abiding in him; walking in the flesh, on the other hand, destroys the peace of Jerusalem (Gal. 5:16–26; Eph. 5:1–7; 1 Peter 5:5–8).

THE PURPOSE OF UNITY

That the world may believe that You sent Me.

The commission of the church, whether local or universal, is to bring honour to the Son of God. Jesus knows that unity in the churches will exert power and spiritual influence in the world when its members are seen to love one another as they should (15:12). When the church is torn apart by division and strife the world is critical and perplexed, and remains unbelieving. The church's task is to bear clear witness to Christ's divine Person and to his atoning work on the cross, declaring one covenant of grace.

Is Christ's prayer a request for visible church unity as expressed in the various ecumenical bodies worldwide? If so, it has failed to be answered. We must look for another solution to its meaning. The phrase 'that the world may believe that You sent Me' does not necessarily imply visible oneness, as desired by some, such as the World Council of Churches. It is a request for the world's acceptance of Christ's divine mission and commission from the Father as Messiah and Saviour. When the churches all over the world meet for worship on the first day of the week, they are united in public witness to the glory of Jesus Christ as Redeemer and Lord. Nothing proclaims the glory of the Son of God more than the universal church's witness to his resurrection one day in seven. The command to meet every Lord's Day-Sabbath is designed to keep the resurrection of Jesus Christ before the world as an event to believe in and remember (Deut. 5:15; see also Rev. 1:10). The world will believe when it sees and hears what the church believes.

It is necessary to understand Christ's request aright. Does he pray that everyone in the world will be saved, implying that if that doesn't happen, church disunity is to blame? Consider the following:

- 'I *do not pray for the world* but for those whom You have given Me' (John 17:9, emphasis added); is it likely that he is praying for the world now?
- 'I ...pray ... for those who will believe in Me *through [the disciples'] word*' (v. 20, emphasis added). Has he changed his mind and is he now thinking that visible unity will be more powerful than the proclamation of the gospel? It may at first seem that he is saying that the salvation of the world will be achieved through the witness of a united universal church; however, it is only by faith in Christ that people are justified in God's sight, and it is the gospel that is the power of God unto salvation (Rom. 1:16–17).
- The world can 'believe' in Jesus Christ in the sense of accepting and not opposing him or his saints. In John 2:23–24 we read that 'many believed in His name ... But Jesus did not commit Himself to them, because He knew all men'. William Hendriksen comments, 'Because of the manner in which his power was displayed they accepted him as a great prophet. This, however, is not the same as saying that they surrendered their hearts to him. Not all faith is saving faith.'[12] Faith is created by the Holy Spirit through 'their word', that is, through the apostles' teaching (John 17:20; James

1:18; 1 Peter 1:3, 23). Jesus's purpose for his churches is that they bear witness to his divinity and his salvation, recognizing that division among believers hinders their good works. The people of God are to let their light shine to bring glory to God (Matt. 5:16).

One body (v. 22)

And the glory which you gave Me I have given them, that they may be one just as We are one.

As a divine Person in the Godhead Jesus shares the same eternal glory with his Father, but that is not the glory that is in view here. Nor does he speak about an 'acquired divinity', but about the Messianic glory given to him as the God-Man and High Priest of the people of God under the covenant of redemption. The source of this glory is the Father's love (12:27–28). The Mediator's glory is that he took upon himself our humanity (apart from sin), joining God and man together in a new indissoluble union, yet he did not cease to be the Word (*logos*) that existed in the beginning (1:1–3). Trinitarian theology calls this the hypostatic union (1:14).[13] The incarnation meant Jesus becoming 'bone of our bones and flesh of our flesh' (Gen. 2:23); nevertheless, we must remember that our Saviour remained always God and always true man, with no confusing or mixing of substance. The purpose of this union was to lift humanity out of its fallen condition of sin and misery, and it is the grounds for all the grace and glory that are bestowed upon the human nature. C. H. Spurgeon comments,

It is a sweet thought that Jesus Christ did not come forth without his Father's permission, authority, consent, and assistance. He was sent of the Father, that he might be the Saviour of men. We are too apt to forget that, while there are distinctions as to the *persons* in the Trinity, there are no distinctions of *honour*. We too frequently ascribe the honour of our salvation, or at least the depths of its benevolence, more to

Jesus Christ than we do the Father. This is a very great mistake. What if Jesus came? Did not his Father send him? If he spake wondrously, did not his Father pour grace into his lips, that he might be an able minister of the new covenant? He, who knoweth the Father, and the Son, and the Holy Ghost as he should know them, never setteth one before another in his love; he sees them at Bethlehem, at Gethsemane, and on Calvary, all equally engaged in the work of salvation.[14]

THE GLORY OF UNITY

And the glory which you gave Me I have given them.

These words have puzzled the commentators. Some think that 'glory' refers to the Holy Spirit, who is elsewhere called 'the Spirit of glory' (1 Peter 4:14); others think that it speaks of 'the happiness of the everlasting state, which is usually called glory in Scripture'.[15] However, I consider that John's words earlier in the Fourth Gospel give a satisfactory answer that fits nicely with the fundamental nature of Christ's prayer. The church is dependent on what the Saviour has accomplished for its salvation and on what he gives it for its sanctification (see John 17:12, 14, 18–19). In the earlier chapters of this Gospel, when John speaks of Christ's 'glory', he means 'grace and truth'; for example: 'And the Word became flesh and dwelt among us, and we beheld His glory, the glory as of the only begotten of the Father, full of grace and truth' (1:14). These two essentials—grace and truth—define 'glory'. Jesus Christ was 'full of grace and truth'; therefore, the granting of grace for salvation (Eph. 2:8–9) and the light of truth to inform and sanctify (John 14:9a, 16–17) seem to be what is meant. His death brought glory to himself and he shares it with his church. This glory is an essential element in the sanctifying work he is accomplishing and the public witnessing he has ordained for the churches to undertake.

It seems, then, that Jesus is speaking of a present glory (Eph. 1:17). Christ described himself as the Vine and believers as the branches (John

15). By faith, sinners are united to Christ, and believing union in Christ is the basis for all grace and truth received. Paul speaks of 'Christ in you, the hope of glory' (Col. 1:27). Because of their union with Christ, Christians are also united to all other believers (Eph. 4:4–6). However, this glory is also a progressive glory because of the work of the Holy Spirit (2 Cor. 3:17–18) and because it is something wonderfully promised to all who are 'in him' at the end of time:

> And we know that all things work together for good to those who love God, to those who are the called according to His purpose. For whom He foreknew, He also predestined to be conformed to the image of His Son, that He might be the firstborn among many brethren. Moreover whom He predestined, these He also called; whom He called, these He also justified; and whom He justified, these He also glorified.
> (Rom. 8:28–30)

THE MYSTERY OF UNITY

That they may be one just as We are one.

The people of God are not only one, but they are also in one another. They are not only in the same family; they are also in the same body.

> For as the body is one and has many members, but all the members of that one body, being many, are one body, so also is Christ. For by one Spirit we were all baptized into one body—whether Jews or Greeks, whether slaves or free—and have all been made to drink into one Spirit. For in fact the body is not one member but many.
> (1 Cor. 12:12–14)

'In the hypostatic union, our nature is united with Christ's nature; in the mystical union, our person with his person … Christ is in us, in that he lives in us, governs us, makes us partake of his righteousness, life and spirit [*sic*]; we are in him as branches in the tree, rays in the sun, rivers in the fountain.' Because of their mystical union, Christ and all Christian believers shall never be parted: 'in death the union is dissolved between the body and the soul but not between us and Christ ... The hypostatic union is the ground of all grace and glory that was bestowed on the human nature ... the mystical union is the ground of all grace and glory which believers receive (2 Cor. 5:21; Gal. 2:20; 1 John 4:4).'[16]

The reason why Jesus gives his people his glory (grace and truth) is 'that they may be one'. The unity between Saviour and redeemed sinner is both profound and real. It is not an option but a salvation reality; thus, Christians are 'all one in Christ Jesus' (Gal. 3:28), being united to one another through a mystical union with Christ and their adoption into the church family (Gal. 4:6–7). They are one body, joined together and cared for by the Good Shepherd of the sheep (John 10:11, 14–16). Their body life will be expressed in care for one another (15:12; Phil. 2:4). Their unity displays the visible and powerful effects of grace and truth to the world around them. We are more than brothers; we are one body in Christ (1 Cor. 12:20). The highest degree of unity is envisaged here, not moral perfection:

> And He Himself gave some to be apostles, some prophets, some evangelists, and some pastors and teachers, for the equipping of the saints for the work of ministry, for the edifying of the body of Christ, *till we all come to the unity of the faith and of the knowledge of the Son of God, to a perfect man, to the measure of the stature of the fullness of Christ.* (Eph. 4:11–13, emphasis added)

FOR FURTHER STUDY

1. What is required in order to pray well (Matt. 6:9–16; James 5:15–16)?
2. What are the marks of a true church?
3. What place has preaching in worship? Support your answer with Scripture.
4. What is meant by Jesus's words 'that they all may be one' (John 17:21)?

TO THINK ABOUT AND DISCUSS

1. What is the minimum of truth that is necessary to unite Christians in local-church fellowship?
2. Are the World Council of Churches and the Churches Together movements in the UK a biblical response to the concept of Christian unity in John 17?
3. How far should local churches of like faith and practice go to achieve outward unity?
4. What is required in order that the world might believe that the Father sent the Son (John 17:21, 23)?

Notes

1 **D. Martyn Lloyd-Jones,** *The Basis of Christian Unity: An Exposition of John 17 and Ephesians 4* (London: IVP, 1968), p. 12.

2 Ibid., pp. 12–13.

3 **Calvin** says, 'Some look upon it as a simple parable; but, as the name *Lazarus* occurs in it, I rather consider it to be the narrative of an actual fact'; *Commentary of the Harmony of the Gospels*, vol. ii, ch. 16 (CD-Rom; Christian Library series; Rio, WI: AGES Library, 2007).

4 See my *Opening Up 2 Thessalonians* (Leominster: Day One, 2008), pp. 37–38, for a short discussion on the doctrine of eternal punishment.

5 **Loraine Boettner,** *Roman Catholicism* (London: Banner of Truth, 1966) says that the practice of praying for the Christian dead began c. AD 300.

6 *First Book of Discipline*, 1560, in **David Laing,** (ed.), *The Works of John Knox*, vol. ii (Edinburgh: James Thin, 1895), pp. 183–260.

7 **C. H. Spurgeon,** *Morning and Evening* (McLean, VA: Macdonald Publishing, [n.d.]), 7 August, p. 440.

8 **C. H. Spurgeon,** *On Conversion As Our Aim*, quoted at www.thespurgeonfellowship.org/Spring09/hr_sp09_3.htm.

9 Quoted at 'Preaching—Defined', at www.thegracetabernacle.org/quotes/Preaching-Defined.htm; accessed March 2012.

10 **Charles Simeon,** quoted at www.preaching.com/resources/past-masters/11563684/page-2/; accessed March 2012.

11 **Herbert Carson,** *Hallelujah: Christian Worship* (Darlington: Evangelical Press, 1980), p. 70.

12 William Hendriksen, *The Gospel of John* (London: Banner of Truth, 1969), p. 127.

13 'The hypostatic union still exists and does so forever': **Robert Letham,** *The Holy Trinity* (New Jersey: P&R, 2004), p. 487.

14 C. H. Spurgeon, *Morning and Evening* (McLean, VA: Macdonald Publishing, [n.d.]), 5 February, p. 72.

15 Thomas Manton, *An Exposition of John 17* (Wilmington, DE: Sovereign Grace, 1972), p. 371.

16 Ibid., pp. 366–367.

The High Priest and his glory (vv. 23–26)

… I in them, and You in Me; that they may be made perfect in one, and that the world may know that You have sent Me, and have loved them as You have loved Me. Father, I desire that they also whom You gave Me may be with Me where I am, that they may behold My glory which You have given Me; for You loved Me before the foundation of the world. O righteous Father! The world has not known You, but I have known You; and these have known that You sent Me. And I have declared to them Your name, and will declare it, that the love with which You loved Me may be in them, and I in them.

One life (v. 23)

… I in them, and You in Me; that they may be made perfect in one, and that the world may know that You have sent Me, and have loved them as You have loved Me.

The believer's mystical union with Christ is described here in terms of the relationship that exists between the Persons of the Godhead, but now it is related to love and progressive sanctification. By God's free grace Christians share the victory of the death and resurrection of Christ and are sustained by the power of his endless life. Because of Christ's fullness, they receive 'grace for grace' (John 1:16), that is, one blessing after another. All the redeemed receive this added and ever-flowing grace in unbroken succession; its source is the fullness of the love and grace of Christ. The Scriptures have declared the love of God from the beginning (Gen. 3:15; Exod. 34:6–7) and Jesus's love reflects this as he is the dispenser of grace and truth in this final dispensation (John 1:17; 14:9b). From grace and truth flow the one life present in all who have believed.

MYSTICAL UNION

I in them, and You in Me.

Jesus speaks here regarding the union that the people of God have with himself and the Father, and there is nothing more basic to the doctrine of salvation than union and communion with him. It is incredible to know that this mystical union can be compared to the union that exists between the persons of the Trinity in the Godhead. Union with Christ means being 'in Christ'. This union is the goal of election love: the Father choosing us 'in Him before the foundation of the world' (Eph. 1:4). The people of God are united to Christ in his death, resurrection and his exaltation to heaven (Rom. 6:2–11; Eph. 2:4–6; Col. 3:3–4). Because of this mystical union, they are created anew and their new life is lived in fellowship with Christ. In death they fall asleep in Christ; because of their union they will be resurrected and glorified (Rom. 8:17; 1 Cor. 15:22; 1 Thes. 4:14, 16). As John Murray says, 'We thus see that union with Christ has its source in the election of the Father before the foundation of the world and has its fruition in the glorification of the sons of God.'[1] Murray also states that the mystical union the people of God have with their Saviour is only known from the Holy Scriptures, being 'revealed unto us by his Spirit and [the means] by which revelation and faith come to be known and appropriated by men'.[2] It is the Holy Spirit who joins the people of God to Christ (1 Cor. 12:13), so their mystical union is with the whole Godhead (1 John 1:3). It is a holy union (1 Peter 2:9), a loving union (S. of S. 1:13) and an eternal union (2 Cor. 5:17) from which flow all the graces required for the people of God to persevere in the faith (Gal. 5:22–23; Jude 24–25).

PERFECT UNION

That they may be made perfect in one.

Christ's prayer is for the ongoing maturity of his people. The NIV renders his words thus: 'May they be brought to complete unity.' Jesus identifies his glory (grace and truth) as necessary for perfecting unity in the one body, in order that one perfect life flowing from the Spirit's work of sanctification may be realized. Progress has to be made and perfection sought. Manton says, 'Our happiness in God is completed by degrees. In this life the foundation is laid ... but the complete fruition we have in heaven; there we are fully made perfect in one.'[3] Until heaven, Christian unity is to be understood in terms of doctrine and practice, accord and amity (1 Cor. 1:10) and comes about by the transforming and conforming work of God's Spirit in the lives of individual saints (2 Cor. 3:17–18). Christ's peace will be present where grace and truth are in abundance. J. C. Ryle says, 'Let us bear much, concede much, put up with much before we plunge into factions and separations.'[4] It takes time to bring the harvest to perfection, and it requires love shared freely and ungrudgingly to achieve happy churches (John 15:9; Phil. 2:5). The work of grace begun at conversion will be completed at the consummation of all things (Phil. 1:6; 3:21). Patience, of the bearing and forbearing type, is also required if happy unity of the faith ((Eph. 4:13) is to be preserved (see Col. 1:11). Christians may not always be of the same opinion on non-essential issues, but they should always have the same aim and purpose, as they have the same Saviour. C. H. Spurgeon writes,

When we were united by faith to Christ, we were brought into such complete fellowship with him, that we were made one with him, and his interests and ours became mutual and identical. We have fellowship with Christ in his *love*. What he loves we love. He loves the saints—so do we. He loves sinners—so do we. He loves the poor perishing race of man, and pants to see earth's deserts transformed into the garden of the Lord—so do we. We have fellowship with him in his *desires*. He desires the glory of God—we also labour for the same. He desires that the saints may be with him where he is—we desire to be with him there too. He desires to drive out sin—behold we fight under his banner. He desires that his Father's name may be loved and adored by all his creatures—we pray daily, 'Let thy kingdom come. Thy will be done on earth, even as it is in heaven.'[5]

EVIDENT UNION

That the world may know that You have sent Me.

Christ asks the Father to vindicate him against the world and that his work will continue. Christian evangelism and mission proclaim Jesus Christ as Saviour of the world (John 1:29). Schism and strife in and among the churches will temporarily hinder the effectiveness of the church militant. The world's judgement of the gospel is linked to the behaviour of the disciples of Christ. With this in mind, Christians are to live so that the gospel will be received well and Jesus Christ recognized as the Son of God incarnate. If offence is taken, it must not be because of the lifestyles of Christians or their bad manners; any offence must come only from the gospel itself.

Here again we see that grace and truth are key. If the churches fail to display the glory (grace and truth) given to them by the Saviour, how will the world know that Jesus Christ is the true Messiah and Son of God? The ongoing witness of the people of God to Jesus Christ as Lord is curtailed and contaminated if division and strife are present in the local churches. God's people are called to bear witness through good works to their union in Christ: 'Beloved, I beg you as sojourners and pilgrims, abstain from fleshly lusts which war against the soul, having your conduct honourable among the Gentiles, that when they speak against you as evildoers, they may, by your good works which they observe, glorify God in the day of visitation' (1 Peter 2:11–12).

LOVING UNION

That the world may know that You ... have loved them as You have loved Me.

Christ is the Father's one and only Son and the first object of his love: 'And suddenly a voice came from heaven, saying, "This is My beloved Son, in whom I am well pleased"' (Matt. 3:17). His dignity and holiness as Mediator are also deserving of God's love: 'My Father loves Me, because I lay down My life that I may take it again' (John 10:17). Jesus is precious to the Father, who has put all things into his hand (John 3:35) and pledges his love to us in and through Christ his Beloved (Eph. 1:6).

The Father loves the church with the same purity and passion; Christ says, 'You ... have loved them [the church] as You have loved Me'. His church is loved freely, everlastingly, purely, genuinely, affectionately, unchangeably and for ever. In his love he bestows the special fruit of the Spirit (Gal. 5:22–23), as well as acceptance, protection, patience and reward.

The love of the Son for the church is clearly demonstrated through the cross: 'Greater love has no one than this, than to lay down one's life for his friends' (John 15:13). The gospel proclaims that Jesus Christ gave his life a ransom for many, and it declares that he was stirred by the highest motives of love. His sacrifice was a clear and powerful reflection of his love for sinners 'lost and ruined by the fall'.[6] He 'loved the church and gave Himself for her' (Eph. 5:25). Thus, his love was of the highest and purest sort.

The Father is pleased with Christ and Christ is pleased with the Bride for whom he died (Matt. 3:17; Eph. 5:25). Manton says, 'As the end of [the Father's] love to Christ's human nature was to bring it to heaven, so the end of God's love to us is to sanctify us, and so to make way for glory.'[7]

One glory (v. 24)

Father, I desire that they also whom You gave Me may be with Me where I am, that they may behold My glory which You have given Me; for You loved Me before the foundation of the world.

Our High Priest is coming to the end of his prayer and his thoughts turn to heaven and the glory to come. He has prayed for the things that concern his people's well-being here below; now he thinks on the things above. Jesus's previous prayers were for the happiness of the church in the present world. Now he prays for them in the world to come. Having recounted the wonderful love of the Father towards himself in the previous verse, he deliberately speaks of it once more, as if to emphasize it and drive home its reality and implications to the minds and hearts of his followers.

HIS LONGING

Father, I desire that they also whom You gave Me may be with Me where I am.

His request concerns his elect ones, those chosen by the Father and given to him as his own possession (compare vv. 2, 6, 9, 11–12). The church is not one denomination but is made up of all the elect from all ages and dispensations: all those who have been washed in Christ's blood, justified by faith alone and indwelt by his Holy Spirit (Rev. 19:6–8). Today, the church militant is rent asunder by denominational division, but the church triumphant is glorified and made perfect through Christ's atoning sacrificial work on the cross. He died to bring his people to glory. They will share in heavenly realities and the eternal blessings found in him alone (Rev. 7:9–10; 21:1–5).

Jesus's deep-rooted, tender care and concern for those the Father has given him comes through strongly. In this prayer, Christ is writing his last will and testament, and it requests that his people be with him in heaven and share in his glory. He is always thinking of them and he always wants the best for them. He has loved them to the end (John 13:1). It is striking that he reveals his personal desire; we see that Christ's desire is God's promise to the people of God. This thought is worthy of meditation. When we realize that our Saviour always did and said what the Father wished, we realize that his prayer requests are indeed the very promises of God. Those issues raised by the Mediator are the plans and blessings that God has ordained for his people.

After Christ's resurrection he ascended to heaven in his glorified body to sit at the right hand of the Father (Luke 24:50–53; Acts 1:9–10; Heb. 1:3–4). He took sinless, perfect human nature to heaven. His ascension bestowed great and essential blessings on the church and now, as he is reigning in heaven, he is praying for the church (Rom. 8:34; Heb. 7:25; 9:24). Heaven for the believer is where Christ is. It has been said that it is the company and not the place that makes happiness flourish. However, it is always to be remembered that heaven is a place prepared for the redeemed (John 14:1–2). Death will not be easy, but heaven will be ecstasy. As soon as the soul of a believer leaves the body, the spirit enters the immediate presence of God and the company of Christ. This is Paradise and joy (Ps. 16:11; Luke 23:43; 2 Cor. 12:2; Phil. 1:23; Heb. 9:24).

Heaven

When one thinks on the Christian view of heaven two distinctions must be grasped. It helps to keep these two ideas separate as this prevents us from confusing the scriptural information on the topic.

Immediately at death we will enter what is best called the 'intermediate state' and which the Bible calls 'heaven'. It is a disembodied state when the spirit is separated from the body. Richard Baxter wrote, 'The spirits in heaven enjoy the general happiness of the love of God and Christ, and the pleasurable review of providence.'[8] Where are the dead who die in Christ? They are in heaven, where God dwells with his holy angels. This is the place to which Jesus Christ ascended after his resurrection. Thus, heaven is not a state of being but a place of dwelling (Ps. 33:13; John 3:13; 6:33–51; 2 Cor. 12:1–4; 1 Peter 3:22). The Holy Scriptures teach that 'to be absent from the body [is] to be present with the Lord' (2 Cor. 5:8). This is the same heaven that Jesus our Lord promised to the thief on the cross, when he died believing Christ to be the Jewish Messiah (Luke 23:43).

Thus there is a *present* heaven; but there is also a *future* heaven, the 'resurrection state' also taught in the Scriptures, which is prophesied to take place when Jesus Christ comes again a second time (1 Cor. 15) and which will consist of God's heaven and the 'new heaven and ... new earth' joined together and made one (Rev. 21:1–4; 2 Peter 3:13). Those in the present heaven are awaiting the resurrection day, when all people will be raised from the dead (John 5:28–29). The present condition of those who died in Christ is still blessed and glorious, even though they are bereft of a body; but this bodiless existence is not their final resting place. They are limited to heaven and not yet in possession of the earth, which, along with new heavens, has been promised to them as an inheritance (1 Peter 1:3–4). In the present heaven, the soul awaits the heavenly shout of the Son of God at the Second Coming, when Christ will bring the redeemed disembodied spirits with him as he returns to earth. God's people are waiting for the Day of the Lord, when they will take possession of their promised inheritance and be given their just rewards (1 Thes. 3:13; 4:14–18; 1 Peter 1:3–4). Augustine said that when in heaven, the saints are clothed in 'immortal and spiritual bodies, and the flesh shall live no longer in a fleshly but a spiritual fashion'.[9]

When one thinks about heaven, then, one needs to remember the distinction that the Bible makes between disembodied spirits and resurrected bodies. The former state follows death while the latter follows the resurrection. One is existence in an ethereal (celestial) body, and the other is existence in the resurrected body. Nevertheless, it is valid to call both 'heaven'. The first is the heaven of 'just men made perfect' (Heb. 12:23), while the second is that of the 'new heaven and a new earth' (Rev. 21:1).

HIS GLORY

That they may behold My glory which You have given Me.

In John 17:1 the Son showed that he longs to bring glory to the Father—that is, he longs to reveal his grace and truth to the world. Now he speaks of 'My glory which You have given Me' and requests that his church, whether in heaven or earth, will 'behold' ('take notice'; thus, look at and survey) who he really is. The word 'behold' in the Bible always calls our attention to something great, wonderful and important (see Ps. 133:1; John 1:36; 1 John 3:1).

On his ascension, Christ was crowned with glory and honour, which inspired the inhabitants of heaven to sing the praises of their Redeemer King in the fullest joy (Ps. 24:7–10). Jesus has taken human nature, in its perfect, sinless and eternal condition, into heaven. He wants his people to witness 'the radiance of his divine attributes as reflected in his exalted human nature'.[10] It is 'My glory' because it belongs to him as the Lamb of God who takes away the sin of the world (1:36), as mighty Liberator of the elect (Matt. 25:31) and as Lord of glory (1 Cor. 2:8). He is also referring to his glory that shall be revealed when he comes a second time with all his angels to judge the world in truth and righteousness:

> Then the sign of the Son of Man will appear in heaven, and then all the tribes of the earth will mourn, and they will see the Son of Man coming on the clouds of heaven with power and great glory. And He will send His angels with a great sound of a trumpet, and they will gather together His elect from the four winds, from one end of heaven to the other.
> (Matt. 24:30–31)

In heaven, the people of God will be able to observe and explore his glory, as well as rejoice in him through all eternity.

> We are happy in his happiness, we rejoice in his exaltation. There is no purer or more thrilling delight to be known this side heaven than that of having Christ's joy fulfilled in us, that our joy may be full. His *glory* awaits us to complete our fellowship, for his Church shall sit with him upon his throne, as his well-beloved bride and queen.[11]

Because of sin and unbelief we have all come short of his glory, but because of God's grace through the gospel of Christ the elect will share in it for ever (Rom. 3:23; 1 Cor. 2:7; Col. 1:27; 2 Thes. 2:14). What the Queen of Sheba said of King Solomon's servants will be said in Jesus's presence in heaven: 'Happy are your men and happy are these your servants, who stand continually before you and hear your wisdom!' (1 Kings 10:8). There all God's people will sing, 'Blessing and honor and glory and power be to Him who sits on the throne and to the Lamb, forever and ever!' (Rev. 5:13b).

HIS ELECTION

... My glory which You have given Me; for You loved Me before the foundation of the world.

Once again Jesus speaks of his incarnation glory (see v. 22), his Messianic office and High-Priestly role. This was not a mere dwelling in a human body in the same way that the Holy Spirit indwells the believer, but the union of Jesus's divine nature with sinless human nature. Liberal theologians say that Jesus the man 'acquired divinity'; however, Christ is two different (diverse) substances united into one Person. It is now an indissoluble union: he has taken our nature into heaven. He is the last Adam and the second Man, which means that the plan of redemption was accomplished by God the Son:

'The first man Adam became a living being.' The last Adam became a life-giving spirit ... The first man was of the earth, made of dust; the second Man is the Lord from heaven. As was the man of dust, so also are those who are made of dust; and as is the heavenly Man, so also are those who are heavenly. And as we have borne the image of the man of dust, we shall also bear the image of the heavenly Man. (1 Cor. 15:45–49)

The doctrine of election is one of the great themes of the Bible, and the

Son, whom God loved before the foundation of the world, was God's 'Elect One' (Isa. 42:1). The Old Testament likewise reveals God's choice of Israel from among all the nations of the world. The ground of eternal election is the love of God, whether it be the election of Christ (Matt. 3:17; Eph. 1:6) or that of the chosen people of God (Deut. 7:7–8a; 14:2; Rom. 9:13). John 17:24 expresses the Father's love for the Son, which flows out from eternity past. As Manton puts it, 'Absolute elective love is the Father's property and personal operation; but then his eternal purpose is brought to pass in and through Jesus Christ.'[12] The expression 'the foundation of the world' is found ten times in the New Testament and it reveals that the Father chose Jesus to be the Saviour of his people as a sovereign act of God's will and a gift of God's grace to the world. Peter tells us that Christ was the sacrificial Lamb of God given for the elect's redemption: 'He indeed was foreordained before the foundation of the world, but was manifest in these last times for you' (1 Peter 1:20). From those words we see that God planned the way of salvation—it was 'foreordained'—through the shedding of the blood of Christ, 'before the foundation of the world'. In the Council of Redemption (sometimes called the Council of Peace or the Council of Eternity) Father, Son and Holy Spirit entered into an eternal covenant to glorify the Son through the saving of the elect (Ps. 2:7–9; 89:3; Zech. 6:13; 1 Peter 1:20). As a result of this covenant of redemption, the Word 'was sent from God, received his assignment from God and received certain promises from God'; 'he did not come of his own initiative alone but on terms agreed with the Father'.[13] The covenant of redemption made before the foundation of the world was that in which the Son consented to be the Surety (Mediator) on behalf of those whom the Father had given him:

- The Father loved the Son (Matt. 3:17)
- The Father loved *us* in the Son (Rom. 8:15)
- The Father *chose* us in the Son (Eph. 1:4–6)

- The Father *saves* us through the atoning blood of the Son (1 Peter 1:18–20)

Love found a way to redeem my soul,
Love found a way that could make it whole ...
(Avis M. Christiansen, 'Wonderful Love That Rescued Me', 1915)

One knowledge (v. 25)

O righteous Father! The world has not known You, but I have known You; and these have known that You sent Me.

As his intercession concludes, Christ is still addressing God as his Father. He has taught his disciples that he does nothing alone, but everything is decided in consultation and in combination with his Father. His knowledge of the Father extends from eternity past and is both perfect and absolute, not only because he is the Father's Son, but also because of their unity and harmony in the eternal Godhead, by which they share one essence and life.

THE ATTRIBUTES OF GOD

O righteousness Father!

This expression speaks of the divine nature of God the Father. God's attributes can be divided into those that he alone possess as the Almighty and Eternal One, and those he has given to man, who was made in his image at creation (Gen. 1:26). God has revealed himself in his attributes, which tell us what and who he is. They reveal those essential qualities that define him as God (1 Tim. 1:17; 6:15–16). Berkhof says that the Being of God does not admit any scientific definition, because it is hidden from us; yet we are not ignorant of God's character, for we have the Holy Scriptures.[14] The Old Testament tells us that God's name is 'I AM WHO I

AM' (Exod. 3:14), revealing that he is self-existent, self-contained and totally independent. The New Testament reveals that 'God is Spirit' (John 4:24), revealing the spiritual nature of God. The early church fathers felt that it was impossible to gain an adequate knowledge of the divine essence because of the transcendence of God. The Reformers agreed that the essence of God is incomprehensible, but they did not exclude the possibility of some knowledge of it. They declared the unity, simplicity and spirituality of God. Thus God in his Being is incomprehensible (Job 11:7), immaterial (John 4:24) and unchangeable (Exod. 3:14–15). These attributes are inherent to him: they are natural to and innate in God.[15] The Bible assumes that God exists and declares him to be omniscient (all-knowing—John 21:17b); omnipotent (all-powerful—Matt. 19:26); and omnipresent (everywhere present—Ps. 139:7–12).

THE KNOWLEDGE OF GOD

The world has not known You, but I have known You; and these have known that You sent Me.

God communicates the knowledge of himself to man and can be known only as he actively makes himself known. He is the *subject* of this communication: it is he who communicates it. He is also the *object* of this communication: the knowledge he conveys reveals himself to us; therefore, if there is no revelation there is no knowledge of God. Revelation is God *actively* making himself known; it is a supernatural act of self-communication mediated through creation and the Holy Bible. However, not all people understand this revelation (1 Cor. 2:14). Nevertheless, Christians believe from the Scriptures that all people are given a natural knowledge of supernatural realities (Rom. 1:19; 2:14–15), and there is also divine external revelation when the gospel is preached (2 Peter 2:5), both of which render all people without excuse. Thus there is an acquired knowledge of God, and there is also an innate knowledge specific to us as creatures made in the image of God (Gen. 1:26; Rom. 1:19). Reformed theologians talk of 'ingrafted or implanted' knowledge, but evolutionary naturalists deny both (they say that there is no God; thus there is no knowledge of God). The innate knowledge is ours by birth, while acquired knowledge is gained through the study of God's revelation both in nature and the Bible (Ps. 19; Rom. 1:19–23). The Reformers said that even natural revelation was obscured by the Fall; thus men and women cannot read it aright. Therefore, God in the Bible, as Louis Berkhof says, 'republished the truths of natural revelation to clear them of misrepresentation and to interpret them for us'.[16] Not only this, but God also 'provided a cure for spiritual blindness in the work of regeneration and sanctification so that we can obtain a true knowledge of God'.[17]

Thus in John 17:25 Jesus is stressing the necessity of a real and personal knowledge of God that the Son alone can give. This knowledge is so vital that without it one cannot be a Christian in the truest sense of the word (John 17:3). It is more than a merely intellectual knowledge (although it is true that the mind is fully engaged), for it is experienced in the soul as well. Christ wants his people to 'know' (*ginosko*) God in a saving and spiritual way. All types of faith require knowledge: saving faith (Rom. 10:14); sanctifying faith (2 Peter 3:18a); persevering faith; and the faith that brings Christians to worship the divine Persons. All acts of faith require knowledge beyond that found solely in creation or the imagination; worship without the knowledge given to us in the Holy Scriptures is blind guesswork.

We have seen from this verse that the knowledge of God is vital to true faith. What and who God is are always relevant questions for every generation. Without this revelation we all remain lost and under condemnation, awaiting judgement. Here we see again the battle for the Bible. We go wrong in religion when we think that Christianity does not need the Bible to teach us about the character and divinity of Jesus Christ, or about man's need of redemption and the knowledge of the way of salvation.

One mission (v. 26)

And I have declared to them Your name, and will declare it, that the love with which You loved Me may be in them, and I in them.

Here we come to the end of the greatest prayer ever made. It contains the Saviour's last words and thoughts before his arrest. How precious they should be to God's people everywhere! He prays again about his mission and how it must continue even after he has ascended into heaven. His burden is for the Father's name to be known and God's love shed abroad in his people's hearts by the Holy Spirit (Rom. 5:5).

GREAT NAME

I have declared to them Your name, and will declare it.

Jesus's mission was to speak of and make the Father known to the world (3:16). This knowledge of the Father is not religious knowledge, such as might be found in an encyclopaedia or dictionary, but that which leads one into the kingdom of God. Christ's words bring saving knowledge that lead to repentance and faith (6:63b). God is understood when *his name* is known. There is no name as such given to the Father in the New Testament; however, the Old Testament reveals the Trinitarian God by degrees through various names and titles, such as Elohim, El Shaddai, Adoni, Jehovah, the Lord of Hosts and so on. However, in John 17 Jesus speaks of the Father as holy and righteous (vv. 11, 25) and as the Father of his elect people (vv. 2, 6, 9, 11–12). The prophetic and teaching ministries of Jesus revealed both what and who God is. Christ says that the world does not know God the Father, but the Son knows him and has made him known to those who believe by revealing 'Your name' to them.

> [Jesus said,] 'If you had known Me, you would have known My Father also; and from now on you know Him and have seen Him.' Philip said to Him, 'Lord, show us the Father, and it is sufficient for us.' Jesus said to him, 'Have I been with you so long, and yet you have not known Me, Philip? He who has seen Me has seen the Father ...'
>
> (John 14:7–9)

God revealed his eternal personality to Moses when he spoke to him at the burning bush: 'And God said to Moses, "I AM WHO I AM." And He said, "Thus you shall say to the children of Israel, 'I AM has sent me to you'"' (Exod. 3:14). This incident was a pre-incarnation appearance of Jesus Christ. Henry Law speaks of it thus:

> 'I AM WHO I AM.' Such is the voice from the burning bush. The Speaker, then, is hid in no mask of mystery. It is the Angel of the everlasting Covenant. It is the great Redeemer. 'I AM WHO I AM.' Jesus, as God, here puts on eternity as his robe. He knows no past. He knows no future. He lives unmoved in one unmoving present. He stretches through all the ages which are gone and which are yet to come ... If there had been a moment when his being dawned, his name would be 'I am what I was not'. If there could be a moment when his being must have end, his name would be 'I am what I shall not be'. But his is, 'I AM WHO I AM' ... That child is the eternal 'I AM'. He whose Deity never had birth, is born of the woman's seed. He, who never began to be, as God, here begins to be, as man.[18]

Isaiah also speaks of Jesus's pre-incarnation glory: 'In the year that King Uzziah died, I saw the Lord sitting on a throne, high and lifted up, and the train of His robe filled the temple' (Isa. 6:1). In Isaiah's vision, he saw 'the LORD of hosts' (Isa. 6:5, Hebrew *Yahweh*); however, it was the pre-incarnate Christ who captured Isaiah's vision. We know this from John 12, where John quotes from Isaiah 6:10 and then notes, 'These things Isaiah said when he saw His glory and spoke of Him' (v. 41, referring to Christ). Jesus is Lord.

Jesus's mission as Prophet and High Priest to God's people was to declare the works and character of God the Father. After Jesus's ascension to heaven the Holy Spirit would take on the role of teacher in his place (John 14:26). He would be sent forth from the Father and from the Son to continue to make known the Father's name through the ministry of preaching, teaching, evangelism and outreach carried out first by the apostles and then by their successors (15:26–27; 16:13–15). Jesus expects the church militant to take the gospel into the entire world. This emphasizes the responsibility that the churches and individual believers have been given by the Saviour in making the gospel known (Matt. 28:19–20; Rom. 10:14b; Eph. 4:11–13). The Lord's work is to continue through the ministry of the people of God empowered by the Spirit. The Holy Spirit speaks through the Word (John 16:12–15). The new birth flows from the ministry of the Word and the Spirit (1 Peter 1:23), producing love as its fruit (1 John 4:7). Missionary work, as the fruit of love, must be the church's continued priority both at home and abroad. Paul wrote,

> To me ... this grace was given ... to make all see what is the fellowship of the mystery, which from the beginning of the ages has been hidden in God who created all things through Jesus Christ; to the intent that now the manifold wisdom of God might be made known by the church to the principalities and powers in the heavenly places.
>
> (Eph. 3:8–10)

GREAT LOVE

That the love with which You loved Me may be in them, and I in them.

When faced with the loneliness of the task ahead Jesus found that falling back on the eternal and tender love of the Father comforted and sustained him. He knew that God's love is as ancient as himself, and there was no time that he did not think on him and love him. Here he uses the word 'love' in the conclusion of his intercession, as it has underpinned all that he has already said and requested. The aim of the gospel is that men and women might know God and possess his love in their hearts, for love is the greatest gift, and from it all divine graces flow to us (Isa. 38:17; John 17:3; 1 Cor. 13:13; Rev. 1:5). His love is the forerunner of all good works done by the people of God. It is this love that causes us to be adopted as the children of God: 'Behold what manner of love the Father has bestowed on us, that we should be called children of God!' (1 John 3:1).

The love of God is not only shown towards us but it is in us when we are in Christ (Rom. 8:38–39; 1 John 4:16). It is important to note that we are loved from eternity, but not justified from eternity. Before we know God we are lost, under the condemnation of a broken law and unconscious of his love towards us. We are not forgiven and cleansed in the blood of the Lamb until we repent and believe. Before we know God as our Father in Christ, the love of God is towards us, but not in us. This love in us has a practical effect in our souls and results in the feeling of assurance of salvation. John Calvin defined faith thus: 'it is a firm and sure knowledge of the divine favour toward us, founded on the truth of a free promise in Christ, and revealed to our minds, and sealed in our hearts, by the Holy Spirit'.[19] The Puritans spoke of assurance as the fruit of faith growing out of faith. Assurance was to them faith fully grown and come of age. There can be faith without assurance, but where assurance is present it is an aspect of faith, organically related to it, not something distinct and separate from it. Faith is thus regarded as containing a measure of assurance within itself from the outset. Assurance is not usually given until faith has been tried, seasoned, ripened and strengthened by conflict with doubt and fluctuation of feeling. For most, assurance is a conscious condition of mind and heart induced by the Spirit's witnessing activity and is a side effect of the sealing of the Spirit, rather than being integral to the act of sealing as such.[20] Assurance flows from both the work and the witness of the Holy Spirit in us (Rom. 5:5). It is possible for believers to have the effects of God's love seen in their lives and not feel it; for, as Manton says, 'the effects of love do always abide, for it is an immortal seed, but the sense of love is flitting and changeable'.[21] Thus Jesus prays that the people of God may have the comfort of assurance and feel themselves beloved of the Father.

FOR FURTHER STUDY

1. How is the union of the three Persons in the Trinity to be expressed in our churches?
2. What are the fruits of the believer's mystical union with Christ?
3. What is the intermediate state, and what does it mean for those who die in Christ and those who die but are not Christians?
4. Write out the incommunicable and the communicable attributes of God. Find Scripture references that demonstrate each one.
5. What is the relationship between the 'I AM' of Exodus 3:14 and the 'I am' sayings of Jesus?

TO THINK ABOUT AND DISCUSS

1. Discuss the significance of Christ being in heaven in bodily form.
2. What is the glory Jesus speaks of in John 17:24?
3. Worship is the regenerate soul coming before God to offer up *spiritual sacrifices* (1 Peter 2:5). Discuss this statement.
4. What does it mean for the love of God to be 'in' believers?

Notes

1 **John Murray,** *Redemption Accomplished and Applied* (London: Banner of Truth, 1961), pp. 161–162.

2 Ibid., p. 167.

3 **Thomas Manton,** An *Exposition of John 17* (Wilmington, DE: Sovereign Grace, 1972), p. 384.

4 **J. C. Ryle,** *Expository Thoughts on the Gospels: John*, vol. iii (London: James Clarke & Co., 1969), p. 221.

5 **C. H. Spurgeon,** *Morning and Evening* (McLean, VA: Macdonald Publishing, [n.d.]), 23 November, p. 656.

6 **Joseph Hart,** 'Come, Ye Sinners, Poor and Needy', 1759.

7 **Manton,** *John 17*, p. 395.

8 Quoted by **W. M. Smith,** *The Doctrine of Heaven* (Chicago: Moody Press, 1977), p. 201, n.

9 Quoted in Ibid.

10 **Manton,** *John 17*, [n.p.].

11 **C. H. Spurgeon,** *Morning and Evening* (McLean, VA: Macdonald Publishing, [n.d.]), 23 November, p. 656.

12 **Manton,** *John 17*, p. 390.

13 **D. Macleod,** 'Covenant Theology', in **Nigel M. de S. Cameron,** (ed.), *Dictionary of Scottish Church History and Theology* (Edinburgh: T & T Clark, 1993).

14 **Louis Berkhof,** *Systematic Theology* (London: Banner of Truth, 1971), p. 237.

15 Ibid., pp. 41–56. I am indebted to Berkhof for what follows.

16 Ibid., p. 237.

17 Ibid.

18 **Henry Law,** *The Gospel in Exodus* (London: Banner of Truth, 1967), pp. 13–15.

19 **John Calvin,** *Calvin's Institutes* (Grand Rapids, MI: Associated Publishers & Authors Inc., 1970), 3:2:7.

20 See **J. I. Packer,** *A Quest for Godliness* (Wheaton, IL: Crossway, 1990), pp. 180–183.

21 **Manton,** *John 17*, p. 444.

A sermon: Help when you need it most

The theme of this sermon is Christ's Priesthood and its continuing benefits to the people of God. This portion of Scripture shows us why prayer is worthwhile and proves to be powerful with God. My text (Heb. 4:16) is an exhortation to come before Jesus Christ in prayer and speak with boldness. It informs us that if we do so, he will meet with us at the throne of grace as our great High Priest. We can come fearlessly to him because of the heavenly sitting of Christ at the right hand of God (his Session), where he is now actively engaged in the continuation of his mediatorial work as our ascended and great High Priest. Here we have a clear view of his Priestly office on behalf of the people of God. From this verse of Scripture, we find great encouragement to be often at the place of prayer, being assured of his willingness to meet sinners at the mercy seat.

> Let us therefore come boldly to the throne of grace, that we may obtain mercy and find grace to help in time of need. (Heb. 4:16)

Here is an exhortation to come fearlessly before God. Our Saviour, Jesus Christ, will meet with us there as our great High Priest and he will guide our prayers into heaven. Thus we find great encouragement to pray and to be found in the place of prayer.

The Epistle to the Hebrews focuses on Jesus Christ and his eternal Priesthood. He is not just one priest among many, but the supreme High Priest and Head of the church. His credentials as Head of the church are established in this epistle, for Jesus has been shown to be superior to the prophets, to the angels and to Aaron, and he is greater than Moses. Hebrews 3:14–10:18 forms the main portion of this epistle. Jesus Christ was no ordinary priest but High Priest *par excellence*. In this section of Hebrews the words translated 'High Priest' literally mean 'great priest' in the Greek, signifying that Christ is the greatest of all the high priests of God. His humanity has qualified him from a human standpoint, while his deity has qualified him from God's perspective. His Priesthood is above that of all others; and he has made all other priests redundant, outmoded and unnecessary as his is an eternal Priesthood, for he ever lives to make intercession for us. Greater than Aaron, Israel's ancient high priest, Christ is beloved and recognized by the Father, being faithful and powerful in his works.

Christ's ascension

In Hebrews 4 we learn that lack of faith in the gospel of our Lord Jesus Christ will keep many from the blessings to come, while faith and trust will be rewarded with salvation and God's promised rest. Thus the readers are encouraged to make every effort, by rejecting unbelief and disobedience (v. 11), that they may know salvation through Jesus Christ alone. This is a warning to us all, for God knows the hearts of everyone (v. 13). However, as always, we are pointed to Jesus Christ, God's Son and the Saviour of the world. He is now in heaven, for he has 'passed through the heavens' (v. 14) into heaven itself. His ascension was a very important event for the church. It reassures believers that the work of Jesus Christ is complete and acceptable to God the Father, and that Christ succeeded in the task of reconciling sinners to God. Because of this, Christ is deserving of exaltation. Ascension Day was Christ's coronation day: 'Lift up your heads, O you gates! And be lifted up, you everlasting doors! And the King of glory shall come in' (Ps. 24:7).

He has entered heaven to reign over his enemies, being crowned with glory and honour (Heb. 2:9). He governs as King from his heavenly throne (Heb. 8:1), and rules over angels (1 Peter 3:22), the church (Eph. 1:22) and the world (Heb. 2:6–8). It was Paul who said, 'For He must reign till He has put all enemies under His feet' (1 Cor. 15:25). Faith in *this* Saviour and *this* Priest is essential to the receiving of God's grace and help in time of need. 'Seeing then that we have a great High Priest who has passed through the heavens, Jesus the Son of God, let us hold fast our confession' (Heb. 4:14).

Let us notice three things:

1. The grounds for coming boldly to the throne of grace (v. 15)

For we do not have a High Priest who cannot sympathize with our weaknesses, but was in all points tempted as we are, yet without sin.

As High Priest, Jesus Christ is at the very centre of our religion, because his Priesthood is fundamentally linked with atonement for sin. 'The priesthood of Christ is invested with great importance ... and is the very turning point on which our Salvation depends' (John Calvin). The concept and office of priest has been highjacked by other religions and the original and pure stream has become polluted; but if one goes back to the Word of God the origin of the priesthood and the scope of its ministry can be found. God recognizes only those whom *he* has ordained as his priests (Heb. 5:1–4). The peoples of all religions recognize the need for priesthood, but God has only one High Priest. Old Testament Jewish priests were a group which foreshadowed the one who was to come as Messiah. They were a model or pattern, a kind, which exemplified the characteristics of holiness. They prefigured and represented the Saviour still to come. God cannot be approached without a priest. Why is this so? Because he says so, and because God is holy! The Priesthood of Jesus Christ is as relevant to the New Testament as the Aaronic priesthood was to the Old Testament. It is essential to the gospel and was ordained by God in the covenant of redemption.

Jesus Christ is God and Man; thus he is full of sympathy for us (v. 15). He understands the problems of living in a fallen world and the power of sin and temptation. He did not sin, being unable to do so; however, he sympathizes with us in our weakness. To 'sympathize' means 'to suffer with' and expresses the feeling of one who has entered into suffering. He was in all points tempted, and experienced every degree of temptation (2:18) because he has shared our humanity; therefore he understands the testings which we now endure. He 'was in all points tempted as we are, yet without sin'. In all our sorrows, we have his sympathy. Temptation, pain, disappointment, weakness, weariness, poverty—he knows them all, for he has felt all. Spurgeon says, 'We are told that the Captain of our salvation was made perfect through suffering, therefore we who are sinful, and who are far from being perfect, must not wonder if we are called to pass through suffering too' (C. H. Spurgeon).

He was tempted in every respect as we are, *yet without sin*. The Scriptures guard the sinless perfection of the Lord Jesus with jealous care, and we should too. He knew no sin (2 Cor. 5:21), he committed no sin (1 Peter 2:22), and there was no sin in him (1 John 3:5). Nevertheless, our risen Saviour understands the problems of living in a fallen world and the attacks of Satan, so we have good reason to look to him and come to the throne of grace in prayer in time of need.

2. The place to come boldly (v. 16)

Let us therefore come boldly to the throne of grace, that we may obtain mercy and find grace to help in time of need.

We are meant to 'come boldly'. By this is meant 'with confidence' (3:6), or with 'plainness of speech'. When we come to the place of prayer, we are of course expected to come with reverence and godly fear, but also with boldness, as this is one of the elements of evangelical faith. We see examples of this in those who are recorded in Scripture as having received answers to their supplications: 'Assuredly, I say to you, I have not found such great faith, not even in Israel!' (Matt. 8:10); 'Then He touched their eyes, saying, "According to your faith let it be to you." And their eyes were opened' (Matt. 9:29–30).

We are therefore to come courageously into God's presence, the place where our Saviour is now seated at the right hand of God, and we can approach him with boldness, knowing that we will find sympathy, mercy and salvation (7:22–25). Here is a gracious invitation extended to us all. It is to be accepted by faith, with the assurance that Christ Jesus died to save us and that he lives to keep us (Rom. 8:34). We are assured of a holy welcome because he has told us to *come boldly*.

The throne of grace is the throne of mercy. God's grace is the free bestowal of kindness and means to show favour. This is the action of God. The Hebrew word translated 'grace' (*chanan*) is used only in association with God in its adjectival form. A similar idea is expressed by the Hebrew word *chesed*, often translated 'lovingkindness' or 'goodness'. It is the 'loyal love' that God freely shows to his people because of his covenant with them. From this flow God's kindly dealings of sympathy and love. Likewise, the Greek word translated as 'mercy' (*eleos*) denotes an outward demonstration of pity, a sympathy that expresses itself in helping a person in need instead of remaining completely passive. *Eleos* is often used in conjunction with the Greek word *charis*, which is translated as 'grace' in Ephesians 2:5; 1 Timothy 1:2; 1 Peter 1:2–3; together they combine to magnify the longsuffering and mercy of our God and Saviour.

3. The reason for coming boldly to the throne of grace (v. 16b)

That we may obtain mercy and find grace to help in time of need.

Because there is a 'throne of grace', love and abundant help are found there. The throne of grace is therefore the throne of help. We are to come to the place of prayer and not to neglect it or deny its reality. 'Come' is from the same Greek word translated as 'draw near' in 10:22. Because of Christ's priestly work, believers can approach God's presence believing his promises. 'Draw near to God and He will draw near to you' (James 4:8). People in Old Testament times could not draw near to God as New Testament believers now can. Only the high priest could approach God, and then on only one day of the year, Yom Kippur. Salvation in Jesus Christ allows believers to come into his presence because the inner veil of the temple was cut in two by the very hand of God when our Saviour, Jesus Christ, died on the cross. Now God's people can enter his holy presence at any time of the day or night and 'obtain mercy and find grace to help in time of need'.

> For He Himself is our peace, who has made both [Jews and Gentiles] one, and has broken down the middle wall of separation, having abolished in His flesh the enmity, that is, the law of commandments contained in ordinances, so as to create in Himself one new man from the two, thus making peace ... For through Him we both have access by one Spirit to the Father. (Eph. 2:14–15, 18)

In Old Testament times the high priest entered God's presence on behalf of the people through the inner veil of the temple. Now, because of the cross of atonement of Jesus Christ, we enter through 'his flesh', that is, his death.

Conclusion

In the lives of God's people there are times when they need his help more than others. This is the moment to pray earnestly and come boldly to our Saviour's side. As the Scripture says, 'Let us draw near with a true heart in full assurance of faith, having our hearts sprinkled from an evil conscience and our bodies washed with pure water. Let us hold fast the confession of our hope without wavering, for He who promised is faithful' (Heb. 10:22–23).

Jesus Christ, our risen Saviour, is able to forgive sins. Here is the good news: our guilty consciences can be silenced; our past sins can be forgiven; our hearts can feel the touch of his cleansing blood. Jesus forgives sins. The paralytic man in Capernaum was forgiven with the words 'Man, your sins are forgiven you' (Luke 5:20). Our sin is our greatest problem, and spiritual health is far more important than physical wholeness. When Jesus saw the faith of the paralytic man, the first thing he did for him was to forgive him all his sins; only after this did he deal with his physical needs. Let none think that they have no sins to confess or transgressions needing forgiveness. Those who come to the 'throne of grace' in repentance and faith will find acceptance, admittance and an answer to their prayers. How wonderful to know that God's lovingkindness allows us access to all spiritual blessings in Christ, and that his grace empowers us (by his Holy Spirit) to do what we should be doing for Christ and his kingdom. 'In time of need' is a translation of a phrase that could be rendered 'in the nick of time'. Therefore, we could read it thus: 'that we may obtain mercy and find grace to help *just in the nick of time*'. Christ gives more grace, just when we need it. This is reminiscent of a phrase in Psalm 46:5 (emphasis added):

There is a river whose streams shall make glad the city of God,
The holy place of the tabernacle of the Most High.
God is in the midst of her, she shall not be moved;
God shall help her, *just at the break of dawn*.

Select bibliography

Berkhof, Louis, *The History of Christian Doctrines* (London: Banner of Truth, 1969)

——*Systematic Theology* (London: Banner of Truth, 1971)

Boice, J. M., *Foundations of the Christian Faith* (Leicester: IVP, 1986)

Brown, John, *Hebrews* (London: Banner of Truth, 1972)

Calvin, John, *Commentary on Ezekiel*, vol. xxi (Grand Rapids, MI: Baker, 1979)

Calvin, John, *Commentary* (CD-Rom; Christian Library series; Rio, WI: AGES Library, 2007)

Calvin, John, *Calvin's Institutes* (Grand Rapids, MI: Associated Publishers & Authors Inc., 1970)

Campbell, K. M., 'The Antinomian Controversies of the 17th Century', in *Living the Christian Life*, Westminster Conference Papers, 1974

Dabney, R. L., *Systematic Theology* (Edinburgh: Banner of Truth, 1996)

Dressler, H. H. P., 'The Sabbath in the Old Testament', in D. Carson, (ed.), *From Sabbath to the Lord's Day: A Biblical, Historical and Theological Investigation* (Grand Rapids, MI: Zondervan, 1982)

Edwards, Jonathan, 'The Perpetuity and Change of the Sabbath', *Works*, vol. ii (Edinburgh: Banner of Truth, 1974)

Finlayson, R. A., 'Anselm and the Doctrine of the Atonement', in *The Story of Theology* (London: Tyndale Press, 1969)

Geisler, N. L., (ed.), *Inerrancy* (Grand Rapids, MI: Zondervan, 1982)

Girdlestone, R. B., *Synonyms of the Old Testament* (Grand Rapids, MI: Eerdmans, 1978)

Hendriksen, William, *The Gospel of John* (London: Banner of Truth, 1969)

Hulse, Erroll, 'Recovering the Doctrine of Adoption', in *Reformation Today*, 105, 1988

Kik, Marcellus J., *Ecumenism and the Evangelical* (Philadelphia: P&R, 1958)

Manton, Thomas, *An Exposition of John 17* (Wilmington, DE: Sovereign Grace, 1972)

Morris, Leon, *The Gospel According to John* (Grand Rapids, MI: Eerdmans, 1971)

Murray, Andrew, *The Holiest of All* (London: James Nisbet & Co, 1895)

Murray, John, *Redemption Accomplished and Applied* (London: Banner of Truth, 1961)

Nelson's NKJV Study Bible (CD-Rom; Nashville: Thomas Nelson, 2005)

Ridderbos, Herman N., *The Gospel of John* (Grand Rapids, MI: Eerdmans, 1997)

Ryle, J. C., *Expository Thoughts on the Gospels: John*, vol. iii (London: James Clarke & Co., 1969)

Sookhdeo, Patrick, *The Challenge of Islam to the Church and Its Mission* (Pewsey: Isaac Publishing, 2009)

Trench, R. C., *Synonyms of the New Testament* (Grand Rapids, MI: Eerdmans, 1976)

Warfield, B. B., *The Person and Work of Christ* (Philadelphia: P&R, 1970)

About Day One:

Day One's threefold commitment:

- To be faithful to the Bible, God's inerrant, infallible Word;
- To be relevant to our modern generation;
- To be excellent in our publication standards.

I continue to be thankful for the publications of Day One. They are biblical; they have sound theology; and they are relative to the issues at hand. The material is condensed and manageable while, at the same time, being complete—a challenging balance to find. We are happy in our ministry to make use of these excellent publications.

JOHN MACARTHUR, PASTOR-TEACHER, GRACE COMMUNITY CHURCH, CALIFORNIA

It is a great encouragement to see Day One making such excellent progress. Their publications are always biblical, accessible and attractively produced, with no compromise on quality. Long may their progress continue and increase!

JOHN BLANCHARD, AUTHOR, EVANGELIST AND APOLOGIST

Taste and see that the Lord is good
Knowing, loving, and enjoying God

JOEL JAMES

208PP PAPERBACK, ISBN 978–1–84625–269–3

How do you relate to God? Moses said to Israel, 'You shall fear the Lord your God; you shall serve Him and cling to Him …' (Deut. 10:20). In other words, knowing God is a perfect paradox: he is both too great to approach and too great not to. When we study the God of the Bible, we should be both overwhelmed by his incomparable majesty and irresistibly drawn to his love.

In this warm and easy-to-read study of the attributes of God, Joel James captures and encourages that worshipful blend of awestruck fear and irrepressible love. Because it is built around key Old Testament 'Sunday school' stories of God's working with people such as Moses, Jonah, Ahab, and Manasseh, this book avoids the pitfalls of philosophical abstraction. It won't simply teach you who God is, it will also help you to love him.

Joel James has an M.Div. and a D.Min. from The Master's Seminary and is the pastor-teacher of Grace Fellowship in Pretoria, South Africa. He and his wife, Ruth, have been married since 1993 and have two children.

Great Gospel Words

COLIN N PECKHAM

128PP PAPERBACK, ISBN 978–1–84625–138–2

Here is doctrine made simple! It is easy to read, necessary to grasp and thrilling to experience! Many people in our churches today do not understand the basic doctrines of salvation. In these important studies, Colin Peckham examines the great gospel words 'repentance', 'justification', 'regeneration' and 'assurance', showing how each aspect is vital in 'salvation' as a whole. Colin Peckham taught biblical doctrine for years and his expertise in making things understandable, as well as his passion for reaching the lost, are clearly seen here. His emphasis is not merely academic, but brings the challenge of an encounter with the God who made this salvation possible.

The late Revd Dr Colin Neil Peckham was born in South Africa, where he had an evangelistic ministry before entering Bible college in Cape Town. He then emigrated to Great Britain and was principal of the Faith Mission Bible College, Edinburgh, Scotland. As principal emeritus he had an extensive preaching ministry in Britain and abroad and authored several books. He was married to Mary (née Morrison) from the Isle of Lewis, Scotland. They had three adult children and two grandchildren. Colin passed away in 2009, followed some months later by Mary.

This further work from the pen of Dr Colin Peckham on 'great gospel words' is most welcome, especially at a time when the average church member has no real understanding of the essential elements of the gospel.
—Revd Tom Shaw BA, MTh, Congregational minister, N. Ireland, and former President of the Faith Mission

The Sovereignty and Supremacy of King Jesus
Bowing to the Gracious Despot

MIKE ABENDROTH

240PP PAPERBACK, ISBN 978–1–84625–267–9

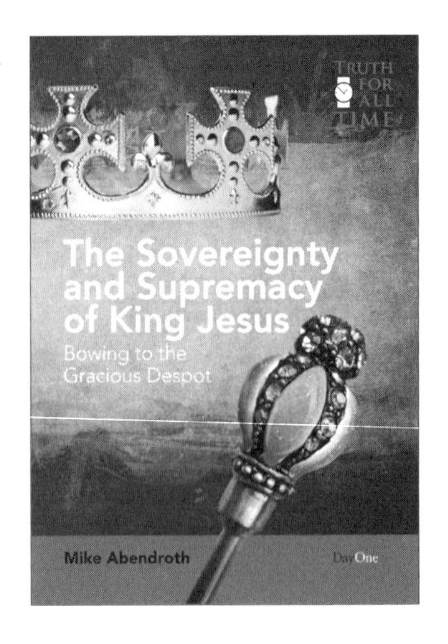

What thoughts flood our minds when we think about God? Do we think of Him as King? If so, what kind of King? In this book Mike Abendroth seeks to address a twofold problem: most Christians do not consider God as any type of Monarch, and, if they do, they think about monarchs that are weak rather than reflecting on the utter Lordship of God, the ultimate King.

In Part 1, Mike Abendroth demonstrates that the whole Bible reveals God as King. In Part 2, he describes the life-changing implications that flow from that revelation. Filled with insightful quotations, worshipful hymns, and thoughtful study questions, this book helps us to biblically embrace God as our King.

Mike Abendroth graduated from The Master's Seminary (M. Div.) in 1996 and became the pastor of Bethlehem Bible Church, West Boylston, MA, in 1997. He received his Doctorate of Ministry in Expository Preaching at the Southern Baptist Theological Seminary in 2006. One of his passions is training men to teach the Bible expositionally. He is the author of *Jesus Christ: the Prince of Preachers* (Day One, 2008). Mike is married to Kimberly and they have four children.

I wholeheartedly endorse this book and strongly encourage you to carefully read its message. Mark up its pages. Devour its truths. Share it with others. Use it as an evangelistic tool. Draw from it to preach. Use it to teach small group Bible studies. You will find this book to be an invaluable resource.
Steven J. Lawson, Senior Pastor, Christ Fellowship Baptist Church, Mobile, Alabama